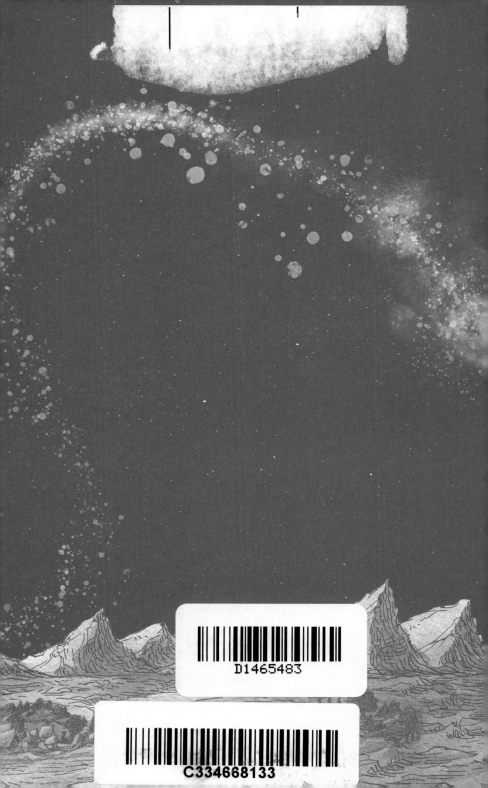

A CLOCK OF STARS

STARS
OF

BEYOND THE MOUNTAINS

Books by Francesca Gibbons

A CLOCK OF STARS: THE SHADOW MOTH

A CLOCK OF STARS: BEYOND THE MOUNTAINS

A CLOCK OF STARS

BEYOND THE MOUNTAINS

FRANCESCA GIBBONS

Illustrated by
CHRIS RIDDELL

HarperCollins *Children's Books*

First published in Great Britain by
HarperCollins *Children's Books* in 2021
HarperCollins *Children's Books* is a division of HarperCollins*Publishers* Ltd
1 London Bridge Street
London SE1 9GF

www.harpercollins.co.uk

HarperCollins*Publishers*
1st Floor, Watermarque Building, Ringsend Road
Dublin 4, Ireland

1

HB ISBN: 978–0–00–835508–1
TPB ISBN: 978–0–00–835509–8
SIGNED EDITION ISBN: 978–0–00–850600–1
SIGNED CANADA EDITION ISBN: 978–0–00–851129–6

Francesca Gibbons and Chris Riddell assert the moral right to be identified as the author
and illustrator of the work respectively.
A CIP catalogue record for this title is available from the British Library.

Typeset in 11.3/18
Printed and bound in the UK using 100% renewable electricity at CPI Group (UK) Ltd

MIX
Paper from
responsible sources
FSC™ C007454

FSC
www.fsc.org

This book is produced from independently certified FSC™ paper
to ensure responsible forest management.

For more information visit: www.harpercollins.co.uk/green

This one's for Mini and Bonnie too

A Cast of Characters

OCHI

ANNESHKA

IMOGEN AND MARIE

MARK

ZUBY

MIRO

PATOLEEZAL

PERLA and KONYA

KAZIMIRA and CTIBOR

BRANNA

Queen Svitla Queen Zlata Queen Blipla Queen Flumkra Queen Yeeskra

SUROVETZ

YEMNI

It's not my mother that I fear
nor my father's rage.
For both my parents need me
to help them in old age.

But there are armoured monsters,
that fill my heart with dread.
They kidnap naughty children –
that's what my mother said.

It's not the darkness that I fear.
It's not for dawn I pray.
For these beasts will go hunting
at any time of day.

Beware the knocking at the door,
beware the krootymoosh.
Beware their rattling cages.
They do not pity youth.

It's not my mother that I fear
nor my father's rage.
For both my parents need me
to help them in old age.

– Nursery rhyme from the Lowlands

PART 1

CHAPTER 1

The trees leaned out of Ochi's way, creating a path through the darkness.

Ochi walked without hesitation. She knew her way through these woods – she was the forest witch, after all.

A pony followed at a respectful distance. There was a pillowcase tied to its saddle with a very strange clock inside.

Anneshka Mazanar followed the pony. There was nothing respectful about the way that she walked. She muttered as she stumbled through the forest. Andel's mechanical dragon had scorched her hands and face. She'd lost a slipper and her wedding dress was in tatters. Brambles trailed from her petticoats, swishing like a long barbed tail.

Although Anneshka's burns were painful, the thought of what she'd lost hurt more. She'd been *this close* to being crowned queen. *This close* to fulfilling her destiny.

Now Drakomor was dead. And it wouldn't be long before all of Yaroslav heard about the things she had done; the people she'd had killed and the prince who'd got away . . .

Anneshka imagined her mother's reaction. *You could have*

married the king, but oh no! You had to have a dragon, had to set fire to the castle. Stupid girl. What will the neighbours say?

No. Anneshka would not return to Yaroslav. The witch was her only hope.

Ochi strode ahead, lantern swinging. She was tall and slender with pale skin and black hair. She'd offered Anneshka shelter. Perhaps she had answers too.

The witch knows where I'm destined to rule, thought Anneshka. She gritted her teeth and limped on. *I can still have a kingdom and a castle. I'll show mother. I'll show everyone.*

Ochi's cottage appeared without warning. One moment, there was nothing but trees, the next Anneshka was standing by an old house. Ochi was busy unsaddling the pony so Anneshka let herself in.

There was a fireplace and higgledy-piggledy furniture. There were lots of clay pots, and a chicken was roosting in a drawer.

So this is what I'm reduced to, thought Anneshka as she collapsed into a chair.

A pot on the mantelpiece rattled. Anneshka looked up. The pot was still.

'This place is driving me mad,' she murmured and she pulled up a stool for her feet. One foot was bloody and bare. The other wore a grubby silk slipper.

'That's right, child, make yourself at home,' said a rasping voice from behind. Anneshka jumped to her feet. The voice belonged to a very old woman. Her skin was wrinkly and her muscles had wasted away. Anneshka scanned the room for a sharp object.

'Don't be afraid,' wheezed the hag. 'It's only me that changes. I'm sure you're as beautiful inside as out.'

Anneshka recoiled. Was that . . . 'Ochi?'

'What did you expect?' said the woman. 'No one stays young for ever.'

Anneshka did not like the way that she smiled, but she knew she was speaking the truth. The young witch and the old woman were the very same person. Anneshka recognised the eyes.

'We'd better see to your burns,' said Ochi-the-ancient. She opened a drawer and removed two snails.

'What are you doing?' cried Anneshka. 'Get those things away from me!'

'You won't be queen of anything if you die of an infection,' said Ochi, hobbling closer. 'Those injuries need treating.'

The snails remained hidden in their shells. Anneshka looked down at her hands where the skin had blistered, caught by the dragon's fire. 'Oh, all right,' she sneered. 'Do what you must.'

Ochi placed the snails on Anneshka's wrists and stroked the shells with her twisty old fingers until their inhabitants emerged.

Anneshka fought the urge to throw the snails across the room. She hated the way they had eyes out on stalks; she hated the way that they moved. Everything about them was disgusting.

'There are burns on your face,' said the witch.

Anneshka wrinkled her nose, but her hands did feel better . . . She let Ochi place a snail on her chin. The creature's cold foot slithered up her cheek and across the bridge of her nose.

By the time Ochi was done, Anneshka's burns were covered in an iridescent layer of slime.

'This had better work,' she grumbled.

The old woman put the snails on the floor and they started the long journey back to their drawer.

'What a queen you will be,' sighed the witch, sitting down.

'Queen of what? Queen of where?' snapped Anneshka. She was growing tired of the way Ochi talked.

'I can ask the stars . . . if you're willing to pay.'

A pot by Ochi's chair started shaking. The witch pushed it back with her heel.

'You're hiding something,' said Anneshka. 'What's in all these pots?'

'I'm not hiding anything, child. Why would I hide things from you?'

Anneshka scowled at the witch. She looked frail; a bundle of bones with an eggshell for a head. *It would be easy to crack her skull open*, thought Anneshka; *see if the secrets fall out.*

The pots by the window were sealed with plugs. Anneshka snatched one and read the label.

W. Lokai

The label meant nothing to her. She grabbed another pot, leaving slime fingerprints.

S. Zárda

She'd never heard of a potion called that.

One of the pots had no stopper. Anneshka peered inside, half expecting a frog to leap out. It was empty so she looked at the label.

V. Mazanar

'That's my mother,' cried Anneshka. 'That's her name!' She took a moment to steady herself. 'Why is there a pot named after my mother?'

'Come,' said the witch. 'It's time to rest.'

'Tell me now!' Anneshka marched over to the snails and raised her single slippered foot above one of them.

'It's too late. I'll tell you in the morning.'

Anneshka lowered her slipper, relishing the crunch.

'My snail!' cried Ochi. Her face twisted in pain.

'Talk,' demanded Anneshka. Her bare foot hovered above the second snail.

'Your mother purchased a prophecy on the day you were born,' said Ochi. 'I told her you'd grow up to be queen.'

Anneshka's toe pressed the snail's shell. 'I already know that.'

'Please! Not Boris!' begged the witch. She talked faster. 'When your mother dies, she'll pay for the prophecy with her soul. I'll keep it in that pot.' The witch paused. She looked ashamed. 'Each soul, freely given, grants me more time in this body.'

Anneshka raised an eyebrow and stepped away from the snail. 'You collect souls to extend your miserable life?'

There were pots on the shelves and stacked up in corners, pots on the table and under the chair. Anneshka turned a full circle. She looked down at the witch. 'Just how old are you?'

Ochi stared at Boris as he inched under a cupboard. 'I'm twenty-three,' she whispered. 'Seven hundred and twenty-three.'

CHAPTER 2

Someone had stolen the keys for the windows in room 32C. Outside, it was one of the last hot days of the year. Inside, a class of Year Sevens were being baked alive.

Mr Morris was being baked too. 'Turn to page eight,' he said, and he plodded across the room, slow as a lizard in a tank.

Imogen flicked through the textbook, enjoying the mini-breeze the pages made as they turned. She paused at a photo of an astronaut gazing out of a bubble-shaped window.

That's Earth, said the text. *That's home. That's where we make our stand.*

Imogen wondered if the astronaut felt homesick or excited when he looked at the Earth from this strange new perspective. *Perhaps*, she thought, *he feels a bit of both.*

She glanced up at her teacher. He wasn't talking about astronauts. He was talking about the differences between liquids and solids.

Sweat is a liquid, thought Imogen, as a drop ran down Mr Morris's face. *Time is a solid*, she continued in her head. *Nothing can make it move faster.*

There were five minutes until the end of the school day. Five minutes until Imogen finished her first week at secondary school.

It hadn't been a bad start. She'd made friends, and she liked her form tutor, but everyone already knew her as 'that girl who disappeared'. At least they didn't know she was seeing a therapist.

Other students kept asking if she'd run away or been kidnapped. Imogen decided against telling the truth. They'd never believe she'd found a door in a tree, made friends with a prince and flown on the backs of giant birds . . .

Three minutes until home time. Imogen tried to focus on the textbook.

Space travel comes at a cost. The astronauts on this mission won't see their families for five years. And when they return, it'll take many more years to adjust to normal life.

Two minutes until home time.

Mum would be waiting at the school gate. Imogen wished she wouldn't. None of the other parents did that, but Mum had been different since Imogen went missing.

It had been her idea to get a therapist. She said Imogen needed 'special support'. Apparently, that was code for hours of talking . . . As if you could be talked into forgetting about a magical world.

One minute until home time.

'At room temperature, water is a liquid,' said Mr Morris. He sounded exhausted. 'But when it's heated, water starts to –' the school bell rang and the children grabbed their books and poured out of the room – 'evaporate,' finished the teacher, flopping back in his chair.

The door banged shut and the classroom went quiet. Mr Morris closed his eyes. Imogen waited to be noticed. The teacher took a deep breath, letting the air in through his nose and out through his mouth. He held a water bottle to his cheek. He was sitting very still.

'Sir?'

Mr Morris jumped. 'Imogen! You're still here!'

'You know astronauts have been to the moon. Have they been to other places?'

Mr Morris lowered the water bottle from his face. 'Well . . . yes. NASA sent probes to Mars.'

'But there are no people on Mars.'

'No, Imogen. Not yet.'

Imogen narrowed her eyes. 'Do you think there might be another planet that the astronauts haven't discovered yet? Like our planet, with people and animals . . . but different?'

'I don't know,' said the teacher. 'But if something like that *does* exist, it's very far away. Even if you had a ship that travelled at the speed of light, it'd take many years to get there. You might be an old woman by the time you touched down.'

Imogen found it hard to imagine that she'd ever be an old woman.

'Why do you ask?' said Mr Morris.

Imogen stood up to leave. Enough time had passed. There'd be no one around to see her meet Mum at the gates.

'Oh, never mind,' she said. 'I was just curious.'

CHAPTER 3

Imogen lay on her sister's bed, surrounded by drawings. There was so much paper stuck to the walls that the room seemed to warp when the wind blew through the window. It felt more like being in a tent than a house.

Marie, who was three years younger than Imogen, was sitting on the floor. She was colouring, and there were pencils scattered across the carpet.

'Mrs Kalmadi says moths can't open doors,' said Marie, 'or recognise people.'

'You've got to stop talking about it at school,' scolded Imogen. 'People will think something's wrong with you.'

'But everyone else is talking about it. Don't people talk at the big school?'

Imogen looked at a doodle of Mum. She had a head shaped like a light bulb and bunches of bananas for hands. Marie had done that one a few years ago.

'Yes,' confessed Imogen. 'They talk about it all the time.'

At the foot of the bed was a more recent sketch; a portrait of a boy with far-apart eyes and ears that stuck out through his hair. Imogen's gaze kept returning to the boy. She had to admit, that one was pretty good.

'I don't like pretending Yaroslav's not real,' said Marie. 'It was just as real as Mrs Kalmadi. It felt more real, at the time.'

Imogen didn't like pretending either. She hated it, in fact. 'I'm sure Mum will believe us eventually,' she said. 'We just need to find a way to convince her.'

Mum's voice echoed up the stairs. 'Girls, time for dinner!'

Marie dropped her pencil and dashed out of the room. Imogen swung herself off the bed and picked up Marie's drawing. It was a sketch of a forest at night. She'd captured it well: the secret shadows, the cold light of the stars. If Imogen closed her eyes, she could almost hear the whisper of moth wings.

'Earth to Imogen!' called Mum. 'Your grandma's here. Come and say hello.'

Imogen dropped the drawing and went downstairs to join the rest of her family.

The weather was warm for September, so they ate dinner outside. Mum lit candles to keep the insects away. Grandma served lasagne and talked about bridge club. She'd been kicked out because she was too good at cards. At least, that's what she said.

After dinner, the girls started clearing the patio table and Mum whispered something to Grandma about Mrs Haberdash.

Imogen's ears pricked up. Mrs Haberdash was the old lady who owned the tea rooms and the gardens where Imogen had found the door in the tree.

'The state of those gardens,' said Grandma, in a low voice. 'I wouldn't be surprised if there *was* something living in them, just like she says. Most likely it's foxes.'

'What's that?' said Imogen, peering at the grown-ups.

'Oh, nothing darling,' said Mum. 'Would you take my plate?'

'Yes . . . But you were talking about Mrs Haberdash, weren't you?'

The women exchanged looks. 'I'm afraid Mrs Haberdash isn't very well,' said Mum.

'She's seeing things that aren't there,' said Grandma. 'It happens sometimes, to old people.' She tapped on the side of her skull as if being old had nothing to do with her.

'Mrs Haberdash is sick because of foxes?' said Imogen, confused.

'No, no,' said Grandma. 'She thinks there's something in her gardens – some kind of monster. She says she saw it at night, round the back by the bins. It was probably a fox, foraging for scraps, but poor Mrs H is all worked up.'

A monster? thought Imogen. *Could it be . . . ?*

'Perhaps we should visit her,' suggested Marie.

'I don't think we're allowed,' said Grandma, and she glanced at Mum.

'Don't look at me,' said Mum. 'You can see your friends whenever you like.'

'I just can't be trusted to take care of your children,' replied Grandma. 'Is that it?'

Mum was making intense eye contact with a scented candle. 'Imogen, Marie . . . take all the plates to the kitchen.'

But Grandma held her plate tight. 'It wasn't my fault they went missing,' she hissed. 'I only took my eyes off them for a minute.'

Imogen had never seen Mum and Grandma argue. Mum backed up Grandma. Grandma backed up Mum. Those were the rules.

'Why don't all four of us go?' said Marie. 'Why don't we go to the tea rooms together?'

Mum looked up, still frowning. 'I'll think about it,' she said.

Later that evening, Grandma put Marie to bed, meaning Imogen got Mum to herself. They sat in the garden, watching the first stars appear.

There was an orange glow on the horizon; an electric glare that even the brightest stars couldn't outshine. The sky above Yaroslav had been black and full of stars. Imogen wondered if a skret attack would make the neighbours turn out their lights. Then you'd see the stars. *It probably isn't worth it*, she thought with a smile.

'What are you thinking about?' said Mum. She put her arm round Imogen and even though Imogen was in Year Seven, she still fitted there snugly.

'Oh, you know . . . Just wondering what it'd be like if you could see all the stars.' Imogen rested her head on Mum's shoulder.

'It's good to have you back, Imogen,' said Mum. 'I've been so worried about you . . . Without Mark, I don't know what I'd have . . .'

Imogen seized the opportunity. 'Is Mark your boyfriend?'

A daddy-longlegs drifted by.

Mum took a deep breath before she responded. 'Yes. He is. I really like him, and I think you will too, if you could only give him a chance . . . He hasn't got any children so it's hard for him, but Mark's a good man. Please. Promise me you'll give him a go.'

'I won't call him Dad.'

'Of course. I'd never ask you to.'

'But I suppose if you like him . . .'

Mum gave Imogen a squeeze. 'That's my girl.'

CHAPTER 4

The people of Yaroslav stopped searching for Anneshka after the first snowfall. If she was hiding in the forest, she would have starved to death by now. No one would give food to a murderer . . . not even one as pretty as her.

Most people thought she'd died crossing the mountains. It was the wrong time of year for the journey. Perhaps they'd find her corpse in the spring, somewhere near the top of a mountain, encased in ice and her wedding dress. Yaroslav's artists were fond of that image. It sold very well.

How were they to know she was neither dead, nor dying, but safe and warm in the forest witch's house?

Anneshka sat by the fire. The chicken was roosting in its drawer and the clay pots were still, as pots ought to be. Anneshka ran a finger over her old burns. The skin had grown back silver.

Through the little window, she could see nothing but trees. They stooped under the weight of the snow. Ochi was out there, shaking powder from their branches.

As each flake fell it seemed to whisper *All hail, hail, hail.*

Anneshka turned her gaze to the fire, where the flames hissed *Queeeeeen*.

Ochi strode into the cottage and Anneshka snapped out of her trance.

The witch shed her cloak and her youth in one go. Then she shuffled towards the fire, slow and stiff. 'Poor trees,' wheezed Ochi. 'They weren't expecting this much snow. Winter's come early.'

All this talk about trees, thought Anneshka, *and she still hasn't told me where I'll be queen.*

Ochi's knees creaked as she sat. Anneshka had stayed with the witch for long enough to know how things worked. When Ochi was outside, she was a young woman, her body lithe as a sapling, but when the witch entered her hut, she was more like a stump. Hideous and old.

Anneshka wondered if Ochi's prophecies would sell so well if people saw her real face. Somehow she doubted it.

'Tell me,' said Anneshka. 'If I won't be the queen of Yaroslav, where will I rule?'

The witch sat back in her chair. 'My prophecies provide a glimpse of the future. What you're asking for is a long, steady look.'

'I'm losing my patience, hag. You promised to tell me where I'll rule.'

'I did no such thing.'

'What's wrong?' sneered Anneshka. 'Losing your touch?'

Ochi turned her eyes to the clock – the one that Anneshka had taken from Andel, the one that rested above the hearth. The clock looked as old as Ochi. It must have stopped working a long time ago.

'I *can* do it,' said the witch, 'but I'd need a little help.'

The pots on the mantelpiece trembled.

'Pah!' scoffed Anneshka. 'That clock won't help. It's broken – doesn't even keep time.'

'Keep time with what?' said the witch. 'Time and motion, motion and time. The older I get, the harder it is to tell them apart.' She gave a gummy smile that made Anneshka want to bash her toothless face in. Curse the witch and her riddles.

'Speak plainly,' demanded Anneshka.

'That clock is tuned to the stars,' said Ochi.

Her words made a memory stir . . .

Anneshka got to her feet.

Drakomor had told her about such a clock. He said it was made by Andel – said it was capable of reading the stars. Is that what this was? Is that why Andel had saved the clock from the fire?

Anneshka inspected it up close. It had five hands, none of which were moving. A smattering of jewels hung before its face.

'With such a powerful tool, I could look deep into the future,' continued Ochi. She raised her voice over the rattling pots. They were all at it now; the pots on the shelves, the pots in the corner, the pots tucked away out of sight.

'I'm sure you're perfectly capable of finding the right kingdom without any help from me,' said the witch. 'It's your destiny, after all. The only question is, how long are you willing to wait?'

Anneshka shot the witch a poisonous look. She had no intention of being as old as Ochi before she sat on her throne. 'Tell me,' she commanded. 'Tell me now.'

The pots shook with all their might. Ochi's chicken hopped down from its drawer and hid under the desk.

'All I ask is a little security . . .' Ochi's tone was casual, but her stare was intense. 'All I ask is your soul.'

Now the room was shuddering with the force of seven-hundred trapped souls. Anneshka looked around. Could the pots be trying to warn her?

'There's no need to be alarmed,' said the witch. 'I won't take a thing till you die.'

But what if the souls in the pots were jealous? What if they didn't want Anneshka to succeed? Her mother had always been jealous. She'd always wished it was *her* that was fated to be queen.

Anneshka turned to the witch. 'I'll do it,' she cried.

The pots juddered as if they were trying to bring down the walls. A lantern fell and smashed. Ochi's chicken squawked.

'Anneshka Mazanar, I promise to read your stars,' said the

witch. She pressed a knife to her thumb and the skin broke like wet paper. She handed the knife to Anneshka.

'On the day that I die, I promise you my soul,' said Anneshka. She cut her thumb and held it to Ochi's. Their bloods mixed. The pots were still.

Everything in the cottage was quiet . . .

Everything apart from the ticking of the clock.

It went slowly at first. Then fast. Then faster. Hands spun in frantic circles. Days chimed by in a moment. The clock's little hatch fluttered open and shut faster than a moth's wingbeat.

Then everything slowed. The jewelled stars drifted into position. The ticking counted seconds. Anneshka put her hands to her face. She didn't *feel* any different. 'Is that it?' she whispered.

The clock's hatch popped open and a wooden crown wheeled out. It was so small and so perfectly made . . . Anneshka wanted to touch it. But the crown spun around, as if doing a dance, and retreated into the clock.

'What was that?' asked Anneshka.

'That was the first of our clues,' said the witch and she hobbled over to her desk.

'Clues? I didn't ask for clues. I asked for a prophecy!'

Ochi picked up a quill. 'It's the first part of your prophecy. Don't worry, I'll work out what it means . . . The clock of stars cannot be rushed.'

CHAPTER 5

By the time Imogen and Marie were allowed to visit the tea rooms, it was almost Halloween. Mum still seemed to think the girls needed an armed guard to leave the house, so 'the whole family' was going.

Imogen, Marie, Mum and Grandma waited until a horn beeped outside. 'Ladies,' called Mark, 'your carriage awaits!' Mum said Mark's car was sporty. Imogen thought it looked squished.

Imogen and Marie scooted into the back of the car, wedging Grandma between them. 'Guess what we've been making!' said Mum, hopping into the passenger seat.

'Brain jelly!' cried Marie.

'How terrifying,' said Mark and he locked eyes with Imogen in the rear-view mirror. 'I hope there aren't any sticky fingers back there. Those seats are genuine leather.' He started the engine.

Imogen rested her forehead on the window. She summoned up memories of summer. She remembered the shadow moth with its silver-grey wings. She remembered the castle and the skret caves and—

'How's school, Imogen?' said Mark. 'I hear you've taken an interest in science.'

Imogen rolled her eyes. 'Not all science,' she said. 'Just space.'

'Space . . .' Mark nodded. 'I used to like space.'

He's trying to connect, thought Imogen, *but he just missed the turning to the tea rooms.*

'You're going the wrong way,' cried Grandma.

'Relax,' said Mark. 'I'm just avoiding country roads. When you've got a nice car, you have to take care of it.' He flashed Mum a smile. 'Same goes for the passengers.'

Imogen mimed being sick and Marie wrinkled her nose. Grandma tried to give them a 'behave-yourselves' look, but even she looked vaguely repulsed.

As they pulled into the tea rooms' car park, Mum swivelled to face the back seats. 'Now, girls, Mrs Haberdash has been having a tough time. Let's stay away from any sensitive topics. Please don't mention the foxes in her garden.'

'And no talking about La-la Land,' added Mark. 'That'll only confuse her.'

Imogen glared at the back of Mark's head. *La-la Land* was his name for the world on the other side of the door. He seemed determined to prove it was a lie.

They clambered out of Mark's car, gravel crunching as they walked. Imogen paused by a gate in the corner of the car park. It was the entrance to the Haberdash Gardens. That's where the shadow moth had taken her last summer. That's where her adventures had begun . . .

But someone had fixed the gate's lock. There would be no more trespassing.

'Come on, Imogen,' said Mum. 'The tea rooms are this way.'

Reluctantly, Imogen followed.

As usual, Mrs Haberdash was dressed as if she was about to have tea with the queen. There were diamonds in her ears and ruffles round her neck.

When she saw she had customers, she angled her mobility scooter towards the door.

'Agnes!' cried Grandma, rushing to her old friend's side. 'I'm so sorry we couldn't visit sooner.'

Mrs Haberdash seemed like she was about to reply, but Grandma got there first. 'We've been terribly busy – what with the police investigation and the children back at school and the foxes – did I say foxes? I meant squirrels!'

Imogen decided to leave the grown-ups to it. She went to join Mrs Haberdash's dogs, who were lounging on a wicker sofa like three fluffy cushions. Marie followed.

'Look what I've got,' said Imogen when she was sure they were out of earshot. She held her rucksack open. Her sister peered in.

'Mum's phone!' gasped Marie. 'Does she know you have it?'

The closest dog lifted its head.

'Of course not. Keep your voice down. I'm going to lend it to Mrs H.'

Marie looked confused. 'What? Why? Mum will kill you!'

'No, she won't. She'll just think she left it. She's always putting things down and forgetting. Besides, if she'd let me have my own phone, we wouldn't be in this situation.'

Marie removed her sketchbook from her bag. 'What's Mrs Haberdash going to do with a mobile phone?'

'Take a photo.'

'Of what?'

'Of the monster, of course,' whispered Imogen. 'The one she keeps seeing in her gardens.'

Marie pressed her lips together, disapproving. 'Imogen, I'm not sure about this. Grandma said it's just a fox, and Mum said we shouldn't talk about it.'

'What if Grandma's wrong? What if they're all wrong? *They* said there's no such thing as a door in a tree. *They* said Miro's my imaginary friend. Now they're saying Mrs Haberdash is seeing things. But look! Does Mrs H look like the odd one to you?'

Mrs H was listening to Grandma. She looked prim and calm. Grandma was describing something big, gesturing with her arms and waving her walking stick dangerously close to the cakes.

'Besides,' continued Imogen. 'We got into another world through the Haberdash Gardens and now Mrs H has seen something strange in the very same place. Don't you think it's a bit of a coincidence?'

'What are you two whispering about?' said Mum. She was carrying a tray stacked with teacups and cakes.

'Nothing,' said the girls in unison. Imogen zipped up her rucksack.

'Nothing?' Mum laughed. 'Now why do I find that so hard to believe?'

After they'd eaten their cake, and when the others were busy petting Mrs Haberdash's dogs, Imogen went to talk to the old lady. She nudged Mum's phone across the counter, whispering her plan and asking Mrs H not to tell.

Mrs Haberdash tapped the side of her nose. 'Don't worry, Imogen,' she said softly. 'Your secret's safe with me . . . I know how to use these camera phones. You just point and tap, point and tap.'

'Do you think you'll be able to find the monster?' asked Imogen.

'I'll see what I can do,' said Mrs Haberdash, slipping the phone into a drawer. 'It's very kind of you to believe me. *They* all think I'm going mad.'

She nodded at Imogen's family, who were on the other side of the room. Grandma was feeding cake to the dogs and Mark was trying to stop her. The smallest dog growled at Mark.

'*They* don't believe anyone,' muttered Imogen.

CHAPTER 6

The next day, when everyone was back home, the landline started to ring. Mum took the call and Imogen fizzled with excitement. It *had* to be Mrs H.

Imogen could hear a woman talking on the other end of the line and there were dogs yapping in the background.

'You've found my phone?' said Mum to the mouthpiece. 'Oh, what a relief! It must have slipped out of my jeans – yes – yes, thank you, Mrs Haberdash. I'll come right away.'

She hung up.

'Can I go with you?' asked Imogen. She couldn't wait to see Mum's face when she was confronted with a photo of THE TRUTH.

'Of course,' said Mum. 'Your grandma can stay with Marie.' She picked up her jacket, and Imogen followed her out of the front door with a little skip in her step.

*

'I caught it,' cried Mrs Haberdash as soon as they stepped into the tea rooms. Imogen had never seen her so animated.

'Caught what?' said Mum.

Uh-oh, thought Imogen. *Mrs H is going to drop me in it. She's going to tell Mum I gave her the phone.*

'I caught the monster,' said Mrs Haberdash.

Mum grabbed Imogen, pulling her close as if a rabid fox might be behind the wicker sofa. 'Where is it?' gasped Mum.

Mrs Haberdash started laughing. She laughed so hard that several spirals of her hair came loose – so hard that Imogen thought she'd fall off her scooter.

'It's not here,' said the old lady, when her laughter had subsided. 'I caught the monster *on camera*.' She opened a drawer and removed a handkerchief-wrapped package. 'I hope you don't mind. I used your mobile phone . . . as it was here, on the counter.'

Imogen watched Mum's face as Mrs H folded back the hanky. The phone was inside and Mum squinted at the screen.

'What is it?' said Imogen. 'Does it look like a fox?'

'I don't know,' said Mum. 'It's such a dark photo.'

Mrs Haberdash wheeled closer. 'What do you mean?' she cried. 'It's a monster! It's clearly a monster!'

Mum zoomed in on the picture. 'It could be a lot of things, Mrs H.'

Imogen took the phone and had a look for herself. The image

was blurry. Only the eyes were clear. Two circular orbs glowed neon in the flash. The shape of the creature was indistinct, but Imogen thought she could see . . . *there*, in the corner of the screen. It was the tip of a hooked claw.

A type of claw she'd seen before . . .

'Are you sure it's not a close-up of a frog?' said Mum.

Mrs Haberdash scowled. 'I know what a frog looks like, Catherine.'

'Or perhaps it's some kids, dressed up for Halloween? The costumes are very realistic these days.'

'Why would children hide by my bins?' Mrs Haberdash looked genuinely distressed and Imogen felt a pang of sympathy. She knew what it was like to be doubted.

Adults don't believe children. They don't believe old ladies either. Perhaps it's just the middle years when you can change people's minds.

'Teenagers do funny things,' said Mum, taking the phone from Imogen and slipping it into her handbag. 'I'm sure you'll feel better when Halloween's over. I'll send Mark to check on you tomorrow.'

On the way home, Imogen borrowed her mum's phone and looked at the photo again. 'The monster has claws,' she said, 'very big claws for a fox.'

'What do you want me to do, Imogen?' replied Mum, exasperated. 'Send for the army? I'm sure the police are inundated with prank calls at this time of year. Try putting it out of your head. It's not good for you to focus on things that aren't real.'

Imogen narrowed her eyes. The army . . . the police . . . that wasn't what she wanted at all. They'd lock up the monster or put it to sleep. That was what people did to things they were afraid of.

'Delete the photo,' Mum instructed.

Reluctantly, Imogen did as she was told and yet her mind was racing. She'd have to find another way of convincing Mum that the door in the tree was real. But how could she do it without putting the monster in danger?

And, most important of all, what was a *skret* doing in the Haberdash Gardens?

CHAPTER 7

Autumn came and went, and so did all talk of monsters. Imogen was too busy getting used to her new school to think up any more schemes. Life was full of homework and house points.

Often, it was easier to pretend that the door in the tree didn't exist. When other children asked about Imogen's mysterious disappearance, she laughed, as if it was a joke – a funny trick she'd played on the adults.

I'm still going to prove that Yaroslav's a real place, she told herself. *I'm just waiting for the right moment.* But the right moment never seemed to arrive. Imogen got good at pretending that she didn't believe in monsters. Sometimes, she pretended so hard that her memories went fuzzy.

And so, time slugged along, inch by inch, hour by hour, until it was Christmas. Imogen and Marie broke up from school. Imogen looked forward to presents and pigs in blankets. But this year, she would get neither.

For time was done slugging. It was ready to break into a gallop. And the days of pretending that our world is the only one that exists were soon to come to a close.

On the first morning of the Christmas holidays, Mum bundled Imogen and Marie into the car. She drove out of town, towards the Haberdash Estate, but they whizzed past the sign for the tea rooms.

'Aren't we going to see Mrs Haberdash?' asked Marie.

'Surprise!' cried Mum. 'We're going to a fancy hotel! It's just down the road from the tea rooms. I've packed your overnight bags.'

Imogen glanced from Mum to Marie. She'd never slept in a hotel before. She'd read about them, so she knew what to expect. 'But I thought hotels are for travelling,' she said, 'and we're not that far from home.'

'This is a special Christmas treat from Mark,' said Mum, as if that explained everything. 'Don't forget to thank him.'

Mum parked in front of a glass-fronted building. The sign by the entrance said:

Welcome to The Lily Pad
Spa – Restaurant – Hotel

A picture by the words showed a frog with a towel on its head and long manicured nails.

'Why are we staying here?' asked Imogen. 'What are we going to do?'

Mum lugged their bags out of the boot. 'Relax!' she said

with a half-crazed smile. 'We've come here to relax!'

'Can we draw too?' asked Marie.

'Of course,' said Mum. 'I've packed your paper and pencils, and we're very close to the Haberdash Gardens. Actually – I'll let Mark reveal the plan.'

Imogen wanted to know 'the plan' right now, but Mum was already marching towards the hotel. The girls followed. 'It's a very trendy place,' whispered Mum as the automatic doors swished apart.

There was a gigantic Christmas tree in the lobby. Mum spoke to the receptionist while Imogen inspected the tree. It was fake. The presents underneath it were fake too.

'No children in the spa after six,' said the receptionist, handing Mum keys for their rooms.

Marie flicked a switch and the tree's lights started flashing.

'Marie!' hissed Mum, without turning round. How had she seen that when she'd been facing the other way? These days, Mum always seemed to be watching.

A porter came and took their bags while Mum checked her phone. 'Mark's got us a table,' she said. 'Aren't you lucky? Not many children get lunch at The Lily Pad.'

The receptionist directed them to the restaurant, and Imogen saw that her mum had been right. All the other diners were grown-ups. They didn't look like they were having much fun. A woman in a baggy dress stared at the waiter. Her partner stared at the bar. An elderly couple picked at their food in silence, as if sitting in different rooms – or perhaps different universes.

'Cathy,' called Mark from a table on the other side of the room. 'Over here! I hope you don't mind, but I've ordered.' He turned to the girls. 'Hello, young ladies. Don't you look lovely?'

Imogen pulled a face and sat down.

Then Mark started talking about his job. Mum reached for the wine. Imogen looked out of the window. A man was moving dried leaves with a blowing machine. Imogen wished she was out there. Even playing with dead leaves was more fun than this.

'We've got to innovate,' continued Mark. 'Go digital or die. That's what I told the board.'

A waiter appeared. He was carrying four plates with piles of colourful vegetables cut into neat little squares.

'Hey, Imogen,' said Mark as the waiter placed their plates in front of them. 'How's it going? Learned any new science facts?'

'Erm, yes.' Imogen eyed her diced vegetables.

Mark moved a vase so he could see her face. 'Care to share with the group?'

'I've been studying how stars die,' said Imogen. 'The really big ones explode and all that's left is a black hole and the black hole eats everything. Even planets. Even light.'

'Amazing,' said Mark, without sounding amazed.

'How can a hole eat light?' asked Marie.

'No one knows what's inside a black hole,' said Imogen. 'It might just be chaos. It might be a portal into another world.' She gave Mark a meaningful stare.

He responded by lowering his voice. 'How's the other stuff going? You know . . . the therapy?'

'Dr Saeed said it's just between me and her,' replied Imogen.

'You can talk to us too,' said Mum. 'We're always ready to listen.'

Imogen shovelled the vegetables into her mouth, buying time. She was only having therapy to keep Mum happy. She didn't have anything to be therapied for. She chewed the vegetables slowly.

'It's going fine,' she said. 'I'm fine.'

'What about you?' said Mark to Marie. 'What have you told the therapist?'

Marie looked at Mum and Mum smiled encouragingly. 'I told her that she shouldn't be afraid of the skret,' said Marie. 'They're not as bad as they look.'

'Right,' sighed Mark. 'So we're still stuck on the La-la Land story.' He clicked his fingers and the waiter brought more wine.

La-la Land. Something stirred inside Imogen. She'd forgotten that Mark used that name. 'Don't take the bait,' she muttered to herself, spearing a line of cubed veg.

CHAPTER 8

'You know,' said Mark, 'the Haberdash Gardens are on the other side of that hedge.' He lifted his chin at the restaurant window. It was hard to believe. The hotel grounds looked so empty, so . . . tidy.

'Dr Saeed said we should take you back to the gardens,' continued Mark. 'She thinks it might unlock the memories from last summer – the real memories, that is.'

But those are the real memories, thought Imogen.

'We could have just visited for the day, but I thought a bit of calming spa-time would do you good. Your mother too. And isn't this place wonderful? It's like all the best bits of the countryside, without any mud.'

'You don't have to worry,' said Mum. 'We'll be with you in the gardens, every step of the way. So will Dr Saeed. She's joining us in the morning.'

Imogen *did* want to visit the gardens . . . but not like this. Not as some kind of experiment. What did they think would happen? That she'd suddenly admit that she'd lied? That she'd made up the door in the tree? Dr Saeed could take her ideas and—

The next course arrived, interrupting Imogen's thoughts. There was a piece of grey meat with a swirl of sauce and a stack of sliced potatoes.

'I bet you've never had a three-course lunch before,' said Mark.

Marie cocked her head. 'When we were staying with Miro, we had seven-course dinners.'

Imogen prodded the potato tower and it fell, splattering sauce across the tablecloth. Mum gave her the evil eye. 'What *is* this?' whispered Imogen, poking the meat with her fork.

'Veal,' said Mum. 'You'll like it.'

'What's veal?' asked Marie.

'A young cow,' said Mark. 'It's got a lovely smooth texture. Very expensive.'

He sliced off a piece and popped it into his mouth.

Imogen moved the vase across the table so she couldn't see him chewing.

'I'm vegetarian,' cried Marie.

'That's not true,' said Mum. 'Try a little.'

Imogen looked back out of the window. The leaf-blower man had gone, but a grey moth was fluttering across the grass. Imogen jumped up from her seat. 'Look!' she gasped, and in her excitement, she knocked over Mum's wine.

'Oh, Imogen!' cried Mum.

'You're missing it!' said Imogen. 'You're missing the moth!'

The grown-ups fussed over the spilled wine, but Imogen had to make them see. This could be her only chance! She climbed on to her chair. 'The shadow moth is *right there*,' she yelled.

Now everyone looked: the woman in the baggy dress, the elderly couple, the waiter by the bar. But they weren't looking out of the window. They were staring at Imogen.

The moth floated up and dropped down in the wind. It didn't look much like a moth any more.

'Mademoiselle,' said the waiter, touching Imogen's arm.

'Imogen Clarke! Get down!' yelled Mum.

'But my moth!' Imogen lowered her hand. Her moth looked a lot like a leaf. 'It was right there . . .'

'She's completely out of control,' muttered Mark, shaking his head in disbelief.

Imogen climbed down from the chair. She knew she was in trouble. The waiter gestured at the grey meat swimming in wine. 'Would mademoiselle like another veal steak?'

'*Mademoiselle* is going to her room,' said Mum.

Imogen cast one final glance at the window, before leaving the restaurant.

CHAPTER 9

Imogen stayed in her hotel room all afternoon. From there, she could see the Haberdash Gardens. Strangely shaped trees stuck up behind the hotel's neat hedge. Weeds poked through underneath. The Haberdash Gardens were trying to expand.

Mum kept popping her head round the door. She always made an excuse, but Imogen knew what was really going on. 'How would anyone kidnap me from here?' she complained. 'This place is like a prison.'

'Just call if you need me,' said Mum. 'There's a phone over there by the bed.'

'I don't know your number,' said Imogen.

'Fine,' sighed Mum and she held out her phone. 'You can call Mark on my mobile . . . I don't like punishing you, Imogen, but we can't go on like this.'

Imogen put the phone in her pocket.

Marie came to join her and, for a while, they sketched in silence. Imogen drew the shadow moth, but she couldn't get the antennae right. Marie copied her and, somehow, her imitation was better than Imogen's original.

Then Marie left to have dinner with the grown-ups. Imogen was alone in the hotel room. She scrunched up her drawing and threw it into the bin, but it didn't make her feel any better.

Later, when Mum returned, Imogen pretended to be asleep. She could hear Mum and Mark talking by the door. 'Perhaps I should wake her,' said Mum. 'She'll be hungry without any tea.'

'Might do her some good,' said Mark. 'Might make her think twice before lying.'

Imogen tried not to scowl. That would be a giveaway. People don't scowl in their sleep.

'She's not lying,' whispered Mum. 'Dr Saeed says the girls really believe in their alternate world. It could be their way of coping with . . . with whatever really happened.'

There was a pause. 'Cathy, you know, the police still haven't found any evidence the girls were kidnapped. It's possible that they just ran away.'

'But why would they run away? They have nothing to run away from.' Mum's voice sounded small, and Imogen wanted to give her a hug.

'Honey, we talked about this,' said Mark. 'It's not a reflection on you. Running away, making things up . . . they're things kids do to test the boundaries.'

'Not mine. Not my kids.'

'Okay,' said Mark. 'Not your kids . . . Shall we go down for a drink?'

The door clicked shut and Imogen lay still as their footsteps faded. She hated Mark. She hated him more than she'd ever hated anyone.

She picked up the hotel phone and called reception, just like she'd seen in films. 'This is room twenty-eight,' she said, using her most grown-up voice. 'I'd like to order room service.'

'Of course,' said the woman on the other end of the line. 'What can I get you?'

'Apple crumble, jelly babies and a banana milkshake.'

The woman hesitated – just for a moment. 'No problem,' she said. 'Would you like to pay now or shall I put it on the room?'

Imogen narrowed her eyes. Mark would be paying. It was his 'treat', after all. 'Put it on the room,' she said.

CHAPTER 10

That night, Imogen only slept lightly. She was woken in the early hours by a clattering sound. She looked around the hotel room. Lights blinked on the TV and the coffee machine. The noise was coming from outside so she slipped out of bed and tiptoed to the window.

There was the moon, like a sideways smile, and there was the hedge that divided the Haberdash Gardens from the hotel. Christmas lights shone from the hotel's trees and spotlights were set into the patio, but the Haberdash Gardens were dark.

Something moved outside, behind the restaurant. Imogen pressed her face against the window, trying to get a better view. A recycling box had fallen over. There was more clattering and a wheelie bin toppled, spilling its rubbish-guts across the patio.

Marie joined her sister at the window. 'What's going on?' she asked.

'Something's messing up the bins,' said Imogen.

Marie squinted at the well-tended grounds.

'There it is – look!' Imogen pointed at a shadow, squatting by the upturned bin. It was tearing at binbags with claws as long as kitchen knives. It had no fur and its arms were strong, with muscles like twisted rope.

'Not a fox,' whispered Marie.

The monster wrestled with a chicken carcass – pulling the legs until they popped free from the body. It turned and raised a bone to its mouth. Imogen recognised him as soon as she saw his enormous tusk-teeth. 'It's Zuby!' she cried. She seized her jumper and pulled it on over her head.

'What's he doing here?' asked Marie.

Imogen put on her coat, jeans and shoes, and slid Mum's phone into a pocket. 'I don't know,' she said. 'I'll ask him.' She was already half out of the door.

'Wait for me,' cried Marie, grabbing her own jeans and coat. 'I'm coming too!'

The sisters sneaked along the hotel corridor and down the stairs. A young woman was sitting behind the reception desk, with her back to the girls. Imogen put a finger to her lips, indicating to Marie not to speak. Then she lowered herself on to all fours and crawled in front of the desk. Marie followed. They were out of the woman's line of sight, too close to be visible.

Imogen stopped near the hotel's exit. If she triggered the sensors for the automatic doors, the woman was bound to look. She'd call Mum and then they'd be in *serious* trouble.

Imogen pulled Mum's mobile out of her pocket and

searched for 'The Lily Pad'. The hotel's web page appeared. Imogen clicked to make a call and the phone at reception started ringing. The receptionist swivelled to take it. 'Hello, this is Eve at The Lily Pad. How can I help?'

Imogen seized her opportunity. She sprang to her feet. The automatic doors slid open. Imogen and Marie rushed out.

'Hello, is anyone there?' said the receptionist's voice from Mum's mobile. Imogen hung up. She was grinning from ear to ear. It had been a while since she'd had this much fun.

The sisters crept round the hotel until they came to the restaurant. Everything was quiet.

'Where is he?' whispered Marie.

There was plastic packaging torn to pieces, and chicken bones stripped of their meat. Patio spotlights and twinkling Christmas lights illuminated the scene.

'Zuby?' said Imogen, looking behind an upright bin. 'Zuby, is that you?'

There was a rustling in the flower bed. The claws emerged first, followed by a pale grey body and a bald head.

'Little humans?' said a familiar scratchy voice.

And Zuby stood before them with an expression of wonder on his face.

CHAPTER 11

'Little humans!' repeated the skret, his voice rasping. 'What are you doing here?'

'What are *we* doing here?' said Imogen. 'This is where we live.'

Zuby stared at the hotel. 'You live in that palace?'

'No, no. Not in the hotel. We do live in this world though. What are *you* doing here?'

Zuby scratched his head. There was something that looked suspiciously like mayo on the tip of his claw. 'The Král found out that I'd released the prisoners without his consent and . . . well, normally, you'd get sliced and diced for that kind of betrayal.'

'When you say "prisoners", do you mean us?' asked Marie.

The skret nodded.

'Oh, Zuby, I'm so sorry!' she cried.

Imogen thought back to their summer adventures. She hadn't realised Zuby would get into so much trouble for setting them free.

'The Král was very understanding,' continued the skret. 'He

sent me into exile as punishment. But I was too late to cross the mountains. When I reached the pass, the winter blizzards had started early. There was so much snow. I could hardly see my own claws . . . The grey moth found me just in time.'

Imogen's pulse quickened. 'The shadow moth brought you here?'

'It led me to the Unseen Door, and I've been hiding in the scrub ever since.' Zuby gestured towards the Haberdash Gardens.

Imogen glanced at the chicken bones and jar of mayo. 'Zuby, how long have you been eating this rubbish?'

'Rubbish?' cried the skret. 'I've been living like a Král! There's all kinds of treasure in these great tall pots.'

'They're not pots!' said Imogen, alarmed. 'They're wheelie bins. You shouldn't eat from them.'

'Why not? There's lots of nutrition.' Zuby picked up the chicken carcass by its pelvis. 'Had a lovely snack from this baby velecour. Such tender meat and nicely salted.'

There was a flash of torchlight on the other side of the restaurant. 'Quick,' said Imogen. 'Someone's coming.' The sisters pushed the skret into the shadows and crouched low. The hedge bristled at Imogen's back.

'They're going to find us,' bleated Marie as torchlight flicked round the bins.

'No, they're not,' said Zuby. 'This is where I came in.' He

reversed through a hole in the hedge.

'Something's been at the rubbish,' said an adult voice. 'Pesky foxes.'

Two security guards lumbered into view. One of them kicked the shredded bin bag. 'Well, I'm not clearing it up,' he mumbled.

'They get in over there,' said the other guard. 'Under the hedge.'

Imogen was already scrambling through the hole after Zuby, into the Haberdash Gardens. 'Come on, Marie,' she hissed.

The security guards' voices were getting louder. Marie crawled through the gap and tucked herself out of sight by the skret.

Long grass brushed up against Imogen's face. She kept still as the men were close now – on the hotel side of the hedge – and any movement might give her away. The men's torchlight cast shadows through the branches. Imogen tried to make herself small.

'I'll get Jim to block the hole in the morning,' said a security guard.

'Jim?' exclaimed the other. 'With his back?'

Marie's eyes shone in the darkness. Zuby's positively glowed.

'I'm not fixing the hedge,' huffed the man. 'That's gardening work, that is. Nothing to do with me.'

The voices faded away.

When Imogen was sure the men had gone, she crawled closer to Zuby. He was crouched with his knees by his ears, tusks sticking out of his mouth.

Imogen wasn't sure if her mum had been serious about calling the army to sort out Mrs Haberdash's monster, but, either way, she didn't want Zuby getting caught in this world. 'You can't stay here,' she whispered. 'If people find you, they'll put you in a zoo . . . or, worse, a museum.'

'What's a muzoom?' asked Zuby.

'Like a prison,' said Marie. 'But you never get out.'

'I wasn't going to stay long,' said the skret in his scratchy voice. 'Just until spring, when it's safe to cross the mountains.'

Imogen could see the hotel's Christmas lights through the hedge. 'But winter has only just started.'

'Your world is ruled by different stars,' said Zuby. 'It was late autumn when I left the Kolsaney Forests, but I found late summer here.' He counted on his claws. 'So, if this is the start of your winter, it should be spring back home. You don't get blizzards in spring - not even in the mountains.'

Imogen thought she saw a smudge of wings.

'I just have to wait for the moth to appear,' said the skret.

Silver glinted in the dark behind him. Imogen didn't dare hope. Was it really her moth or did she just want it to be?

'The Mezi Mûra will come when it's time,' continued Zuby. 'That's one species of moth you can't summon. You can ask for

49

their help when you see them, but they like to do things their own way.'

The shadow moth circled above Zuby's head, giving him a blurry halo.

'But, Zuby, it's here!' cried Imogen.

The skret turned his eyes to the sky. 'Oh!' he said. 'It's you!'

CHAPTER 12

Imogen wanted to whoop with joy, but she was afraid of alerting the security guards so she forced the whoop down inside. Her moth! Her moth with its feathered antennae and beautiful velvety mane. Her moth that Mark said wasn't real. It was right here in front of her, settling on Zuby's claw.

'Its wings are so pretty,' said Marie, leaning in.

The moth's wings trembled as Marie breathed out. Normally, Imogen would have told her to give it some space, but she was so happy!

'No one believes us,' she said, half to Zuby and half to the moth. 'No one believes there's a door in a tree. The police tried to find it, but they couldn't.'

'That's good,' said the skret. 'The Unseen Door is supposed to hide from humans.'

'Why?' said Marie. 'The door didn't hide from us.'

'You can thank the moth for that,' said Zuby. 'Only Mezi Můra can make the door visible to your kind. Not meaning to be rude, but just think what would happen if we had loads of humans slipping between worlds. There'd be wars and diseases and who knows what else. That door was built by skret to cover a rip between worlds – a scratch in time. The portal was never *meant* to exist.'

'But it does exist,' said Imogen, 'and how do you know what is and isn't meant to be?'

The moth crawled along Zuby's claw, up his arm and on to his shoulder.

'Please don't be offended,' said the skret. 'I'm very glad the moth made an exception for you. But that's what it was – an exception. It won't be happening again.'

Imogen felt as if the moth was fluttering inside her belly. Being told it wouldn't happen only made her want it more. She was sick of pretending. Sick of being told what was and wasn't real – what she could and couldn't do.

Besides . . . she'd just had a brilliant idea.

'What if we came with you?' said Imogen, the words rushing out of her. 'What if we all went through the door in the tree?'

The moth crawled up Zuby's neck and on to his face. It sat between his nostrils, opening and closing its wings like a miniature fan.

'Last time I saw you, you were desperate to be here – to be home,' said the skret. 'Why do you always want to be where you're not?'

'Yes,' cried Marie, alarmed. 'We can't get stuck in Yaroslav again! We'd miss Christmas!'

The moth was on Zuby's head now. It looked like it was about to take off.

'It won't be anything like last time,' said Imogen, already wildly excited. 'Zuby can go across the mountains where he'll be safe, and we'll prop the door open so it can't slam shut. We'll only stay for a minute.' She pulled Mum's phone out of her pocket. 'And we can take pictures using *this*. Photographic evidence. You can't argue with that. Then Mum will *have* to believe us! We won't let her find the door, don't worry. We'll just prove to her that it exists!'

The moth took off from Zuby's head. 'Follow that moth!' declared Imogen, rushing into the darkness.

'Wait for me,' cried Marie.

'Little humans,' called Zuby, as he scurried after them. 'I don't think this is a good idea!'

CHAPTER 13

There was no sign telling Imogen that she was trespassing. Not in this corner of the Haberdash Estate. But she knew she was doing it, all the same.

The grass was tall. The shrubs were leggy. The dead leaves lay where they fell. This was the land of the owls and the foxes and the *caw-caw-caw* crows. And, for the last few months, it had been home to Zuby too. 'Careful here,' said the skret. 'The ground gets a bit boggy.'

Imogen activated the torch on Mum's phone, lighting the way for herself and Marie. Zuby could see in the dark and had no need of such 'magic'.

'Promise we won't stay for more than a minute,' panted Marie.

'I promise,' said Imogen, not turning round.

'Promise we won't let the door shut behind us.'

'Promise!' Imogen replied.

'And promise you won't show other humans the way,' cried Zuby. 'Even if you can, even if the moth returns, it's very important that the door stays hidden.'

'I already promised that!' said Imogen with a laugh. 'I'll show Mum the photos, not the real place.'

Imogen thought she heard a sound behind them, but when she turned, there was nothing there – just undergrowth and shadows. She shrugged and carried on, her sister and the skret at her heels.

They paused when they came to the river. The shadow moth was already flying across the water, wings flashing silver in the night. Zuby went first. He scampered along a dead tree that had fallen so it straddled the river.

Zuby crossed the tree-bridge on all fours, claws digging into the bark. Imogen had forgotten how sharp skret talons were. Even though she knew Zuby was a friend, she felt a small shiver of fear.

The phone's light didn't reach to the other side of the river, but Imogen heard Zuby touch down. She climbed up the fallen tree's roots. Her movements were swift, impatient. She couldn't wait to see Mum's face when she showed her the photos. She couldn't wait to prove Mark wrong.

They can't dismiss a photograph of the Kolsaney Forests, thought Imogen, as she inched along the trunk. She could hear Marie breathing not far behind. *I'll get a good shot of Zuby as well. It can't do any harm once he's not in our world.*

Imogen jumped down from the tree, landing hard on the frozen earth. It seemed colder here – on the wild side of the river. Plants waited underground, tucked tight in their bulbs. Trees played dead for the winter.

Imogen helped Marie down from the fallen tree trunk, then she returned her attention to the moth. It was darting about Zuby's head. 'Don't worry, I'm coming,' said the skret in his crackle-hiss voice and they all set off again.

When Imogen glanced back, to check Marie was keeping up, she thought she saw something in the bushes. 'What was that?' she hissed, pointing with the torch on Mum's phone. Marie squinted at the darkness. Zuby lifted his clawed hands, ready to attack.

Everything went very still.

Then a pigeon came bursting from the ivy. With a few panicked claps of its wings, the bird disappeared.

'Silly grey plumptious,' muttered Zuby. 'Nice juicy meat though.'

Imogen opened her mouth, but there was no time to ask Zuby if he really ate pigeons. The shadow moth was getting away. The skret raced after it and the girls followed.

The moth led them to an enormous tree. Imogen recognised it at once, even without any leaves. There was a door in the trunk. It was just the right height for a skret. It was just the right height for a human child too.

Imogen's heart beat double-time.

Zuby cleared the leaves from the threshold, using his claws

as rakes. 'I really don't think you should come with me,' he warned. 'The Mezi Mûra isn't here for you – not this time.'

The moth crawled to the keyhole, wings glistening in the light from the phone.

'What can we use to wedge the door open?' asked Imogen.

Marie grabbed a big stick. 'What about this?'

'That'll do. Smile for the camera.'

Flash! Imogen captured her sister and the skret. Zuby wasn't smiling. He looked more monstrous than ever.

'Perfect,' said Imogen.

The moth folded back its wings and wriggled through the keyhole.

'Are you sure this is going to be okay?' said Marie, biting her bottom lip.

'I don't see what could go wrong,' said Imogen.

Zuby reached for the handle and pulled the door open. He walked into a blaze of green.

'What if—' started Marie, but Imogen wasn't listening. She photographed the door and stepped through.

CHAPTER 14

The forest on the other side of the door was the greenest thing Imogen had ever seen. It was like being inside an emerald. Sunlight streamed through new leaves and birdsong filled the air.

Marie wedged the door open with her stick, taking care to get the position just right.

Imogen waited for her eyes to adjust to the brightness. Then she started taking pictures on Mum's phone. *Snap!* She got a shot of the trees and their buds. *Snap!* She got Zuby, glowering by an anthill.

Imogen felt great. She felt triumphant. *Let's see what Mark makes of this!*

She had photos of spring that were taken in winter, photos of a skret and a door in a tree, photos of forests in the Haberdash Gardens – a place where no forests were supposed to exist.

Perhaps journalists would be interested. Perhaps they'd show the photos in assembly at school. Imogen had better start working on her autograph. But no matter how famous she got, she wouldn't forget her promise. She'd keep the door's location a secret.

She turned to capture it from this new, exciting angle. And there, stepping over the threshold, was a man in a suit. He had to bend to fit through the doorway.

Imogen lowered Mum's phone.

The man was so busy staring at the forest that he wasn't looking at his feet, and he tripped over Marie's stick.

Zuby sprang forward. Imogen shrieked. But neither were fast enough to stop the stick flying out of place. The man tripped into the forest, hands out, mouth open.

Behind him, the door banged shut.

The sound echoed off the trees – slam, slam, SLAM! Like twenty doors closing in rapid succession.

The man was left sprawled on the floor. Even face down, he was unmistakable. The smart shoes. The uncomfortable jacket.

Mark rolled on to his side and groaned. 'Who put that stick there?' he muttered.

CHAPTER 15

Marie rushed to the door, but Imogen already knew it would be locked. She felt the terrible certainty of it, pinning her to the spot. Marie pulled the handle and let out a wail.

Imogen scrunched up her eyes, trying to transport herself back to the hotel. *Just a few photos. Just for a minute.* Why couldn't things ever go to plan?

She opened her eyes. Mark was still lying on the ground. He mumbled something, before lifting his head to blink at the emerald forest. 'Is this some kind of . . . trick?' he asked.

Imogen wondered why Mark was still wearing a suit. It wasn't the kind of outfit you would pull on quickly if you woke up in the middle of the night . . . Hadn't he been to bed?

Mark got up, moving slowly. 'Ah, I get it,' he said. 'This is virtual reality; some kind of cyber forest! They didn't mention *that* in the hotel brochure.'

Marie was running between the trees. 'Come back!' she called to the canopy. But the shadow moth had disappeared.

'It's so realistic!' muttered Mark. He touched the moss on

a branch, inspected the dirt on his shirt. His frown deepened to a scowl. 'All right, Imogen,' he said at last. 'You've had your fun . . . What's going on?'

Imogen could only shake her head. She'd already told Mark the truth and he had called her a liar.

'You can't leave us here!' cried Marie. 'Not again!' She was still searching for the moth.

'It's okay,' said Imogen, turning to the skret. 'Zuby will make the moth return, won't you?'

Zuby opened his mouth to respond. 'My God!' cried Mark. 'What is that?' He rushed over to protect the girls, spreading his arms out wide. 'Stay back,' he shouted at Zuby.

The skret held up his hands to show he meant no harm, but the sight of those claws only panicked Mark more. He picked up a rock. 'Stay back or I'll brain you!'

'Don't!' cried Imogen. She tried to wrestle the rock from Mark's grip.

'It's all right,' said Zuby. 'There's no need to be afraid.'

Mark lowered his weapon – just an inch. 'What the . . . Did it speak?'

'Nice to meet you,' said the skret, with a bow.

'His name is Zuby,' said Imogen. 'He's our friend!'

She couldn't read the look on Mark's face. Disbelief? Anger? Fear?

'This must be a dream,' he said at last. 'A door in a tree? A monster that talks? None of this is real.' He pointed to Imogen and Marie. 'None of *you* are real!'

Imogen watched in stunned silence. How could he still not believe?

'I'm not a dream,' said Marie. 'I'm a girl!'

Mark gave a hollow laugh. 'That's just what Marie would say . . . I never liked children. Never saw the point, but when I met Cathy, I thought, why not give it a go?'

He traipsed to the door and slumped down in front of it, pulling his tie from his collar. 'I tried so hard . . . I did everything I could think of to win those kids round. And what did I get in return?'

'Mark, you can't sit there,' said Imogen. 'You're blocking the door.'

'No,' said Mark, looking straight at Imogen. 'There's none of Cathy's sweetness in her. Nasty, angry thing. Must take after her father . . . Well, I give up. It's not my fault he'd had enough of you brats.'

Imogen took the words like a slap. She stood still for a moment, reeling. Then anger flared in her chest. Mark shouldn't say things like that – shouldn't say things about her father. Imogen was about to let rip when she caught sight of Marie.

The colour had drained from Marie's face. 'Did Dad leave because of us?'

Imogen strangled her rage. Now was not the time for

exploding. She didn't want Marie being upset so she'd have to find a way to distract her. 'Mark, get up,' she snapped.

'I think I'll sit this one out, if it's all the same to you,' he replied. 'I'm waiting for the dream to end.'

'Who is he?' asked Zuby, scratching his head.

'That's Mark,' said Imogen. 'He's friends with our mum. Zuby, will you call back the moth?'

The skret blinked with sad moon-shaped eyes. 'It's like I was telling you, little humans . . . I can't summon that kind of moth.'

'But why did it fly away?' cried Imogen. 'Why has it trapped us again?'

'To be fair,' reasoned Zuby, 'the moth didn't bring *you* through the door. It brought me. How was it to know you'd sneak in? This is all a terrible mistake.'

'Imogen, you promised this wouldn't happen,' said Marie.

Imogen felt the weight of the charge, but she lifted her chin, defiant. 'Don't blame me. Blame *him*.' She pointed to Mark, who'd closed his eyes as if ready to sleep. 'Why did he follow us anyway?' she continued. 'It must have been him hiding in the garden. If he saw us sneak out of the hotel, he should have made us go back! That's what grown-ups are supposed to do!'

'I am sorry,' said Zuby. 'I don't mean to interrupt, but I really must go.'

'What do you mean?' asked Marie.

'The Král sent me into exile. If the other skret find me here, I'll be sliced and diced.' Zuby removed a pole and a sack from the hollow of a tree. 'I put my belongings away for safekeeping. Everything I need to start a new life. I'm going beyond the mountains.'

'But what about us?' cried Imogen.

'You will have to look after each other,' said the skret, opening the sack and removing a cloak. 'Head to Yaroslav. Find Prince Miro. No doubt he'll take you in.' Zuby put on the cloak, protecting his mushroom complexion. 'If I see the silver moth, I will tell it what's happened. I will ask it to take you back home.'

'But . . . it's Christmas.' Marie gave a whimper.

Zuby tied the sack to the pole and slung it over his shoulder. 'I am sorry, little humans, but I did try to warn you. I can only wish you well.' And, with that, he walked away from them, disappearing among the trees.

Imogen watched Zuby go. For a moment, she had a strange feeling, as if someone was watching her in return. 'Zuby's right,' she said. 'We should head to Yaroslav.' She turned to the left. No, that wasn't it. She turned to the right, but those trees weren't familiar either. 'Oh bum-snot!' cried Imogen, despairing.

'Hey,' said Marie. 'What's that?'

'What's what?'

'There's a house over there. Can't you see it? There's a cottage between the trees.'

PART 2

CHAPTER 16

The sudden arrival of three strangers did not go unnoticed in the Kolsaney Forests. The Žal was over, and the woods teemed with life.

A gold-bottomed beetle felt the vibrations of footsteps. It ran for cover, rear end gleaming. Two black squirrels were criss-crossing the canopy. They stopped and stared at the humans below.

The animals weren't the only observers. Bark lids opened. Leaves were lowered so eyes could see – eyes with thin slit pupils. The trees were watching too.

'I don't remember there being a cottage in the forest,' said Imogen. 'I thought people lived up in the trees.'

'I wonder if there's any food inside,' said Marie, stomach growling.

'Let's go and see,' said Imogen. 'Whoever lives there might be able to point us in the direction of Yaroslav.' She began to walk towards the house, trying to keep her gaze fixed on it at all times. She stared so hard that her eyes watered. But the cottage kept slipping out of view, drifting behind trees, reappearing somewhere else.

Mark trailed behind the girls and Imogen cursed him. The one time she could have done with his help and he thought the whole world was a dream.

Daylight was fading when Imogen finally glanced over her shoulder. 'It feels like we've been walking for years,' she complained. But when she turned back, the cottage was in front of her nose.

'Is that what you were looking for?' snorted Mark.

Imogen stared. That was *very* odd . . . She was sure the house had been further away. And it had been facing a different direction. She stomped around the building, confused and slightly annoyed.

At the front of the house, a woman was working in the garden. A white pony grazed with a chicken on its back.

'Good evening,' said the woman, straightening. 'I was wondering when you'd be along.'

Imogen and Marie exchanged looks. 'We're not meant to be here,' said Imogen. The woman made her uneasy. She looked young, but there was something old about her voice.

'And how do you know what is and isn't meant to be?' said the woman.

The hairs on the back of Imogen's neck lifted. Wasn't that what *she'd* said to Zuby?

'It wasn't our plan,' stuttered Imogen. 'It wasn't our plan to let the door close.'

'No, but perhaps it's your destiny.'

Marie peeped out from behind Imogen. 'What's destiny?' she asked.

'It's a story that's written in the stars,' said the stranger, as she brushed soil from her hands.

Mark walked into the cottage garden like he owned the place. 'This dream gets stranger and stranger,' he said, staring at the woman's long robes.

But the woman behaved as if Mark wasn't there. She picked up the chicken and tucked it under her arm. 'Would you like some garlic soup?' she asked the girls. 'I've already got a pot going. It'd be no trouble . . . no trouble at all.'

CHAPTER 17

There wasn't much space inside the cottage. The front room was full of old furniture and pots. Imogen wondered if the woman was a hoarder, like the ones she'd seen on TV.

There was another woman sitting by the fire, but this one had yellow hair. Imogen heard the door shut and she turned to see a very old person step inside, with a chicken tucked under one arm.

'The lady asked us in,' cried Imogen. She didn't want these people thinking she was here uninvited. She wondered where the woman from the garden had gone.

'What lady?' said the ancient one.

'The lady from outside,' said Marie.

The old woman smiled. 'That was me.'

Imogen narrowed her eyes and saw that she was telling the truth. The face of the young woman was still there, although it was hidden beneath wrinkles. She had the same dark eyes, same strange way of speaking.

'But the lady in the garden was different,' said Marie.

'She was young,' blurted Imogen.

'I do look a little older at home,' said the woman. 'That's *time* for you. None of us can escape it entirely – not even me.' She placed the chicken on the floor and watched it toddle away.

'A *little* older?' cried Mark. 'You've lost all your teeth!'

Imogen cringed. Did he have to be so embarrassing? He must still think he was asleep . . .

The old woman seemed not to have heard him, however. 'I'm Ochi, the forest witch,' she said. 'You are most welcome in my home.'

'No!' cried the other woman, the one with yellow hair. 'They're not welcome at all! Who are they and what do they want?' Her gaze flicked from Mark in his dishevelled suit to the children in their waterproof jackets.

Imogen had seen her before . . . although she wasn't sure where. The blonde woman was young and pretty. Her eyes were bright blue, almost lilac.

'They're only travellers,' said Ochi. 'They won't tell anyone in Yaroslav that you're here.'

'They can't stay,' said the yellow-haired woman. 'There isn't enough—' She was interrupted by a bell. Imogen recognised that chiming. But surely it couldn't be?

She turned, and it was! Miro's clock! Miro's clock from the castle, with its face full of stars and its hamster-sized door. What was it doing in here?

But there was no time for such questions. Mark was standing by the mantelpiece. 'Isn't that something?' he said, reaching out. 'They're floating like stars.'

He grabbed at the jewels as they whirled round the clock's face. Imogen wanted to stop him, but she didn't know how.

'Get that man away from my prophecy,' shrieked the yellow-haired woman.

Mark caught a jewel and the clock slowed. 'I haven't had a dream this vivid for years!' He inspected the star, pinned between his finger and thumb.

'Don't do that,' pleaded Ochi.

'Oh, give me a break,' barked Mark. 'It's my dream! I can do what I want!'

The clock's door was opening when Mark caught a second jewel. The clock ground to a halt. It didn't seem to like being touched.

'You're ruining my prophecy!' yelled the blonde woman and she gave Mark a shove. He stumbled and one jewel flew back into position.

The woman tried to free the other star, but Mark's fist closed tighter. 'It's my dream,' he repeated.

'It's my prophecy!' said the woman. She grabbed a pan and swung it at Mark. *Clunk!* Pan collided with skull. Mark groaned and sank to the floor.

'Mark!' cried Marie and she rushed to his side.

'Is he breathing?' asked Imogen, her voice barely a whisper.

Marie held her fingers to Mark's mouth and nodded. His hand must have gone limp because the second star released from his fist. It sailed back up to the clock.

The clock's door opened and a figure trundled out. It was a child in a raincoat. She lifted one arm, pointing at something in the distance.

That was strange . . . The girl from the clock looked just like Marie.

CHAPTER 18

Imogen and Marie sat on the floor facing their mum's semi-conscious boyfriend.

'Do you think he's okay?' whispered Marie.

Mark was deathly pale, staring into space like a zombie.

'I'm not sure,' said Imogen. In one way, she thought the blow to the head had done him good. At least he no longer thought he was dreaming. 'You know when people pinch themselves to see if they're awake?' she said to Marie. 'I think that smack was like a really big pinch.'

Imogen wasn't so sure what to make of the woman who'd done the smacking. You couldn't go around hitting people you'd only just met. And those eyes . . . they were so familiar.

'I don't understand,' said Mark, clasping his head. There was a lump where he'd been struck.

'Garlic soup will make you feel better,' said Ochi and she stirred the pot above the flames.

The yellow-haired woman snatched the spoon from the witch. 'I'll do that,' she snapped. '*You* should be working on my prophecy.'

Ochi's gaze slid over her companion. She seemed to decide it wasn't worth fighting. 'Don't forget the seasoning,' she muttered and she retreated to her desk.

'Can we have some soup too?' asked Marie. The blonde woman nodded. She broke eggs into the pot, tossing the shells on the fire. *Crunch. Crack. Splat.*

'I don't understand,' repeated Mark.

Imogen watched the woman's sharp fingernails as she shredded herbs into the soup. She added other things to it too – things Imogen couldn't name.

When the garlic soup was finished, the woman spooned it into bowls. 'Here,' she said, handing one to Mark and one to each of the girls. 'Drink up.' Then she joined Ochi at the desk. She gave the witch a bowl, but she didn't have one herself.

Perhaps she isn't hungry, thought Imogen.

The young woman peered over the old woman's shoulder. Ochi sipped her soup. The young woman whispered and pointed at the scribbles on the parchment.

Imogen stared at her own dinner. Herbs swam in a milky liquid. She lifted the bowl to her face. It smelled acceptable. She put the bowl to her lips. It tasted delicious – not like eggs and garlic at all, but roasted nuts and cream. The heat filled Imogen's belly, spreading to her fingers and toes.

'It's gone dark outside,' said Marie, slurping her soup.

'Perhaps we should stay here tonight,' suggested Imogen.

Mark nodded, still zombified. He finished his dinner and closed his eyes. He was soon sleeping upright, with his back propped against the wall and his chin on his chest.

On the other side of the room, the women talked in hushed voices. The older one was still scribbling away. The younger one kept glancing at the girls. Imogen stared back. She didn't like the way the blonde woman's eyes flashed. Where had she seen her before?

Imogen wondered what time it was at The Lily Pad. She wondered if Mum was awake and if she'd noticed they were missing. But Imogen was sleepy and these were questions that could wait until morning. Her cheeks were warm and her eyelids were heavy. She lay down on the fluffy fur rug.

'Do you think Ochi can summon the moth?' murmured Marie, her voice blurry with sleep.

'Let's ask her in the morning,' whispered Imogen. 'She did say she's a witch . . .'

The heat from the fire was lovely. The rug was surprisingly soft. Imogen allowed her eyes to close. 'No one believed us,' she murmured. 'They thought we were making it up.' And, quite without warning, sleep took her under.

CHAPTER 19

Imogen was cold when she awoke. The fire had gone out
and Marie was no longer at her side. She sat up and looked
around at Ochi's cottage.

The place seemed sadder in the daylight. The corners had
more cobwebs and the pots looked a little more grey. There was
a snail on the desk, writing messages in slime.

Ochi looked sadder in the daylight too. Her skin was almost
transparent.

'Where's my sister?' asked Imogen, getting to her feet.

'We're too late,' said Ochi.

'What do you mean?' Imogen turned a full circle. 'Where's
my sister?' She said it louder this time.

Mark snored himself awake and blinked at his surroundings.

'We've been sleeping for too long,' said the witch. 'Many
hours have passed.'

Imogen bent down and peered under the desk. 'Marie?'
she called to the shadows. Two beady chicken eyes stared
back.

Imogen ran out of the cottage, through the garden and into

the forest. 'Marie!' she shouted at the trees.

Only birds replied.

Panic started rising in her chest. This wasn't happening. It couldn't be. She'd promised Marie it would all be okay – that they'd only be gone a few minutes – that they'd take a few photos and return to the hotel!

Imogen ran back inside. 'What have you done with my sister?' she shouted, directing her fury at the witch.

'I didn't know she'd take the child,' said Ochi, hiding behind bony hands.

Imogen looked around the room once more. Ochi was right . . . Marie wasn't the only one missing. Where was the yellow-haired woman?

'She must have put a potion in the soup,' said the witch. 'Sent us into an unnatural sleep. They'll be halfway across the mountains by now, riding the pony too hard.'

'Who cares about the pony?' shrieked Imogen. 'What about my sister!'

Mark staggered to his feet with a pained expression. 'Imogen, I've got the mother of all headaches. Please . . . stop shouting . . . Now, what's all this about Marie?'

For the first time in her life, Imogen was glad to hear Mark's voice. No mumbling. No babbling about dreams. He may look a mess, but he sounded okay.

'Marie's been taken by that woman!' she cried.

Mark cradled his head. 'I'm sure she's here. She's just hiding.'

He started opening cupboards, calling Marie's name. He looked under the stairs and checked in the pantry. His movements became frantic. 'She's missing,' he gasped. 'But why – I mean where? She's too young to be out on her own!'

The answer came from Ochi. 'The child has been taken beyond the mountains,' said the witch.

'There are no mountains in this part of England.' Mark looked tired and a little afraid.

'You'll need supplies for the journey,' said Ochi. 'And a couple of horses. It's no easy road.'

'Supplies . . . horses . . .?' Mark shook his head and winced. 'No. I'm calling the police.' He pulled his phone from his pocket and jabbed it three times. The phone beeped. Mark tried again. 'No signal? You have *got* to be joking. This isn't a dream. It's a nightmare! What am I going to tell Cathy? How am I supposed to explain?'

Imogen felt sick. That woman had taken her sister. That woman with the bright blue eyes. Marie would be terrified when she woke – halfway up a mountain, without anyone she knew.

And Imogen had promised it would all be okay.

She had promised they wouldn't stay long.

Mum's mobile was still in her pocket. She took it out and searched for 'The Lily Pad'. The phone said, 'No network'.

Well, that made sense. There was no internet in this world. There was no phone signal either. Mobiles were about as useful as stones.

Ochi took a piece of parchment from her desk. It was covered in diagrams and drawings of stars. 'I've been predicting the future for Anneshka,' she said, 'with a little help from that clock.'

Anneshka . . .

Imogen knew the name. Wasn't Miro's spare mother called something like that? Wasn't she the one who was marrying the king? Now Imogen could place the blue eyes . . .

Anneshka had been wearing a wedding dress. The castle had been on fire and people were screaming and running away, but Anneshka had walked into the flames.

That was the yellow-haired woman.

'Hold up,' said Mark. 'What do you mean, "predicting the future"? What are you? What is this?' He was sounding more like himself by the second.

Ochi smiled. 'I am the forest witch. I could read your stars too, if you're willing to pay.'

A pot on the mantelpiece rattled.

'There's no time,' snapped Imogen. 'Please, Ochi, tell us — what has Anneshka's prophecy got to do with Marie?'

'Prophecies belong to the person who paid,' said Ochi and she pressed her crinkled lips together.

'A child has gone missing,' snapped Mark. 'If you don't

want me reporting you as an accessory to the crime, tell me everything and tell me now!'

The old woman shuffled to the seat by the fire. 'I suppose I could make an exception . . .' She looked at Mark from the corner of her eyes. 'The stars say Anneshka will be queen. She'll rule the greatest kingdom in the world. That is the place that she seeks.'

'And what about Marie?' prompted Imogen.

'The child that came out of the clock looked a lot like your sister, don't you think?'

'A little,' said Imogen, uneasy.

'How does that help us find her?' demanded Mark.

'The child is part of Anneshka's prophecy,' said Ochi. 'Their destinies are tied. I told Anneshka I needed more time to work out the details . . . I should have known she wouldn't listen.'

Imogen was struggling to understand. She thought back to Miro's tower, where little figures had emerged from the clock – a hunter before they'd met Blazen, a running prince before they'd fled.

'You think that clock reads the stars?' she asked Ochi.

'I know it to be true,' said the witch. 'The objects it shows us are signs.'

'This is ridiculous,' muttered Mark.

The chicken strode out from under the desk and flapped its wings in agreement.

'If Anneshka's taking Marie across the mountains, we have to go after them,' cried Imogen. As the words escaped her lips, she felt calmer. *That* was the beginning of a plan. A scary plan, but a plan nonetheless.

'Do I look like I'm ready to go mountaineering?' cried Mark.

Imogen looked him up and down. His smart shoes were caked in mud, his shirt was untucked and the lump on his head was enormous. 'No,' said Imogen. 'You don't look like you've ever climbed a mountain. But I know a boy who has.'

'A boy?' Mark guffawed. 'The last thing this mess needs is more children. We need police or detectives. Preferably both.'

The plan in Imogen's head was beginning to take shape. 'This boy is brave and kind,' she said.

'Bravery will only get you so far,' muttered Ochi. 'Does he have horses?'

'I think so. I think he'll have supplies too.'

'Supplies for what?' cried Mark. 'You're not going anywhere, young lady. You're going back to the hotel where you'll be safe and quiet and do as you're told.'

Imogen narrowed her eyes. 'No, I'm not,' she said. 'I'm going to rescue my sister.'

CHAPTER 20

In Miro's dreams he was always alone. He drifted through the streets of Yaroslav. The statues of his forefathers were lined with frost, but the dream-boy felt no cold.

He peeped in at taverns full of gold-lit faces. He looked in at houses, where children slept in rows. He floated deeper into the city.

There was a dark place in the main square – a space from which no light could escape. There had been a castle here once. There had been a king and a prince.

The black hole swirled, drawing him closer.

The king had loved the prince. He'd loved him more than the most precious stone.

Miro looked down at his feet and saw in the darkness, where no snow could settle, was the heart of the mountain, the *Sertze Hora*.

What was it doing here, glowing so hotly? Glowing so hotly and so far from home? Miro would take it, clutch it tight to his chest. He'd let the warmth spread, let the hearts thump together.

The dream-child reached for the Sertze Hora, fingers

spread wide. He was just like they said. Just like his uncle.

And then Miro was awake.

He sat up quickly. It was only a dream!

He lifted his pillows, one after the other. No Sertze Hora there.

He parted the curtains that surrounded his bed and peered at the rest of the room. No Sertze Hora out there either.

He tiptoed to the shutters and pushed one open. It was morning – early spring. A bird sang on the opposite roof. People walked in the street below. The heart of the mountain was where it belonged.

Miro crept back to his bed. It was only a dream . . .

A man burst into the room without knocking. He was pasty-faced and brightly dressed. 'Good morning, King Miroslav,' he sang. It was Patoleezal, Miro's Chief Adviser. Not that Miro had been given much choice in the matter.

Patoleezal was followed by a long line of servants. 'Light the fire,' he commanded. 'Tie back the curtains. Don't let the king get cold! He'll have grilled sausage for breakfast and that nice lard-soaked bread.'

'I'm not hungry,' said Miro.

'Nonsense,' said Patoleezal. 'We can't have you turning into skin and bones.'

Ever since the fire had destroyed Castle Yaroslav, Miro had been living in Patoleezal's mansion. It was a luxurious place, in an expensive part of town, but Miro never felt quite at home. He didn't feel much like a king either.

When all of the servants were busy, Patoleezal approached Miro's bed.

Miro shoved his toy lion under a pillow. He'd had it since he was born, the last surviving gift from his mother, but Patoleezal didn't approve of stuffed toys. Kings were supposed to be men.

'How are we this morning, Your Highness?' He didn't wait for an answer. 'I was wondering if you'd signed the papers? And I hoped to have a word about my friend. He's been very good at smoothing things over. Perhaps a knighthood's in order?'

Miro watched Patoleezal's mouth as he talked. It was the only part of his face that seemed active.

'There's a dispute to be settled about grain-houses,' continued the Chief Adviser. 'And a complaint about the lesni being allowed to hunt.'

'I won't change my mind,' said Miro. 'The forests belong to them.'

Patoleezal bowed his head. 'You're putting good people out of a job. Don't you want to keep the huntsmen onside? Don't you care about the welfare of your people? There's also a question about taxes. Oh, and two young ladies want to see you.'

Miro's heart did a drumroll. 'Which young ladies?'

'Lady Ropooka and the Duchess of Žaba.'

Miro covered his face with a pillow. 'I don't want to see them.'

Patoleezal lifted the corner of the cushion. 'Between you and me, I think Lady Ropooka would make a good wife, when you come of age. Her family are the wealthiest in Yaroslav, and goodness knows the royal coffers need restocking –' he lowered his voice – 'after the incident with the mechanical dragon.'

'I don't want to see them,' cried Miro, throwing the pillows off his bed. 'I don't want to see anyone.'

Patoleezal gave a simpering smile. 'Being king comes with many duties. Besides, it's already arranged. They'll join us tomorrow for luncheon.'

CHAPTER 21

It didn't feel right being in Yaroslav without Marie. Imogen wanted to point out familiar buildings, but each time she saw Mark walking beside her, the excitement died in her chest.

It was replaced by a sickening guilt when she remembered what had happened to Marie. Imogen had encouraged her to go through the door. She had promised it would all be okay . . .

Mark kept flitting between wonder and panic. He stared at the tall houses and bustling streets. 'How on earth are we going to find your sister? Don't get too far ahead!'

'Don't get too far behind,' mumbled Imogen. She knew where she had to go.

The castle was still a burnt-out shell, but she'd asked a man at the gates for directions and he'd told her where 'King Miroslav' could be found. Imogen had done a double take when the man called Miro that. *Of course*, she remembered. *Miro is no longer a prince. Now his uncle is gone, he's the king.*

She led the way past painted houses and swinging shop signs. All trace of skret bones had gone from the city. There were no more vertebrae decorating doorways, no more skulls embedded in walls. Peace must be holding between the humans and the skret.

In Imogen's arms was a case about the size of a shoebox, but there were no shoes inside. The case rattled a little as she walked.

'You shouldn't have taken that clock,' called Mark, still lagging behind. 'What would your mother say?'

'Finders keepers,' said Imogen, and she held the case a little tighter.

'That is NOT what she'd say! If Ochi wasn't so elderly, she'd be chasing us through the streets, demanding to have her clock back. What put the idea in your head? Since when did you steal from old ladies?'

'I need it,' said Imogen.

'For what?'

Imogen hesitated. She wasn't sure she believed the witch. She wasn't sure if the clock read the stars. It certainly fitted with what Andel had told her, all those months ago . . .

Mark marched ahead and blocked her way. 'Imogen, I asked you a question.'

She stopped and rolled her eyes. 'It might help us find—' She couldn't say Marie's name. Each time she thought of her sister, afraid and alone, it was like a balloon expanded in Imogen's throat. It choked out the words and the air. She swallowed hard. 'The clock might be useful,' she managed.

'It's got five hands!' cried Mark, eyes bulging. 'It doesn't even tell the right time!'

Imogen clutched the case to her chest. 'Finders keepers,' she growled.

Behind Mark, a cart rolled downhill, pursued by an irate farmer. Every moment they stood here arguing, Marie was getting further away. Imogen needed to find Miro. She needed horses and supplies.

Mark raised a hand to the lump on his head and Imogen seized her chance. She darted round him and skipped up the street. Mark said a rude word and followed. Two skret stood on the corner, with clawed feet poking out from under their cloaks. Imogen kept her distance on instinct. *Silly me*, she thought. *They aren't a threat any more.*

But when Imogen glanced over her shoulder, the skret stared back with piranha eyes. She put on a spurt of speed, power-walking towards Kamínek Bridge.

'Did you see that?' cried Mark. 'There were *goblins*! How can people act like it's normal?'

The locals were staring at Imogen too. She must have looked odd in her jeans and her raincoat. Mark stuck out in his dirt-smeared suit. Imogen realised, with a funny brain twist, that *they* were the new monsters in town.

'Where's the police station?' said Mark.

'There isn't one,' snapped Imogen stomping over the bridge.

Statues lined the crossing – warriors, holy men and . . . what was this? Someone new.

Imogen paused at the stone man's feet. He was holding a sword in one hand and a bear's head in the other. He looked as if he could take on the world. The sculptor had made him too slim, but Imogen recognised him all the same.

It was Blazen Bilbetz. The man who'd seduced the Queen of Mikuluka. The man who'd died when the tallest tower fell. Poor Blazen . . . the city was a little less colourful without him.

Mark leaned against the stone Blazen's leg and gazed downriver at the view. 'So, this is what you were talking about . . . It *is* a real city.'

This time yesterday, Imogen would have screamed, 'I told you so,' but proving Mark wrong had lost its appeal. She'd won the debate. She'd got what she wished for. She just hadn't wished for it to happen like this.

She'd give anything to have Marie with her.

'Looks like an interesting place,' said Mark. 'Bit old-fashioned. But I can see that it's got potential.'

'Potential for what?' said Imogen, annoyed. She exited the bridge and turned left. They weren't far from the place they were seeking – the place where Miro now lived.

Surely Miro would be able to help save her sister? Sorting out other people's problems was what kings did . . . wasn't it?

CHAPTER 22

Now Imogen and Mark walked through the wealthiest part of the city. The houses had swirly bits of stonework, and steps leading up to their grand front doors.

Imogen stopped by a seven-storey mansion with elegant, curved windows. Royal Guards were stationed on either side of the entrance.

'This must be it,' she said, and she handed the box with the clock in it to Mark. She strode up the steps and banged on the doors. The Royal Guards stared ahead as if nothing had happened.

'No one's coming,' hissed Mark. He checked his mobile. 'Are you sure there isn't a phone box in this place? Somewhere we can dial nine-nine-nine?'

Imogen was about to knock again when the doors flew open. She nearly knocked on the belly of a man. 'Yes?' he said, peering down his nose. He was dressed in an incredible mishmash of colours. His tunic seemed to be sewn from silk hankies and his mouth was elastic.

'We need to speak to King Miroslav,' said Imogen.

The man smiled a big fake smile. 'Nobody sees the king without an appointment. Especially not waifs and wanderers like you.'

'How do we make an appointment?' asked Imogen.

'You would have to speak to the king's Chief Adviser.'

'Who's that?'

'Why, that's me,' said the man. 'Patoleezal Petska.'

Imogen narrowed her eyes. 'But we're speaking to you right now.'

The man pulled a scroll from his pocket and let it unfurl. He pretended to read. Imogen knew he was pretending because his eyes weren't scanning the page.

'I'm afraid there's a rather long waiting list.' Patoleezal turned down the corners of his mouth.

'We're friends of Miro's,' said Imogen. 'I don't think he'd mind if we skipped the queue.'

'The king never mentioned any friends. He's expecting a visit from Lady Ropooka and the Duchess of Žaba. Are you a lady?'

Imogen shook her head.

'Or a duchess?'

She shook her head again.

'Didn't think so.' Patoleezal rolled up the scroll.

He was about to leave when Mark bounded up the steps. He tapped Patoleezal on the shoulder. 'Hello, I'm Mark. Mark

Ashby. I'm used to dealing with important people. If I could just have five minutes with the king—'

The guards drew their swords with a synchronised swoosh. Mark held up the clock case as if it was a shield.

'What is this nincompoop selling?' demanded Patoleezal.

The Royal Guards didn't answer. They were ready to split Mark in two.

Imogen slipped behind the men. With her back against the wall, she inched sideways. Maybe they wouldn't notice . . . Maybe if she moved very slowly . . .

'I'm not in sales, actually,' said Mark. 'I'm an expert in strategic growth.'

'Growth?' Patoleezal puffed himself up. 'I don't need any help with growth. I think you'll find I'm taller than many.'

'That's not what – look – none of that matters,' cried Mark. 'A child has been taken! I'm reporting a crime.'

Patoleezal wafted his hand. 'Get this clown off my doorstep. He can sell his growth potion elsewhere.'

The guards grabbed Mark and threw him backwards. Imogen winced as he rolled down the steps. The case landed by his head with a clunk. She hoped that the clock was okay.

'Clear off,' shouted one of the guards. 'The king doesn't want what you're selling.'

Mark lay spreadeagled on the cobbles, chest heaving with outrage. 'I am *not* in sales! I'm a business revenue consultant!'

'And I'm all five queens of Valkahá,' said Patoleezal. He seemed to have forgotten about Imogen. If she reached with her fingers, she could touch the front doors.

'I'll have you reported,' cried Mark. 'There are elected officials – regulators – OMBUDSMEN! No one's above the law! Not even advisers to the king!'

'I *am* the law,' muttered Patoleezal.

Imogen slipped into the mansion. She needed to find Miro and get help for her sister. Mark would just have to look after himself.

CHAPTER 23

Inside the mansion, Imogen crept across the hall. Her image was reflected in the marble floor. From this angle she could almost see up her own nose.

Which way should she go? Right, through the archway? Left, through the double doors? Straight up the extra-wide staircase?

Patoleezal was talking to the guards, but it wouldn't be long before he turned and saw her. Imogen would have to think fast. Something told her the king wouldn't live on the ground floor. She dashed upstairs, trying to make each footstep silent.

But her attempts to go unnoticed were in vain. There were two more Royal Guards up here. Imogen met their eyes as she climbed the last step. There was no point running. She straightened her shoulders and walked towards the men.

'I'm here to see the king,' she said. She could feel the guards eyeballing her jeans and coat. *Just look confident*, she thought. *You'll be no use to Marie if you can't get past these two.* She stood even taller.

Somewhere downstairs a door slammed shut.

'Chop, chop,' piped Imogen. 'I haven't got all day.' She thought that was what a lady or a duchess might do.

The guards exchanged looks. 'And who shall I say is calling?' asked the man on the left.

Imogen tried to remember the names Patoleezal had mentioned at the door. 'Lady Ropooshka,' she tried.

'You mean Ropooka?' said the other guard, suspicious.

Footsteps echoed across the marble hall. Imogen was running out of time. 'No,' she cried. 'I don't mean Ropooka. I'm sick of people mispronouncing my name.'

'Sorry, m'lady. I didn't mean to be rude.' He turned and indicated for Imogen to follow. Her performance had worked!

The guard led Imogen down a windowless corridor, where the ceiling was covered in gold. *Don't look impressed*, she thought. *Lady Ropooka wouldn't be fazed by a little gold leaf.*

The Royal Guard ushered Imogen into a room with mirrors on every wall. A chandelier drooped from the ceiling. A throne stood alone on a plinth. And there, staring out of a curved window, was a boy who looked just like Miro.

'Your Majesty, you have a visitor,' said the guard.

'Don't want visitors,' said Miro, still facing away.

'But Your Majesty, it's the Lady Ropooshka.'

'Especially not her,' said Miro. 'Besides, you fool, it's *Ropooka*.'

The guard turned to Imogen. 'Sorry, m'lady. The king's not receiving any visitors today.' He tried to steer her out of the mirrored room, but Imogen shook herself free.

'Not even friends?' she asked.

Miro's head snapped in her direction. His eyes were dull. His face had paled. He was the ghost of the boy that she'd known.

'Miro, it's me!' Her voice made the chandelier tinkle. 'Marie's been taken and I need your help!'

But Miro seemed caught in the mirrors – reflected, refracted and bent out of shape. There were infinite kings with far-apart eyes. Infinite kings in a lovely glass cage. None of them were quite like the boy who'd been prince.

Imogen's confidence floundered. Perhaps Miro had forgotten. Perhaps he wouldn't help her rescue Marie.

The guard took Imogen's arm. 'Miro!' she cried. 'It's me!'

'You heard the king,' boomed the guard. 'He doesn't want any visitors – lady or duchess or anything else.' He pulled her out of the room.

Imogen tried to break free, but the guard's grip only tightened.

There were people at the far end of the corridor: Patoleezal and the other Royal Guard.

'There she is!' cried the guard, pointing. 'She said she's Lady Ropooka! She said she was here for the king!'

Patoleezal positively growled.

Imogen grabbed on to anything she could – candlesticks, paintings, the edge of a door – but the guard dragged her down the passage. 'Miro!' she screamed. 'I need you!'

What had happened to her friend? Why wouldn't he make it stop?

'No one sees the king without my permission,' cried Patoleezal. He was only a few steps away now. 'Especially not the likes of you!'

Then, from behind, came the voice of a boy. 'Oi, you! Let go of my friend!'

CHAPTER 24

Imogen stood in the mirror room. It was just her and Miro now – her and Miro and all their reflections. They were far apart, facing each other.

'You look the same,' muttered Miro.

Imogen hesitated. He seemed so different. What could she say? 'Of course,' she replied. 'It's only been a few months since we left.'

'Feels like longer,' said Miro.

Outside, the sun was low in the sky. Inside, the room was full of crystal light. It splintered from the chandelier, casting strange shapes on the children's faces.

'Why did you come back?' asked Miro.

Imogen realised, with a lurch, that he was hoping she'd reply, *I came to see you*. But she couldn't say that. It wasn't the truth. She wished Marie was there to smooth things over.

'You should have come home with us,' she said.

'I belong here,' said Miro. 'I'm the king. It's my duty.' His voice was as hard as the glass in the mirrors.

Imogen glanced at the throne. It was the room's only

furniture and it looked kind of lonely. 'I need your help, Miro,' she said. 'I'm going to rescue Marie.'

'Rescue Marie? From what?'

'She's been kidnapped by Anneshka.'

Miro faltered. 'Anneshka Mazanar is dead. She tried to cross the mountains in winter.'

'No. She's crossing the mountains as we speak, and she's taken Marie. She's obsessed with some magic prophecy. She thinks Marie's part of it.'

Miro half tripped to his throne, landing on the seat with a thump. He looked small sitting there. He looked like a child pretending to be a king.

'Anneshka is not a good person,' he said.

'I know that. She's stolen my sister!'

'No, but I mean . . . she's evil. She killed Yeedarsh and Petr and she tried to kill me.'

'Oh,' said Imogen. That balloon feeling was back in her throat, inflating so her voice went all tight.

'Marie is in great danger,' said Miro.

Imogen's mind was racing. Marie was in danger – needed rescuing fast – but Miro was in such a weird mood. Would he give her supplies for her journey? She couldn't chase Anneshka without her friend's help . . .

Suddenly, Imogen felt very tired. 'Is there space on that throne for two?'

Miro shuffled over and she sat down beside him.

Imogen looked at the glittering room. She looked at her reflection and wished, for a second time, that Marie was there. Marie had always been better at understanding their friend, with his sulks and his royal bravado.

She imagined Marie in the mirror – her waterproof coat zipped up to her chin, her red hair tied in a scraggly knot. The imaginary sister started smiling. The solution was obvious. Imogen started smiling too.

It could be just what he needs . . .

'I'm going to save my sister,' said Imogen, turning to face Miro. 'I'm going to cross the mountains. It will be a long and dangerous journey. I'd hoped you'd give me a horse and some food . . . But since you're so miserable about "doing your duty", why don't you come with me too?'

CHAPTER 25

'I can't just run away,' said Miro, jumping down from the throne. 'I've got a kingdom to rule!'

'Why not? Everyone needs a break . . . Patoleezal can look after Yaroslav while you're gone. Anyway, I'm not suggesting you *run* anywhere. We'll take horses.'

Miro started walking back and forth and the reflected kings copied. Millions of Miros paced like lions at the zoo. 'Running away, taking a break . . . It's all the same. It's irresponsible!'

Imogen lifted her feet on to the throne and sat there cross-legged. 'What's the worst that could happen?' she asked.

Miro stopped pacing and stared. 'We could get stabbed or mauled. We could die a slow, painful death.'

'And what, exactly, are you doing *here*?' said Imogen.

'How DARE you ask such a question! I am king! I am very busy all of the time.'

'It doesn't seem to be doing you much good,' she said stiffly. 'You look ill . . . You've been alone for too long.'

Miro ran to the nearest mirror. He inspected his curly brown hair and the dark half-moons under his eyes. 'I'm not alone,' he murmured. 'I have Patoleezal . . . and the Royal Guards. There are thousands of people in Yaroslav.' He was still gazing at his reflection. 'Some of them think that I shouldn't be king. They say I'm too like my uncle.'

'Nonsense,' said Imogen. 'Your uncle stole the Sertze Hora. You'd never do anything like that.' She drummed her fingers on the side of the throne, wondering when they'd be able to leave.

'Others say I'm not like him enough,' muttered Miro. 'I don't look like other kings.'

'You look like your dad,' said Imogen simply. 'You showed us his statue.'

'My mother didn't look like Yaroslav's other queens. They said her skin was too dark.'

'They're wrong,' cried Imogen. 'It doesn't matter what you look like.'

Miro placed both his palms on the mirror. 'It might not matter when you look like *you*.'

'I didn't mean—' Imogen swallowed her words. Miro was watching her reflection intently. 'Perhaps I meant that it *shouldn't* matter . . . and that isn't the same thing, is it?'

'No,' said Miro. 'It's not.'

Imogen slipped down from the throne and her face hovered behind her friend's in the mirror. 'What was your mother like?' she asked.

Miro's hands left fuzzy marks on the glass. The fingerprints were spread wide as if reaching for something – or someone.

'I can't remember,' he whispered, and he sounded so sad that Imogen almost forgot her own fears. 'I know that she came from far away. A princess from beyond the mountains . . . but I don't remember much else.'

'Miro . . .' Imogen placed her hand on his shoulder. 'Come with me.'

'I can't. I've got to be a good king. I've got to show them I'm not like my uncle.'

'Forget about the people who think you're like him,' pressed Imogen. 'They don't sound very nice. Come with me to rescue Marie! It can't be that bad beyond the mountains if that's where your mother was from.'

'Why do you think she came here?' cried Miro. He paused, then he turned to face Imogen. 'The merchants used to bring stories.' There was an impish gleam in his eyes.

Now *that* was more like the boy Imogen remembered. 'What kinds of stories?' she asked.

'Stories from beyond the mountains. Terrible tales . . . My old nurse said there are armoured monsters who steal children. They have furry bodies and they carry big clubs. If you see one, you should run and hide.'

'What else did your nurse say?'

'There are people with gills and webbed hands who live in rivers. They smell like fish and they swim like them too.'

'I don't believe it,' said Imogen, although she thought that she might. Her belly did a flip.

Miro was getting into character and he lifted his hands as if they were claws. 'There are cats the size of wolves that miaow in the moonlight.' He put back his head and let out a yowl. 'There are grottoes and waterfalls and mountains without names.'

He paused for breath and Imogen saw the colour return to his cheeks. 'Go on,' she prompted. 'What else?'

'There are marshes so vast that no one's ever reached the other side. There are buvol and slipskins and hundreds of hobashi. There's even a realm with a water dragon!' Now he was positively jumping on the spot.

Imogen nodded, encouraging him to go on, but Miro slowed and collected himself. 'It's a terrible place . . . beyond the mountains. We're much better off here.'

'But what about my sister?' cried Imogen. 'If those stories are true, Marie isn't only in danger from Anneshka. There's danger all around!'

Miro rotated the rings on his fingers. He moved them one by one, as if trying to crack a puzzle, as if setting his jewellery at just the right angle would fix everything.

'Why does Anneshka Mazanar think your sister is part of her destiny?' he asked.

'I'll explain on the road.' Imogen turned to leave.

'Wait!' cried Miro.

Imogen sneaked a glance over her shoulder.

'If we're going that far,' said Miro, 'we'll need horses . . . and plenty of food.' He pointed at Imogen's raincoat. 'You can borrow some proper clothes too.'

Imogen almost smiled.

CHAPTER 26

It didn't take Imogen long to find Mark. He was loitering near Patoleezal's mansion with the clock case under one arm. 'Imogen!' he cried when he saw her. 'There you are!'

His shirt was missing buttons. He looked dazed and lost – like he'd popped out for lunch and found himself in a jungle. 'I've searched this whole town,' he said. 'There's no phone box, no police station, no nothing. They don't even have a pharmacy. I can't even buy painkillers for my head.'

'I told you so,' muttered Imogen.

'There's nothing else for it,' said Mark. 'We'll have to go after your sister ourselves.' He put one hand on his hip, as if this was great news.

Imogen couldn't help wondering, and not for the first time, why her mum liked this man. 'That's what I've been saying all along,' she grumbled.

Mark pretended not to hear. He squinted at the distant mountains. It was dusk and the peaks had faded to outlines, with the forest a dark shadow at their feet. 'I think we should leave soon,' Mark declared.

Imogen was so angry that she had to stop herself kicking a statue. 'I know,' she said. 'We're going in the morning. Miro's sorting the supplies.'

'Miro?' Mark wrinkled his brow.

'My friend,' snapped Imogen. 'The King of Yaroslav, remember? He's coming with us to rescue Marie.'

Imogen and Mark were allowed to sleep in Patoleezal's mansion. Patoleezal didn't look very happy about it, but Miro was the king, so Patoleezal had to agree. Imogen was given the room next to Miro's. Mark slept in a chamber downstairs.

A candle lit the space by Imogen's bed, but its light couldn't reach the ceiling. The room was taller than it was wide and Imogen felt boxed in, like she was sleeping in a luxurious grave.

She placed the clock of stars under the bed, checking its case was still shut. Then she changed into the massive nightdress that had been provided by Patoleezal's servants.

There were voices outside the mansion – a man shouted, a woman laughed, a door banged shut. It was strange hearing people in Yaroslav at night. Imogen still remembered the calls of the skret . . .

She blew out the candle and let her head sink into the pillow. She would need as much sleep as possible before beginning her quest . . . *Beyond the mountains*. There was a mythic ring to the words. She wondered where her sister was sleeping right now.

Something stirred behind the curtain. 'Hello?' said Imogen, lifting her head. 'Who's there? Why are you hiding?' The curtain's tasselled hem lifted and Imogen held her breath. 'It can't be,' she whispered. 'I got rid of my worry creatures.'

But there it was. Defying all logic. The worry creature crawled into view. It was as tall as a garden gnome, with a potato-shaped body and pale skinny limbs.

You can't get rid of us, it hissed. *We're always in the shadows, getting fat on your fear.*

'I'm not afraid,' gasped Imogen. But as the words left her lips, she knew it was a lie.

The worry creature reached towards her and Imogen's chest tightened, her breaths coming shallow and sharp. 'You're not real,' she whimpered. 'You can't be.'

Imogen hadn't told anyone about the worry creatures. Not her therapist. Not her mum. Not even Marie.

You should be ashamed of yourself, it snarled. *Luring your sister away from the hotel . . . bringing her here just to prove that you're right. You love having an audience, don't you?*

'Leave me alone,' said Imogen, trying to keep the wobble from her voice. 'Everything's going to be fine.'

The creature gave her an evil smile. *Marie will be dead before you find her.*

'Go away!' Imogen's voice was a squeak. She sprang out of bed, but the worry creature wouldn't back down. They never did.

It was all coming back to her now – the long lonely nights, the bad thoughts, the terror that seized her by the throat. She'd thought it was over. She'd thought that, if only she could forget about the worry creatures, they'd forget about her too.

The creature drew its finger across its neck. *Dead, dead, dead. Dead before you find her.*

That was enough. Imogen flung the curtains apart. The worry creature grabbed the hem of her nightdress and started to climb the outside. *Dead, dead, dead.* It swung on to her shoulder, sharp little fingers tugging her hair.

Imogen opened the window and wrenched the creature from her neck. *DEAD, DEAD, DEAD!* It writhed and screamed.

'Leave me alone,' cried Imogen and she hurled it out of the window. The worry creature hit the cobbles with a splat.

She listened for a reply . . .

None came.

But the creature would soon pick itself up and begin climbing the gutter. Imogen shut the window and secured the latch.

'Everything's going to be fine,' she sobbed as she ran back to her bed.

CHAPTER 27

Imogen was woken by a candlelit face. 'We need to go,' whispered Miro.

Pink-purple light peeped between the curtains. It was very early in the morning, and as Imogen stirred she remembered what had happened to her sister. 'Marie,' she cried, sitting up.

'It's all right,' said Miro. 'We're going to find her. But we have to leave now.'

Imogen felt her sister's absence like a hole in her chest – a horrible, hollow ache. She raised a hand to the pain and tried to rub it away.

Miro placed the candle by her bed. In his other arm was a heap of clothing. 'I think these will be the right size,' he said. 'I'll wake Mark and we'll meet you outside. If anyone asks what you're doing, just say that Patoleezal knows.'

'Hang on,' said Imogen. 'Does he not?'

Miro shook his head. 'He'd never let me go beyond the mountains. But don't worry. The guards won't wake him unless they get *really* suspicious.'

'But you're king,' said Imogen. 'And he's just an adviser.

He can't tell you what to do.'

'You don't know Patoleezal,' mumbled Miro and he dumped the clothes at the end of her bed.

Imogen reached for them – drawn to the gold thread and brocade. There were trousers, a cloak and a quilted jacket, a yellow sash and fur-lined boots. 'Thank you,' she said. The ache in her chest was still there, each time she thought of Marie, but it helped to know Miro was coming with her.

'It's my honour,' he said rather grandly. And, with that, he slipped out of the chamber.

Imogen dressed in the half-light of dawn. Yesterday's outfit was scrunched on the floor. Jumper. Raincoat. Jeans. Mum hated it when she left her clothes like that. 'What are you?' Mum used to tease. 'A girl or a snake? It looks like you've just shed your skin!'

As Imogen fastened her cloak, she couldn't help feeling that Mum had a point. She *was* shedding her skin. She hoped this new version of herself would be better than the old one – the one who'd led Marie through the door in the tree and slept while she got kidnapped, the one who'd let Anneshka get away.

Imogen took the magic clock from under the bed, blew out the candle and left the room.

The sun hadn't risen, but its rays ran on ahead, turning the mountains lilac and bathing the city in gold. Mark and Miro were waiting on the street with horses and a puzzled Royal Guard.

For a moment, Imogen didn't recognise her mum's boyfriend. His suit had been replaced by a tunic and cloak. His shiny shoes had been swapped for fur-trimmed boots. He looked like he belonged here.

Miro had changed too. He seemed happier, lighter. He skipped along the cobbles as if his ankles had wings. 'This one's for you,' he said to Imogen, leading a pony towards her.

'I thought it was for the Lady Ropooka,' said the guard, looking Imogen up and down. 'The *real* Lady Ropooka.' Then he glanced from the king to Patoleezal's mansion, as if wondering which master to obey.

Please don't wake Patoleezal, prayed Imogen.

There were saddlebags on the pony and Imogen peeked inside, curious to see what Miro had brought. One pouch was stuffed with food – smoked meat and wax-sealed cheeses. The other held mittens and a purse. Rolled furs were tied on top. Imogen put the clock case with the furs, securing it with a loose strap. 'You've got better at packing,' she said to her friend.

'Lofkinye was a good tutor,' said Miro, smiling, and he held out his hands to give Imogen a leg-up. She scrambled into the saddle, trying not to pull the pony's mane.

'I wish horses came with seat belts,' said Mark, climbing on to a brown mare. And then, in case anyone thought he was afraid for himself, he added, 'They're wild animals. Not safe for children.'

Miro mounted the third horse, a stallion with a glossy black coat. In the golden sunrise, he looked every inch the king.

'Does Lord Patoleezal know you're going riding?' asked the guard.

'Yes,' said Miro, Mark and Imogen all at once.

Behind the guard, the mansion was stirring. Candlelight flickered in the mirror room.

Imogen wondered if this would be a good time to mention that she'd never ridden a horse before. Not even a small one. But then a window opened and Patoleezal leaned out.

'Miroslav,' he called from three storeys up. 'Where are you going at this ungodly hour? The Lady Ropooka is visiting today. You can't just take off!'

The Royal Guard grabbed the stallion's bridle. Imogen sighed. They were caught.

Chapter 28

Miro tried to make his horse move, but the guard only tightened his grip on the bridle.

'This is really not on,' said Mark, squinting up at Patoleezal. 'First you accuse me of being a salesman. Now you're harassing a child.'

Patoleezal disappeared from the window.

Miro tugged at his horse's reins and the stallion's nostrils flared. Imogen didn't know a lot about horses, but she could see this one was annoyed. It didn't like being encouraged to move while the guard was holding it back.

'Please, Your Majesty,' said the guard, getting nervous.

Panic was spreading among the horses. Mark's mare let out a squeal.

That did it.

Miro's stallion reared.

The guard was forced to let go of the bridle, and Imogen gasped, expecting Miro to fall. But the boy leaned forward and held on to the horse's neck.

The doors of the mansion flew open.

'Miroslav, get down from that beast!' Patoleezal was standing on the top step in a very long nightshirt.

Miro nudged the stallion with his heels and the horse bolted.

'Stop them!' roared Patoleezal, hopping on bare feet.

Mark did something with his legs and the brown mare leaped after Miro. Imogen realised, with horror, that she didn't know how to make her pony go. She was the last rider outside the mansion.

The guard lurched towards her, but Miro had chosen the pony well. It gave a high-pitched whinny and took off after its friends.

It was all Imogen could do to stay on. *Bumpety-bump.* Her bum left the seat. The guard was chasing, boots slapping stone. But he couldn't keep pace with the pony.

A scream escaped Imogen's lips. *Bumpety-bump.* She tried to cling on with her legs, but the tighter she squeezed, the faster her mount seemed to go.

'Stop,' cried the guard, 'in the name of—'

Imogen never heard who the man thought he worked for. The pony careered round the corner, leaving the Royal Guard behind.

It didn't slow until they reached Kamínek Bridge, where Miro and Mark were waiting. Imogen's chest heaved. Her body was jangling with nerves.

'Imogen, are you okay?' cried Mark.

She nodded, unable to speak. Flying velecours had been easy compared to this. She hadn't known ponies were so bouncy.

'I released the guards' horses from the stables,' said Miro. 'They won't be able to follow.'

Imogen was genuinely impressed, but too out of breath to say.

'Uh-oh,' said Mark. 'Here comes the cavalry.'

There was one man approaching on horseback, nightshirt flapping in the wind.

Patoleezal.

His horse was small. Far too small. He must have taken it from someone else.

'Let's go,' said Miro, and he spurred his stallion.

'Imogen,' said Mark. 'This isn't safe. You don't know how to—'

But her pony was off, following in the stallion's wake. Imogen's heart jolted. *Bumpety-bump.* This time, she didn't think she'd stay on.

Mark's mare was overtaking her pony. 'Hold the saddle horn,' he yelled as he passed her. 'Don't you dare fall off!'

Imogen didn't know what he was talking about, but when she glanced down, she saw a strange lump at the front of the saddle. It looked a bit like a car gear stick. She grabbed it and felt more stable. Houses flew by in a blur.

Mark was ahead now, hot on the heels of Miro's black horse.

He kept looking over his shoulder, shouting instructions to Imogen, but the rushing air tore at his words.

Imogen clasped the saddle horn with both hands, wishing for the race to end. An old man dropped a loaf as she passed. Two children whooped from a window.

Imogen risked a look back. There was Patoleezal. His nightshirt flapped dangerously high up his legs. He was whipping his pony, shouting commands. 'The gate!' he bawled. 'Shut the gate!'

Imogen turned to see the city's entrance ahead. The gridiron gate groaned into action. But Miro was already through it. Mark wasn't too far behind.

Imogen's heart matched the drumming of hooves. *Bumpety-bumpety-bump!*

As the sun rose, the gate began winding down. Spikes gleamed along its lowering edge. Imogen wasn't going to make it. A memory flashed into her mind. The first time she'd come to this city, Marie's hoodie had got caught on those spikes. Imogen had pulled her to safety.

Imogen set her face, determined. She *had* to get under that gate.

The pony put on a last spurt of speed and Imogen ducked her head. The spikes raked her hair as horse and girl passed to freedom.

When the pony slowed, Imogen twisted, looked back. The

gate was shut and Patoleezal was on the wrong side. Imogen could see him through the criss-cross of iron. He brandished his fist and shouted in her direction, but she couldn't hear a word that he said.

CHAPTER 29

Imogen, Miro and Mark peered into the Kolsaney Forests. They were at the first line of trees. Their horses stood in a row, ears twitching at the smallest of sounds.

'That's the Old Road,' said Miro, pointing to a path between the trees. 'I think it leads to the mountain pass. It should be the fastest way to follow Anneshka and Marie.'

'You don't sound very sure,' said Mark.

Imogen had been thinking the opposite. Miro seemed to know so much. The prince she'd met in the summer had known nothing beyond his own walls.

'Won't Patoleezal send people after us?' asked Imogen.

The city was visible behind them, curled at the bottom of the valley.

'He'll never guess where we're going,' said Miro. 'People don't cross the mountains unless they have to.'

The grass growing down the centre of the Old Road confirmed this. It didn't look like it had been used for years. Deep in the forest, a wild velecour squawked.

'Is Patoleezal your legal guardian?' asked Mark. He shifted

in his saddle, uneasy. 'I don't want people thinking you've been kidnapped.'

'Patoleezal's not a guardian of anything,' said Miro.

'That must be tough,' said Mark. 'Having no guardian, I mean – especially when you're such a young ruler. It's like you've inherited the family business, with no one to show you the ropes.'

Miro's gaze lingered on Mark's face and Imogen wondered why . . . She coughed, breaking the moment. 'How do I make the horse go?'

Miro looked startled. 'Can't you ride? Even peasants know how! Oh – not that you're—'

Mark laughed. 'A peasant?' He nudged his horse into action. 'It's okay, Imogen, we'll go slowly. Your pony will fall into line.'

Imogen's face felt very hot. She squeezed the reins with both hands. 'Since when did you know about horses?' she called.

'There's a lot you don't know about me,' said Mark, saddlebags jangling at his back.

Miro and Imogen rode side by side. They had a lot to catch up on. Since the last time they'd met, Imogen had become a Year Seven. Miro, meanwhile, had become king.

Imogen told her friend about the prophecy – how Anneshka was going to rule the greatest kingdom, whatever that might be, and how Marie was going to help her succeed.

Miro was outraged. 'Marie would never help Anneshka!'

'I know,' said Imogen. 'It doesn't make sense.'

Perhaps if Imogen hadn't been so busy chatting, she would have noticed the trees. They were whispering to each other. Then again, perhaps she wouldn't. For the language of trees is often mistaken for the rushing of wind through leaves.

Daylight was fading when the riders approached the far side of the Kolsaney Forests. The mountains were close. Their snowy shoulders eclipsed half the sky.

'This looks like a good place to stop,' said Mark, gesturing at a clearing among the trees.

Imogen dismounted her pony with very little grace. Her bottom was sore. Her legs were jelly. It no longer felt natural to stand.

Mark began making a fire, claiming he'd learned how at Scouts.

'How fascinating,' said Miro.

Imogen thought he was too easily impressed. Even cavemen knew how to make fire.

Miro secured the horses and Imogen laid out the furs. Then the travellers filled their bellies with bread and tender herb-crusted meat. Miro had even packed sweet mustard for dipping.

'Are there more of those skret in the forest?' asked Mark, eyeing the trees round the clearing. Their branches seemed to tremble in the firelight. The burning wood crackled and popped.

'Skret mostly live in the mountains,' said Miro. 'But you don't need to worry about them. The Maudree Král and I are allies. There's no . . . disagreement any more.'

Imogen chewed slowly, basking in the warmth of the flames. Sitting by the fire, with furs beneath and stars shining above, she felt a little glow of contentment. She could almost forget why she was here . . .

Imogen hoped Marie had a fire and something nice to eat. She hoped Marie wasn't too cold.

She's cold all right. She's frozen to death.

Imogen's head jerked to the left. A worry creature stood behind Mark, loitering at the edge of the firelight. It stared at Imogen and gave a low hiss.

It's not real, she told herself. *It's my imagination playing tricks.*

Miro lay back and sighed. 'There are so many stars,' he said. 'I wonder whose side they're on. Surely, they can't want Anneshka to be queen?'

'Exploding balls of gas don't take sides,' said Mark.

'Actually,' corrected Imogen, 'stars are mostly plasma.'

The worry creature approached the fire. Its face was scrunched as if it had been shrunk in the wash. *Your sister has frozen in the mountains*, it snarled. *Frozen to death and it's all your fault.*

Imogen glared at the creature. Mark shifted, not sure if she was scowling at him.

'The stars see everything,' said Miro, as he stuffed bread into his mouth. 'Everything we are. Everything we're destined to be . . . that's what my uncle used to say.'

'There's no such thing as destiny,' said Mark.

'Yes,' said Imogen, in her most innocent voice. 'Just like there are no doors in trees.'

Mark's upper lip twitched. She'd hit a nerve.

Sparks and smoke rose into the darkness. *Frozen to death*, cried the worry creature. *Frozen to death and it's all your fault.*

Imogen lay back, forcing her attention away from her tormentor. The longer she looked at the sky, the more stars there seemed to be. They hung out in clusters. They peeped through the clouds.

Imogen gazed at the sky a little longer and the worry creature's voice grew quiet. 'The stars see everything,' she whispered, speaking to no one in particular.

The worry creature made a 'harrumph' noise, as if it was fed up with being ignored. Then it turned on its heel and stomped off.

CHAPTER 30

Imogen woke early with dew on her face. The fire had gone out and the others were asleep. Imogen knew she should stay put, but she was cold. She decided to go for a walk, just until Miro and Mark woke up. Perhaps she'd collect some firewood.

The Kolsaney Forests were stirring as she walked into the trees and away from the camp. Somewhere in the distance, a wolf howled. Closer, a bird with go-faster stripes was busy ripping moss from a stump.

Imogen crouched to inspect the bird. *Peck, peck, peck.* It tore at the moss with its beak. The forest seemed much busier now that the mountain had got back its heart. Imogen was so busy watching the bird that she didn't realise she was being watched too.

A twig snapped. The bird took flight and Imogen sprang to her feet.

'The trees said you were here.' The voice belonged to Ochi. She was youthful again, and tall. 'I've come for my clock.'

'What clock?' said Imogen.

'I think you know, child . . . It wasn't yours to take.'

'It's not yours either,' returned Imogen.

Ochi seized her by the shoulders. 'I need it!' She gave Imogen a shake. 'You don't even know how to use it! You don't even know what it is!'

Imogen moved to stamp on Ochi's toes, but something held her foot fast. She looked down. A root had grown over her boot, wrapping itself round her ankle.

Imogen met the young witch's eyes. She was in there – the old woman, the *real* Ochi. Imogen's skin prickled at the thought. She'd heard someone say there's a child in every adult; the shadow of a younger self. She'd never heard of it working the other way round – of an old soul wrapped in young skin.

'It's just a mask,' said Imogen, staring.

'The clock,' repeated Ochi and she pressed Imogen's shoulders as if trying to grind her into the earth.

Imogen wasn't sure how far she'd walked from the clearing. Would Miro hear if she screamed?

'You can have the clock when I've got my sister. If you're so desperate to have it back, why don't you help me find Marie?'

'I don't interfere in such things,' said the witch.

Imogen's fear turned to anger. How could Ochi speak like that? As if she wasn't part of this world?

'But you've already interfered!' cried Imogen. 'You invited us into your house. You let Anneshka kidnap my sister. And now you're here, bothering me!'

A cloud passed over Ochi's face. 'Your sister's kidnap is not my fault. I was drugged, like the rest of you . . . Besides, it's the child's destiny. You can't argue with that.'

Imogen narrowed her eyes. 'Destiny. Is that what you call it?' A second root looped round her leg.

'I won't ask you again,' said the witch. 'Where's my clock?'

'Let her go,' said a voice from behind. The witch glanced over her shoulder. It was Mark, holding a sword. Imogen was pretty sure he didn't know how to use it, but as he lifted the point she felt a flicker of doubt.

She was very glad to see him. The roots uncurled from her legs.

'We were just talking,' said Ochi lightly, but she let Imogen go. Imogen rushed to Mark's side.

'She's stolen my clock,' said the forest witch. It sounded petty, like one child complaining about another. 'Your daughter is out of control.'

'He's not my dad,' muttered Imogen.

Mark didn't lower the weapon. 'I quite agree,' he said to Ochi. 'The child's an absolute nightmare. Liberal parenting. That's what's to blame.'

'I want my clock back,' demanded the witch.

'I'm afraid you can't have it,' replied Mark. He tucked Imogen behind him and started backing away.

'Why not?' cried the witch, cheeks aflame.

'Finders keepers,' said Mark. 'That's why.'

Ochi gave Mark such a dirty look that her young face gathered lines. Then she tossed her cape over one shoulder and stalked away, disappearing between the trees.

CHAPTER 31

On the third day of riding, the travellers approached two tall mountains. There was snow underfoot, and Imogen's breath made white clouds. She was glad of her pony's warmth.

'No sign of Patoleezal's men,' muttered Mark, glancing back at the valley.

No sign of the forest witch either, thought Imogen. She could feel her sister's absence again – that hole where Marie ought to be. But this time the void was outside Imogen, giving her energy, drawing her on.

'Look,' cried Miro, pointing. 'It's the mountain pass! Those peaks are called The Twin Brothers.'

Imogen steered her pony, eager to see for herself. The Twin Brothers had grown very close to each other. They shielded the path from the sun so the snow on the ground didn't melt. Their slopes were rocky and steep. *You are not welcome*, the mountains seemed to say. *We turn our backs on you and all your kind.*

Imogen shivered and wrapped her cloak tighter. She was jealous of Miro's fur cap.

'Are you cold?' asked Mark. 'Want to borrow my cloak?'

Imogen shook her head.

Miro rode on, his horse leaving prints in the snow, and Imogen seized her opportunity. Ever since Mark had rescued her from Ochi, something had been on her mind.

'Mark,' she said, trying to sound casual. 'Why didn't you let Ochi have the clock? I thought you didn't agree with stealing from old ladies.'

When Mark spoke, it was in a clipped voice that Imogen hadn't heard before. 'I don't like people threatening my family.'

His family? Imogen wasn't sure how she felt about that. Mark cleared his throat. 'Imogen, that night in the gardens . . . when we went through . . .'

He couldn't even say it.

'The door in the tree?' she suggested.

Mark nodded. He sat a little straighter in his saddle. 'I'd had an argument with your mother. We fell out in the evening and she went straight to bed. I was at the bar on my own when I saw you and your sister sneaking about outside the hotel.'

Not so long ago, Imogen would have been pleased to hear about Mum and Mark arguing. Now she was just tired. She was tired of the cold and of not being able to feel her bum. She felt like she'd fused with her saddle.

'Your mother refused to believe that you'd run away last summer. It made me so angry. I don't know why, but it did. I said things I shouldn't have said.'

'What things?' Imogen looked sideways at Mark.

'About discipline and bringing up children. That one day you'd have to stand on your own two feet – have to explain figures to the board. And then what would you do? You couldn't just make up a magical kingdom. Hard work. Statistics. That's what counts. You've got to live in the real world.'

Imogen bit her lip. Mark's version of the real world sounded made up.

'But now . . .' He glanced at the belt of sky between the mountains. 'Now I'm not so sure.'

There was silence apart from the crunching of hoofs. The Twin Brothers pressed in on either side, their rock faces icy and stern. Ahead, Miro's stallion was a black splodge on white snow.

'I suppose what I'm trying to say,' continued Mark, 'what I'm trying to say, is that I'm sorry.'

Imogen was so shocked that she almost dropped the reins.

'The door in the tree exists,' said Mark, 'and so does this incredible world. When we get home, I'll put everything straight. I'll make sure your mum knows the truth . . . How does that sound?'

'That sounds good,' said Imogen. 'Really good.'

And so they passed between The Twin Brothers. They passed from one kingdom to the next – leaving behind what had gone before and facing events yet to come.

PART 3

CHAPTER 32

On the fourth day of riding, Imogen, Miro and Mark reached the far side of the mountains. A great expanse of land rolled before them, divided by rivers and lakes. The hills weren't too big. The valleys cradled villages.

'Beyond the mountains,' whispered Imogen. 'It doesn't look so bad.'

Miro sidled by on his black horse. 'Looks can be deceiving,' he said, but he was smiling. He appeared to be relaxed . . . excited even.

Brooks threaded the mountain slopes. It seemed to Imogen that the streams were laughing – a joke about meltwater and rushing round bends, a punchline she'd never understand.

The horses followed the water downhill. Sometimes they waded through the shallows. Sometimes they dipped their heads for a drink.

By the sixth day, the travellers had finished their descent. The mountains were at their backs, and a wide river and low hills lay ahead.

'Where are we?' asked Imogen.

'I believe this is the Lowland Kingdom,' said Miro. 'They say it hasn't been invaded for centuries.' Imogen felt this to be true. There was something peaceful about this waterlogged place. Perhaps it was the smell of damp earth and things growing. Perhaps it was the size of the sky.

Imogen couldn't help feeling hopeful. Of course they'd find Marie. Of course it would all be fine. Her worry creatures seemed as unreal as snow in summer.

'Why hasn't the kingdom been invaded?' asked Mark. 'I don't see any towers or walls.'

'You don't need walls when you have a water dragon,' said Miro.

Mark glanced left and right. 'Dragon? I hope that's a figure of speech.'

Imogen looked at Miro. He smiled and shrugged, but he didn't say any more.

They stopped for a lunch of cheese and dried crackers. Miro smeared his biscuits with lard. Mark stacked them into a triple-decker sandwich. Imogen nibbled her cheese by the river, which wound its slow way between woods and meadows.

A dragonfly was hunting in the rushes. Imogen crouched to see it up close. The dragonfly had a gleaming body. *Snap, snap* went its jaws. It was devouring flies mid-flight.

Suddenly, a long tongue flew up and hit the dragonfly with a splat. Imogen was so shocked that she dropped her cheese. The tongue recoiled, taking the insect underwater.

It was all over so quickly.

Hunter was hunted. River ran smooth.

Imogen searched for the tongue's owner. She parted the rushes . . . There was nothing there. She leaned over the river, holding on to the grass so she wouldn't fall in.

She could see her own blurry reflection, face bending with the current. But under her face was another. Blue eyes watched from below. Imogen scrambled up the bank, suppressing a scream.

Miro was at her side in an instant.

'There's a face in the water!' cried Imogen. 'It had blue eyes and a long sticky tongue!'

'Are you sure that it wasn't a frog?' But as Miro spoke something surfaced in the river. Webbed fingers emerged first, then the crown of a head, then a face with deep rockpool eyes.

'I think that's a river sprite,' whispered Miro. 'Back away . . .'

Imogen stayed where she was. She wanted to ask the water-creature if it had seen Marie. But before she could say anything, Mark grabbed her with both hands. 'Hey!' she cried. 'Get off!'

He dragged her away from the river and deposited her in the long grass. 'You were too close!' he yelled. 'What were you thinking?'

'I wanted to ask it about my sister!'

'You wanted to have a *conversation*?' said Mark. 'I just saved your life! God knows what they're putting in the water. Must be something nasty to make monsters like that.'

'*You're* the only monster around here,' muttered Imogen. But when she looked at the river, the sprite had disappeared.

CHAPTER 33

The travellers came to a town by the river. It was the first settlement on this side of the mountains.

Most of the buildings were made out of wood, with small windows and pointy roofs. Sprouting vegetables filled the gardens and geese grazed by a brook.

The houses were much shorter than in Yaroslav and they looked very snug inside. Imogen could see in through the windows.

'Let's split up,' she said when they reached a green near the centre of town. 'We should ask if anyone's seen my sister.'

'I'm not leaving you,' said Mark. He nodded at Miro. 'And he shouldn't be left alone either.'

Miro looked strangely pleased by this statement.

'Fine,' said Imogen. 'But it's going to take ages.'

The lord of the town did not want to help find Marie. He eyed the travellers with suspicion. 'Children go missing all the time,' he said. 'I cannot be expected to keep track of them. That is the job of their parents.'

The priest hadn't seen Marie either. 'I will pray for her soul,' said the grey-faced minister. 'The krootymoosh have taken so many. Would you like to light a candle for the child?'

'Hang about,' said Mark. 'Krooty-what?'

'Krootymoosh,' said the priest without blinking. 'They're beasts that take sinful children.'

Mark didn't know what to say. It was clear from his startled expression. Luckily, Imogen did. 'Marie's not sinful. She's a goody two-shoes.'

'It was a woman who took her,' added Miro.

The priest pushed his glasses up his nose. 'Is that so? You children should be careful not to speak out of turn . . . or the krootymoosh might take you too.'

'Thank you,' said Mark, steering them out of the church. 'We'll keep that in mind.'

The town's apothecary was a thin man with a sallow, hungry look. 'What seems to be the problem?' he asked.

There were hundreds of bottles on the shelves behind him, filled with bright powders and jellies.

'I'm looking for a girl with red hair,' said Mark. 'She went missing a week ago.'

'Not another,' mumbled the apothecary.

'Another what?' asked Miro.

'Another child taken by the krootymoosh. They're a plague on the Lowlands. There's no cure . . .' He paused and sniffed. 'But what about you? Are you sick?'

Imogen, Miro and Mark shook their heads.

'Then I'm afraid I can't help,' said the man.

The travellers turned to leave.

'That'll be five crowns,' the apothecary called after them. 'I don't give advice out for free!'

Imogen, Miro and Mark stopped searching for Marie at dusk. They walked to a cluster of willows on the edge of town, where they'd left their horses to graze.

The river babbled and firelight spilled from houses. Imogen leaned against a tree and felt her energy drain with the last of her hope. No one had seen her sister. No one even cared that she'd gone.

Imogen tilted her face to the sky. There was so much space . . . How far away was Marie now? As far as the moon? As far as the stars?

She imagined her sister drifting in the darkness, hair floating as if she was underwater, her body tracing a line across the sky. That was what happened in zero gravity. You had to find things to push off from and then you'd keep moving in the same direction forever . . . no way of stopping. Unless you hit an asteroid, that was.

Please, thought Imogen. *Don't hit an asteroid.*

'It doesn't make sense,' said Mark. 'This is the first town we've come to. Marie and Anneshka must have done the same.'

Behind him, willow branches reached for the stars. Mark froze, half turned. 'Unless they didn't cross the mountains.'

'What do you mean?' said Miro.

'Something about this doesn't add up.' Mark was pacing now. 'What if Ochi lied? She said Marie had been kidnapped and we took her word for it. She said go "beyond the mountains" and, look, here we are. What if Marie is still in Ochi's cottage? What if she's tied up in the woods?'

'Ochi's never stolen children before,' said Miro, although he didn't sound certain.

'Think about it logically,' continued Mark. 'Anneshka didn't seem interested in you or your sister and no one's seen her passing this way. Not a single person.'

'We haven't asked every single person,' cried Imogen. 'We haven't even asked the river sprite.'

'We've asked all the responsible adults,' replied Mark. He ran his hand across his stubble. 'And now I hear children are being taken by krootymoosh. Ochi didn't mention that, did she?' He turned to face Imogen. 'Young lady, I'm taking you home.'

'NO!' cried Imogen.

'Already?' whispered Miro.

'Yes,' said Mark with the calm certainty of a man whose decisions were final.

'I'm not going,' yelled Imogen. 'You can't make me! The

door in the tree's sealed shut!'

'I'll make it open,' said Mark, and he placed his hands on his hips.

'But you've only just got here,' muttered Miro.

'I'm not leaving without my sister,' said Imogen.

Mark shook his head. 'Better to return with one child than none. We'll send the professionals after Marie. This world is too big . . . too strange. It's like trying to find a needle in a haystack.'

The calmer Mark was, the wilder Imogen felt. 'No, no, no!' she screamed. 'I want to find her NOW!'

'Imogen, this is for your own protection.'

Imogen was so angry that she couldn't even think. Just when Mark seemed like he might be okay . . . How could he abandon her sister?

'It's your fault we're here!' she cried. 'It's your fault I went through the door in the tree! If you hadn't been so keen to prove me wrong, I wouldn't have needed to prove myself right!'

'Don't you blame me,' said Mark, temper cracking. He caught himself – took a deep breath. 'You're going back, and that's the end of it. We'll leave first thing in the morning.'

CHAPTER 34

There was a tavern not far from the cluster of willows, with a large sign reading THE WATER HOUSE.

'We'll stay here for the night,' said Mark, in a fake cheerful voice, 'and set off for home in the morning. I'm sure you'll feel better then.'

Finding Marie would make me feel better, thought Imogen, but she followed Mark and Miro inside.

A group of ruddy-faced men with fisherfolk hats and beer-foam moustaches huddled round a table. A skret was gnawing on a leg of roast lamb. Three old ladies hogged the fire.

They all turned to stare at the new arrivals. 'At least pubs work the same way as at home,' muttered Mark and he plonked himself down at the bar.

'You must be thirsty,' said the landlord. He had dark-brown skin and friendly eyes. 'The road from Yaroslav is a hard one.'

'How did you guess where we're from?' said Mark, sounding spooked.

The landlord chuckled and pointed. 'Your clothes. They give you away.'

Mark glanced at his borrowed cloak and tunic, as if seeing himself for the first time. He did look different from the landlord; formal and dressed for the cold. The landlord's shirt was billowy and loose. He wore a waistcoat and a little necktie.

Miro scrambled on to the stool next to Mark, propping his elbows on the bar. Imogen hesitated. She wanted to sit with her friend. She did not want to be near *that man*.

'Tell me,' said the landlord, 'how are things in Yaroslav? It's been quiet on the Old Road. Did the tussle with the skret get resolved?'

Imogen felt a glimmer of pleasure as Mark struggled to respond. He didn't know anything about Yaroslav. 'Surely,' prompted the landlord, 'King Drakomor's got things in hand?'

'King Drakomor is dead,' blurted Miro and, for a moment, he looked like he'd cry. But he mastered himself and shook his hair from his face. 'I am Drakomor's heir.'

The landlord slammed down the beer mug so hard the handle came off in his hand. 'You're the king of Yaroslav?' He glanced at Mark for reassurance. Imogen scowled at them both. Why did grown-ups only ever trust each other?

'It's true,' said Mark. 'He is.'

The old ladies and the fishermen twittered. The tips of Miro's ears turned red.

'Welcome to the Lowlands, Your Majesty,' said the landlord. 'I want to hear Yaroslav's news. But first, what will you drink?'

Imogen decided to leave Miro to it. She was not in the mood to join in . . . She spotted a table in the corner. It had high-backed benches with wings. That looked like a good place to sulk.

She slid on to a bench, but a girl was sitting opposite. She had a wild cat at her side – like some kind of giant lynx or snow leopard.

'Oh, I'm sorry,' said Imogen. 'I didn't realise this table was taken.'

The girl was about Imogen's age, with amber-brown skin and tightly coiled hair that framed her face like a cloud. She wore a plain top and a flowery skirt, as seemed to be the fashion round here. 'That's okay,' said the girl, with a shy smile. 'You can stay if you like.'

The big cat didn't blink but kept its eyes fixed on Imogen. There was something predatory about the way that it stared. Imogen would have been terrified if the girl hadn't seemed so at ease. She wasn't behaving as if the cat was dangerous, even though it was as large as a wolf.

Under the girl's hand was a piece of parchment. 'What are you drawing?' asked Imogen, tilting her head.

'Oh, it's not finished,' said the girl, and she hid her sketch under the table. She studied Imogen, apparently deciding whether or not to speak. Imogen must have passed the test. 'That's my papa,' said the girl, 'behind the bar. He loves it when new people arrive. He'll talk your papa to death.'

'Mark's not my dad,' snapped Imogen. It came out angrier than she'd intended and the girl went quiet. Imogen could hear Mark laughing. At least with the high-backed benches she could no longer see his face.

The big cat continued to stare and Imogen shifted, uncomfortable. 'What's the deal with your wolf-cat?' she asked, trying to sound confident, but feeling more like a mouse by the second.

The girl stroked the cat and the animal relaxed. 'She's not a wolf-cat,' said the girl. 'She's a sněehoolark.'

Imogen felt a nub of jealousy. She wished *she* had a pet sněehoolark. The cat had white stripes under its eyes, great tufted ears, and whiskers as long as paintbrushes. 'Where do you get a snee-who-lark from?'

'She was given to my parents by a monk,' said the girl. 'He'd walked all the way from the Nameless Mountains. Sněehoolarks are common up there . . . Her name is Konya.'

The jealousy nub put down roots. Imogen bet Konya wouldn't give up on Marie. She bet Konya killed worry creatures like rats. The sněehoolark rubbed its silky head against the girl's shoulder. Its purr was like a helicopter. It made the table vibrate.

'What's your name?' asked Imogen.

'Perla,' said the girl, and then, after a moment's hesitation, 'what's yours?'

'Imogen Clarke. My sister's been kidnapped and I'm here to find her and take her back home.'

The girl gave Imogen a curious look. 'Was your sister kidnapped by the krootymoosh?'

Imogen shook her head. People kept mentioning the krootymoosh, but she still didn't know what they were. Perhaps she'd gloss over it . . .

That's it, hissed a worry creature. *Pretend that you know. You don't want to look like a numpty.* It skulked out from under the table.

'What's a krootymoosh?' asked Imogen as she stamped on the worry creature.

Perla looked surprised by the question. 'I can show you . . . if you like. I've got one upstairs. But you mustn't laugh at my room.'

Imogen wondered what might be funny. 'I promise,' she said, getting up from the bench.

Miro was surrounded by fishermen, all jostling to talk to the king. His face was flushed. He was loving the attention. Imogen spoke into his ear. 'I'm going to see a krootymoosh,' she whispered. 'Want to come?'

CHAPTER 35

Perla led Imogen and Miro away from the bar and up a flight of stairs. There was no krootymoosh here, whatever it might be.

The children climbed a ladder into the attic, and Konya the wolf-cat leaped up behind them.

Surely, thought Imogen, *the krootymoosh can't be that dangerous if Perla keeps it up here?*

But there was no sign of a krootymoosh in the attic either.

'Is this your bedroom?' asked Imogen.

Every inch of the room had been painted. But it wasn't painted like her bedroom at home – it was painted like a gigantic map.

Perla gave a nervous nod.

There were footpaths drawn on the floorboards, mountains over the door. Imogen looked up, and the ceiling was spectacular. Between the criss-cross of beams, the roof had been coloured bottomless black. A galaxy of stars blinked down on them, connected by fine silver lines.

'It's a star chart,' breathed Miro. 'Incredible!'

'You like it?' Perla clasped her hands.

'It's amazing!' said Imogen, squinting at a huge painted wetland that was labelled *Mokzhadee*. The wetland's details were exquisite: bogs and rising fog, flooded meadows and grassy isles. 'Why would we laugh at this?'

'Some people think it's strange,' said Perla. Her voice was low, as if sharing a secret. 'But I like making maps.'

'*You* did this?' gasped Imogen. 'How? Who taught you?'

'I taught myself.' Perla's eyes gleamed with delight. 'Lots of travellers come to our tavern – people from far-off lands. I don't like asking them questions, but Papa does enough of that . . . Some of them talk about their homes. Others talk about places they've been to. I listen . . . Then I add what I've learned to my map.'

Miro had found Yaroslav, right in the corner of the attic. 'That's my kingdom,' he said, pointing to a city no bigger than a button.

Perla eyed Imogen. 'Is that where you come from too?' she asked.

Imogen wasn't sure how to reply. She was so tired of having to explain herself, tired of not being believed. Would Perla understand if she told her she'd come through a door in a tree?

'Yes,' said Imogen. 'I'm from Yaroslav.'

Miro opened his mouth. He was about to contradict her so Imogen changed the topic, fast. 'I thought you were going to show us a krootymoosh. Where is it? Do you keep it locked up?'

Perla picked up a leather-bound sketchbook. 'I'll show you a krootymoosh in *here*.'

Imogen and Miro gathered round. On the first sheet of parchment was a drawing of a monster.

It was standing on its back legs, like a human, but it was covered all over in fur. It had powerfully built shoulders clasped in spiked armour. A jagged helmet covered its face.

Just like she had with the maps on the walls, Perla had captured every detail. '*That* is a krootymoosh,' she said, tapping her finger on the page.

'It's an armoured monster!' cried Miro, his eyes wide with horror – or was it delight? 'My old nurse knew of those beasts. She said they take naughty children.'

'That's what the nursery rhymes say,' whispered Perla. 'That's what I used to think too.' She was much quieter talking about krootymoosh than when she'd talked about maps.

'And what do you think *now*?' asked Imogen.

Perla sat on the bed. She kept her eyes trained on Konya. 'It's not true. I know it's not. My brother *was* well behaved, but the krootymoosh took him anyway.'

Imogen felt a wave of sympathy. She knew what it meant to miss a sibling, to think about them all the time. 'I'm sorry about your brother,' she said.

Perla was frowning and chewing her lip. 'At least I've still got Konya. The krootymoosh don't mess with her.' The sněehoolark was grooming herself on the mattress.

Miro seemed a little wary of the wolf-cat, but Imogen sat at the other end of the bed. 'How did it happen?' she asked Perla. 'You don't have to tell us if you'd rather not,' she added quickly.

Perla was quiet for a long time. She ran her fingers through the sněehoolark's fur.

'It was early,' she said. 'My parents were sleeping but Tomil, my brother, he wanted to go fishing. I could see him and his boat from my bed.' She looked through the little round window, as if her brother was still outside.

Imogen felt a little queasy. She couldn't help picturing Tomil as Marie.

'Tomil was always up early,' said Perla. 'He always had lots of plans. But he was so busy launching his boat that he didn't see the krootymoosh coming.'

Miro was about to speak, but Imogen shook her head. Perla was deep in her memory. It was best just to let it flow.

'I saw the krootymoosh coming to the river – seven feet tall with a cage on its back. I called Konya and we sprinted downstairs. Together, we could have stopped it. Together, perhaps—'

Konya gave a mew that belonged to a much smaller cat. She reached out a paw to her mistress.

'We were too late,' whispered Perla. 'The krootymoosh and

my brother had gone. I found Tomil's boat a mile downstream. Maybe if I'd run a bit faster – maybe if I'd—'

'It's not your fault,' said Imogen with some force. Perla's deep brown eyes met hers.

For a moment, there was silence in the attic. Adult voices travelled through the floorboards. They were laughing and shouting at the bar.

'Why doesn't your king do something?' asked Miro. 'How many children have gone?'

'I don't know,' said Perla. 'It only started recently. People thought the krootymoosh were fairy-tale monsters. We didn't know they could come true.'

She turned to Imogen with a curious expression. It was the same look she'd worn in the bar when Imogen had mentioned Marie. 'What took your sister, if it wasn't a monster?'

'A woman with yellow hair.'

Perla's face fell. 'Do you believe in fate?'

'Of course,' answered Miro.

'I'm not sure,' whispered Imogen.

'I've never told this to anyone,' said Perla, 'but, sometimes, I think the stars do things on purpose. They bring people together for a reason.'

'Me too,' said Miro, nodding vigorously.

Imogen's stomach squeezed tight. Did Perla know something about her sister?

Perla turned the page of her sketchbook. What Imogen saw next made every muscle in her body go tense. There was a drawing of . . . her. Well, of a girl with a face just like hers. She had freckles on her nose and short hair. Imogen ran her fingers across the parchment.

'I thought I'd seen you before,' said Perla.

Imogen looked at the sketch of herself. It had been done in a style that she knew. It had been done in the style of Marie.

'Did . . . *you* draw this?' asked Imogen.

'No,' said Perla. 'But the girl who did was here, and she was travelling with a blonde woman too.'

CHAPTER 36

'She was here?' cried Imogen. 'My sister was here in this house?'

'I didn't know she'd been kidnapped,' said Perla. 'I thought the blonde woman was her mother.'

'Did you talk to her?' asked Miro. 'How did she seem? How long ago did she leave?'

Perla thought for a moment. 'She seemed sad. That's why I let her borrow my sketchbook . . . It was only a few days ago.'

Imogen tried to laugh, but it came out more like a sob. She looked back at the drawing. It was Marie's work. She could tell from the nose. Marie always made Imogen look like she'd got a snout.

'Did the woman say which way they were going?' asked Imogen.

'She didn't say anything much. I think she wanted to be left alone.'

Imogen lifted the attic's trap door and placed her foot on the top rung of the ladder. 'Where are you going?' said Miro.

'To rescue my sister, of course!'

'You can't!' cried Miro. 'We don't know where they went.'

But Imogen wasn't listening. Marie had been here and she could still be close. Perhaps, with a torch, Imogen would be able to get to the next village before daybreak and then, and then—

'We should tell Mark,' said Miro.

'No way!' cried Imogen. 'He's already decided he's taking me home. He won't let me go after Marie.'

'But if he knew she'd been seen—'

'What's wrong, Miro?' said Imogen. 'Scared?'

Miro retreated, stung by the accusation. 'I just think we should stick together.'

Imogen climbed down from the attic. Miro, Perla and the sněehoolark followed. In the bar, Mark was talking to Perla's dad. They had their backs to the children, heads bent close, so Imogen slipped out unseen.

It was a relief to feel cool air on her skin. *There* was the whoosh of the river. *There* were the fast-moving clouds. Everything was speeding by and Anneshka was getting away.

Imogen ran to the stables – a rough wooden building nearby. Miro and Perla were behind her, neither quite daring to speak.

Inside the stables it smelled of straw and horse poo. The light from the tavern streamed in through the doors. Horses shifted in the shadows, not sure what to make of their visitors.

'I need you to help put the saddle on my pony,' said Imogen to Miro.

'You don't even know where you're going,' he pleaded. 'What am I supposed to tell Mark?'

'Tell him what you like,' she cried, spinning round. 'Mark's not my dad! He's just a bossy man who keeps following me about!'

'I think he'd be a nice father,' mumbled Miro.

Perla and Konya watched from the doors.

'Fine,' snapped Imogen. 'I'll get the pony ready myself.' She hauled the saddle from the stand and staggered under its weight, before dropping it on the ground. Her pony flicked an ear in her direction.

'Pass me the bags,' she commanded.

'You should give Mark a chance,' said Miro grabbing a saddlebag and holding on tight.

Imogen tried to take it from him, but Miro wouldn't let go. She tugged at a strap and the seam ripped. A box fell. Something clunked to the ground.

Imogen and Miro's eyes met in the half-light.

'What?' asked Perla. 'What did you break?'

The case lay open on the stable floor.

'My father's clock,' wailed Miro, throwing himself on to all fours. He couldn't have looked more distressed if his uncle's head had rolled out.

'I thought it was destroyed in the fire!' Miro glared at Imogen, accusation writ large on his face. 'How did you get it? Why didn't you say? It's my clock! My clock from the castle!'

Imogen gulped. 'I wasn't sure you'd approve.' She crouched next to her friend. 'I wasn't sure if you believe in finders keepers.'

'Finders keepers,' muttered Miro. 'I remember that phrase.' A jewelled star shone among the dried mud and straw.

'I took the clock from Ochi,' said Imogen, choosing her words carefully. 'I don't know how she got it.'

Miro's expression shifted from fury to disbelief. 'You stole from a witch?'

'Ochi says the clock reads the stars. I thought if I could get it working again, it might help us find Marie. It might show us where Anneshka is going.'

Perla joined them, kneeling on the stable floor. Konya sniffed the clock's face like she'd found a dead rat. There was no movement, no ticking heart.

The clock's little door hung open, as if it had been forced. A chunk of wood lay beside it.

'Something's fallen out,' said Perla, and she picked up the piece of wood. 'It looks like a toy.'

'It's not a toy,' said Imogen. The world seemed to tilt. 'It's a carving of three children . . . it's a carving of us.'

CHAPTER 37

Back in the attic, Imogen, Miro and Perla stood in a triangle. They faced inwards, holding hands, just like the children that had come out of the clock. 'Is it working?' asked Perla. The clock lay at their feet.

'Not yet,' said Imogen. 'Keep still.'

Konya watched from a nest of quilts on the bed. Only the tip of her tail moved, flicking from side to side.

'Nothing's happening,' said Miro, letting go of the girls' hands. He was still in a bit of a grump.

'But Ochi said the clock reads the future,' said Imogen.

'It's broken,' grumbled Miro as he slumped on to the bed. 'You've broken my father's clock.'

'Perhaps we're not thinking the right way,' said Perla. 'When I get stuck with a map, I try looking at it from a different point of view.' She turned the carved figures upside down.

But the wooden children held on to their secrets. Perla gave them a shake, before tossing them towards Konya. The snĕehoolark switched into hunting mode. 'Hey!' cried Miro, snatching the figures. 'That's a part of my clock!'

Konya swiped at the carving, and her claws clipped Miro's hand. Blood oozed from his finger. *Drip, drip, drip, tick.*

'Oops,' said Perla. 'Konya thought you were playing.'

'Quick!' cried Imogen. 'Lick it clean.'

Miro went a little cross-eyed, staring close-up at his cut. Imogen was afraid he might faint. 'I know,' he said – and then, more excitedly – 'I know how to fix the clock! What if the wooden children aren't holding hands? What if they're making a pact?'

Of course, thought Imogen. *Why didn't I think of that?*

Konya chewed at the carving, teeth squeaking on wood.

'How do we make a pact?' asked Perla.

Miro pulled a knife from his belt. 'We need blood. Everyone's blood.'

The children stood in the middle of the attic with the broken clock at their feet and a sky of painted stars overhead. 'I pledge to rescue Tomil and Marie,' said Miro. 'I'll do whatever it takes. On my honour, I swear it.'

Imogen wanted to ask how they'd save both children at once. They could be at opposite ends of the world, and Miro had promised her first – but he was already cutting his hand.

Imogen took the knife. 'I promise to save Tomil and Marie,' she said, and she pressed the blade to her palm. The edge bit her skin and she passed the knife on.

Perla did the same, brows crinkling with concentration. 'For

Tomil and Marie,' she whispered. The children pressed their hands together.

That was it. The pact was sealed. The tavern sounds faded and the world fell quiet.

Then the ticking began.

The hands of the clock started moving. Jewelled stars whizzed around. The children crouched to see what would happen. Just when it seemed that the clock would take off, propelled by the spinning of its hands – it slowed.

The little hatch opened and a figure walked out. It was a man with a crown. 'That's King Ctibor,' breathed Perla. The wooden man gave a royal wave before striding back into the clock.

'Excellent,' said Imogen. 'Let's pay him a visit.' She'd never met a king before . . . except for Miro, but he didn't count.

'Imogen! It's time for bed!' Mark called from below.

Imogen rolled her eyes. 'One minute,' she yelled back. She lowered her voice for Miro and Perla. 'Where does this King Ctibor live?'

Perla dashed to the wall, almost colliding with it in her excitement. 'Here,' she cried and she pointed to her map. By her finger was a city surrounded by rivers. 'Vodnislav, capital of the Lowlands.'

'Great,' said Imogen. 'We'll leave tonight, while the adults are asleep.' Miro was about to protest, but Imogen raised her hand. 'No. We're not telling Mark.'

'But we can't just disappear,' said Perla, round-eyed. 'What will my parents think?'

Imogen felt a sharp twist of guilt. Perla's parents would be terrified. Just like Imogen's grandma and mum. 'What would they say if we told them?' she asked. 'Do you think they might let you go?'

Perla pursed her lips. 'They say I'm safe in the attic. They're afraid of the krootymoosh.'

'Exactly,' said Imogen. 'Mark's the same. He wants me to give up and go home.' She rounded on Miro. 'And you ran away from Patoleezal. This is no different, if you think about it.'

'It's *very* different,' said Miro, stiffening. 'Mark is nothing like Patoleezal.'

'Imogen!' boomed Mark. 'Get down here! It's way past your bedtime!'

'Coming!' she shrieked. She turned back to her friends. 'Look, you can stay if you want – pretend that everything's fine. But I'm not playing by adult rules any longer. I'm going to track down Marie. And if the clock says she's with King Ctibor, that's where I'm going too.'

'But what if Mark needs us?' asked Miro.

Imogen looked at him hard. Being king had given Miro some funny ideas. 'Mark's a grown-up,' she said. 'Grown-ups look after themselves.'

CHAPTER 38

Imogen had been put in the tavern's smallest bedroom. Mark was in the room next door. She waited for an hour after she heard him go to bed, then she slipped out from under the covers and pulled on her trousers, quilted jacket and boots.

Her plan was to run away before dawn.

She didn't know what made her look through the window. It was dark – not much to see. But there, on the other side of the glass, was a moth with silver-grey wings.

'Oh, *now* you're here,' said Imogen. She opened the window to let the shadow moth in, but it flew away from the tavern, trying to lead her back the same way she'd come.

'Not you too,' sobbed Imogen. 'I can't go home. Not yet. Anneshka has taken my sister.'

Imogen was no longer so sure about her plan. She couldn't tell Miro or Perla, but she felt torn – pulled between her mum and her sister. It was like a physical sensation, like her heart was ripping in two. She pushed her palm against her chest.

She knew that every day she was missing, her mum would be getting more upset. She knew that this was all wrong . . . But if she didn't go after her sister, Marie might never come home.

What would Mum do, wondered Imogen, *if she was here, instead of me?* Mum had dealt with lots of tough situations, and she always seemed to know what was best.

And, there, Imogen found the answer. Mum would never leave without both of her girls. Imogen felt certain of that.

The shadow moth settled on the window ledge and closed its papery wings, folding them like a tiny silver umbrella. Imogen fancied that the moth understood. For a while they sat in silence, just breathing and watching the moon.

'I'm worried about Mum,' said Imogen, at last. 'She might think we're not coming home.' At the thought of Mum's face, all tired and teary, Imogen's hand returned to her heart. She kneaded the place between her ribs. 'I just wish I could let her know.'

The moth moved its antennae to the left and Imogen couldn't help wondering. 'Do you think . . .? Could you take Mum a message?'

The moth turned its body to the right. Imogen didn't know what that meant. It was a lot to ask of an insect, and Imogen was pretty sure it couldn't speak, but she remembered what she'd been told. Moths can carry messages. They used to take messages between humans and skret. So why not send a message to Mum?

'I just want her to know we're okay,' said Imogen, 'and that

we'll be back as soon as we can. If you could make her feel even
a little bit better . . . I'd really appreciate it.'

The shadow moth shook its wings open and fluffed up the
fur on its back. It seemed to know what to do. 'Thank you,' said
Imogen as the moth flew away. 'If there's anything I can do in
return—'

But the moth had disappeared into the night.

'Right,' muttered Imogen. 'It's time we did the same.'

Imogen, Miro, Perla and Konya crept across the deserted bar.
The floor was sticky with beer. They unbolted the front door
and dashed out.

Someone had locked the stables, but Miro took a pair of
cloak pins and wiggled them into the keyhole. There was a
click and the stable doors swung free. Imogen had to admit
Miro was good at picking locks.

Inside the stables, they readied the horses. Imogen hoped
Perla didn't notice her struggle to get on to her pony. After all,
she was pretending to be from this world.

Finally, the children rode out. It was dark, but the horses
could see well enough. Miro led the way on his black stallion.
Perla rode her mother's horse. Konya, the wolf-cat, trotted at
her side.

Imogen's pony followed. The clock of stars was snug in its
case, fastened behind her saddle along with the other supplies.

And, as the pony moved beneath her, carrying her away from the tavern, Imogen felt a wave of relief.

She had made her decision. No more Mark. No more orders. No more 'I know what's best'. She was going to Vodnislav to rescue her sister and no one could make her turn back.

CHAPTER 39

Anneshka rode the white pony through Vodnislav. The city was built at the meeting of three rivers and, everywhere Anneshka turned, there was water eating earth.

Marie walked behind the pony, tied to the saddle by a rope. 'I'm hungry,' she said in a small voice.

'I don't care,' said Anneshka.

The buildings in Vodnislav were low, like the land. There were no great walls. No mansions. Even the church steeples lacked ambition. If it hadn't been for the ridiculous number of boats, Anneshka would have thought she was in the wrong place.

'Where are we?' asked Marie.

'The capital of the Lowlands,' said Anneshka. 'This is the realm I'm destined to rule.' She slid off the pony and untied Marie's hands. There were people about – people who weren't used to seeing children on leads.

'I thought you were going to rule the world's greatest kingdom,' said Marie. 'How do you know this is it? Are the people very happy? Do they have robots that do all the chores?'

Anneshka stared at the girl. She was white-faced and dirty from the road, with dark circles round her eyes and a bruise on one cheek.

Robots . . . Chores . . . What was she talking about?

'It's the only realm with a dragon,' said Anneshka, and she boosted the girl into the saddle. Let the townsfolk think they were mother and child. They'd draw less attention that way.

'What kind of dragon?' said Marie. She looked around with wide eyes.

Anneshka remembered the fire at Castle Yaroslav – her wedding turned to ashes, her dreams gone up in smoke. 'Not *that* kind of dragon,' she muttered. 'A water dragon. It's a powerful weapon.'

An old man was smoking a pipe by a well.

'Excuse me,' said Anneshka to the man. 'Where can I find the Queen of Vodnislav?'

He eyed her through a cloud of yellow smoke. 'There's no queen round here.'

Anneshka's pulse quickened. It was fate. The throne was waiting for her!

But the man continued. 'There's only King Ctibor and his daughter.' He glanced at the girl on the pony. 'You're not from these parts, are you?'

'No,' said Anneshka, before Marie could answer. She wafted smoke from her face.

'Most folk hide their children,' said the man. 'Although it isn't always enough. My neighbour hid his son in an eel trap. Got taken by the krootymoosh last summer. My niece puts her twins in the oven. They come out smelling like cake.'

The old man was rambling. Anneshka turned to leave. 'Even the king lost his firstborn,' said the man. 'Terrible fuss that caused.'

Anneshka hesitated. 'The king lost a child?'

'A girl. Many years ago.' The man sipped his pipe and seemed to count in his head. 'She'd be about your age now . . . Was long before the krootymoosh turned up, but King Ctibor still says it was them. Folk have talked about the monsters long enough. Think we talked them into existence.' His eyes returned to Marie. 'Make sure your daughter stays close.'

To Anneshka's horror, Marie replied: 'I'm not her daughter! I've been kidnapped!'

'Excuse me,' hissed Anneshka and she yanked the pony's reins, tugging it down the street. Sharp left. Out of sight.

Anneshka pulled Marie from the saddle and the child fell face down in the mud. 'Don't you dare cause me trouble like that!'

'I want to go back to my sister!' sobbed Marie. 'I want to go back to my mum!'

There was a face at the window of a nearby house so Anneshka heaved the girl to her feet. 'The stars sent you to me for a reason,' she whispered. 'But be careful . . . it might not be a reason you like.'

She held Marie close and pretended to comfort her. The child's shoulders shook as she cried. Eventually, the face disappeared from the window.

'I'll do you a deal,' said Anneshka, pushing Marie away. 'If you make my life easy, I'll set you free when I'm done.'

Marie stopped weeping and looked up, eyes shining with tears and new hope.

'If you make my life harder,' continued Anneshka, 'I'll feed you to the water dragon. Understand?'

King Ctibor's castle was tucked in the bend of the river. Anneshka thought it a rather unimpressive building. It seemed to cling to the earth, as if afraid of slipping in.

Only a thin strip of land connected the fortress to the city. On this, stood three armoured guards. Anneshka approached with the girl and pony in tow. It would be too easy to fall in the river; she could hear its liquid roar as it rushed by on either side, but she kept her gaze fixed on the men.

They were soldiers of some kind – not like the Royal Guards she knew. Instead of plumed helmets they wore iron buckets. Instead of smart jackets they sported chain mail. Two of them were very short. 'Who goes there?' asked the smallest, voice grating like metal on stone.

Anneshka paused and tried to hide her surprise. Luminous eyes peered at her through a slit in the helmet's visor.

Skret.

What were they doing in the Lowlands?

Only one of the guards was human.

'Please fetch the king,' said Anneshka.

'We asked you a question,' growled the skret.

Anneshka looked over her shoulder, casting a warning glance at Marie. It was a look that said *Keep your mouth shut.*

'We've come a long way,' said Anneshka, appealing to the human guard.

'But who *are* you?' he asked.

'You don't recognise my face? I suppose it has been a while . . .' She let herself swoon, sinking to her knees, as if her legs could no longer support her. The man lifted his helmet and lowered his spear.

'Careful,' warned the skret. 'She could be up to something.'

Anneshka made her voice a whisper. 'Please . . . tell King Ctibor his daughter has returned.'

The man dropped his spear and caught her, just as she pretended to faint.

CHAPTER 40

The sun was low in the sky when Imogen, Perla and Miro reached the Klikatar River. Imogen couldn't help glancing over her shoulder, checking if they were being followed. But if Mark was searching for the children, he was either riding too slowly or in the wrong direction. Imogen, it seemed, had escaped.

'That's strange,' said Perla. 'The map says the crossing should be here.' She'd brought as many of her drawings as she could manage – sketches of the Lowlands, the Scrublands and beyond.

Imogen surveyed her surroundings. The river was wide and fast-flowing. Red-brown trees grew near the water and the air throbbed with insect life. There was no sign of a bridge. Perhaps Perla's maps were more imagined than real . . .

'Let me have a look,' said Miro, and he took the map from Perla.

Imogen clambered off her pony, saddle-sore and exhausted. She approached the water on foot. In the middle of the river it whooshed and whirled, but it ran slower at the edges. There were rocks downstream – not the kind left by nature. They had flat sides and sharp corners.

'Hey,' called Imogen. 'Come here. Look at this!'

A stone arch stuck out from the rushes. There was another arch on the far side of the water. It was all that was left of the crossing.

'That's our bridge,' said Perla, at Imogen's shoulder. 'Or, at least, it was.'

Konya sniffed at the rubble.

'What are we going to do?' asked Miro.

'There must be another route to Vodnislav,' said Perla. 'What does it say on the map?'

Miro studied the parchment. 'There's a crossing to the north, but it would add days to our journey.'

'We haven't got days!' cried Imogen. Perla raised her eyebrows and Imogen felt ashamed. 'Sorry . . . I didn't mean to shout.'

The children tied up their horses and ate dinner in silence. None of them knew how to make a fire so they huddled close for warmth, with Konya the wolf-cat wedged in the middle.

Imogen unpacked the clock and propped it against a tree, but the timepiece provided no answers. As the sun set, biting insects appeared. One droned near Imogen's ear. 'I'm glad Mark can't see us,' she muttered. 'Stuck already.'

'Same goes for Patoleezal,' said Miro, and he put on a funny voice. 'Kings don't sit on the ground. Kings don't eat with their fingers.' He glanced at Perla. 'What would your parents say?'

'Something about krootymoosh, I expect.'

*

Night had fallen on the river when a deep noise cut through the air. It sounded like a broken bassoon, playing the same note on repeat.

'What's that?' whispered Imogen.

Miro reached for his knife.

But Perla only giggled. 'Don't you have frogs where you're from?'

More noises joined the frog fanfare. A high-pitched trumpet came from under a log. A rhythmic croak rose from the water.

'We don't have frogs like that,' said Imogen. 'Not in England, anyway.'

Perla paused. 'What's England?'

Oops! Imogen had forgotten her lie. She'd told Perla she was from Yaroslav . . . She fumbled for a response and was saved by another strange sound.

'Good evening, fingerlings,' said a silky voice.

All three children looked up. There was a face among the bulrushes – a woman, with her legs underwater . . . or perhaps she had a tail?

Imogen got to her feet.

'Careful,' warned Perla, and Konya gave a hiss of agreement. Even the frogs had gone quiet. 'River sprites are dangerous . . . Do you have them back home?'

'No,' whispered Miro. 'We don't.'

But Imogen wasn't about to let *this* sprite get away. The woman propped her elbows on the riverbank. She didn't seem to mind the mud. Green hair cloaked her shoulders.

'Hello,' said Imogen. 'Do you know how we can cross the river?'

The woman blinked with eyelids that closed sideways. 'That's easy,' she said. 'You can swim.'

'The water's too fast,' said Perla.

'I don't trust her,' added Miro, under his breath.

The river sprite caught a fly with her tongue. Somewhere in the distance was the thunder of hooves.

'We're not swimming,' said Imogen to the woman. 'Is there another way to get across?'

The sprite parted the rushes, revealing three enormous lily pads. Each leaf was as big as a hula hoop, with a waxy sheen and upturned edges. 'I can take you,' she said, smiling sweetly. Her teeth were pearly white and needle-sharp.

Miro started turning the rings on his fingers, as he always did when he was afraid.

The hoofbeats grew louder and there, beneath the full moon, Imogen saw two riders approaching. The one in front she recognised as Perla's father. The other shadow was shaped like Mark.

Imogen's blood drained from her face. The men hadn't spotted them . . . not yet. But it was only a matter of time.

'I'm waiting,' sang the river sprite, and she wiggled a giant lily pad.

CHAPTER 41

The King of Vodnislav welcomed his long-lost daughter with open arms. He ordered a feast to be prepared in her honour. Anneshka did not want to eat. She wanted to see the water dragon, but this was King Ctibor's castle and she had to play by his rules.

'Is everything all right, my darling?' asked Ctibor from his seat at the head of the table.

'I've got no appetite, Father,' said Anneshka. 'It's been such an emotional day.' She'd never been fond of fish and there was a pile of brown clams on her plate, along with a whole roast trout. The trout's eyes had turned to jelly. Disgusting.

Marie appeared to feel the same way. 'I'm a vegetarian,' she whispered.

Anneshka wondered what that meant.

'When is the lady going to play with me?' asked the girl sitting next to Marie. Her name was Princess Kazimira. She was Ctibor's younger daughter; six years old and heir to the throne. That is, she *had* been the heir before Anneshka showed up.

'As I've already told you,' said King Ctibor, 'the lady is your sister, Princess Pavla.' The king's eyes glazed over. 'Returned after all these years . . .'

'Sister,' said the princess as she gazed at Anneshka. There was fish oil dripping down her chin. 'When will sister play dollies with me?'

The king smiled at his youngest. 'Pavla is tired, my little plum cake. I'm sure she'll play dollies in the morning.'

Princess Kazimira grabbed a fork and stabbed her fish in the head. 'But I want to play NOW!'

Marie's face carried a look of horror. *Yes,* thought Anneshka, warming to Marie. *The king and his daughter are both as repulsive as their food.*

But then Marie took Anneshka by surprise. She turned to Kazimira. 'I'll play with you if you like.'

'Now, there's an idea,' said King Ctibor.

A servant presented Anneshka with a platter of small boiled eggs. 'Vodnislav's finest,' said the king.

Anneshka's lip curled but she managed a nod. Even the eggs here smelled fishy. She popped one into her mouth. Urgh! It was salty! She gagged. Should she swallow it? No, it was too much. She spat the egg out, catching it in her napkin.

Am I in the right place? she wondered. *Can the greatest kingdom have food this bad?*

The king raised an eyebrow.

'It was off,' said Anneshka, and she reached for her wine. *It's not the food that makes Vodnislav great*, she reminded herself. *It's the water dragon and its power.* She took a big gulp from her goblet to wash the foul taste away.

'So, tell us,' said Ctibor. 'Where did the krootymoosh take you? What did the monsters want?'

'Oh . . . I'd rather not talk about it,' said Anneshka. 'It's been very traumatic.'

'My poor little poodle!' cried Ctibor. 'Did they hurt you?'

'I'm exhausted,' snapped Anneshka. 'Save your questions.'

'Of course,' said Ctibor, but his face showed disappointment.

Anneshka's mind returned to the dragon. With a monster like that at her side, she could conquer the world . . . 'Father,' she said in her smoothest voice, 'when can I see the dragon?'

The king rubbed his red nose and sniffed. 'Why would you want to see that?'

'I've heard so much about it,' said Anneshka. 'Can it really flood entire towns?'

'Don't you worry, my darling dumpling. The water dragon is ready to defend Vodnislav. I keep it deep in this fortress, safe under lock and key.'

'Does it eat children?' asked Marie. She looked rather pale.

King Ctibor seemed stumped by this question. 'It eats our enemies,' he said.

Princess Kazimira bounced in her seat, chanting, 'Dragon,

dragon, dragon!' She squished a boiled egg with her fist. 'I want to see it too!'

The king's face dropped like a half-baked pudding. 'I'm afraid it's out of the question.' Kazimira let out a wail and Marie covered her ears.

Anneshka peered at Ctibor. What was he hiding? 'Of course, Father,' she said. 'Whatever you think is best.'

Under the table, she removed a vial of sleeping potion from the pocket of her skirts. She'd taken the bottle from Ochi. It had worked in the witch's hut. Why not use it again?

Tucking the vial up her sleeve, Anneshka got to her feet. 'I'd like to propose a toast,' she said. She tilted her hand over the flagon of wine, allowing a few drops of potion to fall in.

'What a marvellous idea,' cried the king. He was grinning from ear to ear.

Anneshka filled the king's goblet. Then she poured a small glass for the princess.

'I haven't got a drink,' said Marie.

Anneshka ignored her. 'To family,' she said, and she raised her goblet. Ctibor and Kazimira did the same.

'To sisters!' squeaked the little princess.

Anneshka watched them drink.

CHAPTER 42

'Perla's dad and Mark are coming,' Imogen whispered to her friends, ducking down into the rushes. 'We have to get on those lily pads – now!'

'But what about the horses?' said Miro. 'They won't fit!'

He was right. The lily pads were big, but not *that* big. 'We'll have to go without them,' said Imogen.

She dragged the saddlebags to the river. Miro cut the horses loose, but Perla had gone very still.

'Don't be afraid,' said Imogen. 'The sprite is on our side. I can tell.'

'I'm not afraid,' replied Perla. She lowered her chin to her chest. 'I don't want to upset Papa.'

Imogen remembered how she'd encouraged Marie to go through the door in the tree . . . How she'd promised it would all be all right. She didn't want to make the same mistake twice. So, instead of speaking, she crawled on to a lily pad, lugging the saddlebags behind her. The leaf felt rubbery and strangely solid, more like a dinghy than a plant.

The riders were close now.

'What's that, by the river?' called Mark. His silhouette was black against the moonlit sky.

'Perla! Is that you?' shouted Perla's father.

Perla made her decision. She stepped on to a lily pad, arms out for balance. Konya followed with her paws spread wide.

The sprite drew the leaves away from the bank. 'Good fingerlings,' she whispered. 'Nice fingerlings.'

But the third lily pad was still empty. Imogen spun round. Where was Miro? Why hadn't he come?

'Hey!' cried Mark. 'Stop that boy!'

Miro came into view. He was racing to the riverbank with a box in his hands.

Of course.

The clock of stars.

Imogen must have left it on the grass.

Miro sprinted towards the lily pads. Mark had got down from his horse and was just a few feet behind, running hard.

The sprite kept swimming, towing the leaves.

Miro jumped from the mud, feet above water, box clutched to his chest. He fell on to the third leaf and it dipped with his weight. The clock of stars skidded to the edge. It was saved by the lily pad's rim.

Imogen looked back at the riverbank. The world was cast in shadows; outlines of trees and tall grass. She could make out Perla's dad and Mark, by the rushes.

'PERLA, WHAT ARE YOU DOING?'

'IMOGEN, MIRO – COME BACK!'

The gap between the leaves and the land was getting wider. Too wide for the men to jump. Mark waded into the river, but Perla's dad held him back. 'No,' he said. 'The current's too strong.'

Imogen felt a stab of guilt – even though it was Mark, even though he couldn't tell her what to do.

'Papa,' whispered Perla to the darkness and she lifted a hand to the shore.

The lily pads drifted downstream, carrying the children away.

'Good fingerlings,' said the river sprite. The water hardly stirred as she swam.

CHAPTER 43

The river sprite pulled the leaves by their underwater stems. She was a very good swimmer. The lily pads bobbed like balloons.

Imogen could no longer hear Mark shouting. She sat in the middle of her leaf, clutching the saddlebags and trying hard to smother her doubts. She'd *had* to go after Marie . . . She'd *had* to sneak off in the night . . . but it still didn't feel very good.

The moon hung low and as orange as a nightlight. The frogs took up their songs.

'I think we've gone far enough,' said Miro. 'I'd like to get off this leaf.'

Perla nodded her agreement.

Konya's eyes were the same shape as saucers. Like many cats, she didn't seem to be a big fan of water. She wanted to get off the leaf too.

But the sprite showed no sign that she'd heard Miro's request. She continued to tug them along.

Imogen was mesmerised by their rescuer. She didn't care what Miro and Perla said. She thought river sprites were amazing. 'What's your name?' asked Imogen.

'Odlive,' said the sprite, swimming on.

Imogen peeped over the side of her leaf. It was hard to guess the depth of the water. Something swished where Odlive's legs ought to be. A tail? A passing fish?

'You're not local, are you?' said the sprite. 'That bridge hasn't been passable for years . . . What brings you fingerlings to my river?'

'Fate,' whispered Perla.

The sprite stopped and turned in the water. 'I've always liked fate,' she mused. There was food stuck between her incisors. 'Fate is a little like my river. It doesn't matter how hard you try, fate always wins in the end.'

'Is that your advice?' said Imogen. 'Just let bad stuff happen?'

'I don't give humans advice,' said Odlive and a sly smile crept over her face. 'But if I did, I'd say you should go with the flow. Stop trying to swim upstream.'

Imogen's admiration for river sprites took a hit. She didn't agree with that. Perhaps Odlive wasn't quite what she'd imagined . . .

'Now,' said the sprite, 'it's time that you paid.'

Imogen thought she must have misheard. Frogs filled the silence that followed. There was one that sounded like a kazoo.

The sprite sank lower in the water. 'Most people don't like to pay at the start. They're even less keen at the end, but in the middle –' she let out a happy sigh – 'in the middle they *always* pay.'

'Uh-oh,' mouthed Perla.

Konya glanced at her mistress, trying to work out why they'd stopped.

'Excuse me,' said Miro, in his most regal voice, 'but that wasn't part of the deal.'

'What deal?' snapped Odlive. 'It's not a deal if I get nothing.'

Miro clenched his jaw. 'I am King Miroslav Yaromeer Drahomeer Krishnov, Lord of the City of Yaroslav. I don't do deals.'

Imogen glanced at her friend. His name used to be longer, didn't it?

Odlive ran her tongue over her sharp little teeth. 'Kings pay double.'

'He was joking!' cried Imogen. 'He's not really a king!'

'Please,' said Perla, 'let us go! I have to rescue my brother!'

Odlive laughed, then she slid underwater. Her tail snaked to the surface. It was long – very long – more like an eel than a mermaid. Imogen swivelled on her knees, trying to keep track of Odlive's shape. The sprite swam under the moon's reflection. She swam under the floating leaves.

'We shouldn't have trusted her,' hissed Miro.

'We didn't have any choice,' replied Imogen, angry that he seemed to think it was her fault. It was easy to criticise other people's ideas – harder to think up your own.

When Odlive resurfaced, she had weeds in her hair. 'Pay me what you owe!' she cried. 'Pay me now!' She grabbed Imogen's leaf and it wobbled.

Imogen seized the saddlebags, fumbling to find a purse. 'How much?' she asked and she held out a fistful of gold. Coins plopped into the water, but Odlive let them sink.

'I'm not interested in money,' she said. 'I'm only interested in meat.'

Imogen's stomach lurched.

'You can't eat us!' cried Miro.

'Not *you*, silly fingerlings! I've already tried human. It's far too fatty and sour. I have fish to eat every day. I want something new, from the land. I want wolf!'

She found the stem of Perla's leaf and started reeling it in. Konya fluffed up her tail and hissed.

'Not Konya!' cried Perla. 'She's my friend!'

Odlive curled her webbed fingers over the rim of Perla's leaf.

Imogen would have to think fast. She rifled through the saddlebags. Cheese? No. That wasn't right. Old bread and berries? Those wouldn't do either. Something was wrapped up in cloth . . .

'I wonder,' said Imogen, as casually as she could. 'Do river sprites like ham?'

Odlive released Perla's leaf. 'Ham? What is *ham*?'

Imogen narrowed her eyes. 'I suppose it's a kind of land fish.'

The river sprite licked her lips and swam closer. 'Sometimes the fishermen give me land fish,' she said. Her eyes were greedy and round. 'It has transparent skin and there are no bones inside.'

Imogen almost laughed. 'You mean sausages? This is even tastier than that.'

The sprite opened her watertight nostrils and sniffed. Imogen held out the smoked meat. She tossed a piece in the water. The sprite attacked it with her pincer-like teeth. *Chew, chew, chew, swallow.*

'Land fish,' she whispered, eyes bright with delight. 'I love land fish.'

Chapter 44

King Ctibor slumped back in his chair, mouth open. Princess Kazimira was face down on the table, forehead resting on her half-eaten trout.

'What did you do?' cried Marie.

'Quiet,' replied Anneshka. 'They're sleeping.'

The servants looked uneasy, but Anneshka spoke with such confidence. 'My father and sister have had too much to drink,' she said. 'Take them to their chambers.'

The attendants carried Ctibor and Kazimira away. Anneshka and Marie were alone.

'I'm tired,' said Marie. 'Can I go to bed?'

'No,' said Anneshka. 'You're coming with me.'

She marched Marie through the castle until they found a servant – a young woman who didn't know that visiting the dragon had just been banned by the king. The servant led them to the dragon's keeper. Like many of Ctibor's guards, he was a skret.

'I'm Princess Pavla,' said Anneshka, 'daughter of King Ctibor and heir to the throne. I want to see my dragon.'

'Yes, Your Highness,' said the skret. He hadn't been there

when Ctibor said she couldn't, and who was he to refuse the king's daughter?

Anneshka and Marie followed the dragon's keeper through the castle. The rooms weren't especially grand. The fires were lit, but it wasn't enough to chase out the damp. Beyond every window, the river rushed by.

Marie kept slowing, as if hoping she'd be forgotten. But Anneshka did not forget. 'Keep up,' she commanded, 'and tell me . . . what is a vegetarian? Why did you say that you're one?'

Marie hid behind her curls. 'It's a person who tastes like a vegetable,' she said. 'You can't feed me to the dragon. Dragons don't like carrots and beans.'

Anneshka sensed this wasn't the truth, but Marie looked stubborn, and it didn't really matter, so she turned her attention to the skret. 'How big is the dragon?' she asked. 'It must be as tall as a church.'

'I don't know,' replied the skret. 'I've never been allowed in the chamber. King Ctibor feeds it himself.'

'Then in what sense are you the beast's keeper?' said Anneshka, an edge creeping into her voice.

'In the sense that I keep the door locked,' said the skret, and he paused by a floor-length tapestry. The wall hanging showed a mighty dragon with creatures fleeing on all sides. Birds were in flight, deer galloped, people ran. Presumably they were Vodnislav's enemies.

'Are you sure about this?' said the dragon's keeper. His enormous eyes turned on Marie. 'It might not be safe for the small one.'

'I don't want to see the dragon,' cried Marie, grabbing the skret by his arm.

'The girl's coming with me,' snapped Anneshka. 'I won't ask you again – open up!'

The skret looked uncertain, but he bowed his bald head. 'Yes, Princess Pavla,' he said. He drew back the tapestry, revealing a door, which he unlocked with three different keys. Anneshka's heart bounced in her chest.

'That is where you'll find the dragon,' muttered the skret as he pushed the door open wide. A passage disappeared into darkness. 'Does King Ctibor know that you're—'

'Yes!' yapped Anneshka. She took a torch from the wall and shoved Marie down the passage. The child could go first. If the water dragon was going to eat anyone, it wasn't going to be Anneshka.

Perhaps that was the girl's fated use . . .

Anneshka followed the tunnel, keeping Marie one step ahead. The air grew so clammy that she could feel moisture on her face. Her clothes became heavy with damp.

'Please,' wailed Marie. 'I don't want to!'

Anneshka jabbed the child between the shoulders. 'Keep going.'

Marie whimpered and walked on.

When the passage widened, the girl tried to retreat. 'I won't tell anyone you're not Pavla,' she cried. 'I'll be good! Please don't feed me to the dragon!'

Anneshka grabbed Marie's hair with one hand and lifted the torch with another. It was hard to see in the dim light, but they seemed to have entered a chamber. There were no windows and water covered most of the floor. And there, chained above the black pool, was a dragon.

Anneshka's pulse quickened. She dragged Marie towards the beast, the girl fighting like a cat in a sack. 'When my sister finds out—'

'Your sister's not coming!' Anneshka tightened her grip on Marie's hair. The dragon was smaller than she'd imagined, barely the length of two men.

She held Marie at the edge of the water. The child was trembling with fear. 'Are you hungry?' said Anneshka to the dragon. The monster didn't struggle in its chains. 'Do you eat *vegetarians?*'

The dragon didn't respond.

Anneshka forced Marie to look up. 'Why doesn't it move?' she hissed.

There was a pause, a sharp intake of breath . . . After all of that wriggling and shouting, the girl went very quiet and still.

'I asked you a question,' said Anneshka.

'That's not a dragon,' said Marie. She sounded weak with relief.

'Lies!' cried Anneshka but, as her eyes adjusted, she saw that the child was right. She let Marie sink to the ground. The girl began to cry, softly this time.

Anneshka felt as though she'd been kicked in the stomach. She raised the torch higher still.

The dragon was stiff.

The dragon had no wings.

The dragon was a stuffed crocodile.

CHAPTER 45

Miro and Perla walked down the hill with Konya trotting at their side. Imogen paused at the summit. From here she could see Vodnislav, with three rivers bending to meet, just like on Perla's map. There was so much water flowing into the city that the land seemed held together by bridges.

This was the home of King Ctibor – the man who'd come out of the clock. If the clock really did predict the future, if the things it revealed were clues, this must be where Marie was too.

Imogen felt light at the thought, despite her heavy load. She was carrying one of the saddlebags, with the clock case strapped to the top. For the last few days, since releasing the horses and escaping from the adults, the children had been forced to carry their own things. It hadn't been easy, lugging saddlebags across the Lowlands. Still, it had been worth it because they'd managed to shake off Mark.

Imogen hoisted the saddlebag up her shoulder and followed her friends down the hill.

'Why do you think the clock showed us King Ctibor?' Perla asked Miro. She was frowning at the ground as she walked. 'Do you think the king knows something about my brother?'

'Maybe,' said Miro. 'King Ctibor probably doesn't know all those children are getting stolen, otherwise he'd have done something to help. Perhaps he'll rally an army, fight the krootymoosh on open ground.'

As the children approached the city, Imogen noticed that the houses were similar to the ones in Perla's hometown – wooden with sharp-sloping roofs – except here, there were thousands of them.

When the travellers passed the first clump of cottages, two women in shawls came out to stare. Imogen could hear them talking: 'Three youngsters . . . not even hiding . . . won't last long when the krootymoosh come.'

The children and the sněehoolark trudged over a bridge, heading deeper into Vodnislav. River sprites peered out from under the crossing. The water was heaving with barges and boats. Nutshell-shaped craft carried one or two people. Or, occasionally, one person and one sheep.

Miro pointed to an overloaded boat. 'Look! Look at that!' Then he turned to a pair of white birds, who were fighting over what appeared to be fish guts. 'Yuck! What are those birds?'

'Rivergulls,' said Perla.

They look like vultures, thought Imogen, eyeing the birds' hunched shoulders and bald necks. The rivergulls tore at the innards, which gleamed like scarlet jewels.

'Rivergulls are revolting,' said Miro.

'No, they're not,' said Perla. 'Rivergulls can swim underwater and fly higher than anything else. They swallow fish for their babies and sick it up in their nests.'

Miro didn't look convinced by this information, but Imogen's mind was elsewhere. Her sister . . . her sister was in this strange wooden city . . . She wondered if she was close. As if conjured by her thoughts, she glimpsed a child up ahead. It was a girl with red hair, who was exactly the same height as Marie.

Something twisted in Imogen's chest, like a rope winding tight. She called out: 'Marie?'

The girl didn't hear, but Imogen knew what she'd seen. That was her sister!

A man in leather waders led the girl away, tugging her by the hand. Adrenaline flooded Imogen's body. She dropped her saddlebag and gave chase. Perla and Miro were calling, but Imogen ignored them both. She couldn't lose her sister again.

The man towed the girl down a busy street. 'Marie!' cried Imogen. 'MARIE!' The crowd thickened. 'Excuse me, I need to get to my sister. Excuse – can I get past?'

Imogen smelled the fish market before she saw it. She paused on the edge of a square. Before her was a wall of people, through which Marie must have disappeared.

Imogen climbed up the side of a cart and scanned the scene.

The square was packed with people gossiping, haggling and manhandling fish. A carp had whiskers as long as a human.

Buckets held oysters and mud. There were small silver fish laid out on stalls, flapping and panting for air. Imogen wanted to put them back in the river – but not before saving Marie.

Her gaze found a flash of red hair. Marie was at the heart of the crowd. Imogen jumped off the cart and bodies crushed in all around her: armpits, skirts and stern frowns.

Someone threw a fish and Imogen ducked, avoiding a tail-slap in the face. Mud-coloured eels were hanging in rows, and Imogen slipped in-between.

Marie's bright hair bobbed into view, before vanishing down a dirt alley.

'MARIEEEEE!' cried Imogen. Her voice was drowned out by bells. In this city, they clanged like old pots. Imogen hurtled after her sister, sprinting down the dirt track, not stopping until she reached more water. And there was Marie by the riverbank.

'MARIE!' shrieked Imogen.

Finally, Marie heard. She let go of the man's hand and turned.

But the girl was wearing the wrong face.

It wasn't Marie after all.

A jittery sensation spread down Imogen's limbs.

I promised I wouldn't let the door shut behind us. I promised it would all be okay.

She tried to breathe deeply, tried to focus on the ground and how firm it was under her feet. Stumbling, she knelt by the river. Perhaps she was going to be sick.

Was this what it felt like for Mum – always waiting for her girls to reappear, seeing their faces wherever she turned?

I promised – I promised –

'Imogen!'

She swallowed and looked back the way she'd come. Miro and Perla were rushing towards her, weighed down by saddlebags. Konya leaped out in front of her mistress and people made way for the giant cat.

'What happened?' asked Miro when he got to Imogen's side. 'You almost lost the clock!' He and Perla were lugging Imogen's bag between them, and they were both out of breath.

'Oh,' gulped Imogen. 'I thought . . . It was nothing . . . I just got carried away.'

Perla and Miro exchanged glances, and Imogen knew what that meant. They must have been thinking that she was a weirdo.

'Are you all right?' asked Miro.

Imogen struggled to her feet and decided not to answer. 'Where do we find King Ctibor?' she asked.

'I think he has a castle,' said Perla. She pulled out one of her maps and squinted at the parchment. 'It should be on the banks of the Pevnee River, with water on all sides. A bridge of land stops the castle being an island . . .'

'Like that place?' said Miro, and he pointed to a fortress that loomed above the wooden-tiled roofs.

'Yes,' laughed Perla. 'Just like that!'

CHAPTER 46

Inside Vodnislav Castle, skret guarded the throne room.

What are skret doing in Vodnislav, thought Imogen, *serving a human king?*

The throne room was lined with pillars. Each one was shaped like a river sprite, with a long tail curling at the bottom and its head supporting the roof. Imogen peered between the pillars, wondering if her sister was here.

Perla was doing the same. She must have been looking for Tomil, but she kept herself tucked behind her friends with Konya prowling at her back. Perla didn't like talking to adults – especially those she didn't know.

A man was slumped on a throne at the far side of the room. He looked like he'd just woken from a nap. A little girl wearing a frilly bonnet stood on a smaller throne. She was almost as white as her dress. 'Daddy, who are they?' she asked.

'I'm not sure, my little cherry,' replied the man, 'but I think we're about to find out.'

A skret guard took a deep breath. 'I present King Miroslav Yaromeer Drahomeer Krishnov, Lord of the City of Yaroslav,

Overseer of the Mountain Realms and Guardian of the Kolsaney Forests.'

It was funny hearing someone else call Miro those names. Imogen always thought he'd made them up.

'Actually,' cut in Miro, 'King Miroslav will do.'

'And this is the noble King Ctibor,' said the skret, 'Protector of the Lowland Realm, Lord of the Three Rivers and Commander of the Great Water Dragon.'

Miro bowed with a flourish. Imogen waited to be introduced, but the skret turned on his claws and left.

How rude, thought Imogen. *Better do it myself.* 'And we're Miro's friends,' she cried.

Perla looked embarrassed, as if Imogen had done something wrong.

'*What?*' mouthed Imogen. Perla was the one being odd.

'I knew your father well,' said King Ctibor to Miro, ignoring Imogen. Then he gestured to the girl in the bonnet. 'This is my daughter, Princess Kazimira. It's been a long time since we had word from Yaroslav. To what do we owe this honour?'

'I'm on a quest,' said Miro, and he stood a little taller.

Ctibor shifted on his throne. He didn't seem pleased by this news. 'If you wish to borrow my water dragon, I'm afraid it cannot be spared.'

'That's not what we want,' said Imogen.

'Then what?' barked Ctibor.

Miro's kingliness was slipping away. Imogen wasn't surprised – it wasn't easy to say that they were there because of a figure in a magical clock. 'Actually,' said Miro. 'I'm not quite sure.'

'Daddy, I want to play with those children,' said the princess, and she stamped her foot on the throne.

'What a splendid idea,' said King Ctibor. 'Why don't you take the girls to your chambers? Show them your dolls. I'll talk to Miroslav, king to king.'

CHAPTER 47

Much like her bonnet, Princess Kazimira's chambers were covered in frills. There were frills on the tables, frills on the chairs, frills all over the rugs. She skipped through the rooms, picking up dolls. When her arms were full, she dumped the dolls on her bed.

A silk skirt ran round the bottom of the mattress. Konya stuck her head underneath.

'Bad kitty!' cried Kazimira, and she seized Konya's tail. The sněehoolark turned, claws out, but Perla saw it coming. She pulled the princess out of range.

'Cat hurt me!' cried Kazimira.

'She didn't touch you,' said Perla, confused.

But Imogen recognised the look on Kazimira's face: the princess was green with envy.

'Say sorry NOW!' she screamed. And then, more quietly, 'Say sorry or give me your cat.'

Behind Kazimira, something crawled out from under the bed. 'What's that?' said Imogen, hoping to distract her.

The princess squealed with delight, her rage forgotten in an instant. The crawling thing was a lizard or some kind of newt, no bigger than a pencil case.

'There you are!' cried Kazimira as she grabbed the newt, wrapping her fingers round its middle. It had black skin with bright emerald spots.

'Is that how you're supposed to hold it?' asked Perla.

'My dolly,' said the princess, giving the newt a shake.

Imogen wanted to say that it was a living animal, not a doll, but she needed to keep Kazimira happy. She needed to buy Miro enough time to ask the king about Marie.

Konya glanced at Perla, requesting permission to hunt the newt. But Perla pointed to the floor by her feet and Konya slunk over, reluctant.

'What's your pet called?' Imogen asked the princess.

Kazimira climbed on to the bed and plonked the newt in the middle. 'Pavla,' she said. 'I named it after my sister.' Imogen joined Kazimira as she tore a dress off a doll. It was similar in style to the one she was wearing. In fact, all the dolls looked a little like the princess.

Kazimira started wrestling the doll's dress on to the newt. Imogen watched with horror. She didn't have the words . . . Perla was rooted to the spot, unwilling, or perhaps unable, to move closer. 'Are you sure that's a good idea?' Perla asked.

'Of course,' said the princess, peering at Perla from under her droopy white bonnet. 'Don't want little Pavla being naked.'

'Is the newt – I mean, is *Pavla* – named after your younger sister?' asked Imogen. She hadn't seen another princess in the throne room.

'No, silly,' laughed Kazimira. 'The real Pavla's much older than me. She's got golden hair and a pretty nose. Pavla's beautiful. When I grow up, I'm going to be beautiful too.'

The princess forced the newt's front legs through the sleeves of the dress.

'Yes,' said Imogen. 'I'm sure you'll look just like Pavla.' She smirked at that. The newt *was* beautiful, in its own newty way.

'Take this one,' commanded the princess, handing Imogen a doll with a ball-shaped head. 'Pavla is going to be queen and your doll is her servant.' And then – in case Imogen needed further clarification – '*You're* the servant.'

Imogen bit her lip. Miro had better be getting some useful information from King Ctibor.

It felt like they played dollies for hours. Perla watched from afar. Her face said all there was to say. Konya was on her best behaviour, but her eyes were fastened to the newt.

Imogen made her doll do the things servants do. Pavla-the-newt was now wearing a bonnet as well as a dress. She'd gone sort of floppy.

'Naughty Pavla,' scolded the princess.

'I think Pavla wants a cup of tea,' said Imogen. She emptied some water from a vase into a toy teapot. Then she poured the newt a miniature cup of water. The poor thing stuck its whole face in.

'She's playing that newt to death,' muttered Perla when Kazimira left the room to fetch another doll.

'I know,' said Imogen. 'But how can we make her stop?'

Perla leaned forwards and whispered.

Imogen smiled. For a shy person, Perla had some very good ideas.

Kazimira's footsteps echoed in the next chamber. She was coming back. Imogen picked up the newt, as gently as she could, and slipped it into her trouser pocket.

Then Perla sprang into action. She whooped at Konya, pretending to chase. The sněehoolark ran, delighted by the game.

'What's going on?' asked Kazimira, standing pink-faced at the door.

'Konya's eaten Pavla!' cried Imogen, fighting to keep a straight face. Konya ran faster, knocking over a table. Imogen joined the chase.

Kazimira's eyes widened. 'BAD KITTY!' she yelled and she lunged at the sněehoolark. She managed to catch the cat's tail, but Konya was half wild with excitement. She didn't slow down, even with a princess in tow. She sprang over the bed, dragging Kazimira behind her.

'Baaaaaaaaad kitty!' screamed the princess as her belly hit

the floor. Konya turned the corner and Kazimira let go, sliding across the floor until she collided with a frilly footstool.

The snĕehoolark scrambled up the curtains as a skret guard burst into the room. Imogen and Perla were breathing hard and laughing.

'Princess Kazimira,' cried the skret, 'is everything all right?' His orb eyes went from the girl on the floor to the snĕehoolark sitting on the curtains.

'The cat ate my dolly!' wailed Kazimira as she thrashed her fists. 'I want it punished! I want *all* of them punished!'

CHAPTER 48

The stove in King Ctibor's library was taller and broader than the king himself. It was covered in tiles and radiating heat, but even the stove couldn't chase out the damp. Orange mould bloomed on the spines of the books. Paint flaked from the ceiling.

'Vodnislav grows wetter each year,' grumbled Ctibor, taking a seat near the ceramic stove. 'Not a problem you must have at home.'

'No,' confirmed Miro. He was armed with three rolls of parchment and his father's magic clock. He placed them on the table and sat opposite his host. This was it. This was Miro's chance to discover why the clock had sent them to Ctibor. His friends were counting on him.

'Tell me,' said Ctibor, 'what happened to your uncle? The last I heard, Drakomor was king . . . Don't tell me you've come of age already?'

Miro turned the ring on his thumb.

Drakomor . . .

His uncle . . .

The memories were more real than Ctibor's library. Drakomor lying unconscious on the floor. The castle consumed by flames. Miro could taste the smoke, feel the—

'Miroslav, are you well?' asked King Ctibor.

Miro was back in the room. 'Yes,' he said, blinking. 'My uncle is dead.'

'Oh. I'm sorry.' Ctibor spoke with such genuine feeling that Miro almost forgot not to cry. 'There's nothing worse than losing a member of your family . . . You have to fight for those you love, fight to keep them safe.'

'Yes,' said Miro, thinking of his friends. 'I believe the same.'

Ctibor smiled. 'Enough of such talk! You need fattening up. Shall I have my servants bring us something sweet?'

Miro nodded. He liked the way Ctibor looked at him. There was an indulgent twinkle in the old king's eyes.

Ctibor sent a man to fetch food, then he turned to the clock. 'So what's this?' he asked.

Miro managed a smile. 'It's an heirloom of my father's. A clock that reads the stars.' He opened the box and was about to say more when the clock's bell started to chime.

'How charming,' said Ctibor. The little hatch opened and a wooden skret crawled out. It had unusually long front teeth.

Zuby! thought Miro. Where was he? What did this new clue mean?

'Astonishing!' said Ctibor. 'What a marvellous contraption.'

The tiny skret scuttled into the clock, pulling the hatch shut behind him. Before Miro had time to puzzle over the meaning of the miniature Zuby, a real skret entered the room – carrying pastries and fiddleweed tea. He poured the drink with glinting claws. Miro had to remind himself not to be afraid. The skret weren't his enemies now.

'Here – get some food down you,' said Ctibor.

Miro bit into a pastry and it puffed sugar in his face. The skret bowed and left the room.

'You know,' said Ctibor, 'you look just like your father.'

'I do?' Miro looked at his blurry outline, reflected in the stove's tiles. He wished he could see the similarities himself. He'd spent hours in the mirror room, studying his face, searching for his parents' features. He'd even tried to stand like his father's statue. He'd done it for so long that his legs had gone numb, as if he was made from stone too.

'The likeness is quite uncanny,' said Ctibor. 'Hasn't anyone told you before?' He popped a whole pastry into his mouth and sugar clouds puffed from his nostrils. 'I can see your father now, looking out of your eyes.'

Miro reached for his tea and hid his face behind the cup. 'Th-thank you,' he stammered.

Ctibor chuckled. 'I didn't say it was a good thing. Here – have another pastry.'

Miro knew he should ask Ctibor a question, make conversation, like Patoleezal had taught him. Miro said the first thing that entered his head: 'Do you know what's going on with the krootymoosh?'

King Ctibor's face darkened. 'Both of my daughters are safe, if that's what you mean.'

'But what about other people?' asked Miro. 'The krootymoosh are kidnapping children. If you released the water dragon, that'd soon chase the monsters away!'

'You cannot protect everyone,' said Ctibor. 'Especially not peasants. They're breeding like cats . . . Sometimes I think the krootymoosh are a blessing in disguise.' Ctibor caught sight of Miro's face. 'You'll understand when you're older,' he muttered. 'It's like I was saying . . . you have to look after your own. Decide who you will – and won't – save. Remember that, Miroslav.'

Miro wanted to agree. He wanted King Ctibor to like him, but he couldn't help thinking that it was better to protect everyone's children, if you could.

'So,' said Ctibor, sitting back in his chair, 'what's all this talk of a quest?'

Miro reached for the parchment, unfurling one scroll at a time. They were portraits, drawn on the road. Miro had done his best to capture Anneshka; Imogen had sketched Marie; and Perla had drawn Tomil like his face was a map – lots of details that made a whole.

Miro showed the portraits to Ctibor. Two missing children. One would-be queen. 'I'm looking for these people,' he said.

King Ctibor saw the sketch of Anneshka and froze. 'Why . . . that's my Pavla!'

Miro shook his head. Perhaps his drawing wasn't good enough. Perhaps it looked like someone else. 'Her name's Anneshka. You can't see on the drawing, but her eyes are brilliant blue. She's very dangerous and she's taken my friend. I'm going to bring her to justice.'

Ctibor leaned forward so his head almost touched Miro's. Up close, Miro could see every pore on the older king's face.

'I'll only warn you once,' said Ctibor. 'Don't talk about Pavla like that.'

'But she's not called—'

'Am I a fool?' cried Ctibor, bristling. 'Do you think you can throw cream in my eyes and tell me the world's made of milk?'

Miro was bewildered. 'Cream? No, I—'

'I know my own child when I see her! That's Pavla, my pumpkin pie! Everyone said she was dead. Everyone said that she drowned. But I knew my Pavla was too smart for that . . . She was abducted by the krootymoosh and now she's escaped.'

Miro faltered. He pointed to the drawing of Marie. 'Does Pavla have this girl with her?'

'Yes,' snarled the king. 'So what? She's taken the child to Valkahá. They had to go on urgent business, left several days ago . . . but Pavla will be back. I know she will.'

Miro would have to choose his words carefully. 'How did

Pavla prove she was your daughter?'

Ctibor lifted his eyes. 'How have you *proved* you're Miroslav Krishnov?'

'You said I look like my father,' said Miro.

'I was lying. You look nothing like him.'

Miro flinched as if he'd been struck.

'I'll have your head on a spike!' boomed Ctibor. He grabbed Miro's collar and pulled him close. 'Coming to my castle, threatening my daughter. Who are you really?'

A skret guard rushed into the room. 'Your Majesty,' said the skret, before hesitating when he saw that one king had the other by the throat.

'What is it?' growled Ctibor, not breaking eye contact with Miro.

'It's about the snĕehoolark,' said the skret. 'It's eaten Princess Kazimira's lizard. I wouldn't have come, but the princess is beside herself. She wants the animal executed. The little girls too.'

'Well then,' said Ctibor. 'It seems Kazimira and I have come to the same conclusion.'

CHAPTER 49

From a distance, Valkahá looked like an anthill. It was the right shape, with steep sides and, like an anthill, it had several queens.

But this mound was not built by insects. It was a city, made out of rock.

Anneshka and Marie approached on horseback, with a pack of skret marching in their wake. The skret had been sent by King Ctibor to keep his daughter safe.

Anneshka had left Vodnislav in a hurry. It wasn't the place that she sought. She'd realised her mistake as soon as she met the 'dragon' and, instead, she'd turned her gaze west . . .

Valkahá was the greatest. *This* time, she was sure.

Between Anneshka and her goal lay the Scrublands. It was a place of scorched earth and thorns, of boulders and flowering shrubs. It was also a place of potholes.

'It's like being on the moon,' said Marie, eyeing the pits.

'Don't be ridiculous,' snapped Anneshka. 'The moon is perfectly smooth.'

'My sister says it's covered in craters.'

'Your sister is a very stupid girl.'

'She is not!' cried Marie. 'Imogen saved the shadow moth! And she found the way into this world! My sister knows all sorts of things.'

Anneshka glanced back at the skret soldiers, wondering if they'd heard. She made her voice soft and gentle. 'Found the way into this world? What exactly do you mean by that?'

Marie pressed her lips together, thinking. Anneshka knew that look: *I'll know her better than my own mother before this is over. I'll probably hate her just as much. But our fates are tied, for better or worse . . .*

'I'm thirsty,' said Marie.

'I don't care,' said Anneshka. 'Explain yourself and you might get a drink.'

Marie cast a longing glance at the waterskin tied to Anneshka's horse. 'I'm not from Yaroslav,' the girl whispered.

'Oh yes?'

Marie licked her dry lips. 'I'm from another world.'

An ordinary adult would have cursed her for lying, but Anneshka had a nose for the truth. *Another world . . .* That would explain the child's strangeness.

Anneshka ordered the skret to stop, then she handed the waterskin to Marie. The child glugged. 'How did you get out of your world?' asked Anneshka. 'Is there some kind of bridge?'

Marie looked wary. 'There's a door.'

'How interesting . . . And what is it like, this realm that you're from?'

A dumpling-sized bee buzzed from one bush to the next. Marie followed it with her eyes. 'Oh, I don't know. It's pretty boring . . . Compared to this world, that is.'

'Does it have dragons?'

Marie shook her head.

'Are you rich? Are the streets paved with gold?'

Marie shook her head once again.

'Is your king married or single?'

'Actually, we have a queen,' said Marie. 'But she's not allowed to do very much. They only let her out on special occasions to cut ribbons and wave at crowds.'

Well. It didn't sound very promising . . .

Anneshka encouraged the horses on, weaving between potholes and rocks.

'How do you know that *this* kingdom is the greatest?' asked Marie. She'd perked up now she'd been watered.

'Have you no eyes?' cried Anneshka. 'Behold!' The sun glinted off the termite city. Each building knelt on the shoulders of its neighbour, straining to be taller than the rest, but nothing could compete with the palace at the top. It shone so brightly that Anneshka had to lower her gaze.

Yet Marie didn't seem to understand. 'You think this place is the greatest because of how it looks?'

'Don't be ridiculous,' said Anneshka. 'Valkahá is a very wealthy city. Its five queens hold more silver than Vodnislav, Yaroslav and the Nameless Mountains combined. I bet your world can't compete with *that*.'

Oh, the things Anneshka could do with such silver! The swords she'd command. The people she'd bend to her will.

The child seemed to think for a while. 'But if Valkahá already has five queens, there might not be room for another.'

Anneshka smirked. 'I'll make room.'

'How?' asked Marie.

'Same way as always. Find out what people want. Make them think I have it.'

The girl didn't say anything to that. Behind them, skret chain mail clinked.

The streets of Valkahá were visible now, burrowing between buildings. *There* was the city's semicircular entrance. *There* were the famous silversmiths.

'Is that what you did to King Ctibor?' said Marie. 'Made him think you had something he wanted? King Ctibor missed his eldest child. He *wanted* to believe she was you.'

Anneshka tossed her head. She didn't like having her methods picked apart, strung up with their wobbly bits on show. 'Do you know,' she said, 'there's a type of ant in the Kolsaney Forests that impersonates its enemies? She slips into a rival ants' nest, kills the queen and makes herself at home.'

Marie was listening with wide eyes.

'The worker ants can't tell the difference between the two queens and they continue to feed the impostor. When her eggs hatch into ants, they kill all the workers and claim the nest as their own.'

The child stared at Anneshka blankly. She clearly had no idea what was going on. Anneshka sighed, and nodded at the city.

'This is *our* new nest,' she said.

CHAPTER 50

Imogen, Miro and Perla were sentenced in King Ctibor's throne room. They were surrounded by skret claws and spears. This is not how Imogen had expected their visit to end. King Ctibor sat on his throne, wearing a special gown and a floppy velvet hat. Princess Kazimira was at his side.

'Your crimes are grave,' said King Ctibor. 'You stand charged with high treason, plotting against Princess Pavla, impersonating royalty and – ' he cleared his throat – 'not playing nicely.'

Imogen clenched her hands. Not even half of that was true, and the rest of it certainly wasn't fair.

'How do you plead?' cried Ctibor.

'Not guilty,' shouted the children.

The king turned his attention to Konya. 'And *you*, foul beast, are accused of murder. A poor defenceless lizard . . . Kazimira's favourite! What have you got to say?'

Konya hissed at the guards standing between her and the thrones. Several of the humans stepped back. Even the skret guards flinched.

'Konya's not guilty,' cried Perla, finding her voice at last. 'Leave her out of it!'

'That cat ate my dolly!' screamed Kazimira.

Imogen slipped her hand into her pocket. She could feel the newt's heart tapping beneath its cool skin. Perhaps she should give it back . . . confess that it had been a trick.

But she couldn't bring herself to do it. The newt was so small and limp. It was like Perla said – Kazimira had been playing it to death.

'I have considered all the evidence,' said King Ctibor, 'and decided that you are a threat to my daughters. You are, without any doubt, guilty.'

'No!' cried Miro.

'Kitty,' shrieked Kazimira. 'I want the KITTY!'

'I'm sorry, my little plum cake,' said her father. 'The kitty must be punished. I'll get you a different one, I promise.' Then Ctibor spoke to his guards. 'Take them away!' he commanded. 'I want them executed at first light.'

CHAPTER 51

The guards threw the children into a cell. There was no furniture, no window, no way out. Just four walls and a bucket.

'This isn't fair,' cried Imogen. She pummelled the prison door, screaming at the top of her voice.

Miro stood and stared. Perla curled up in the corner with her hands clamped over her ears. Konya did the same with her paws.

But Imogen didn't care what the others thought. She had to get out of the cell. She had to get to her sister. She started kicking the door instead.

'Imogen, stop it!' said Miro. 'I've got something to tell you.'

'What's the point?' Imogen kicked the door harder. 'We're going to be executed in the morning!'

'It's about Marie. She was here – in this castle.'

Imogen paused. 'How do you know?'

Miro told the girls what he'd learned – how King Ctibor thought Anneshka was his long-lost child, how she'd left before they'd arrived. 'The clock brought us to the right place,' finished Miro. 'We just got here too late.'

'Did King Ctibor say anything about the krootymoosh?' asked Perla.

Miro shook his head and Perla hid her face between her arms.

'To tell you the truth,' whispered Miro to Imogen, 'Ctibor doesn't seem to care about the krootymoosh . . . so long as *his* children are safe.'

'It's hopeless, isn't it?' said Perla without looking up. 'I'll never see Tomil again. What's the point in making maps and talking to kings . . . what's the point of anything?'

Perla's despair echoed in Imogen. She thought she knew what Perla meant . . . Being without Marie was like being followed by a shadow. No, not a shadow – a black hole. A space where there should be a sister. A void that sucked joy from the world.

Perhaps this was even harder for Perla. Her brother hadn't been seen for a while. And Imogen hadn't thought of it before, but Perla was the youngest sibling. Surely it was the oldest child that should be doing the rescuing?

Imogen shuffled closer to her friend. She wasn't very good at giving hugs, but maybe she could give words instead. 'You know, Perla, someone once told me that the stars do things on purpose.'

Perla lifted her head. 'That was me . . . I said that.'

'The stars bring people together,' said Miro. 'Me and Imogen and you.'

'But look where it's got us,' said Perla. 'We're going to be killed at first light!'

Konya let out a sad mew.

Imogen tucked her hands under her armpits. They ached from hitting the cell door. 'Look,' she said, 'I don't know where Tomil is. I don't know how we'll get out of this mess. And I certainly don't know what's written in the stars.'

Perla looked at her with apprehension. These words weren't cheering her up.

'But I do know that we made a promise,' said Imogen. 'This mission isn't over – not yet.'

Perla gave a sniff. 'I just wish I knew where my brother was.'

Imogen remembered how she'd felt earlier – when she'd realised the red-haired girl wasn't Marie. In that moment, she'd wanted to curl up and hide, but Perla and Miro had come running.

'We're not going to stop until we've found your brother,' said Imogen. 'You don't have to do this alone.'

Miro nodded his frantic agreement.

Perla looked from friend to friend. Then she got to her feet, pushed her springy hair back from her face and shook off the worst of her sadness. 'Okay,' she said with a bob of her head. 'It's not over till the bullfrog sings.'

CHAPTER 52

'Ctibor says Anneshka has gone to Valkahá,' said Miro. 'Not that I know where that is.'

'It's the capital of the Scrublands,' explained Perla. 'The kingdom in the west. I wonder what Anneshka wants there . . .'

'She must have decided it's greater than this place,' said Imogen, gesturing at the bucket in the corner of the cell. 'To be fair, you can see what she means.'

Miro snorted and Perla looked like she was about to disagree, but there was a noise from outside the cell door. 'What have we got here?' said a skret.

Konya hissed.

Imogen turned. That voice had sounded familiar . . .

A peephole opened and a yellow eye filled the gap. 'They told me they don't have enough little humans – said they keep getting taken away.' The skret unlocked the door and stepped into the cell. 'Now I've got three pups at once! Does that make me lucky or cursed?'

'Zuby!' cried Imogen, as she wrapped her arms round his neck. His body was bony and hard. It wasn't a comfortable hug, but Imogen was so pleased to see him.

'What are you doing here?' gasped Miro. And then, in a whisper, 'You came out of the clock.'

'This is my prison,' said the skret. He gestured to the cell, as if proud.

Imogen pulled back. She thought he had come to set them free . . .

'Moths and prisoners,' said Zuby. 'That's what Zuby does best. Humans have no interest in moths. But prisons . . . every kingdom has those.'

'You can't work for Ctibor,' cried Imogen. 'He's evil!'

Zuby looked uncertain. 'He's no Král. On *that* we can agree. But tell me, little humans, why are you in my prison? Why aren't you at home with your kin?'

Imogen thought of her mother. She hoped the moth had delivered her message. She hoped Mum wasn't worrying all night or searching the gardens all day. She hoped someone had visited Mrs Haberdash . . .

Zuby pointed at Imogen. 'I sent the moth to find you – asked it to escort you home. And yet here you are, causing trouble!'

'My sister's been kidnapped,' cried Imogen.

Zuby scratched his head. 'Oh. I see.' His great circular eyes turned to Perla. 'What about you? What's your excuse?'

Perla shrank at the question. Strange adults. Strange skret. She didn't seem to like either. 'I'm rescuing my brother from the krootymoosh.' Her voice was as soft as a moth.

'And you?' said Zuby to Miro. 'I thought you were supposed to be king?'

'I'm helping my friends,' said Miro.

'Ah, so kings *do* have friends.' Zuby's face softened. 'And how do you like being king?'

'Oh . . . it's great . . .' Miro wasn't very convincing. He was turning his rings round again. 'I get to stay up until midnight and have enormous feasts.'

'I see,' said Zuby, studying the boy. 'Is that what it means to be king?'

Imogen felt something stir in her pocket. The newt! She'd forgotten it was there. She lifted it out with both hands. The newt didn't squirm or try to escape; it just lay across her palm, like a bean bag.

'What's that?' asked Miro, moving closer.

'It's Kazimira's newt,' said Perla. 'Konya didn't *really* eat it.'

'Why don't you give it back?' cried Zuby.

The newt seemed exhausted. It could hardly lift its head. 'Kazimira was killing it,' said Perla.

'Didn't you hear the guards?' shouted Zuby. He waved his claws with distress. 'They're going to kill *you*. Give back the newt and they might let you go!'

'You wouldn't say that if the newt was a moth,' muttered Imogen. The newt had suckers on its toes. Imogen felt them attach to her palm, as if it was clinging on, as if it was asking for her help.

'But it's not a moth,' said Zuby. 'It's a tadpole with legs. Think of your family. What would they say? You can't save everyone all of the time. Sometimes you have to think of yourself.'

'You sound like Ctibor,' said Miro.

Zuby's shoulders slumped and his claws skimmed the floor. 'Perhaps I do.' He looked at the children with sad eyes, like the world's ugliest puppy. 'There's no honour in working for that man.'

Imogen tucked the newt back into her pocket. 'Why are *you* here, Zuby?' she asked.

Zuby eyeballed Imogen's pocket, where the newt's black tail poked out. 'This place is good,' said the skret, 'even if the king is not.'

'What's good about Vodnislav?' asked Miro. 'Everything's rotten with damp.'

'Hey,' said Perla, scowling.

Zuby waved a claw. 'I'm not talking about that.'

'He's talking about the people,' said Perla. 'Papa says we're friendly in the Lowlands. Much friendlier than anywhere else. And Papa knows *a lot* about people.'

'Your father has a point,' said the skret. 'The humans in Yaroslav have hemmed-in brains. Too much time stuck in their valley.'

Perla smiled, satisfied. Miro opened his mouth to object.

'But I wasn't talking about people,' said Zuby. 'A city isn't all about humans, you know. It's shaped by its forests and trees, by its rivers and mountains, and sometimes – if you're lucky – it's shaped by its sertze too.'

Sertze? Imogen knew that word . . . Miro's uncle had a Sertze Hora. He'd stolen it and hidden it away. The whole kingdom had suffered because of him.

Miro turned the bucket upside down and sat on it, resting his elbows on his knees, and putting his head in his hands. 'I thought Yaroslav was the only place with a sertze,' he murmured.

Imogen wondered how this news made him feel. The old Miro might have got upset – the new Miro just seemed very tired.

'There are many kinds of sertzes,' said Zuby. 'Beautiful life-giving stones. And the Lowlands have a sertze of their own . . . I can feel it.'

The skret laid a hand on his chest, as if he could feel it right there and then. Imogen did the same. She held her breath, waiting, but she only felt the pounding of her heart.

'It's not like the sertze I grew up with,' said Zuby. 'It doesn't beat for the mountains and trees. It beats for the sprites and the streams. The Sertze Voda. That's what it's called.'

Imogen pressed her ear to the cell wall. *Rush, rush, russsssssshhhhh*, said the river. It must have been running nearby.

'We skret are sensitive to these things, or more sensitive than humans anyway.' Zuby wrapped his long arms round his body. 'It's nice to feel it beating . . . It reminds me of home.'

'Tomil and I used to hunt for the sertze,' said Perla. She looked unsure about saying this out loud. 'Konya didn't approve.'

'Konya was right,' said Miro, and the snĕehoolark glanced up at the mention of her name. 'You shouldn't hunt for Sertzes. Those stones belong where they are.'

'It was Tomil's idea,' said Perla, defensive. 'He's always daring me to do things – climb up a tree to search a crow's nest, stick my arm in an eel trap. Once he dared me to put my head underwater and I thought I'd found the sertze, but it was just an old fishing buoy.' Her cheeks dimpled at the memory. 'We did . . . you know . . . sibling things.'

I wouldn't have done what Tomil told me, thought Imogen. Although, if she was honest, it sounded like a scarier version of the things that she did with Marie.

'Anyway,' finished Perla. 'We never found the Sertze Voda. Wherever it is, it's well hidden.'

'Good,' said Zuby and Miro at once.

Then, quite suddenly, the skret cleared his throat. 'Right, enough reminiscing,' he announced in his metallic voice. 'No matter what trouble you've caused, we can't have little humans being killed.'

'You're going to set us free?' said Imogen, hopeful.

The skret ran his claws over his scalp. 'Erm . . . I suppose you could put it like that . . .'

CHAPTER 53

Imogen looked down at the swirling water. She was standing on a wooden balcony at the back of King Ctibor's castle. 'You can jump from here,' said Zuby, 'and the river will take you away.'

The river didn't look very fast, but Imogen knew looks could be deceiving. Mum's brother had nearly drowned trying to save a dog from the River Trent. In the end, the dog had saved him. There were currents beneath the surface – that's what Mum said. You didn't always know what you were jumping into . . .

'Do little humans float?' asked Zuby.

'Yes,' said Perla. 'Although Konya doesn't like getting her paws wet.' The sněehoolark had her tail between her legs.

'I'm not sure that I'm very floaty,' said Miro.

The river ran beneath the balcony. There were rocks on the far side and deep-rooted trees. The water babbled as it swerved past the castle, round the corner and out of sight.

'Now listen to me,' continued Zuby. 'I wouldn't be suggesting this if I could think of another way. The guards will see you if you leave through the castle.' He glanced at the water. 'Boats aren't allowed on this stretch of river, but that doesn't mean it's safe.' The skret counted hazards on his claws. 'Mind the mudslicks and the fiddleweed. It's tangly stuff. Don't talk to the sprites and, whatever you do, watch out for eel traps.'

The children nodded.

'The water will carry you towards a circle of trees called the Ring of Yasanay. I'll meet you there.'

'You're leaving because of us, aren't you?' said Imogen. 'Because you've helped us escape . . . again.'

'You can thank me later,' muttered Zuby, 'by going safely home. I'll try to bring your magic clock with me. And some horses too – it sounds like you're going to need them.'

'But King Ctibor might catch you,' said Perla.

'Oh, don't you worry,' smiled Zuby. 'The skret here are lazy and the humans . . . well, they're humans. King Ctibor won't know you're missing till nightfall. By then, I'll be long gone.'

'Thank you, Zuby,' said Miro. 'I'll see that you're justly rewarded.' He used a snooty tone that Imogen had come to think of as his 'king voice'.

'Never mind that,' said Zuby, wafting his claws. 'Just focus on not drowning. It's time to jump, little humans.'

Imogen opened her mouth, but fear had taken hold of her tongue. What if she did a belly flop and split her tummy open? What if she landed on an underwater rock? What if there were fish with giant teeth and—

Perla jumped off the balcony.

Imogen and Miro looked down. Perla was falling, falling . . . *splash*! She hit the water feet first.

'Watch out!' cried Zuby. The children parted as Konya came galloping towards them. In a blur of fur the sněehoolark sprang off the balcony wall.

Konya made a bigger splash than Perla. She bobbed to the surface and fixed her gaze on her mistress. The wolf-cat swam with surprising speed, paws paddling hard underwater, tail up straight like a fin. Perla took hold of Konya and the river carried them away.

'Now it's your turn,' said Zuby. 'Go quickly, before someone sees.'

Imogen's stomach churned.

'I don't want to drown!' cried Miro. He'd abandoned his king voice.

Imogen was sick with nerves, but she needed to be brave for the two of them. She climbed on to the balcony wall, finding strength in Miro's fear. 'Come on,' she said. 'We can do it together.'

The wind lifted her fringe from her forehead. The sky was billowing, bright. The tip of her boots stuck over the wall's edge. There was water below, dark and deep. *You don't always know what you're jumping into. You don't always know—*

'The circle of trees,' called Zuby. 'That's where I'll be. Don't forget.'

Miro clambered on to the wall too. He stood next to Imogen and she took his hand. 'Don't let go,' she said. Her hair whipped across her face and, for a moment, she felt like it was Marie at her side – Marie's hand in hers.

Miro nodded, wordless. And with that, the friends jumped.

CHAPTER 54

Imogen collided with the water.

A shock of cold.

The rush of it over her knees – belly – face.

Hair pulling up.

Body dropping down.

She was freefalling, twisting in space.

Imogen opened her eyes and the river snatched Miro's hand, tugging him away. His fingers disappeared in a whirl of bubbles. 'NO!' cried Imogen, but her throat filled with water.

Which way to the surface? Which way to the light?

The weeds down here were taller than trees.

She needed to breathe. *Which way to the light?*

Sunken-star eyes peered out of tall grass.

Her lungs started aching, flooded with panic.

She needed to breathe. *Which way to the light?*

Face finds the surface.

Flooded with air!

Imogen gasped once, twice. 'MIRO!' she screamed at the sky. Somewhere above, rivergulls were laughing. A smooth body brushed against Imogen's leg, but she was swept round the bend of the river. There was the castle, pulling away. But where were her friends?

She paddled hard to stay afloat. She passed fish traps, watermills and broken boats. A couple were smooching on a bridge. Some things were the same in both worlds.

Imogen was swept under a bridge, through a watery tunnel. Rats shrieked in the darkness. It was a relief to be spat out the other side.

The river carried Imogen out of Vodnislav. She tried to look for the circle of trees, but it was hard to see anything much. From her position in the water, geese on the riverbank towered like cows. Even the flowers looked huge. If only she could grab a low-hanging branch and pull herself on to dry land.

The river grew wider and there was no sign of the others. What if Miro really didn't float?

A weed wrapped round Imogen's ankle. She stuck her head under to set herself free, but the grass wasn't grass. It was a long eel. Imogen resurfaced, breathing hard. 'Miro?' she called. The river babbled back. She kicked her foot and the eel wound tighter. 'MIRO!' she screamed. 'HELP!'

The eel pulled her down.

Down through the bubbles.

Down through the slippery weeds.

Now Imogen could see that the thing round her ankle

wasn't an eel at all, although it was the right shape. It was the tail of a river sprite – half man, half moray – with cloudy eyes and green hair.

He drew Imogen closer and she tried to kick free, but his tail corkscrewed up her legs, webbed fingers closed round her neck, and Imogen knew she was beaten.

The last thing I'll see is that face, she thought. *A face with alien eyes.*

Bubbles escaped from her lips and terror filled her as the thick tail squeezed her torso.

I'll never save my sister! I'll never see my mum!

Imogen didn't feel the newt leave her pocket, but it must have done, because suddenly it was swimming – swimming between her and the sprite.

You don't always know what you're jumping into . . .

Things happened fast after that. The newt attached itself to the river man's forehead and brightened, turning glowstick green. The sprite looked shocked and his eyes went wide.

Was the newt . . . communicating? If it was, Imogen didn't know what it said. She needed to be free, needed air.

The sprite released Imogen.

Hands grabbing wrists.

Hands grabbing, pulling her up.

Up through the weeds.

Up through the bubbles.

Up through the prisms of light.

Her head broke the water and lungs heaved in air.

Gasping, spluttering. Arms round chest.

Her rescuers fought with the current. There were four hands, some of which wore rings. Feet crunched on pebbles and Imogen was laid out like a prize-winning fish. Upside-down faces appeared above her. One was Miro's, grinning, breathless. One was Perla's, concerned. The third was a wolf-cat's, with fur slick like an otter.

It was very good to see them. Very good to be alive.

CHAPTER 55

Imogen's throat and nose stung like she'd swallowed a jellyfish. She lay on the pebbles, taking big gulps of air, waiting for her breathing to go back to normal.

Miro and Perla crouched nearby, water dripping from their hair. 'Crusty catfish!' cried Perla. 'That was close!'

Imogen didn't know what *crusty catfish* meant . . . She guessed it was something like *wow*.

'Are you all right?' asked Perla, more quietly. Konya nudged Imogen with her nose, as if asking the same question.

'I think so,' said Imogen. The back of her throat hurt and she'd swallowed some water, but other than that she felt okay.

'We made a human chain and pulled you out,' said Miro, clearly excited to tell the tale.

Imogen nodded. She wasn't used to being saved, and she didn't think she liked it very much. It felt better to be the person doing the saving.

'Thank you,' she said to her friends.

'That's all right,' said Miro, grinning from ear to ear. 'It's all in a day's work for a king.'

Imogen sat up and looked at her surroundings. They were on a shingle beach; beyond that was a strip of mud and reeds, and beyond *that* meadows and hills.

There was no sign of the river sprite. No sign of the newt either.

Konya shook water from her fur. 'What happened?' asked Perla. 'One minute you were floating, next you were gone.'

'A river sprite happened,' said Imogen. 'He was going to drown me, but the newt made him stop . . . at least, I think it did.'

Perla looked puzzled. 'How did that tiny thing defeat a sprite?'

Imogen shook her head. The truth was, she didn't know. Had the newt really glowed green or was it just her imagination? Perhaps she'd glugged too much river water.

'Well, in that case, we're quits,' said Perla. 'We saved the newt. The newt saved you.'

Miro turned his face to the sky. 'What goes into the forest comes out of the forest.'

'That's Lofkinye's saying,' said Imogen sharply.

Why was she being so mean? Miro had just saved her life . . . *Because I'm never going to be able to rescue Marie*, she thought, *if I can't even rescue myself.* Hot shame flooded her body. 'Of course,' she added. 'You can say it too, if you like.'

'We have a phrase like that,' said Perla. 'What goes into the water comes out of the water.' She upended a boot and weeds sloshed out. 'It means if you're good to the river, good things will happen to you.'

Imogen got to her feet. The sun was beginning to set, but Vodnislav was still visible in the distance. The river looped in the other direction, mild-mannered and smooth, as if it wouldn't hurt a fly . . . let alone drown three children.

'How are we going to find the circle of trees?' asked Miro. 'Zuby will be waiting for us.'

'I painted those trees once,' said Perla. She traced her finger through the air, as if she was back in her attic, as if she was studying the map. Her lips were slightly parted. Her eyes had a faraway look.

Grandma would call Perla 'eccentric', thought Imogen. *People at school would use other words* . . . But Imogen thought she was brilliant.

Perla lowered her hand. 'The Ring of Yasanay is in the Southern Lowlands,' she announced. 'Twelve ash trees planted high on a hill. Papa told me it was made as a lookout. On a clear day, if you stand between the trees, you can see all the way to the Nameless Mountains.'

'Great,' said Imogen. 'Which way do we go?'

Perla shrugged. 'No idea.'

Even Konya looked disappointed.

'You mean you did all that air-pointing for fun?'

'I can remember the *map*,' said Perla, defensive. 'I just don't know where we are.'

Chapter 56

The newt swam against the current. It wriggled its body from side to side, forcing its way upstream. It swam through a forest of fiddleweed and brushed against the belly of a trout. The newt didn't pause. It knew where it was going.

There was a hole in the side of the river – the mouth of an underwater cave. The newt floated in. The water in the cave was as warm as blood, and there, tucked in the corner, was the Sertze Voda. The heart of the river.

The Sertze was a deep oblivion blue. It pulsed and the water rippled. Tiny eggs were clustered nearby. Inside the eggs' jelly, black blobby things squirmed. Things with tails and gills. The newt checked each one, nudging them closer, helping them bask in the stone's gentle heat.

Finally, satisfied with the arrangements, the newt settled down. It wrapped its body round the Sertze Voda. Time to recharge. The newt would need all the strength it could get.

PART 4

CHAPTER 57

Zuby had never understood the human obsession with horses. He liked the smell of them – dry grass and mushrooms. He liked the feel of their velvety fur. They even tasted fairly good, served with a rich berry sauce.

But to *travel* by horse? That was another thing altogether. And yet the little humans would need horses if they were to succeed on their quest.

The skret approached King Ctibor's stables with a belly full of nerves. He didn't like being out in the daylight – it made him twitchy, even with a long cloak protecting his skin.

The magic clock was in a bundle on his back. He'd felt like a thief, taking it from Ctibor's library, but Zuby had no choice. He had to help his friends.

'What are you up to?' asked the human in charge of the stables.

Stealing horses, thought Zuby. *Releasing prisoners. Throwing it all away!*

'I'm acting on orders from the king,' said the skret. 'He wants me to fetch three small horses.'

The man pulled a face and Zuby thought he'd been found out, but the stablemaster raised a finger. 'Look at those teeth!' he cried. 'Should have them filed off. You'll scare the ponies with tusks like that.'

Zuby forced a smile.

The stablemaster brought out three ponies with bridles on their heads.

'I need the horse chairs too,' said Zuby.

The man rolled his eyes, but he went back into the stables, muttering to himself – 'I suppose you mean saddles . . . silly skret.' He secured the leather seats to the animals' backs.

Zuby thanked the stablemaster, then he led the ponies away, towards the neck of land that connected the castle to the city. The river flowed on either side. Three guards stood in metal clothes. Zuby saluted them. The ponies clip-clopped behind. So far, so good.

'Where are you going with those horses?' asked the human guard. The other two were skret.

'The king wants them sold,' said Zuby.

The skret guards parted to let him through, but the human wasn't done. 'Why?' he asked. 'That's a well-bred pony. Shame to let someone else have her.'

'I don't make the decisions.' Zuby forced another smile.

The human shook his head and stepped aside. 'Make sure you get a good price.'

Zuby felt a thrill. He was getting the hang of this lying business.

He led his straw-scented companions through the streets of Vodnislav, not stopping until he reached the city's outskirts. The Lowlands rolled in every direction. But beyond those soft slopes lay other kingdoms. The Scrublands stretched out in the west. The Nameless Mountains dominated the south.

A rivergull called a sharp warning and, for a moment, Zuby had the feeling he was being watched. He glanced over his shoulder. 'Must be my guilty conscience,' he muttered and checked that the clock was still secure at his back.

He climbed on to the smallest pony and sat, human-style, with one leg dangling on either side. The pony started trotting and Zuby bounced in the seat. *Smack, smack, smack.* The leather hit his rump with each stride.

He tried crouching instead, claws digging into the saddle. That was better. The pony zipped along and the others followed, with Zuby grasping their reins.

It was getting dark when he neared the circle of trees. He secured the ponies, removed his cloak and approached the Ring of Yasanay on foot. 'Little humans?' called Zuby. He couldn't hear their voices. Perhaps they'd fallen asleep.

He was close to the top of the hill when the wind whispered through the trees.

Zuby carried the magic clock in his claws now. It felt so very precious, like he was cradling a freshly born skret. So perfect and delicate, familiar and strange, in a way Zuby couldn't explain.

The skret stepped into the circle of trees, eyes swivelling left and right. He could see well in the low dusk light, but there were no little humans up here.

Zuby would never forgive himself if his friends had sunk. 'There's no point in worrying,' he said out loud. 'I'm sure they'll be here soon enough.'

Travelling by horse wasn't as easy as it looked and Zuby was very tired. He sat down in the middle of the trees. That was when he heard a chiming from the clock. He untied the bundle and held the clock to his face.

There was a door at the top, small enough for a moth. The door opened and Zuby jumped. A miniature woman in a cape trundled out. She raised both her hands, as if grabbing at something.

'Hello,' said Zuby. 'Nice to meet you.'

The woman didn't reply, for she was made of wood. She wheeled back into the clock.

CHAPTER 58

Zuby lay down in the centre of the circle of trees. The magic clock was tick-tocking on his stomach, the grass was cool under his back and the sky between the branches was a hoop of deep blue.

Something tickled the skret's ankle. It felt like a spider. He wriggled his foot and the tickling stopped.

Zuby sighed. He couldn't go back to Vodnislav. Not after what he'd done . . . Ctibor wouldn't be as kind as the Král when he discovered that his prisoners had escaped.

The spider returned. This time it was crawling up the skret's arm. He moved to shoo it away, but it wasn't a spider. It was a root. 'Oh,' said Zuby. 'Didn't see you down there.' He lifted the rootlet, as gently as he could. It was fine, with wispy hairs.

Then he lay back down on the grass. *Tick, tock*, said the clock. 'There, there,' said Zuby, and he gave it a stroke. Talking of time, where were those little humans? He thought they'd be here by now . . .

A root hooked over Zuby's ankle – earthworm thick and anchored on each side. Zuby tried to pull his foot free, but he couldn't. 'Sorry,' he mumbled, and he sliced off the root with one claw.

A third root came wriggling towards him. Zuby jumped to his feet, still holding the clock. The grass where he'd lain was writhing with roots. The trees were coming to life!

The skret backed away. There was a tree at his shoulder, closer than Zuby had expected. He bumped into its trunk, and was about to apologise when the tree wrapped a branch round his middle.

'Wh-what's going on?' cried Zuby. He held on to the magic clock as the rustle of leaves filled his ears.

There was a woman in a cape. She was standing very still in the centre of the circle of trees.

'Watch out,' called Zuby. 'It isn't safe! The roots are—' A bunch of leaves inserted themselves into his mouth.

The woman stepped closer. She had rosewood eyes and silver-birch skin. 'Child of the mountains,' she said in a low voice, 'what are you doing so far from home?'

Zuby tried to speak through the leaves, but he couldn't.

'Not to worry,' said the woman, holding a lantern to his face. 'You don't need to talk . . . I've come for my clock.'

CHAPTER 59

'Does this mean we're lost?' asked Miro. He shivered in his damp clothes. Quilted jackets were great for crossing snow-swept mountains, less good for jumping in rivers.

'You could call it that,' mused Perla.

'Let's just walk,' said Imogen, impatient. 'We'll catch our deaths standing still.' That was Mum's phrase. Saying it out loud made Imogen feel braver.

And so the children and the snĕehoolark set off. Imogen's wet clothes clung to her body, her hair dripped water down her neck. She wondered where Mark had got to. Was he back at the Water House, enjoying a hot meal with Perla's dad?

The sun dipped beneath the horizon. Rushes swayed in the breeze. The mellow hills that had felt so friendly by day seemed to arch like the back of a beast.

Odlive's words returned to Imogen: *You should go with the flow. Stop trying to swim upstream.*

'Go with the flow, my foot!' muttered Imogen. She marched into the gathering night.

'Oi,' said Miro. 'What's that?' He was pointing to a clump of trees, silhouetted on a hilltop, that came into view as they walked.

'It's the Ring of Yasanay!' cried Perla, and she started to run towards the knoll. Konya bounded in her wake. Imogen and Miro fell in line, wet boots sploshing with each step.

The children rushed through meadows and brooks. They scrambled over rickety stiles. A worry creature popped out of a molehill. *You're too late to save your sister*, it hissed. Imogen squished it with her heel.

At the base of the hill were three ponies – shadows shifting in the gloom. Zuby must have left them to graze while he waited for the children at the top.

'Shall we – catch our – breath?' panted Miro. Imogen was relieved that he'd broken first. She didn't want to suggest it, but she needed a moment before tackling that slope.

'What's going on up there?' whispered Perla, glancing at the clump of trees. They were thrashing their branches as if caught in strong winds.

Imogen didn't know the answer. When her heart rate steadied, she started to climb the hill. She was near the summit when she heard the leaves swooshing. It was so loud – like waves crashing in a storm.

A woman's voice carried over the noise. Imogen couldn't yet see who was speaking, or who they were talking to. The voice was coming from the other side of the trees. 'I don't want to hurt you,' it said.

Imogen peeped round a trunk.

Ochi was standing in the circle of trees. She was young and strong and doing something awful. Imogen clamped her hand to her mouth. She wanted to look away but she couldn't.

Branches flailed, wood splintered, roots rose from the earth and the witch's lantern illuminated the scene. A skret was pinned to a tree trunk, with bark spreading over his skin. His legs were covered in rough ridges. Lichen crusted his face.

It was Zuby, half sealed in a tree.

'Let go!' said Ochi. 'Let go and I'll stop!' Zuby's eyes were full of terror, but he couldn't even speak. There were shoots growing into his mouth, wedged between his tusk-teeth.

He held his claws together, protecting something. Imogen squinted and realised it was the clock. Zuby was refusing to give it to the witch.

He's already dead, hissed a worry creature. *He's already turning to wood.*

Perla and Miro hid behind neighbouring trees. 'Imogen,' yelled Miro. 'We need to save Zuby!'

Imogen nodded in desperate agreement, but the worry creatures were holding her back. They dropped from branches and burrowed up through the soil. They clung to the hem of her jacket. *You're not good enough*, they whispered. *Not brave enough either. There's something very wrong with yooouuuu.*

Imogen saw Miro running – running to the centre of the

ring. He let out a wordless battle cry, brandishing his dagger with one hand. But a root caught his foot and he skidded to his knees.

Ochi didn't even turn round. The roots bound Miro in an instant. The trees prised Zuby's claws apart.

Not good enough. Not brave enough. Now your friends know the truth. You failed Marie, and you're about to fail Zuby too.

Imogen pulled a worry creature from her neck as several more swarmed up her back.

Then Perla charged across the Ring of Yasanay. She was fast and light-footed as a hare – but roots chased her heels, caught her ankle. Perla fell in slow motion.

Imogen tore worry creatures from her body and bashed them against the tree. *Splat. Crunch. Squelch.* They felt like baked potatoes. She crushed them one after another.

Then Imogen wrenched herself out of hiding. 'Ochi,' she called across the hilltop. 'Let them go!'

CHAPTER 60

Imogen sprinted towards Zuby. His claws had been forced open by the encroaching bark, his body was encased in the tree. Ochi only had to stretch out and the clock would be hers.

Imogen leaped over a great snaking root. A branch swiped at her head and she ducked. She was close to the witch, ready to jump – but then she was jolted back. She didn't see the root that got her, just felt it close round her waist.

Imogen tried to pull free, but the root was like a boa constrictor. 'It's not even your clock!' she screamed as the trees dragged her away from the witch.

Zuby was barely visible. Bark covered all but his face. Perla and Miro were as helpless as Imogen, roped down by roots.

Ochi reached for the clock.

But there was one soul she'd overlooked.

Konya came flying across the circle of trees, paws barely touching the grass, fur on end, claws out. The snëehoolark meant business.

She leaped at the witch, and the trees creaked and groaned. Ochi let out a scream. Imogen gave a whoop of triumph as Konya brought her prey to the ground.

Then the witch and the wolf-cat were a tumbling whirl of claws and cape, fur and skin. Perla was shouting to Konya, egging the sněehoolark on. Finally, Konya was on top of the witch. Paws pinning shoulders. Whiskers in face.

Good, thought Imogen. *See how she likes being restrained.*

The root round Imogen's middle went slack and then, squirming, it retreated underground. The children were free from the trees.

Perla and Miro rushed to Zuby. There was a rift in the tree that had attacked him, as if it had been lightning-struck. Zuby was sprawled at the bottom of the trunk.

'Zuby!' cried Miro. 'Are you hurt?'

The skret opened his big yellow eyes. 'Zuby is as tough as old mushrooms,' he croaked.

Imogen hesitated, a little way back. She wondered if her friends had noticed that she'd been the last one to help, the last one to enter the circle of trees. They must think her a terrible coward.

But she couldn't tell them the truth, couldn't say that worry creatures had held her back. They'd think she was crazy. They'd call her a liar. They wouldn't be her friends any more.

'There are still bits of tree on you,' said Miro to Zuby.

He was right. Most of the bark had dropped off the skret, but some of it clung to his legs like scabs.

'Please,' came a voice. 'Have mercy.'

Imogen had almost forgotten about the witch. She turned and saw Ochi, under the snĕehoolark's paws.

'You wouldn't hurt an old woman?'

Konya looked very much like she would.

'Old?' said Perla, visibly perplexed.

'Ochi looks different in her house,' explained Imogen.

The clock was at the witch's feet. It was scratched, but it still seemed to be working. Five hands ticked in harmony. Jewelled stars hovered above its face.

Imogen picked up the clock and glared at the witch. 'If we let you go, do you promise to stop following us?'

Ochi grimaced. 'I do as I wish.'

Konya yowled in her face.

'I promise,' cried the witch.

Imogen joined the others. 'What do you think?' she whispered.

'There are only two options,' muttered Miro. 'We either kill her or we set her free.'

Perla's eyebrows went up in the middle. 'We can't kill her,' she gasped. 'She's a person, not a rat.' Perla gestured to Konya, and the snĕehoolark backed off.

Ochi stumbled to her feet.

'You're free to go,' said Miro in his king voice. 'But if you ever hurt Zuby again, I'll have you—'

'What?' laughed the witch. 'Sent beyond the mountains?'

Her eyes flashed. 'You think you're on such a valiant quest. Think you can slay the krootymoosh and the world will fall at your feet? Well, let me tell you, *boy king* – I've seen your stars, and there's nothing in your future but blood and death.'

Miro turned a shade paler. Konya growled.

'Leave us alone,' shouted Imogen at the witch.

'And you,' said Ochi, pointing to the girls as she backed away. 'The krootymoosh are the least of your worries.' She was at the edge of the circle of trees and their branches swayed in the wind – or perhaps they still danced to the witch's command. 'Fear the men of burning light. Fear their molten forms. Fear their deep volcano eyes and yawning, hungry jaws!'

Imogen wasn't sure what to say to that. Was it some kind of poem?

Ochi gave the clock one final look before stepping into the darkness and disappearing down the side of the hill.

The children helped Zuby sit up, propping him against a tree. Miro brought the witch's lantern closer. She'd left it behind when she fled.

'I'm all right,' said the skret. 'Really . . . I just need a moment.'

'That was amazing,' said Perla. 'We were like "no!" and she was like "yes!" and the trees were like –' Perla... wiggled her arms – 'I didn't know tree roots could do that.'

'Me neither,' said Miro, with considerably less excitement. 'What did Ochi mean about blood and death?'

Imogen's worry creatures were slinking off with smug looks on their faces. The children had saved Zuby and they'd got the clock. So why did it feel like the worry creatures had won?

'Don't let Ochi get to you,' said Imogen to Miro. 'I think she wanted us scared.' She crouched next to Zuby and handed him the battered clock. 'Zuby, I'm so sorry we put you in danger.'

'I don't know what came over me,' said the skret. He turned the clock round, as if it was a riddle. 'I should have let the witch have it, but it feels so special.'

The children sat in the circle of trees, taking it in turns to doze and keep watch, until the rivergulls began calling to the slow-rising sun.

The trees were just trees once again, dark stripes against the rose-tinted sky. And, as the first rays peeped through the branches, the clock of stars started to chime.

Zuby held up the timepiece and the children gathered round. Konya pushed her nose between Perla and Imogen, whiskers flattened to her face.

The clock's door opened and two figures came out. The man wore a wide-brimmed hat. The woman had ribbons in her hair.

'It's Branna and Zemko,' cried Perla. 'They're my parents' friends.'

Miro sighed. 'The clock's sending us in circles.'

'No,' said Perla. She pointed to a spot in the air. '*This* is where we are now.' She pointed to another spot, brandishing her finger like a wand. '*This* is Valkahá – where Anneshka took Marie.' Then Perla pointed somewhere else. 'And *this* is where Branna and Zemko live.'

Thank you, thought Imogen. *I have no idea what any of that means.*

Perla glanced at her friends, waiting for the penny to drop. In the end, it was Zuby who explained. 'If you little humans are going to Valkahá, then Perla's friends live on the way.'

CHAPTER 61

The five queens of Valkahá wore their jewellery like armour – pearl-dotted cheekbones, silver-plated necks, breastplates caked in crystals. Anneshka could hardly see the women beneath. Only the blink of an eye or the twitch of a lip gave them away.

She felt ashamed, standing before them. Her dress was made of Lowland wool. Her hair was tied with ribbons, in keeping with the Lowland style. But here, in Valkahá's great hall, she felt more like a milkmaid than a visiting princess. She was glad she'd left Marie at the door.

'Your Majesties,' trumpeted a servant. 'This is Princess Pavla of Vodnislav.'

Anneshka curtseyed and took in the hall. The room was adorned with silver. The thrones were silver too. The queens wore silver headdresses of varying heights and designs.

So this was what greatness looked like. Anneshka had found her kingdom at last.

The first queen tilted her headdress. She had watery blue eyes and a silver centipede hanging over one cheek. 'To what do we owe this honour?' she asked.

'I am here to visit your cathedral,' said Anneshka, 'to pray for my father's good health.'

The second queen's bodice was stiff with jewels. 'You seek a safe place to stay?'

Anneshka nodded, trying to look meek.

The fifth queen got to her feet. There were so many pearls dangling before her face that only the tip of her white chin could be seen. 'Please, be our guest,' she said. Her voice was hoarse, almost like a loud whisper. 'The Princess of Vodnislav is always welcome.'

So Anneshka made herself at home in the palace. She locked Marie in her chamber. Couldn't have the girl escaping . . . not before she'd helped Anneshka become queen.

But things were not as simple as Anneshka had hoped. The queens did not mingle with their guests. They spent the next day in their quarters – a self-contained part of the palace. Here, they had private walkways, private chambers and even a private church.

Anneshka was beginning to understand how they'd stayed in power so long . . .

That evening, the palace guests gathered to feast, as was their nightly ritual. They congregated in the great hall, where tables were arranged in long rows.

Many of the noblemen wore red cloaks. The ladies favoured

silver headdresses, like those worn by the queens. Anneshka bought one for herself, eager to shed her Lowland ribbons. She may be the heir of King Ctibor, but that wasn't *all* she intended to be.

Anneshka sat at a table and took in the scene. The silver thrones remained empty – the five queens were dining alone – but no expense had been spared on the food. Every plate was an artwork. Birds were baked inside birds. Pork was minced and disguised as fruit.

Anneshka ate very little. She was here to listen instead.

'I don't see why we have to give so much away,' said a young man sitting to her right.

Anneshka pretended to be concentrating on taking soup from inside a hollow boar's head. She leaned in so she could hear more clearly.

'All they have to do is sit on their thrones,' said the man. 'We're the ones doing the work.' His friend only grumbled in reply.

Anneshka raised a spoonful of peas to her lips and was surprised to find they were sweet.

'Come on, Surovetz,' insisted the man. 'You're the queens' favourite. Renegotiate the fees. Let's keep more silver for ourselves!'

The man called Surovetz did not respond. Anneshka risked a glance in his direction and realised, with a jolt, that he was already looking her way. He was fair-haired, with a strong chin and sharp eyes.

Anneshka lowered her gaze. She would have to be more careful than that.

'We'll talk later,' said Surovetz to his friend. 'There are too many spies in this place.'

So, thought Anneshka, as the men turned away. *The nobles are dissatisfied with the queens . . . Looks like I've found a way in.*

CHAPTER 62

Branna and Zemko's cottage was almost entirely hidden by blossom.

'What's that ponging stink?' asked Zuby.

Imogen sniffed. She couldn't smell anything bad.

'It's blossom,' laughed Miro. 'Most people like it.'

The cottage was painted white with wooden tiles nailed to its roof. A dog came rushing round the side of the building. It was a small wiry thing, shaped like a footstool. It yapped at the children, but fell quiet when it set eyes on Konya. *That's a big cat*, the dog seemed to say.

The children climbed down from their ponies, stiff and tired after riding all day. Zuby had insisted on walking, even after Ochi's attack. 'The horses and I are on a little break,' the skret had explained.

A young boy sprinted through the cottage's front garden – grass-stained, barefoot and barking. He was chasing the dog and, from the sounds of things, pretending to be a dog himself. He slowed when he saw the visitors. 'Mama,' he called. 'Mama, there are people!'

A woman stepped out of the house, wiping her hands on her apron. She had a rosy complexion and a birthmark on one cheek. At first, she looked confused when she saw the creatures in front of her cottage: three children, three ponies, one snĕehoolark and a very bedraggled skret.

'Branna,' said Perla, shuffling forward. 'It's me, Michal's daughter.'

'Perla!' cried the woman. She opened her arms and gave Perla a hug, lifting the girl clean off the ground. Imogen wanted a hug like that – a hug that would sweep all the bad things away.

Konya rubbed her head against Branna's skirts, as if trying to join the embrace. When the hugging was over, Branna inspected Perla.

'Your clothes are filthy,' she said, disapproving. 'And what's that?' She picked fiddleweed from Perla's blouse. Imogen's hand went to her own hair. It was full of dried river gunk.

'Where did they come from?' the boy asked his mother.

Branna ignored her son and, instead, fixed Perla with an intense stare. 'Do your parents know that you're here?'

Perla puckered her lips. She seemed a bit wary of Branna . . . family friend or not.

'That's just what I asked them,' put in Zuby.

Branna glanced at the skret's bark-crusted legs. Then she turned on Imogen and Miro. 'And what about you?' she demanded. 'Aren't your families worried?'

Imogen didn't reply. Branna was the kind of woman it was hard to tell lies to.

Branna's face settled into a frown. 'I think you'd better come inside.'

*

The cottage's front room smelled of herbs and bread. There were embroidered cushions on a rocking chair and seedlings in pots on the ledge. The air near the oven danced with heat. Imogen already knew she wouldn't want to leave.

'First things first,' said Branna. 'The piano is our best place for hiding. If the krootymoosh come, that's where you must go.'

Perla nodded as if this was a normal way to welcome children into your home. Imogen eyeballed the black and white keys. She'd never been inside a piano. She wondered if there was space . . . and hoped she wouldn't have to find out.

'Luki, fetch the soap,' commanded Branna.

The barefoot boy trotted off with the little dog in tow.

Branna turned her attention to Perla. 'So, young lady. Do your companions have names?'

Perla nodded. 'This is Zuby,' she said. 'He's a gaoler . . . at least, he *was*.' Zuby grinned and waved a clawed hand. '*This* is Imogen. She's my friend from across the mountains. And that's Miro, the King of Yaroslav.'

Branna squinted at Miro. She didn't seem very impressed. Perhaps she thought kings should be taller.

'It's an honour to meet you,' said Miro.

'Yes,' said Branna. 'You're filthy too. I'll heat some water for a bath.'

Miro glanced at Imogen and Perla. That wasn't the response he'd expected.

'We can't have you looking like that when your parents arrive,' continued Branna, busying herself by the oven.

'My parents?' said Perla. 'Are they coming?'

'I'm sure they'll leave as soon as they receive my note. Poor things must be worried. I'll send a letter by rider tonight, let them know that you're safe.'

Imogen thought of her message . . . the one she'd sent by moth. She hoped that Mum had received it. She hoped she'd understand.

If Mark was still with Perla's father, he was bound to read Branna's letter too. Imogen could picture the way he'd respond. He'd come striding in through the front door. Imogen would be in so much trouble. She didn't even know what he'd say . . . he'd definitely make her go home.

But she couldn't have Mark ruining things. Not after she'd travelled so far, not now she knew where Anneshka had gone. 'Don't,' she cried. 'Don't send a letter.'

Perla gave a tiny head shake – a warning? Of what?

Branna stopped what she was doing and looked square at Imogen. 'I don't know what it's like on your side of the mountains, but it's adults that give orders round here.'

'But—' tried Imogen.

Branna tightened the strings of her apron. 'I don't want to hear it. I'm sending those letters tonight. Now go and get ready for your baths.'

CHAPTER 63

Branna scrubbed the children clean one by one. Imogen didn't like being bossed, but she did like the hot water on her skin. The tub was a barrel, like the ones made for beer.

She liked having her hair washed too. And she certainly enjoyed eating redcurrant cake while she dried in the oven's warmth. She'd never seen a stove like it. The mouth was big enough to crawl into.

'Branna,' said Imogen, licking cake from her thumb, 'I don't suppose you've seen a girl with red hair?'

Branna shook her head. 'Can't say I've seen anyone much. We're very tucked away down this lane.' Imogen pulled the towel tighter round her shoulders.

'I think these will fit,' said Branna as she placed a stack of clothes by the stove.

Imogen inspected the stockings. 'Whose are they?' she asked.

'They belonged to my daughter,' said Branna.

Imogen wondered if Branna's daughter had grown up and left home. Branna must have seen the question on her face. 'Krootymoosh,' she said. 'Six months ago.'

'Oh,' said Imogen, and she felt a little chill, despite the oven's heat. Everywhere she went in the Lowlands, she heard the same stories: children snatched from their families, parents trying to forget. The krootymoosh cast a long shadow.

Imogen stepped into the skirt and slipped on the bodice. Branna did up the buttons at the front.

'You can keep the clothes,' said Branna. 'My daughter . . .' Her fingers fumbled with the top button. 'She won't be coming back.'

Imogen looked at Branna more closely. She had a nice face – as round as an apple. 'Are you sure?' asked Imogen.

'Yes,' said Branna. 'No one's wearing them.'

But Imogen hadn't meant the clothes.

Branna stepped back to look at her creation. 'There,' she said. 'Perfect fit.'

Imogen felt like she was wearing fancy dress. The skirt swished when she moved, the stockings itched, and there were ribbons in her freshly washed hair. 'Thank you,' she murmured.

She hoped Mum wasn't giving away *her* clothes: her jeans and trainers, her coat with the nice fluffy hood. She tried not to think of Mum's hugs. After Imogen had returned from her summer of adventures, Mum's hugs had become a little longer . . . a little tighter.

'I *am* coming back,' whispered Imogen. 'As soon as I've rescued Marie.'

'What?' said Branna.

'Oh, nothing,' said Imogen. 'I was just talking to myself.'

Branna emptied the bath tub, one bucket at a time. She'd been so very generous. Perhaps there was one thing Imogen could fix right away. 'We're going to find out where the krootymoosh take the children,' she said. 'We'll search for your daughter too.'

Branna paused. Her face wavered. 'Do not say such things.'

'But isn't that good news?' asked Imogen.

'Krootymoosh are a curse,' said Branna. 'They're a punishment for something we've done. The more you tell lies, the more children go missing. Is that what you want? Do you want Perla to get taken? Do *you* want to get taken too? Because that's what's going to happen if you keep running around on your own.'

Imogen shook her head, confused. Why did adults always think she was lying? 'We're going to rescue Perla's brother,' she said. 'King Ctibor isn't doing anything to help, but—'

'King Ctibor is trying,' snapped Branna. 'He's doing what he can.'

Imogen had met King Ctibor. He didn't seem like he cared for anyone other than himself and his daughters. He certainly wasn't doing what he could.

'Besides,' continued Branna, 'if all of the priests and the men of great learning have been unable to find our children, what makes you think *you* can?'

Imogen didn't have an answer to that. She just *felt* it . . .

When her worry creatures didn't have her by the throat, she felt like she could do anything. Especially with the help of her friends and the clock.

'You're just a child,' muttered Branna and her sweet apple face turned sour. 'You know nothing of life and its monsters.' Then her anger seemed to subside. 'Still . . . I have my son. I'm luckier than many. Far better to count your blessings than to fret over what cannot be.'

Imogen sensed that there was no point in arguing, so she didn't respond, but Branna's outburst had not changed her mind. She felt more determined than ever that she'd keep searching for Tomil and Marie.

CHAPTER 64

That evening, Imogen sat at the kitchen table with Perla and Miro. Konya lay at their feet like a great snĕehoolark rug. Zuby sat opposite, with his injuries treated and cleaned. There was still a bit of lichen at the back of his head, but Branna had soaked the rest off.

Nobody was allowed to touch the food until Branna had said a prayer. Her husband, Zemko, had spent the day working in the garden. Now he stared at the roast goose with loving eyes. Their son, the barefoot boy called Luki, looked ready to pounce on the parsnips.

When Branna was done, they all leaped at the food. More swede mashed with bacon. More buttered parsnips with herbs. Imogen couldn't chew fast enough. Zuby stripped a goose leg in seconds. Konya and the little dog, Klobasa, begged for scraps.

When the feeding frenzy was over, Zemko sat back in his chair. 'So, what are you doing here, Perla?' he asked. 'Come to help me make boats?'

We're on a rescue mission, thought Imogen, *and we're taking directions from a star-reading clock. We've run away from our parents, escaped from King Ctibor and defeated an evil witch.*

'Oh, we're just travelling,' said Perla. Her raised eyebrows gave her away. But Branna and Zemko seemed not to notice – or perhaps they weren't after the truth.

'I'll need to know how to reach all your parents,' said Branna, 'before you go to bed.'

'Mark is with Perla's father,' said Miro, before Imogen could stop him.

Branna nodded. 'Is Mark your father?'

'No,' replied Miro. 'He looks after Imogen. I'm—' Imogen nudged him hard in the ribs. 'No one looks after me,' he finished.

'Papa, is that boy really king?' asked Luki. He was staring at Miro with undisguised awe.

'No, son,' said Zemko. 'He's a child, just like you.'

Miro opened his mouth, but Imogen nudged him again. 'Save your breath,' she whispered. 'If they don't know who you are, they can't send you home.'

'Is he going to banish the krootymoosh?' asked Luki.

'No, son. He's not. Eat your greens.'

Imogen was reaching for more parsnips when she noticed something silver on her plate. She blinked, thinking her eyes must be tired – but then the silver thing moved.

'Hello,' she said to the shadow moth.

Branna reached to swat it away and Zuby raised a protective claw. 'Please don't,' he said. 'It won't hurt you. I think it's got something to say.'

Branna looked baffled, but she sat back in her chair. The moth fluttered on to the table and opened its wings.

'What's it doing?' asked Luki, leaning in.

'It says it delivered your message,' said Zuby. His eyeballs swivelled Imogen's way.

'My message?' she gasped. 'For my mum!'

The moth wiggled its feathery antennae and stomped its tiny feet. Was it . . . doing some kind of dance?

Zuby cleared his throat. 'I'll translate. The moth says . . . the moth says it did a dance on the wall of your mouse.'

Imogen looked up. 'That doesn't make sense.'

'*House*,' said Zuby. 'Sorry. It did a dance on the wall of your house.'

The moth ran up and down the table, tracing patterns across the wood. A hush fell over the room. Even Branna and Zemko were listening.

So moths can talk, thought Imogen and, after everything that had happened, she wasn't really surprised. *They use a language of movement instead of words.*

'At first, your mother didn't notice,' said Zuby. 'So the moth did its dance again.'

The insect looped round the salt cellar and Imogen's world

seemed to narrow. The piano. The oven. The giant cat and small dog. None of that mattered right now. 'What happened next?' she whispered.

'Your mother didn't scream. Didn't put the moth out. But her eyes overflowed.'

Mum was crying, thought Imogen and her stomach twisted. *I should have known she wouldn't understand.* Under the table, Imogen squeezed her hands hard.

The moth danced round glasses and plates. Perla pulled her dish out of its way.

'The moth told your mother you'd come home with Marie. Your mother made patterns with an ink stick.'

Imogen squeezed her hands tighter. Was an ink stick a pen? Had Mum made notes?

'Your mother seemed to know what to chew,' said Zuby. 'Oh . . . not chew. Sorry. Your mother seemed to know what to *do*.'

Branna and Zemko looked stunned. Like a bomb had gone off in their faces.

'Where did you learn to speak moth?' whispered Perla. She was looking at Zuby.

'You can learn it from books,' said Miro, as if he was some kind of expert. 'My father – he used to know how. He used to send messages to the skret of Klenot Mountain.'

Zuby reached for the teapot, saying, 'One more drink for

the road.' He wedged the spout between his tusks and started glugging, throwing his head right back. Luki stifled a laugh.

'You're not *leaving* us?' cried Miro.

'I have to,' said Zuby, and the moth flew on to his head. 'Skret travel best at night and I have a little quest of my own.'

Miro dropped his fork with a clatter. 'What if I command you to stay?'

'You are not my Král,' said the skret. His tone was mild, but it was clear that he'd chosen his path. 'Take care of yourselves, little humans. Take care of that magic clock.'

Imogen should have said something. She should have asked about Zuby's quest and thanked him for his help, but she was still thinking of her mother. Had Mum understood the moth's message? What would she do with those notes?

Zuby bowed to Branna and Zemko. He picked up his cloak and, with that, the skret and the moth left the house.

CHAPTER 65

After dinner, the children were bundled upstairs. Luki's bedroom was lit by a candle. There were toy horses and a big knitted dragon, two beds and a flat-lidded trunk.

Miro lay next to Luki. Imogen and Perla shared the spare bed. Imogen wondered if it used to belong to Branna's daughter, but she decided against bringing it up. There was something very comforting about being tucked in by Branna – even if the tucking was tighter than any Imogen had experienced before.

Klobasa the dog lay on the floor like a sausage with legs. Konya settled by the window with her tail curled round the clock. It was still ticking along nicely. A silver moon slipped behind the clock's longest hand. Mechanical stars twinkled on.

Outside, it had started to rain and Imogen could hear the patter on the roof, like hundreds of impatient fingers. Inside the cottage, she could hear something else – a rustling in the front room, a scampering sound on the stairs. Her worry creatures were on their way.

Imogen wanted to take her mind off the creatures. If Marie

had been there, she would have asked for a story . . .

Imogen waited until Branna left the room. 'Hey, Luki,' she whispered. 'Do you know any stories?'

'Oh yes,' said the boy. 'Loads.'

'Go on then,' said Imogen. 'Tell us your best one.'

'Hmm,' said Luki, and he wriggled out of bed. 'I'm not normally allowed to tell *that*.'

He stood by the room's only candle and its light threw his shadow to the wall. 'Once upon a time, there was a land plagued by monsters.'

'What kind of monsters?' asked Imogen.

Luki moved closer to the candle so his shadow filled the room. He spread his fingers on his shoulders like spikes.

'Krootymoosh,' whispered Perla.

'Yes,' said Luki with a grin. 'The king of this land was brave. He wanted to make the monsters go away.' The boy spaced out his fingers so his shadow had a crown.

Luki's pretty good at shadow puppets, thought Imogen, and she would have said so if her worry creatures hadn't been under the bed. It took all of her energy to ignore them.

'The king challenged the krootymoosh to a duel,' said Luki. 'The Lord of the Krootymoosh accepted. They met on Mlok Island, and everyone came to watch. The king charged, sword flashing in the sun. It looked as if he would win! But no one can defeat the krootymoosh. The beast clubbed the king on his head.'

'No!' cried Imogen.

Perla gasped.

'As the king lay dying, the water dragon appeared.' Luki grabbed his toy dragon and made it swoop round the room. He bounced from one bed to the other.

Klobasa wagged his tail, excited. Would he get to play the game too?

Branna burst into the bedroom. Luki froze. Perla pulled the covers over her head.

'What are you doing?' cried Branna. 'You're supposed to be asleep!'

'Sorry, Mama,' said Luki, dropping the toy dragon and slinking back into bed.

Branna blew out the candle and slammed the door shut, plunging the room into darkness.

But Luki wasn't finished with his story. 'The water dragon killed the krootymoosh,' he whispered. 'Neither were seen again.'

The clock ticked into the silence that followed. Even the rain on the roof seemed to hush.

'I've not heard that story before,' said Miro.

Imogen could feel Perla's warmth at her back. She had to keep reminding herself that it wasn't Marie. 'Do you think the dragon really exists?' she whispered.

'No,' said Perla in the darkness. 'A real dragon would have helped us by now.'

CHAPTER 66

Imogen was woken by the chiming of a bell. It was morning. She sat up with a start. 'Quick!' she cried. 'It's the clock!' She sprang out of bed as the little hatch opened, and Perla and Miro did the same.

The figure that emerged from the clock was big, or bigger than the others had been. It had to duck to fit out of the hatch. In one hand it carried a club.

'What's happening?' asked Luki. 'What's going on?'

The miniature krootymoosh swung the club a few times, then it prowled back into the clock.

'Well, I don't see how that helps,' said Miro.

As the words left his lips there was a scream from outside. The children hurried to the window to see people running down the lane. The overnight rain had left the garden gleaming, and at the top of the hill, behind hedgerows full of blossom, stood a hulking figure. It was so tall that its head was hidden behind the lower branches of a tree. It was carrying a weapon that looked a lot like a club.

Imogen's belly did a flip.

'The krootymoosh are coming,' stammered Luki.

'What do we do?' cried Miro.

'Hide!' yelped Perla.

The children ran down the stairs, Konya and Klobasa hot on their heels. Perla unhooked the end of the piano. The soundboard and strings had been removed. Outside, the screams were getting louder.

'Quick,' said Perla, 'get in.'

Miro and Imogen squidged into the hollow piano, wedging Luki between them. Perla got in last and clawed at the side panel, trying to make it close, but her hands were shaking. 'I can't do it!' she cried. Miro reached across Perla and pulled the panel shut.

The back of Imogen's head touched the back of the piano. The fluffy hammers, designed to hit strings, tickled the tip of her chin. There wasn't much room to move, but, if Imogen slouched, she could see through a crack in the wood.

There were Branna's seedlings, in pots on the ledge. There was Konya, guarding the door. A shape moved behind the lace curtains. The krootymoosh was in the front garden.

Luki started chanting under his breath. 'Beware the knocking at the door. Beware the krootymoosh. Beware their rattling cages. They do not—'

'Hush,' hissed Imogen. Her legs felt strangely liquid. Her heart was going too fast.

Branna and Zemko came hurtling in from the back of the house. They looked around and checked the children were hidden.

Boom. Boom. Boom. The krootymoosh knocked on the door. Imogen felt Luki tremble.

'There are no children here,' shouted Zemko.

'You heard him,' called Branna to the beast. 'We haven't got what you want.'

The voice that replied was deep and terrible. 'That's not what they say in the village.'

Imogen glanced at Miro. His eyes shone in the piano's darkness.

Boom. Boom. Boom. The krootymoosh wasn't knocking any more. It must have been hammering with its club. When Imogen looked back through the crack in the piano, the front door was hanging off its hinges.

Klobasa yapped and snarled. And there was the krootymoosh, head cropped by the doorframe.

The beast stooped to enter the house. It was covered in white fur, but spiked armour shielded its shoulders. It walked upright, on thick hind legs. 'Where's the child?' it demanded, as its helmet scraped the ceiling.

Branna and Zemko cowered by the sink. 'L-l-look around,' said Zemko. 'There are no children here.'

The krootymoosh swung its club, splitting the kitchen table

in two. Branna screamed and grabbed her husband.

'Why would your neighbours lie?' growled the beast.

'They were trying to send you away from their houses,' cried Branna. 'You've already taken my daughter! I've got nothing left to give!'

The krootymoosh grunted at that. It stomped over to the oven and peered inside. 'No children in there.' It paused by the piano, blocking Imogen's view. She could see the matted bits in its fur, smell the sour stink of its sweat.

Imogen wanted to sneeze. She held her nose and the sneeze went away.

The krootymoosh advanced on Branna and Zemko. Imogen could see its tail was little more than a scraggly stump. 'If you don't have children, then why are you washing their clothes?' The krootymoosh pointed to Luki's trousers, drying above the oven.

Branna and Zemko didn't have an answer for that. The krootymoosh picked up a pot of seedlings and threw it across the room. It smashed above Zemko's head. 'I'll crush your skulls,' the beast bellowed.

Imogen didn't see what happened next, but she heard shattering and shouting. The krootymoosh was swinging its club. Somewhere out of sight, Klobasa was barking. Then the dog squeaked and went quiet.

Among all the chaos, Luki started screaming. Imogen and

Miro tried to stop him. But he was screaming with his eyes scrunched shut. It was like Luki had broken, like he'd flipped. Perla was screaming now too.

The top of the piano was torn off. Imogen looked up and there was the beast. It wore a flat metal mask and its eyes were black pits.

'There you are,' growled the krootymoosh, as it reached into the piano.

Then Konya attacked from behind – claws into shoulders, fangs into throat. The krootymoosh roared and stumbled, trying to shake the sněehoolark off.

The children jostled to get out of the piano and now Imogen could see the full scene. The front room was smashed into pieces. Branna lay on her back, arms flung overhead. Zemko was throwing plates at the krootymoosh.

'Mama?' said Luki. His mother lay still.

A second krootymoosh was coming down the lane. Imogen could see it through the smashed front door. Zemko turned to the children. 'What are you waiting for?' he cried. 'Run!'

CHAPTER 67

Imogen burst out of the back door. She scanned the garden for somewhere to hide. Apple trees. Bean poles. Compost. Could she dive into that?

Two boats were stacked in the corner – circular, one-man crafts. Perla pulled one over herself and lowered it to the ground, like a tortoise going into its shell.

Konya leaped up a tree, tail disappearing into blossom.

There was more crashing inside the house. Imogen ran after Perla and took hold of the second boat – it was surprisingly easy to lift. She crawled underneath.

The boat was made from willow, bent into hoops and bound tight. Animal hide was stretched round the outside, turning the sunlight orange. Imogen crouched in the warm amber air.

'Imogen?' came Miro's voice. She lifted the boat by its rim. There he was, standing in the garden. A shadow was spreading down the side of the house.

'Pssst!' said Imogen. 'Over here.'

Miro dashed towards her, hurdling over cabbages and leeks. The shadow stretched across the garden as Miro scrambled under the boat. It was a tight squeeze for two.

'What were you doing?' whispered Imogen.

'Waiting for Luki,' Miro replied.

Imogen's heart tripped up. She'd forgotten about the fourth child. 'Where is he?'

She was answered by a high-pitched scream.

Miro and Imogen lifted the boat. A krootymoosh held Luki by his ankle. The boy shrieked again, dangling in mid-air. There were more krootymoosh approaching, with caged children on their backs. Some of the children were screaming like Luki. Others were crying instead.

Miro moved, as if to help, but Imogen grabbed his wrist. 'No,' she hissed. 'You'll get taken.'

'I don't care,' he replied, wild-eyed.

'She's right,' whispered Perla, from under the neighbouring boat. 'There are too many krootymoosh. We don't stand a chance. Even Konya can't fight six at once.'

The krootymoosh stuffed Luki into a cage. The boy pulled at the bars and howled.

'I want to save him,' said Miro.

'Me too,' whispered Imogen. 'But you'll just get caught like the rest.'

She scrunched up her eyes and tried not to think of Branna, lying so still on the ground. Had Branna been breathing? Imogen didn't know.

The krootymoosh were very close now. The earth shook with the clomping of giant paws. Imogen prayed that they wouldn't be uncovered. Grass brushed against her face. Soil seeped damp at her knees.

When the tramping sound faded and everything was quiet, the children lifted the boats. There were no krootymoosh in the garden.

Imogen crawled out of hiding. There were no krootymoosh in the fields.

'We can't let them get away with this,' cried Miro.

Imogen was shaking and she didn't know why. Was she angry or was she going to weep?

Perla was already running – across the garden, towards the back door. Konya sprang out of her tree in a blizzard of blossom and galloped after her mistress. The girl and the sněehoolark didn't look back. They disappeared into the cottage.

CHAPTER 68

Branna was sitting up when Imogen entered the house, although she looked very pale. 'They took Luki,' she mumbled.

Perla, Imogen and Miro were quiet. None of them knew what to say.

Zemko carried his wife upstairs and laid her on their bed. 'You'll be okay,' he said. 'You just need some rest.' But for all his reassuring words, Zemko didn't leave Branna's side.

So the children were left in charge of the house. The place felt empty without adults. Without Luki. Without Klobasa the dog.

The children dug a hole at the bottom of the garden, where the ground was soft. They'd wrapped Klobasa in a blanket.

Konya nudged the dog with her nose, trying to get him to stand. But Klobasa had stood for the last time, defending his family from the krootymoosh. His wiry tail stuck out of the blanket.

Imogen bit her lip, tried to hold back the tears, but they rolled down her cheeks. It wasn't fair. None of this was. She bowed her head so the others wouldn't see her cry.

Miro placed the dead dog in the ground. As he stepped back, Imogen realised that he was crying too. She looked at Perla. Tears spilled down her cheeks.

'This wasn't supposed to happen,' sniffed Perla. 'This can't be what's written in the stars.' The children's tears fell to the earth. Above them, a rivergull called.

Zemko didn't come downstairs all day, so the children made lunch using whatever ingredients they could find. The result was lettuce sandwiches. Not exactly delicious, but at least they had something to eat.

After lunch, they tidied the front room. Perla hung fabric across the bashed-in door. Miro collected splinters of furniture and Imogen swept up broken pots.

'I can't stop thinking about Luki,' said Miro, picking up a severed chair leg. 'Where do you think the krootymoosh will take him?'

'If we knew that, we'd already be there,' muttered Imogen. She looked at the trampled seedlings. Branna had taken such care of the plants, turning them each day so they got enough light. Now it had all been destroyed.

'At least Luki won't be alone,' said Miro. 'He might already be with Tomil, or his sister.'

'He might already be dead,' whispered Perla. They worked in silence after that.

Imogen found a clump of earth among all the smashed-up pots. There was a seedling sprouting from the soil. One survivor. A pale green shoot, too young to have any leaves.

Imogen bent to rescue it, but as she got on to all fours she noticed something under the dresser. The something was a roll of parchment. She pulled it out and read the writing within:

Here lies Valkahá, City of Stone

Imogen's breath caught in her throat.

Valkahá . . . That was where Anneshka had taken Marie.

Beneath the writing was a piece of abstract art – a puddle of inky lines and intricate loops. There were squiggles in cobalt and navy, in indigo and aquamarine. It was as if the artist had dipped their quill in all the blues of the world.

'Hey,' called Imogen. 'Look at this.'

Perla's face changed as she studied the scroll. Some of her sadness seemed to lift. 'It's a map!'

Imogen looked again. Lines squirmed along the parchment, wriggling back on themselves. They were fidgety lines that couldn't sit still, lines with junctions and dead ends . . .

Perla snatched the scroll and bolted upstairs. She returned a few minutes later, excitement writ large on her face. 'The map doesn't belong to Branna or Zemko,' she declared. 'They've never seen it before. It must belong to the krootymoosh! They must have dropped it during their attack!'

Why would monsters need a map? wondered Imogen.

'I bet it shows krootymoosh secrets,' said Perla, her words were galloping fast. 'I bet it shows where they're going to next and where they take their hostages.'

Miro pointed to the words at the top. 'Valkahá,' he muttered. 'Isn't that where Anneshka has gone?'

Imogen felt a tilting sensation, like the ground was shifting beneath her feet. It was the same feeling she'd had when three wooden children had tumbled out of the clock . . . As if things were circling and spinning – joining in ways that she couldn't understand.

'Sometimes the stars bring people together,' said Perla. She turned the map upside down. 'We just need to work out how to read this thing.'

'That might not be so easy,' said Miro, and Imogen was inclined to agree. The blue lines were layered on top of each other, like five cities had been drawn on one scroll.

'We'll crack it,' said Perla, her positivity returned. 'We should leave for Valkahá at once.'

CHAPTER 69

Anneshka waited for Surovetz in the cellar of the five queens' palace. After overhearing his conversation about silver, Anneshka had tracked him down and requested a meeting in private.

She paced through the vault, where wine bottles were stacked on either side so they formed a narrow passage. Footsteps echoed down the staircase. Was it him?

'A place of silent fermentation,' said Surovetz. 'Or should that be contemplation? I always forget.'

He was on the other side of the wall of bottles. Anneshka could see his shape through the glass. It made him look taller than he was.

'So, what is it you want, Princess Pavla? All this talk of you being kidnapped by the krootymoosh . . . we both know it's a terrible lie.'

'I know who you are,' said Anneshka. She moved down the wine-lined passage and Surovetz followed. She paused and he paused. She moved and he shadowed.

Was she supposed to be afraid?

'You are the daughter of a Lowland king and I am a nobleman's son,' said Surovetz. 'It sounds like the beginning of a long boring poem.'

'You are something else too,' said Anneshka. 'My servants have been watching.'

It was true. Marie had proven herself useful. The girl could fit in small places where grown men did not think to look.

'Oh yes?' said Surovetz, and he peered through a gap between the bottles. 'And what did your servants say?'

Marie had reported back to Anneshka. She'd heard many things – some things that couldn't be repeated. *It's amazing what people say when they think they're not being overheard*, thought Anneshka.

'You source silver for the queens,' she said. 'You're the reason Valkahá continues to be wealthy. The real reason this kingdom is great.'

Surovetz sucked air between his teeth. 'Did your servants say nothing about my good looks?'

'You call yourself a lord,' said Anneshka, tapping the bottles with her nails. 'And yet you hardly get to keep any of the silver for yourself. A nugget here. A few coins there. You come running when the five queens whistle. You are little more than their dog.'

Surovetz did not like that. He rushed to the end of the passage, rounding the corner fast. 'I won't ask you again,

Princess Pavla. What is it you want?' His hand touched the hilt of his sword.

He wouldn't dare, thought Anneshka, and she forced herself not to flinch. 'I am favoured by the stars,' she replied.

'The stars favour no one,' said Surovetz with a self-assured curl of his lip.

'Help me and you will have more silver . . . much more. You will be my right-hand man. In return, I seek assistance. I wish to dispose of the queens.'

Surovetz's smile vanished and Anneshka knew that she'd won.

'Who are you *really*?' he asked.

CHAPTER 70

Imogen made cheese soup for breakfast. 'This should give us some energy for the journey,' she said as she poured the melted cheese into bowls.

Miro readied the ponies. They'd been grazing in the field by the house. Now they looked at the boy, weighed down with bridles. *Here he comes to disturb our peace*, the ponies seemed to be saying.

Perla wrote a letter for Zemko and Branna – thanking them and explaining where she'd gone. Zemko was asleep at Branna's bedside, dressed in yesterday's clothes. Branna, too, was sleeping and a pinkish glow had returned to her cheeks. Perla left her note by the door.

With full bellies and freshly packed saddlebags, taken from Zemko's barn, the children rode away from the house with Konya trotting behind. At the top of the lane, Imogen glanced back. The scene looked the same as on the day they'd arrived: a pink and white cloud of blossom, a cottage half hidden from view.

But it wasn't the same. No Luki. No Klobasa. And Branna

was sick in her bed. The krootymoosh had done this. Imogen felt something harden within her, like a stone forming between her ribs. She couldn't dig it out. She wasn't even sure that she wanted to.

'Rescuing Tomil isn't enough,' said Perla. 'Everyone's so busy protecting what they've got that they only think of one child at a time. Well, it doesn't work. We've got to rescue *all* the kidnapped children, not just the ones that we know. And we've got to stop the krootymoosh from ever doing this again.'

Imogen looked sideways at her friend. Perla sounded angry. Perhaps there was a stone growing inside her too.

The children rode west. By noon, the green of the Lowlands was fading, the rolling hills levelling out. Imogen felt relieved to be moving, even though her body was tired. Her pony rocked steadily beneath her. The saddlebags creaked on either side.

There was no sign of Mark or Ochi, no sign of King Ctibor's guards. Imogen had almost lost count of all the people who wanted her to turn back.

As the afternoon wore on, the ponies' hoofs began clip-clopping on rock. The children had entered the Scrublands – the land of flat earth and tangled vegetation. The ground here was dusty and pockmarked with pits. Some holes were no bigger than rabbit burrows – others would swallow a cow.

Occasionally, the holes were so huge that they seemed to have a gravity of their own. Imogen could feel them pulling her closer, inviting her to look in. She slid from her saddle and crouched at the edge of one. 'Helloooo,' she called into the darkness. Her voice seemed to echo to the centre of the Earth. But, of course, no one replied.

By the evening, Valkahá appeared on the horizon. It rose from the scrub like a shark's fin – steep-sided and impossibly tall. *Marie is there*, thought Imogen. *My little sister . . . all alone.*

The children set up camp before dusk. They tied the horses to a big flowering bush and sat down with their backs against a boulder. Here, they ate leftover parsnips, the last of Branna and Zemko's home-cooked food. It made Imogen think of Mum's cooking. Mum made parsnips taste like a treat – roasted them until they went crispy, smothered them with honey and salt.

Perla squinted at the krootymoosh map as the first stars came out. She traced the blue lines with her finger. Konya watched with moonlit eyes. Imogen and Miro watched too.

Imogen couldn't make sense of the diagram. It still reminded her of modern art – loads of squiggles and colours that left one big question: what's it supposed to be? She glanced at the city on the horizon. It didn't look much like the map.

'Can you read that thing?' Miro asked Perla.

'I'm working on it,' she said. There were little dimples in her cheeks. 'Maps are all about patience. The more you study, the more you can find . . . I want to be a mapmaker when I'm older.'

'*You* don't get to decide,' scoffed Miro. 'You have to do the same job as your parents. Unless you want to be a monk and live off turnips.'

Perla's dimples disappeared. 'That's what Papa says too. He wants me to look after the tavern . . . but I'm not the same person as him.'

'Don't listen to Miro,' said Imogen. 'My mum works for the council and I'm going to be an astronaut. You can be whatever you want!'

Perla didn't ask what an astronaut was, but Imogen knew she was just being shy. 'An astronaut is someone who travels in space. Mark says I need a fall-back career, but I've already made up my mind.'

'But I have to be king,' blurted Miro.

'That's different,' laughed Imogen. 'Being king's fun! Everyone wants to be king.'

Miro didn't say anything to that. He got up and went to the ponies, mumbling about checking on the clock. Imogen wondered if she'd said the wrong thing. Didn't Miro *want* to rule Yaroslav? She thought he liked being in charge.

'You're not from Yaroslav, are you?' said Perla, when the two of them were alone. 'You're from England. The place with no frogs.'

Imogen swallowed. 'Oh . . . yes.'

She'd hoped Perla might have forgotten what she'd said, but Perla seemed to be waiting, expectant.

Imogen's mouth went all dry. She'd lied about where she came from. She'd been so tired of being mistrusted – by Mark and the police and her mum – she couldn't face being doubted by Perla too. She didn't want her to think she was weird.

An end-of-day bee bumbled by.

But there was something even worse than not being believed, and that was lying to a friend.

'No, I'm not from Yaroslav,' said Imogen. 'The truth is, I'm from another world.' She braced herself, waiting for Perla to laugh or demand that she told the truth.

'Crusty catfish!' exclaimed Perla. 'Does your world have mountains or rivers? Forests or deserts or bogs? Is there some kind of gateway? Have you got any maps?'

Imogen smiled at the questions. Perla's face glowed with a curious light and Imogen felt silly for not telling her sooner. 'Well,' said Imogen, 'we do have *some* frogs, for a start . . .'

CHAPTER 71

Anneshka sat in her chamber inside the five queens' palace. She was brushing Marie's hair. 'I've worked out why the stars sent you to me,' she said.

'You have?'

The girl sounded excited. Stupid thing.

Anneshka liked combing Marie's hair. She enjoyed the repetition of teeth running through curls – of snagging, smoothing, starting again.

'All you need to do,' said Anneshka, 'is break into the queens' private quarters. Look for a window or a chimney. It should be easy enough . . . you're good at fitting into small spaces.'

Anneshka started to plait, dividing the child's hair into strands. *Cross, twist, repeat.*

'But aren't private quarters supposed to be private?' asked Marie. 'Why do you want me to break in?'

'To give the queens a goodnight kiss,' said Anneshka. *Cross, twist, repeat.* 'Are you going to do it or shall I give you to the krootymoosh?'

The girl stiffened at that.

'Remember,' purred Anneshka, 'if you do as you're told, I'll set you free. Your sister's bound to be looking for you.'

'She is?' Marie tried to glance over her shoulder, but Anneshka used the braid to steer her head back.

'Keep still,' she hissed. 'I'm not finished.'

Cross, twist, repeat.

'Yes, your sister is here,' said Anneshka, and she smiled at her lie. She remembered Marie's sister from the witch's cottage – a bony thing with speckled skin. There was no way she'd make it out of the forests, let alone all the way here.

'Your parents are in Valkahá too,' said Anneshka, warming to her tale. 'They're ready to take you back home – back to your own little world. But only once you complete this task.'

Cross, twist, repeat.

'Parents?' Marie sounded confused. 'Do you mean Mark and Mum?'

'Yes,' snapped Anneshka. 'Whatever they're called.'

The child's braid shone in the candlelight. Anneshka pinned it in place. 'There,' she said. 'It's finished.'

Marie raised a hand to her hair. 'Thank you.'

'So,' said Anneshka, 'do we have a deal?'

'Okay,' said Marie, 'I'll do it. If you promise to let me go, I'll sneak into the queens' private rooms.'

'What a good girl,' said Anneshka. 'I promise. It's all agreed.'

CHAPTER 72

The sun was setting as Imogen, Miro and Perla rode towards Valkahá. They steered their ponies round a thorny shrub, before joining the stream of people heading through the city's stone entrance.

There were wagons weighed down with goods, wanderers travelling on foot, a pack of children riding on the back of a cart. Imogen caught herself staring. She hadn't seen that many children for a long time – certainly not out in the open. Weren't they afraid of the krootymoosh? Miro and Perla stared too.

The guards at the entrance were collecting a fee. 'Three crowns for travellers,' they said.

Imogen took some coins from her purse – money Zuby had 'borrowed' from King Ctibor.

'No wonder Valkahá's so wealthy,' muttered Miro, 'if they charge you for just walking in.'

The children rode under the archway and Imogen couldn't help being impressed. The city of Valkahá looked like a sculpture carved from a single piece of rock: pale, gleaming buildings, silver-capped steeples, stone streets worn smooth as glass.

Perla gaped at the shining city. Her mouth was shaped like the word 'wow'. The people here were lavishly dressed. They sported round headpieces and silver gowns.

Birds with sharp wings swooped overhead, using the alleys as racetracks. They were too fast for Konya and she watched them with envious eyes.

'Do you think Valkahá is more beautiful than Yaroslav?' asked Miro.

'It's . . . bigger?' said Imogen, trying to be diplomatic. She could see why Anneshka thought *this* kingdom was the greatest. London was modest by comparison. It made Vodnislav look like a swamp.

And somewhere, among all these twisty pale streets, was her sister . . . Imogen could hardly believe it. What if King Ctibor was lying? What if Marie had been taken somewhere else?

But the clock brought us in this direction, she remembered. *And the clock has been right so far.*

Perla unfurled the krootymoosh map. 'Valkahá is built in layers,' she said, and she pointed at the top tiers of the city, where buildings stretched into the clouds. 'I wonder if each blue on the map is a different layer of the town.'

'Interesting,' mused Miro. 'That would explain why the map's such a mess.'

'The deepest blue is the tip of Valkahá,' said Perla, 'where the five queens live in their palace. The palest blue must be the level we're on now.'

That makes sense, thought Imogen. But there was a missing piece of the puzzle. If the map belonged to the krootymoosh, if this was where they'd gone next, why couldn't Imogen see any of them? A krootymoosh would hardly blend in.

The children steered their ponies up a broad street. Imogen kept her eyes peeled for monsters, but people here seemed very relaxed. They didn't seem to expect a krootymoosh attack . . .

A sign caught Imogen's attention:

The Courtyard Inn
Feather beds. Strong beer. Hot food.

There was a painting of a smiling woman, her arms open wide. Imogen wasn't interested in beer, but she longed to sleep on a mattress, and they'd eaten most of the food that they'd packed. 'It's getting late,' she said. 'Perhaps we should get ourselves a room.'

Perla and Miro nodded their agreement. Even the horses looked tired.

Inside the Courtyard Inn, a woman stood behind the bar. She was wearing about ten silver necklaces. She looked like the woman on the sign, except she wasn't smiling and her arms were crossed.

'Do you have any free rooms?' asked Imogen.

The woman leaned across the bar, necklaces jangling. She took in the children's Lowland clothes and the sněehoolark at their side. 'Free rooms?' she replied. 'Nothing in Valkahá's free. If you want a bed, you must pay.'

'Oh, we can pay,' said Imogen, tipping out the last of her coins.

Now the landlady smiled and opened her arms, just like the woman on the sign.

CHAPTER 73

The city of Valkahá breathed easy that night. A soft breeze blew through the Courtyard Inn. It played across the faces of three sleeping children and ruffled a sněehoolark's fur.

Then the wind swept up through the city. It twirled around spires and bell towers. It whispered down steep stone streets. It travelled all the way to the top of the hill, where it rustled Anneshka's skirts.

She was outside the palace, with her ear pressed to a door. It was the servants' entrance to the queens' private quarters. Locked from the inside, of course.

Surovetz stood next to her, leaning against the wall. His red cloak was tossed over one shoulder. 'No need to look so smug,' said Anneshka. 'You haven't done anything yet.'

'Can't blame me for taking pleasure in my work,' replied Surovetz.

There were footsteps inside the palace. Anneshka drew back. The door opened.

And there, on the other side, stood a ghost.

But it was no phantom. It was a child coated in flour. 'I

climbed in through the flour chute,' said Marie. 'I didn't know it was full.'

Anneshka stared. 'Stupid child! You've left footprints!'

'You said you didn't care how I got in!'

Anneshka dusted flour from Marie, muttering under her breath. Then she stepped into the queens' private quarters. Surovetz followed, quiet and quick as a shadow.

They found Queen Svitla asleep in her chamber. Her headdress was propped on its stand. Her jewellery was mounted on the wall – necklaces, rings and rosary beads. Some of the rings were so long they looked like fingers reaching from stone.

Anneshka bolted the door and stalked to the end of the bed. Marie hesitated by the entrance. 'What are we doing?' she whispered.

'Hush,' said Anneshka. 'Don't wake her.'

Without her jewellery and pearls, Queen Svitla was decidedly human – vulnerable and faintly ridiculous, with greying hair and pallid skin. There were lines about her downturned mouth. She reminded Anneshka of her mother.

Surovetz removed his knife. 'Don't hurt her,' cried Marie, rushing across the room, but Anneshka caught hold of the child. Queen Svitla mumbled in her sleep.

'Make it quick,' said Anneshka.

'NO!' cried Marie.

Surovetz leaned in, knife in hand, just as Queen Svitla awoke.
The old woman blinked at her assassins. There was a
question half formed on her lips. Surovetz answered in one
swift movement.

Marie screamed and Anneshka covered the child's face.
Was she trying to muffle Marie's shrieks or protect her from
what must occur? Anneshka wasn't quite sure.

But Marie bit Anneshka's finger.

'Little rat!' she exclaimed, letting go of the girl. The sight
of her own blood made Anneshka light-headed. She steadied
herself against the bed.

It took her a long dizzy moment to realise Marie's screeching
had stopped. The girl was slumped at Surovetz's feet. His grey
eyes met Anneshka's. 'The child wouldn't be quiet,' he muttered.

'Is she . . . dead?' asked Anneshka.

Surovetz bent and felt Marie's neck. 'Unconscious.'

'And the queen?'

'Definitely dead.'

There was a knock on the bedchamber door. The palace
guards had come too late. 'Your Majesty,' said the man
outside the chamber, 'I thought I heard some commotion. Is
everything all right?'

Anneshka rolled her eyes because it didn't seem to matter
how far she travelled; soldiers were made from the same type
of dough. She eyed the dead woman on the bed. 'I'm fine,' said

Anneshka, mimicking Queen Svitla's dry voice. 'I had a bad dream, that's all.'

As the guard's footsteps faded, Surovetz swung Marie over his shoulder so the girl's arms flopped down his back. 'Shall I give the child to the krootymoosh?'

Anneshka glanced at Marie. Her clothes were coated in flour, her plait hung upside down. Anneshka had no further use for the girl – and yet—

'Did you hear me?' pressed Surovetz, with the hint of a sneer on his face.

'Do as you wish,' said Anneshka. 'The child has fulfilled her fate.'

CHAPTER 74

Imogen had a dream that night.

She dreamed she was at home, standing outside her house.

'Come on, Marie, let's fly!' She pushed off from the pavement and her feet left the ground. Out went her arms and she willed herself higher, fingers skimming car roofs.

But Marie was anchored below. 'I can't do it,' she called. 'I'm stuck.'

Imogen bobbed down and took hold of her sister. It was easy to give her a boost. Hand in hand, they soared along the street. 'See,' said Imogen, 'it's simple.'

They flew between chimneys and treetops. They waved to a nesting bird. Mr Green was scowling at his newspaper. Mrs Kowalski sang in the shower. But at the end of the street, Marie started sinking. She fell like a punctured balloon. 'Imogen!' she cried and she kicked at the air. Imogen had to let go.

Marie was screaming and tumbling, tumbling, tumbling to the tarmac below.

Imogen woke with a falling sensation, as if she'd dropped

into bed. She was in a small room. There were stains on the ceiling and squished insects on the walls.

I'm in Valkahá, she remembered. *The Courtyard Inn.*

Miro and Perla were already awake, studying the krootymoosh map. Konya sat guarding the door.

Imogen's mind went straight to her sister. Where was Marie? Had something bad happened? She couldn't shake that feeling from her dream – the vision of Marie falling. She hoped it was just her worry creatures. They'd been scrabbling at her chest all night.

'The streets in the city are in the wrong place.' Perla was frowning at the map.

'Are you sure you're holding it right?' asked Miro.

Perla knitted her eyebrows. She turned the map this way and that.

'What's going on?' said Imogen, swinging her legs out of bed.

'The map of Valkahá doesn't match the real place,' said Miro. 'We'll never find Tomil and Luki like this. We should go to the palace and speak with the five queens.'

'What will we say to them?' asked Perla. She looked a little afraid.

'We'll say, "We need your help finding the krootymoosh,"' said Miro. '"We're here to rescue the children and rid you of the beasts."' He drew an imaginary sword and jabbed at his shadow on the wall.

Imogen couldn't help wondering at Miro's faith in people who wore crowns. Drakomor, Ctibor, Kazimira . . . they hadn't been very helpful so far.

'Do you think that'll work?' asked Perla.

Imogen had her doubts too, but perhaps there was no harm in trying. Besides, if Anneshka wished to become queen, she couldn't be too far from the thrones . . .

Imogen's thoughts were interrupted by a noise from the clock. It began to chime, so the children and Konya scrambled closer.

The clock looked a bit worse for wear: its jewels floated in bumpy orbits and its hands limped round its face. The little hatch opened and a man stepped out. He held a teapot in one hand.

'Who's that?' asked Imogen as the figure poured make-believe tea.

Perla shook her head. 'I don't know.'

Konya batted the wooden man with her paw. He tipped and fell flat on his face. The clock of stars reeled him back in.

'He looked like a servant,' said Miro. 'I bet he works for the five queens. Come on, let's go to the palace. Anneshka might be there too.'

CHAPTER 75

Valkahá had more tiers than a wedding cake and every street seemed to lead uphill. Imogen, Perla, Miro and Konya climbed all the way to the top. The Palace of the Five Queens looked over the city. It was an ornate building with towers shaped like long strings of pearls.

Miro marched to the entrance, where two smartly dressed men stood guard. 'I am King Miroslav Yaromeer Drahomeer Krishnov,' he said, 'Lord of the City of Yaroslav. I wish to see the queens.'

The guards paused, as if holding their breath, and then dissolved into laughter. Miro stiffened. Imogen felt her anger bubble up. How dare they laugh at her friend!

'You're not the king of anywhere,' said a guard. 'You're just a little boy.'

Miro glanced at Perla and Imogen. The tips of his ears had gone red. 'You'd better be nice to him,' said Imogen, 'or he'll have you thrown in the Hladomorna Pits.'

'Oooh, scary,' said the same man. He wiped tears of laughter from his cheeks. 'Look . . . I've been doing this job for a while,

and I know what a king looks like. He arrives with banners and servants. Not two little girls and a cat.'

'I *am* the King of Yaroslav,' said Miro, voice rising. 'I command you to let me inside!' But the more upset Miro got, the less he sounded like a king. The guards started laughing again.

'This is hopeless,' muttered Imogen. 'How can we get them to listen?'

'Tell them the queens are in danger,' whispered Perla.

'You tell them,' said Miro. 'I'm not speaking to these peasants any more.'

Perla pursed her lips, reluctant.

'Fine,' said Imogen. 'I'll do it.' She advanced on the men. 'There's a woman pretending to be Princess Pavla, but she's not a princess at all. She's planning to steal Valkahá's thrones! We've come to warn the five queens.'

The second guard looked uncertain. 'If this is a joke, you'll be in trouble.'

'It isn't,' said Imogen. 'It's real!'

'Wait here,' said the first guard, and he stepped into the palace.

Imogen waited as patiently as she could, but it was hard knowing Marie might be close. She couldn't wait to see the surprise on her sister's face. It would be like that time when Grandma came out of hospital and they made her a massive cake. Or when Mum said they were going to the dentist, but, instead, she drove them to the beach. Or, on Imogen's tenth birthday, when—

The palace doors flew open and a group of men, all wearing red cloaks, stepped out. 'Ah, children!' cried the tallest. 'I hear you've come to stop Princess Pavla.'

'Who are you?' demanded Miro.

'My name is Surovetz,' said the tall man. 'Not that it matters . . . I'm afraid you're a little too late. Princess Pavla left Valkahá overnight.'

There was a wolfish gleam in his eyes and Imogen knew something was wrong. 'Where's my sister?' she demanded. 'She was with Princess Pavla. She has red hair. She's about *this* tall.'

Recognition flashed across Surovetz's face. 'Your sister is with the krootymoosh,' he said. 'I handed her over myself. And that's where you're going too.'

He moved to grab Imogen, but Konya let out a low warning yowl. The sněehoolark's body was coiled tight as a spring.

'I'm more of a dog person,' said Surovetz as he tried to sidestep the giant cat, but Konya was too fast. She sprang up and boxed him in the face. Surovetz staggered back, raised a hand to his cheek. There was blood. Three red slashes, where Konya's claws had cut.

'You'll regret that,' he whispered, unsheathing his sword. The other men gathered round.

'What do we do now?' hissed Miro.

'I think,' said Imogen, 'we should run.'

And with that she turned and bolted. A hand came at her face. She ducked, scrambling across flagstones. Perla and Miro fled too, with Konya bounding ahead.

'Catch them!' cried Surovetz. 'On the orders of the five queens!'

CHAPTER 76

Imogen picked a street and sprinted down it. The others didn't seem to be following. They must have gone a different way.

Now that Imogen was heading away from the palace, all roads led downhill. Her feet could barely keep pace with her body.

She dodged to the left, narrowly avoiding a woman with a stack of silver plates. The men chasing her were not so nimble. There was a terrible clatter, but Imogen didn't look back. She skidded down an alley. There were footbridges above, criss-crossing the street. Perla dashed over the nearest one.

'Hey!' cried Imogen. 'How did you get up there?' But Perla was gone in a flash, followed by a streak of sněehoolark. Miro came next, dashing after his friend. He didn't look down to see Imogen, standing in the alley below. Surovetz and his henchmen came last. They crossed the bridge in three strides, red cloaks flowing from their necks.

'Go, Miro, go!' cried Imogen. But it was time to take her own advice. The men chasing her had found the alley. She dashed under the bridges, feet striking stone. Above her, the sharp-winged birds squeaked and sliced through the air.

Monks were approaching in the other direction – plump and slow-moving as geese.

'Coming through!' yelled Imogen. The gaggle of monks inched aside and Imogen disappeared through a sea of dark robes.

She flew out of the alley and on to a wider street. Behind, the monks were protesting as Surovetz's men tried to force their way through. Ahead, the city was a mass of pale spires.

Imogen kept running. She didn't know where she was going, only that she mustn't be caught. There were guards coming down the hill. Were they looking for her too? Imogen didn't wait to find out. She darted into a shop and pulled the door shut.

Heart hammering, she peeked through the window. Out on the street, the men from the palace were talking and pointing – looking for her. Imogen ducked so they wouldn't see her head. She counted her breaths and waited, hoping that her pursuers would continue down the hill.

'How can I help you?' asked a sunny voice. Imogen turned to see a young blond man sitting behind a workbench.

'Oh . . . I don't think you can,' she replied.

'Nonsense,' said the man. He gestured about the room. 'It's just a question of finding the right style.'

The shop walls were lined with glass-fronted cabinets. Inside were all kinds of glittering jewels: bracelets inlaid with garnets, decorative clasps and buckles for belts. There was a tiara made out of pearls, and strings of coral beads hung from the ceiling.

'I work with the finest silver in Valkahá,' said the man. 'All the designs are my own. Are you sure I can't tempt you to something small? Perhaps a ring or a brooch?'

'I'm not looking for a brooch,' said Imogen with a fresh wave of bitterness. 'I'm looking for my sister.'

'Ah,' said the jeweller, giving her a sympathetic smile. 'I'm afraid I don't have any of those.'

But Imogen wasn't listening. She remembered what Surovetz had said. *Your sister is with the krootymoosh . . . and that's where you're going too.*

Imogen had come too late. A lump formed in her throat. *My sister has red hair; she's about* this *tall.* The lump in Imogen's throat swelled. Talking about Marie wouldn't make her appear.

But the jeweller was waiting for Imogen to speak so she let her words flow. 'Marie has red hair, a big freckle on her nose and a scar where she once cut her hand. She's only eight, but she's really good at drawing . . .' Tears pricked Imogen's eyes.

'She's lucky to have a sister like you,' said the man.

Imogen's tears broke. 'No,' she cried. 'She's not! It's my fault Marie got kidnapped! It's my fault she left the hotel!'

The jeweller didn't contradict her – didn't say that it wasn't so. Instead, he waited for her tears to subside. 'Would you like a cup of tea?' he asked.

Imogen glanced through the window. The men in red cloaks had gone.

'Yes, please,' she said. 'That would be nice.'

CHAPTER 77

The jeweller cleared some space on his workbench, moving aside hammers and tweezers and gems. Then he brought out a pair of cups with silver rims. They were the kind of thing Grandma would have loved.

The cogs in Imogen's head started whirring as she watched the jeweller pour tea. He had pale eyebrows, nearly invisible, and his hands looked capable and strong. But it was the teapot that her eyes kept returning to ... Where had she seen it before?

'I'll add a little honey for sweetness,' he said, handing Imogen a cup.

'I know who you are,' she cried and she nearly spilled her drink with excitement. 'You're the man from the clock!'

The jeweller looked confused.

'Do you know something about my sister?' said Imogen, wondering why the clock had showed her this man. He shook his head and sipped his tea. 'Do you know something about the krootymoosh?'

The jeweller almost spat out his drink. 'No,' he replied. 'We don't have krootymoosh in Valkahá.'

A CLOCK OF STARS

'Yes, you do,' said Imogen. 'My sister was given to them *in this very city*. Besides, why would the krootymoosh have a map of a place they never attacked? They're *here* and they've got to be stopped!'

The man put down his cup. 'Who sent you?' he asked.

'No one.'

'Whoever you've been talking to—'

The door opened and a woman stepped in from the street. She hesitated when she saw Imogen. 'Am I interrupting?' she asked.

'Not at all,' said the man, attempting a smile.

'I'm looking for a hairpin,' said the woman. 'I don't want anything too fussy.'

'This shop is closed,' snapped Imogen.

The woman glanced from Imogen to the man. 'I'm sorry, I didn't realise.' Imogen stared until the woman backed out. Then she got up and dropped the latch so no one else could enter.

'What do you think you're doing?' cried the jeweller. 'That was one of my best customers!'

Imogen returned to the workbench. 'I'm going to ask you some questions,' she said, channelling her inner detective. 'And I need you to tell me the truth. What's your name?'

'Yemnivetz,' he whispered. 'Yemni for short.'

He looked scared, and Imogen would have felt bad if her mission hadn't been so important. She wasn't interrogating him for fun. She was doing it for Tomil and Luki and Marie – and all the children who'd been taken by the krootymoosh.

'What do you know about my sister?' she asked.

'Nothing,' said Yemni.

Imogen placed her hands behind her back. 'What do you know about the krootymoosh?'

'Nothing,' he said, although this time it sounded like a question.

'That's not true, is it?' said Imogen.

'Would you like some more tea?' Yemni poured a second cup. 'It's very good for frayed nerves.'

The door to the workshop rattled. Imogen caught a glimpse of red cloaks through the window. 'Sorry,' called Yemni. 'I'm closed.'

Boom, boom, boom. They knocked harder.

'It's the men from the palace,' hissed Imogen. 'They're looking for me! Don't let them in!'

'I have to,' said Yemni. 'They'll break down the door.' He opened a chest at the back of his workshop. 'Quick,' he cried. 'Get in.'

Is it a trick? wondered Imogen. But there was no time to argue. The men were hammering with their fists.

'One minute,' called Yemni as Imogen scrambled into the chest and he lowered the lid over her head.

Imogen could see through the chest's keyhole. Yemnivetz opened the door and three men burst into the room. 'What took you so long? Why was your door locked?'

'I was just making tea,' said Yemni. 'Would you like some?'

The men glared at the two silver-rimmed cups. 'Who are you drinking it with?'

For a terrible moment, Imogen thought Yemni was about to betray her. It would be easy to hand her over now she was inside a box. Had that been his plan all along?

'Oh, I always make two cups,' said the jeweller. 'One is never enough.'

A man picked up Imogen's teacup and threw it at the wall. She recoiled as she heard it smash.

For a peculiar moment, Imogen's mind leaped to another time and place. She was back at Branna and Zemko's, hiding in the piano, cowering as the krootymoosh attacked . . .

She shook her head and looked through the chest's keyhole. Two men had Yemni pinned against the wall. A third was rifling through the cabinets. He was a thick-set man with a meaty neck. He opened the dressers one by one, tossing jewellery aside.

'What are you doing?' cried Yemni. 'You've no right—'

The bull-necked man sent a cabinet crashing to the ground.

Imogen flinched. 'Please don't hurt him,' she whispered. Perhaps she should try to help? But if she got caught now, it would all be for nothing. She'd be no use to Marie.

'You like to think you're above us, don't you?' said the man, rounding on the jeweller. 'You with your silver hands . . . But your hands are as grubby as mine. Just because you don't come raiding, it doesn't mean you're guilt-free.' He glanced around the workshop with disgust. 'You'd be nothing without us, Yemnivetz.'

Imogen kept her eye to the keyhole. The man spoke as if he knew Yemni, but they didn't seem to be friends. She wished they'd leave him alone. Three against one wasn't fair.

'What do you want?' asked Yemni.

'We're looking for a child,' said the thick-set man. 'A Lowland girl. About ten or twelve. She was heading in this direction. Did you see which way she went?'

The jeweller hesitated and Imogen drew back. Yemni was about to give her up. If only she'd been a bit nicer . . . The men still had hold of his arms and neck.

'No,' he replied. 'I haven't seen a girl.' Imogen let go of her breath.

'You'd better be telling the truth. Surovetz wants her dealt with.'

'Honestly,' cried Yemni, 'I've been working.'

They released him and he sank to the floor.

'You always did hold your nerves in a bucket,' smirked the bull-necked man. He pushed a ring on to the tip of his finger. 'My wife likes silver,' he muttered. 'Thanks very much for the gift.'

The men helped themselves to jewellery as they filed out of the shop. The door banged shut behind them.

CHAPTER 78

Miro, Perla and Konya ran through the streets of Valkahá. They sprinted over footbridges and across stone squares. Miro kept glancing back, hoping they'd shaken the men off, but there they were, red cloaks flapping.

Miro could see the archway ahead – the city's semicircular entrance. Beyond that was only scrub and Miro didn't want to go there. The land was flat, nowhere to hide. But Surovetz's men were coming from every direction. Miro had no choice.

'This way,' he called to Perla, then he ran to the archway, knees knocking, lungs bursting with each breath.

There were guards collecting fees at the entrance. They hesitated, unsure whether to let the children pass.

Then they saw Konya – ten stone of snĕehoolark careering towards them. Both guards stood aside.

Miro, Perla and Konya hurtled under the archway and into the scrubland, feet beating dirt from the earth. A weasel squealed and shot out of their way, disappearing down a small hole.

'Where are we going?' panted Perla. She slowed, but Miro

did not. There was no time to lose. He scanned the barren landscape as he ran.

'That boulder, over there. It might do.' But Miro was so busy searching for somewhere to hide that he forgot to look at his feet.

Miro's boot plunged down – down through the place where he thought there was rock, down through the hole in the ground. He grabbed a bush and tried to stop himself falling. For a split second, he was hanging on the edge of a pothole, dangling from a fistful of leaves.

There were flowers above, thin air below. Miro's feet scrambled for a hold. Then the leaves tore free and he fell.

Smooth rock rushed against his trousers.

His shirt flapped like wings in his face.

He was sliding, sliding.

Couldn't see where.

Even his scream got left behind.

The chute levelled out and Miro skidded to a halt. He pushed his shirt out of his face and checked his arms, legs, body. Nothing seemed to be broken . . .

Perla came whizzing down the pothole after him. Her feet collided with Miro's bottom. 'Ow!' he cried, half turning. Konya joined the pile-up, skidding on all fours. Miro groaned as her skull struck his back.

They lay still for a moment, panting. Miro blinked in the

rising dust. It was dark down here, under the scrubland. It was dark but it wasn't pitch-black. Above, he could hear men's voices.

'Good hiding place,' whispered Perla.

'Yes,' said Miro, getting to his feet and hoping she'd think that this had been his plan.

They seemed to have fallen into a steep-sided cave. The voices overhead faded.

We did it, thought Miro. *We escaped.* But as his eyes adjusted to the cave's darkness, shapes appeared in the gloom. Krootymoosh armour and krootymoosh legs. Krootymoosh bodies and claws.

Miro's heart counted beat after beat. Perla's breathing sounded frantic.

'Just keep very still,' Miro whispered.

The krootymoosh didn't move. They stood like warriors before battle.

Why didn't they try to attack? It was as if the beasts hadn't noticed the children. Miro glanced at Perla. She was trembling and backing away. He'd never seen anyone look so fearful. It made him more afraid too.

But something wasn't right . . .

Miro's knee clicked, and a blue light buzzed into being. It came from a tiny glowfly.

Still the krootymoosh didn't budge. The monsters stood

shoulder to shoulder, row after row, disappearing into the shadows at the back of the cave. Miro took a small step towards them. Konya let out a low growl.

Was it Miro's imagination, or were the beasts slumped in awkward positions? They looked thin and saggy, like old clothes in a wardrobe.

The glowfly drifted to the nearest krootymoosh and disappeared up the helmet's nose-hole. The cave was plunged into darkness. The fly reappeared and so did its light, sailing out of the beast's furry ear.

'They're not real,' said Miro, not believing his own words.

'What do you mean?' whispered Perla. Her voice was as small as a mouse.

Miro forced himself to take a few steps closer, fighting every instinct he had. He lifted his fingers to the krootymoosh's pale pelt. *Tick, tock*, went Miro's heart. The beast's body was cold.

'These things aren't krootymoosh,' said Miro. 'They're hollow.'

'No,' gasped Perla. 'They can't be.'

Miro inspected the torso. Even though his mind knew the beasts weren't a threat, the fear wouldn't quite leave his body.

The krootymoosh were made out of animal skins, stitched into crude human shapes. Two arms. Two legs. A hole for the neck. The fake tail was tacked on at the base of the spine.

A helmet shielded the head, with fur sticking out

underneath. It had extra teeth fitted in front of the mouth and eyeholes so the wearer could see.

Strangest of all were the krootymoosh boots – huge fake paws wrapped in fur, with claws on the outside and platforms within. They must have made the person wearing them taller.

'They're *outfits*,' said Miro, more confident this time. 'They're not krootymoosh at all.'

CHAPTER 79

Imogen climbed out of the chest. There was shattered glass across the workshop, upended cabinets and trampled treasures. Yemnivetz got to his feet.

'Are you okay?' asked Imogen.

The jeweller nodded. He looked exhausted. 'I think that went rather well . . . all things considered.'

'Thank you for not telling them I was here,' said Imogen. She waited for a moment, let Yemni regain his composure. He straightened his waistcoat and smoothed down his hair.

'Who are those men?' she asked. 'And how do they know you?'

Yemni fixed her with mournful eyes. 'We'll start from the beginning,' he said. 'You tell me what you're up to and I'll tell you what I know. But, first, let's go upstairs. I can't stand to look at this mess.'

Imogen followed the jeweller to the room above his shop. It had a vaulted stone ceiling and chairs with Bambi-thin legs. In the corner, a mannequin wore a sparkling silver headdress. There weren't many objects up here, but those that were had been made with great care.

Imogen resisted the urge to touch the headdress. She wanted to show Yemni she was ready to talk. She sat on a chair and slid her hands under her legs.

'You go first,' said the jeweller. 'I'm listening.'

So Imogen told Yemni her story. She explained how her sister had been kidnapped. How she was determined to get Marie back. How children were getting taken by the krootymoosh and how she and her friends were going to make it stop.

Yemni sat quietly, nodding at the right moments and making reassuring sounds. Imogen hadn't meant to tell him everything, but somehow the whole story spilled out.

'You're doing a very brave thing,' said the jeweller when Imogen had finished. 'I wish I was as courageous as you.'

Imogen wondered what he meant. He'd protected her from those men in red cloaks – refused to tell them where she was, even when they smashed up his workshop. That had been brave, hadn't it?

Yemni lit a fire under a kettle and waited for the water to boil. Then he fetched two new cups and a pot of honey. 'Look,' he continued, pouring the tea, 'I don't like the krootymoosh any more than the next person, but what I'm about to say . . . well, you didn't hear it from me. All right?'

Imogen nodded, impatient to hear Yemni's tale.

'Very well,' sighed the jeweller. 'I'll begin. Before Valkahá existed, many hundreds of years ago, only the toughest could survive in these lands – wandering nomads and deep-rooted plants.

'You've seen what it's like out there. The ground is naturally riddled with holes. Nobody thought it was a good place for a city, especially one as fine as this. But when silver was discovered, everything changed. A child slipped down a pothole and found a huge seam of the stuff, running like lightning through rock.

'Word got out and people flocked to the Scrublands, hoping to get rich overnight. The town they built was called Valkahá – a small mining outpost in the middle of the scrub.'

'What's this got to do with the krootymoosh?' asked Imogen, shifting on her chair.

'I'll get to it,' said Yemni. 'But you need to understand the history of this place if you want to learn its secrets . . . When the first seam of silver ran dry, the miners started to dig. They found more metal threading the rock. Valkahá and its people became rich.

'A few miners disappeared, but no one worried about that. The miners should have taken more care. That's what everyone said. Meanwhile, the rock that was cut from the earth was used to build palaces, churches and streets. The deeper the mines went, the taller Valkahá became.'

Imogen glanced at the headdress over the rim of her cup. It glinted in the low light. So *that* was where all the silver came from . . . There were mines, hidden underground.

'Eventually,' continued Yemni, 'the silver became more and more difficult to find, and so many miners had gone missing that it grew hard to persuade people to go down the pits. Dark stories emerged – tales of monsters that lived in the rock.'

'Krootymoosh!' cried Imogen, almost spilling her tea.

But Yemni shook his head. 'No,' he said. 'I'm afraid not. Last year, the five queens closed the mines. They said it was no longer worth the risk. Besides, Valkahá was already so prosperous. What need had we of more wealth? That was what they *said* anyway.'

Imogen helped herself to honey. It was supposed to go in the tea, but she was hungry. She let the crystals melt on her tongue.

'What do you mean?' she asked.

Yemni massaged the back of his neck. 'Most people believe the mines are abandoned. They think they're an empty shell . . . hundreds of miles of deserted tunnels lying beneath our feet.' He tapped his toes on the tiled floor. 'But the mines didn't close. Not then. Not ever. The five queens still run them in secret.'

Imogen was about to ask how they could have a mine without any miners, but the answer leaped into her head. Ugly and bold. Too terrible to say.

'The five queens filled the mines with children,' said Yemni. 'They're easier to control than grown-ups and they don't disappear quite so fast.'

'Don't disappear?'

'Yes. The things that live in the rock . . . they only eat adults.'

Imogen's head was whirling. How could the queens do such a thing?

'There was only one problem,' said Yemni. 'Valkahá is a civilised city. We couldn't send our own children down pits. Perhaps we could send someone else's . . . And so the krootymoosh were born.'

'The five queens discovered the krootymoosh?' asked Imogen.

'*Invented*,' said Yemni with a grimace. 'The krootymoosh are not real.'

Imogen put down her teacup with a clatter. She couldn't believe her ears. 'What do you mean? I've seen them!'

'The five queens sought help from the wealthiest families in Valkahá.' Yemni stared at the arm of his chair. For a moment, he seemed hypnotised.

'Go on,' prompted Imogen. 'What happened next?'

'The families give their strongest sons to the cause. Young men with plenty of vigour, who don't mind spilling some blood. These men get a share of the silver. In return, they kidnap children from neighbouring kingdoms and put them to work underground.'

'You're saying the krootymoosh are *people*?'

'They're the nastiest people I know. Think of the men who destroyed my workshop – it's them, they're krootymoosh.'

Yemni's hand crept up to the place where the intruders had held his throat.

'But the krootymoosh have fur!' cried Imogen.

'Costumes,' said Yemni darkly. 'And not very good ones if you ask me. They wear costumes when they go raiding. The rest of the time, they look like anyone else. Only their red cloaks mark them out – a sign of their secret club.'

'No,' said Imogen. 'That can't be right! The krootymoosh aren't new. People have been talking about them for centuries! There are stories and nursery rhymes!'

'Where do you think the five queens got their inspiration?'

Imogen felt something snap. Perhaps it was that angry stone – the one she'd imagined hardening between her ribs. 'How do you know?' she demanded. 'Where is your proof?' She sounded a little like Mark.

'The Lord of the Krootymoosh is my older brother,' confessed Yemni, hanging his head. 'His name is Surovetz.'

Thoughts flicked fast through Imogen's head. Surovetz was the man at the palace – the one who'd smiled like a wolf. He'd said Marie was with the krootymoosh, said he'd given her to them himself.

But all of those stolen children . . . Perla's brother . . . Branna's daughter and son . . . It was done by humans? It was done for silver?

Imogen scowled at the jeweller. 'If the Lord of the

Krootymoosh is your brother, then why don't you make him stop?'

Yemni glanced up. 'Surovetz is answerable to the queens. There's nothing I can do! Besides, he's not the kind of man you can reason with. It's not – *he's* not – my fault.'

Imogen studied Yemni's pale face. He did look a little like Surovetz. He had the same angular jaw, silver-grey eyes and fair hair, although Yemni's hair was even lighter, almost white. 'You're afraid, aren't you?' she said. 'You're afraid of your own brother.'

'Like I said,' muttered Yemni, 'I wish I was as brave as you.'

CHAPTER 80

It was late afternoon when Imogen returned to the Courtyard Inn. She crossed the tavern, ignoring the landlady's stare. She climbed the stairs towards the room at the back – the one she shared with Perla and Miro, praying they had got away too. She had to tell them what she'd discovered.

But when she pushed the door open, the room was empty. No sněehoolark. No friends.

They've been caught, hissed a worry creature. *Taken by Surovetz.*

Imogen steadied herself. It wasn't true . . . It couldn't be. She couldn't do this on her own.

Imogen crawled into bed, without removing her clothes, and pulled the sheets over her head. She hated to think of Marie, afraid and deep underground. There would be no sun in the mines, no moon, no stars. Just layer upon layer of time-hardened rock.

Imogen closed her eyes.

Marie didn't like dark places. She made Mum leave the landing light on.

Why had Anneshka let the krootymoosh have her? Wasn't

she part of the prophecy any more? Didn't Anneshka want to be queen? Imogen didn't understand.

You're the only one left, hissed the worry creatures. *It's just you and usssssssss from now on.*

Imogen hugged a pillow to her chest. 'I just need to be patient,' she whispered. 'Miro and Perla will come back.'

Miro wanted to go to the surface. This cave was giving him the creeps. Even if the krootymoosh weren't real, he didn't like being surrounded by their skins.

Perla was in no such hurry. She kept sticking her hand up the sleeves of the outfits and turning the giant paws around. Konya chewed on a krootymoosh glove. 'They're empty,' muttered Perla. 'All this time I've been hiding, but what have I been hiding from? Wait until Papa finds out.'

Papa . . . the word filled Miro's head. What would his father say about the krootymoosh? What would a good king do? He peered through the hole in the cave roof – the one that he'd fallen down. He couldn't see the men who'd pursued them, just a circle of weeds and sky. Every so often a bird flickered past; the small ones with bow-shaped wings.

Miro might as well have been looking through a telescope. The birds felt that far away.

He pushed his shirt sleeves to his elbows and gave himself plenty of space. Then he sprinted up the chute, arms pumping.

He almost reached the top. Fingers grasped at leaves. But his foot slipped and gravity did the rest.

Perla and Konya stared as Miro skidded across the cave.

'I'm all right,' he said, pretending to brush dust from his trousers. The truth was, he could feel the blood rushing to his face and he didn't want Perla to see. 'We'll have to find another way out,' he mumbled. 'It would be easier if it wasn't so dark.'

Perla clicked her fingers and a glowfly turned on. Its blue light illuminated her face. 'How did you do that?' cried Miro.

'Observation,' said Perla, voice soft.

'Observation? What kind of observation?' Miro had no idea what she meant.

'Your knees clicked before the first fly appeared. I thought it might be a reaction to the noise.'

Miro and Perla stood clicking their fingers, until a swarm of flies lit the cave. Konya watched, tail twitching, glowflies reflected in her eyes.

The insects floated past the krootymoosh costumes, congregating up near the roof. In this eerie light, Miro could see the far side of the cave. 'Over there!' he cried, pointing.

There was a passage within the rock.

Miro and Perla stepped into the rift, sněehoolark at their heels. The ceiling above them was punctured with holes. The holes were too high up to climb through, but at least they let some sunlight in.

The children came to a junction where the rift split five ways. 'This isn't just one cave and a tunnel,' whispered Miro. 'It's a whole underground network.'

Konya sniffed at the air. 'What is it?' asked Perla. The snĕehoolark tensed, before tucking herself in a dark corner. Perla and Miro followed, pressing themselves out of sight.

They were just in time. A line of men marched along the passage. They carried krootymoosh helmets under their arms. Then more figures came down the rift; these ones were disguised from head to furred foot.

'There are so many,' whispered Perla, forlorn.

The earth vibrated with the stomping of feet. Dust shook from the passage walls.

Miro felt his spirits waver.

Even though he knew the krootymoosh were men, he couldn't help being afraid. People could be just as scary as monsters if they'd got an evil intent.

You would know all about evil, said a voice in Miro's head. *Don't forget what your own uncle did.*

'I'm not like my uncle,' whispered Miro.

The last of the krootymoosh had gone.

'We need to get out of here,' said Perla. She rushed towards a different rift and Konya followed, nose to the ground.

'We need to stick together,' said Miro. 'Wait – wait for me!'

CHAPTER 81

Imogen meant to wait up for her friends. Really she did. But sleep must have crept in when she wasn't looking. She woke with a start, face down on the bed. It was early dawn and there were voices outside the Courtyard Inn. A few moments later, Miro, Perla and Konya came bursting into the room.

'Where were you?' cried Imogen. 'I thought you'd been taken by those men! I thought—' She paused. Her friends were covered in dust. Konya's fur was thick with the stuff.

'You will not believe what we've seen,' said Miro, shutting the door behind them.

And so the friends exchanged stories. Miro and Perla told Imogen about their escape – how they'd fallen down a hole in the scrub and discovered a cave full of krootymoosh.

Imogen tried to tell them what she'd learned from Yemni. She was still half asleep and the story kept getting tangled, but Perla and Miro got the key points. 'Surovetz is the Lord of the Krootymoosh,' said Imogen. 'He takes children to work in the mines, which everyone else thinks are closed.'

Perla reached for the krootymoosh map and staked out its

corners with candles. 'What are you doing?' asked Imogen. Perla pointed to the map's title:

Here lies Valkahá, City of Stone

'Remember how we thought that the map wasn't right?' said Perla without looking up. 'We thought it didn't match with real life?'

'Yes . . .?' said Imogen.

Perla tracked the blue lines with her finger, following each twist and turn. 'Well, there's nothing wrong with the map. It isn't a drawing of the city above ground. It's a drawing of the city *below*.'

Imogen knelt beside her friends and inspected the scroll for herself. She felt as if the world had done a cartwheel; streets that had seemed impossible on the surface made sense if they wriggled through rock. Churches transformed into caves. Spires became underground shafts.

'Perla, you're a genius!' cried Imogen. 'It's a map of the mines!'

Perla gave a shy smile.

'What are we waiting for?' said Imogen, scrambling to her feet. 'Let's start this rescue mission now!' In her mind's eye she saw Marie falling down an impossibly deep and dark hole.

'Erm,' said Miro, 'I'm not sure that's a good idea. We had to try about thirty different routes before we found our way out. When we finally got above ground, the men who were chasing us had given up and gone home. That's how long it took us to escape! And we weren't even in the mines – just stuck in the level above.'

Konya shook the dust from her fur, creating a little white cloud.

'Okay,' said Imogen, trying her best to sound patient. She was itching to rescue her sister. 'But this time we'll take the map.'

'We had to hide in the shadows every time a krootymoosh came past,' said Miro. 'It wouldn't work with a load of kidnapped children. They'd see us before we escaped.'

'In that case, we'll fight!' declared Imogen, clenching her hands into fists.

But Miro shook his head. 'Imogen, you don't understand. There were so many krootymoosh down there . . . There's no way we could take them all on.'

Imogen sank to the floorboards. 'Then what are we going to do?'

Perla put a finger on the tip of her nose – that meant she was thinking hard. Imogen put her head in her hands – that meant she was out of ideas.

'We could create a diversion,' said Miro. 'Something to draw the krootymoosh out.'

The clock ticked a little bit louder. 'You mean like an earthquake?' said Perla.

'Maybe something a *bit* smaller than that.' Miro's voice had gone strangely calm. 'How about a duel, like the one in Luki's story?'

The clock of stars seemed to be ticking on the side of Imogen's head.

'I could challenge the Lord of the Krootymoosh to a fight,' said Miro. 'People would come to watch. Even the five queens of Valkahá. Even the krootymoosh!'

'But Miro,' said Imogen, scrunching up her eyes, 'the king in the story . . . he dies.'

Miro studied his rings. 'Oh . . . you don't need to worry . . . it would just be a duel to first blood. That should be enough to distract the krootymoosh. Meanwhile, you can get the kidnapped children out.'

'My parents would never let *me* fight a duel,' said Perla, as if she was annoyed. 'A duel with the Lord of the Krootymoosh . . . it's like the ultimate dare!'

Imogen couldn't help feeling that Perla was missing the point.

'That's one of the perks of being king,' said Miro. 'You can do whatever you want.'

'But how would you challenge the Lord of the Krootymoosh?' asked Perla. 'They don't exactly have a headquarters.'

'I'll ask the town crier to shout about it. Word will reach Surovetz soon enough.'

Imogen shook her head, exasperated. How could she make Miro stop? 'Miro,' she tried, 'Marie isn't your sister. You can't—'

'She's my friend,' replied Miro, flicking hair from his eyes. 'Besides, I'm King Miroslav Krishnov, son of Vadik the Valiant. What's the point in being a king if I can't put things like this right?'

CHAPTER 82

News of the duel travelled quickly. The boy king of Yaroslav had challenged the Lord of the Krootymoosh to face him in single combat. The battle would be held on Mlok Island, just like in the legend of old.

Nobody thought the child would win, but they couldn't stop talking about it all the same. Whispers spread at places of worship. Bets were placed. Riders were sent to distant lands.

When Patoleezal heard the news, his elastic smile dropped. 'He's gone *where*? He's doing *what*?' Patoleezal's fist closed round the letter. 'Does that boy think of no one but himself? What is to become of me if the king dies in battle? Dead men don't need advisers!'

King Ctibor was getting ready for bed when a servant knocked on his door. 'Your Majesty, we've received a letter. The King of Yaroslav has challenged the Lord of the Krootymoosh to a duel, on Mlok Island.'

Ctibor dropped his nightcap. 'What business has he got doing that? Hasn't he heard the stories? It's supposed to be the King of Vodnislav that banishes the armoured beasts!'

'I think,' said the servant, choosing his words with care, 'he may be trying to end the krootymoosh raids.'

'Nonsense,' shouted Ctibor. 'He's trying to make me look bad. That's what he's doing. He's stealing my glory! He's after my throne!' But King Ctibor calmed himself. Perhaps there was a way . . . 'Is it the same child who escaped from my prison? The one with the girls and the cat?'

'The description does sound very similar,' said the servant.

'Excellent,' said Ctibor. 'Fetch my quill. I'll write to the boy at once.'

Meanwhile, in Valkahá, the five queens sat on their cold silver thrones, thinking their cold, silver thoughts. Anneshka was seated among them, trying very hard to be still.

She was no longer Princess Pavla. Pavla was yesterday's news. After disposing of Queen Svitla's body, Anneshka had dressed in her clothes – headdress, breastplate, jewellery and gown. It was lucky that Queen Svitla wore a face-net, for, nobody could see Anneshka's true face under the veil of pearls.

As Anneshka sat there, doing her best to impersonate a queen, Surovetz strode into the hall. He had three red lines slashed across his face, as if he'd been struck by a monstrous cat.

'The boy king has challenged me to a duel,' he declared. 'A fight until first blood. The whole city's talking about it!'

Anneshka didn't move, but a muscle in her neck went tight. The boy king of Yaroslav. That was Drakomor's heir. What was he doing on this side of the mountains?

'Why does the child want a duel?' asked Queen Yeeskra.

'He seems to think the krootymoosh have kidnapped his friends.' Surovetz looked like he expected a laugh. He was greeted by stony-faced silence.

'The krootymoosh are supposed to be legends, not men you can fight in the field.' That was Queen Blipla, ever cautious. Anneshka wanted to agree. She'd already tried to have Miroslav murdered and that hadn't gone very well . . .

Surovetz squinted at the queens. 'I can't refuse – word is out! People are travelling from far and wide. The duel will be held on Mlok Island, not far from Vodnislav itself. It would be shameful if I didn't turn up . . . It would look like I was scared.'

'Blast your honour,' cried Queen Zlata. 'Nobody knows that it's you!'

'Do you really want the krootymoosh to look like cowards?' said Surovetz. 'If the people of the Lowlands stop being afraid, they may start to fight back.'

That set the queens clucking. Anneshka did her best to join in, but she had a bad feeling about this.

'You're right,' said Queen Yeeskra. 'Much better to crush their hopes. Show the people of the Lowlands what happens when they challenge the krootymoosh. Let them see how the real story ends.'

'What do you mean?' said Queen Flumkra, always the last

to catch on. 'It's only a duel to first blood. It'll be over when the boy gets a scratch.'

Surovetz's eyes seemed to pierce Anneshka's face-net. He knew it was her underneath. After all, it was he who had killed Queen Svitla – he who'd helped Anneshka transform.

'Sometimes,' said Surovetz with an evil smile, 'there's a lot of first blood.'

CHAPTER 83

The landlady of the Courtyard Inn burst into the children's room. 'There's a man in the yard. Says he's got a message for King Miroslav. Is that some kind of stage name?'

Miro sat up in bed, half blinded by his own hair. He pulled on his boots and ran past the woman, down and out into the yard.

The messenger bowed and handed Miro a scroll:

Dear King Miroslav,

My sister was taken by the krootymoosh. I don't know if she's still alive, but I hope that you win the battle. I hope you cut off the krootymoosh's head. Here is a pressed flower for good luck.

Fondest regards,

Milena

Miro felt the blood rise to his face. He folded the parchment in two.

The next day more letters arrived. They were sent by the

people of the Lowlands – shepherds, boatmakers and grateful fisherfolk. There were letters of thanks and encouragement. People seemed to think Miro was a good king. He hoped he wouldn't let them down.

One letter was sent by King Ctibor. Miro could tell by the special wax seal. He broke it and looked inside.

Dear Miroslav, heir of Vadik the Valiant,

You are your father's son! For what could be more valiant than a duel against the krootymoosh?

Please accept my apologies for the misunderstanding that occurred during your visit. In these difficult times, we kings must band together.

I would like to make amends. You must stay with me for the duration of the duel and the festivities that will follow. My castle, my skret and my servants are at your disposal.

I am sure your father would be touched to think of his child and his old friend, Ctibor, fighting on the same side. I have always looked upon you as an ally, as dear to my heart as a son.

I will have the guest chambers prepared for your arrival.

Fare thee well,

King Ctibor,

Protector of the Lowland Realm,

Lord of the Three Rivers,

Commander of the Great Water Dragon

Back inside the Courtyard Inn, Miro showed the letter to his friends. 'Why is King Ctibor speaking like that?' asked Perla.

'He has to,' said Miro. 'That's how kings write.'

'"*Fighting on the same side*",' muttered Imogen. 'He's not the one doing any fighting.'

'I think it's a nice letter,' said Miro. He wished Imogen and Perla would stop criticising and focus on being impressed. He'd made up with King Ctibor. They were allies. Wasn't that enough? 'Anyway,' he continued, 'I'd much rather stay in Vodnislav Castle than some soggy guesthouse. I'll need a good sleep before the duel.'

'But Ctibor was going to have us executed!' cried Imogen.

'Well . . . he's clearly changed his mind. Ctibor hates the krootymoosh. He's on the same side as us.' Miro tucked the letter into his top pocket, so it sat close to his heart. 'I don't know if I mentioned it before, but he used to be friends with my father.'

CHAPTER 84

Imogen and Perla were sitting outside the Courtyard Inn, studying the krootymoosh map, when they heard the clatter of hoofs. Konya got to her feet as a carriage came into view.

It wasn't as fancy as Valkahá's coaches. It looked like a shed on wheels, but it was drawn by four strong horses and manned by two skret wearing chain mail.

Imogen stepped back as the carriage pulled up right in front of the inn. 'We're here for the human child,' rasped a skret with a helmet shaped like a blowfish. 'Which one of you will it be?'

Imogen was stunned into silence. She couldn't take her eyes off the claws sticking out from iron shoes. 'It's that one,' cried the other skret, pointing at Perla.

'You sure?' said his partner.

'I dunno. They all look the same. Does it matter which one we take?'

Perla and Imogen exchanged glances.

The first skret flicked the other skret's helmet and it dinged like a bell. 'Of course it matters, you great toothless ninny!

We're supposed to bring King Ctibor his champion! Not any old human pup.'

Imogen was about to intervene when Miro dashed out of the inn. 'Sorry I'm late,' he called to the skret. He had a saddlebag slung over his shoulder and the clock of stars under one arm. The girls had agreed he should take it with him. It was Miro's clock, after all.

The skret tipped back his blowfish helmet to get a better look at the boy. 'How do we know you're the right one?'

'Why would it lie to us?' asked the other skret. 'We're taking it to fight with the krootymoosh, not offering it a glass of black wine.'

The skret with the blowfish helmet shrugged. 'Fine,' he said. 'Hop aboard.'

Imogen and Perla stood aside while Miro climbed into the carriage. Imogen wished he wasn't going on his own. Perla must have been thinking the same thing because she called, before the door closed, 'Take Konya with you!'

Miro looked surprised. 'Isn't Konya supposed to protect you?'

But Konya wasn't just a bodyguard. Perla and the snĕehoolark were more like best friends, attached by invisible strings.

'Right now you need more protecting than me,' said Perla. 'And even kings need companions.'

Perla rubbed the soft bit under Konya's chin. The wolf-cat gave a seismic purr. Then Perla encouraged her into the carriage. Konya peered out of the little window, confused. 'I need you to look after Miro,' said Perla. Konya gave a soft mew.

Miro's face appeared at the other carriage window. He didn't look much like the boy that Imogen had found in Patoleezal's mansion – the one who thought the world was a terrible place. Miro's complexion had deepened to hazelnut-brown from long days riding in the sun. His curly hair almost covered his eyes.

Something strained at Imogen's chest. A low-level tugging. An ache. Perhaps she had an invisible thread too, connecting her to the people she loved. 'Are you sure this is a good idea?' she asked Miro. 'Are you sure you're not going to get hurt?'

Miro raised his hand to the carriage window, palm pressed to the glass. Imogen brought her hand up to meet it. They would only be separated for a few days . . . But Imogen felt sad, as if they were parting for a very long time.

With a crack of a whip, the carriage jolted into motion. Imogen and Perla stepped back. Konya's face was still at the window. She put her head back and howled.

Imogen felt something within her answer and, for a moment, she was too choked for words. That invisible thread was pulled tight.

'I hope Miro knows what he's doing,' said Perla. Her eyes sparkled with tears.

Then the carriage turned the corner, disappearing into Valkahá's crowded streets.

Chapter 85

Miro wasn't the only one travelling to Vodnislav. Many were drawn by the duel. Spectators came from the flooded meadows, eager to see something new. Skret journeyed from the north, slipskins came from the south, and a witch, who was older than she looked, turned and walked with the rest.

But most of the people arriving in Vodnislav came from the neighbouring towns. They travelled by boat and on foot. It was their children who'd been snatched by the krootymoosh: their siblings, their daughters, their sons. They were Lowland folk and they'd come to see justice done.

Anneshka travelled across the Scrublands in a silver-plated carriage. The queens had one each, but Anneshka was not alone. Surovetz sat opposite.

'You do a good impression of Queen Svitla,' he said as the carriage rattled along. 'Keep this up and you might turn into her. Imagine that – you go to sleep as Anneshka, you wake up wearing the old queen's face.'

Anneshka shuddered. It was not an idea she relished. 'There's more chance of you waking up as a krootymoosh,' she muttered, but Surovetz's smile only widened.

The landscape outside grew greener. Moonscape rolled into hills. 'You shouldn't be so relaxed about the duel,' said Anneshka. 'I know Miroslav Krishnov. He never dies when he should.'

'I'm touched by your concern,' replied Surovetz. 'But we all know how this fight's going to end. I will splatter that boy's brains across the island.'

Anneshka drew the carriage curtains shut. 'I'm telling you,' she said, 'he's up to something.' First she removed her headdress. Then she removed her rings. They were long with jointed knuckles – uncomfortable things. 'I'm sick of this costume,' she murmured. 'I'm not staying in hiding for ever.'

'What choice do you have?' laughed Surovetz. 'You're chained to your mask, just like me.'

'I'm not chained to anything,' snapped Anneshka. 'I'm the queen of Valkahá!'

'You're *one* of the queens,' corrected Surovetz. Anneshka glowered. She wanted to stab him in the face.

'Why are you in my carriage?' she demanded. 'Shouldn't you be out riding with your men? Or whatever it is that you do when you're not dressed as a beast?'

Surovetz leaned forward. 'We had an agreement,' he said. 'I help you become queen – you make me rich.' His eyes twinkled in the low light and Anneshka had the sudden desire to tear open the curtains.

'Now you sit there in your fancy jewels,' continued Surovetz. 'Where's my slice of silver? Where's my cut of the wealth? Us krootymoosh aren't known for our patience.'

'It's like you said,' returned Anneshka. 'I'm only *one* of the queens. You'll get your payment when I'm the last ruler standing. Just make sure you don't get killed first.'

The carriage trundled on.

CHAPTER 86

Imogen and Perla stepped into Yemni's workshop. The jeweller had tidied the broken glass and the room was back in order. Precious stones glimmered on the shelves.

Yemni was hammering a piece of silver. He glanced up when he heard the door, as if expecting a customer. His face fell when he saw Imogen. 'I can't do any more,' he grumbled. 'Whatever it is you're asking, the answer is no.'

'Nice to see you too,' said Imogen. 'This is my friend Perla.'

Yemni nodded and went back to his work. *Ting, ting, ting* went his hammer.

'Perhaps we should go,' whispered Perla. 'He clearly doesn't want to help.'

But Imogen wasn't leaving. 'We're going into the mines,' she declared. 'To rescue the children – my sister, Perla's brother, all of them.'

Yemni paused, hammer in hand. 'You can't. It's not safe . . . You're just children.'

'There are *already* children down there,' said Imogen. 'We're going to set them free.' Her mind summoned images of her sister sitting on the floor with her sketchbook, humming as she coloured something in. Imogen couldn't bear to think of Marie being held captive underground.

Yemni put down his hammer and ran his hands over his face. 'Look. I know this is hard, but there are some things you don't understand. Without mines, there'd be no silver. Without silver, there'd be no trade. You can't have a city without commerce – that's just the way the world works.'

Imogen looked around the workshop. She took in the coronets and bracelets, the brooches, the cloak pins, the pearls. Finally, she understood. 'You don't want to help,' she gasped.

Yemni sighed. 'That's not what I said.'

'Your brother is the Lord of the Krootymoosh. He makes children work in the mines. And you're using the silver they dig up to make jewellery! You don't want the children to be free!'

'No,' cried Yemni. 'That's not true!'

Imogen paused. Her chest was heaving. She'd never felt such rage. Yemni pretended he was all nice and friendly, but he was profiting from this. She could feel the angry stone in her ribcage. It was diamond-hard and sharp as a knife.

'If it's not true, why don't you prove it?' said Perla.

Yemni hesitated. 'What?'

Perla still didn't like talking to strangers, but this was too important to go unsaid. She raised her voice and looked square at the jeweller. 'If it's not true, why don't you prove it?

We've come to ask for your help.'

Yemni's arms fell limp at his sides. 'What exactly do you want me to do?'

'Come with us,' cried Imogen. 'Show us where the children are being held!'

Yemni started shaking his head. He didn't just shake it once or twice. He was like a nodding dog – the ones people keep in their cars – except he was saying *no, no, no.*

'Didn't you listen to my story?' he asked. There was a pleading note in his voice. 'There are monsters in the mines that eat adults. I'd never get out alive.'

Perla unfurled the krootymoosh map. She held it so Yemni could see. 'You don't need to come with us,' she told him. 'Just mark the right place on the map.'

Yemni took hold of the parchment. 'All right,' he said. 'I'll do it.'

CHAPTER 87

The night before the duel, Miro had a bad dream. He woke up wrapped in clammy sheets, alone in a four-poster bed. Well, that was nothing new.

But he wasn't completely alone. Konya was asleep by the door, the clock of stars was ticking nearby, and this wasn't the castle that Miro had grown up in. It was King Ctibor's fortress, in Vodnislav.

The pillows here smelled of mildew and there was a candle by the bed. It was shaped like a river sprite, with a plump human body and a long snaking tail.

Miro wouldn't be able to get back to sleep. Not after a nightmare like that . . . He'd dreamed that his dead uncle was the Lord of the Krootymoosh – that it was Drakomor who he had to fight.

The terror that Miro had been carefully repressing, squeezing it into a hard little ball, had exploded into thousands of pieces. He was surrounded by fragments of fear.

There was his fear of losing the duel, his fear of being a bad king. *There* was his fear of pain and of death, and his fear of failing his friends . . .

It's only a duel to first blood. But Miro didn't want to bleed.

Konya looked at him with half-open eyes, perhaps wondering why he wasn't asleep.

'I'm going outside,' said Miro. 'I need to clear my head.'

Konya stood and arched her back, flexing her big fluffy paws. *I'm coming with you*, she seemed to reply. Miro was grateful for that.

There were skret outside his chamber. Ctibor said they were there to keep him safe, but Miro couldn't help feeling their real job was to stop him running away. It was only a matter of hours till the city awoke and the duel began.

'I'm going for a walk,' mumbled Miro. The skret stared with bulging eyes. 'Don't worry,' he added. 'I'll be back before dawn.'

Soon he was striding through Vodnislav, with Konya at his side. It felt good to be out of the fortress, to feel the fresh air on his skin. Miro walked between some houses and a river. He didn't know which river it was, he didn't have a plan, he only knew that he had to move his body if he wanted to keep the fear from his mind.

Miro pulled a piece of parchment from his pocket. It was a letter in Patoleezal's hand.

Dear Miroslav,

The guards have been searching for you, but we never guessed where you'd gone . . .

Beyond the mountains. Are you out of your mind?

You must not go through with this duel. Yaroslav would be lost without its Royal Family. I'd be lost without you too.

Miro could see Patoleezal saying that line. He'd have a big stretchy smile on his face.

I would come to see you in person, but I am needed here. I must attend to the kingdom in your absence.

In the meantime, I pray that you call the fight off. You cannot possibly win.

Your humble servant,

Patoleezal Petska,

Chief Adviser to the King

Miro dropped the letter in the mud. He wasn't a 'Royal Family'. He was just a boy.

The cottages were dark by the river, but a few lanterns bobbed on the boats. Konya was drinking from the river. Miro picked up a pebble and tossed it in.

He wished sunrise would never happen. He wished the battle would never commence.

'No need to panic,' he whispered to himself. 'It's only a duel to first blood.'

He picked up another pebble and cast it high above his head. It whistled through the air and plopped into the water. Konya watched with her ears back.

Miro wondered how Perla and Imogen were doing. Had the krootymoosh been lured from the mines? He hoped his friends were all right.

He picked up a third pebble and threw it into the current, but this time there was no plop. Perhaps the pebble had landed in the reeds . . .

Miro scanned the slow-flowing river and saw a hand reaching out of the water, webbed fingers closed round the stone.

Konya leaped to Miro's side as Odlive's head arose.

CHAPTER 88

Odlive swam closer and Miro backed off. The sprite's nostrils sealed shut as they dipped underwater and opened when she raised her head. 'Is this yours?' she asked, placing the stone on the riverbank.

'No,' said Miro. He didn't want to upset Odlive and he thought it might be considered rude to throw pebbles into her home.

'Strange,' said Odlive, glancing at the crescent moon. 'It must have come from up there.' She wore a mischievous look and Miro wondered what she was after.

'I don't have any land fish,' he warned.

'I'm not here for food,' replied Odlive. 'I'm here because I've changed my mind. I've been watching you and your friends . . . You're not like the other kings.'

Miro scowled. He wasn't trying to be different. He was trying to be just like his father.

'I saw you escape from King Ctibor,' she continued. 'I didn't think you'd survive.' Her tail was visible beneath the black water, worming from side to side. 'Now I hear about this duel with the krootymoosh, and you return to the place that you fled. I wasn't expecting such bravery . . . I didn't know kings could be good.'

Konya growled and Miro was inclined to agree. He didn't trust Odlive one bit. Perhaps she would try to persuade him to run away. Perhaps she'd try to drown him instead. 'What do you want?' he asked.

On the other side of the river, a night fisherman pulled up his line. A fish was flapping against the side of his boat.

'It goes against the current,' said Odlive, 'but I've decided to give you advice.'

'I don't need it,' said Miro.

The river sprite flicked her tongue at a fly. 'Kings need advice more than anyone,' she said, swallowing the insect in one gulp.

There was a thump from the fisherman's boat and the fish fluttered no more.

'I know things that you don't know,' said Odlive in a sing-song voice.

If Miro was going to leave, this would be a good time to do it. But perhaps Odlive was right. Perhaps he did need a little help. Perhaps everyone did, from time to time . . .

'I'm listening,' he said.

The sprite smiled with her sharp little teeth. 'The water dragon will come if you call.'

'Water dragon?' yelped Miro. 'It's real?'

'Of course,' said the river sprite.

'I knew it!' Miro cried. 'But the dragon only comes for the king of the Lowlands. That's Ctibor. That isn't me.'

Odlive threw back her head and laughed. 'That fusty old fart? He wouldn't know a water dragon if it came along and sat on his lap.'

'What do you mean?' Miro was intrigued.

'Anyone can summon the dragon,' said Odlive. 'You just need to know how.'

Miro was listening intently.

'Tomorrow, when you're duelling the beast, be sure to spill your blood in the river.'

'If that's all it takes, I can cut my hand now,' said Miro, drawing his knife.

'No,' cried the sprite. 'Not now. It has to be done the right way. Your blood must mix with your enemy's. Both of you need to bleed.'

Miro sheathed his knife. 'You want me to get blood from the Lord of the Krootymoosh?'

'I never said it was easy,' murmured Odlive. She was swimming away from the bank. 'I just said I'd give some advice.'

And, with that, Odlive slipped under the water, leaving a mini whirlpool in her wake.

CHAPTER 89

Miro and Konya crossed the starlit castle. They were making their way back to their chamber, but the sněehoolark paused in the throne room. She must have sensed that they weren't alone.

'What's wrong?' asked a voice. 'Couldn't sleep?'

Miro froze. The king of the Lowlands was sitting on his throne. Why was he waiting in the dark?

'I suppose you think the water dragon will save you?' said Ctibor.

Had he followed Miro through the city? Had he heard the conversation with the sprite?

Miro said nothing. He wanted to be friends with his father's old ally, but there was something about Ctibor's tone that made him uneasy.

'You must have heard the stories,' continued Ctibor, 'about the king who saves his realm from the krootymoosh. Bet you fancy yourself as a sword-swinging hero. Bet that's why you declared the duel. Go on, tell me I'm wrong.'

Miro couldn't tell Ctibor the truth – that there was a rescue going on in the mines, that the krootymoosh needed drawing out, that the five queens must be distracted.

Ctibor chuckled without sounding happy. 'Let me tell you something,' he said. 'There are no heroes. Not really. Just like there's no water dragon.'

Miro wanted to keep walking. He wanted to run to his chamber and slam the door shut. But, instead, he found himself saying, 'How do you know?'

'Come with me,' said King Ctibor, and he got up from his throne. 'I haven't shown this to anyone.'

Miro felt a little cheered by those words. Ctibor was going to show him a secret – a secret only shared between kings.

Ctibor strode out of the throne room and Miro trotted to keep up. *He must like me*, thought Miro, *must think of me like a son*. Hadn't Ctibor said as much in his letter?

Konya brought up the rear, eyes darting from boy to man.

Ctibor paused by a tapestry. It showed a dragon eclipsing the sun. Ctibor pulled back the wall-hanging, revealing a hidden door. He unlocked it and said, 'After you.'

Miro stepped into the tunnel beyond. It was even damper in here. Ctibor took a torch from the wall and the two kings walked side by side. Konya followed, head down.

The tunnel gave way to a large chamber. It was gloomy, without any windows. As Ctibor lit the torches, Miro saw the shape of a beast. It had a long snout and a tapering tail. It hovered above a dark pool.

'Behold the great water dragon,' said Ctibor. But the beast didn't move. Miro gaped at its outline. It was held in mid-air by chains.

King Ctibor studied Miro's face before going on: 'The dragon died long ago . . . many years before I was born. This *thing* is my only inheritance – a stuffed brute with glass eyes.'

'I don't understand,' said Miro, his energy draining away.

'It's stories that protect my kingdom,' said Ctibor. 'People believe that the dragon exists. That's why we haven't been invaded . . . that's why we still live in peace.'

But you are being invaded, thought Miro. *What else are the krootymoosh raids?*

Konya paced to the edge of the pool and stared up at the stuffed beast. Her tail was as straight as a feather duster, her ears were twitching, alert.

Ctibor nodded at the snĕehoolark. 'I'm glad you brought the cat. Kazimira is very excited. I've promised her she can keep it . . . assuming you don't return from the duel.'

'It's only a duel to first blood,' said Miro. *There's no water dragon*, he thought, with despair. *Odlive was horribly wrong.*

'Anyway,' sighed Ctibor. 'I thought you should see the truth before you went into battle. Didn't want you trying to act the hero; thought it best that you knew.'

He spoke with a smile in his voice. And that was when Miro

realised. Ctibor did not love him. He did not consider him a son. To Ctibor, he was just another man's child – another body for the krootymoosh to claim.

'How could you not mention this sooner?' asked Miro.

King Ctibor was already turning to leave. 'I don't know, Miroslav,' he said with a shrug. 'It must have slipped my mind.'

CHAPTER 90

If you were to flip Valkahá on its head, the shape would remain the same – like a tree with its roots becoming branches. For there was one city above and one city below.

All of that stone was cut from the ground. All of that silver was smelted from rock. You can't make the world's greatest kingdom without unmaking something else.

Above there were towers. Below there were shafts. Above there were streets where children played. Below there were tunnels where they worked in the dark.

Imogen was perched between the two worlds, sitting on the edge of a pothole. At her back was a wiry shrub. Her legs dangled into the pit. 'Are you sure this is the right one?' she asked.

'Think so,' said Perla. She was sitting next to Imogen with the krootymoosh map tucked into her belt. Perla kept very still, as if trying to blend into her surroundings. Imogen was the opposite. Every inch of her wanted to move. She was full of a jittery energy.

Yemni stood behind them. 'I'll wait here,' he said, glancing over his shoulder. 'You might need help when you resurface.'

Perla inched closer to the edge of the hole. Her expression was set like a mask, but when she glanced at Imogen a flicker of fear crossed her face.

Perla's different without Konya, thought Imogen. *Like a sentence without a full stop.*

'It's okay,' whispered Imogen. 'I'll be right behind you.' Perla nodded, accepting the promise, then she slipped into the hole. Imogen counted the seconds, giving Perla time to move out of her way.

Then she let herself slide into the shadows.

Stone swished under her stockings.

Darkness gobbled up light.

Imogen was falling, falling . . .

Skidding to a stop.

It was cooler down here in the underground cave.

'Everything okay?' called Yemni. His face was visible through the hole – small and far away.

'Yes,' replied Perla. 'We're fine.'

'Good,' said Yemni. 'I'll be waiting. Be careful down there.'

Imogen got to her feet. As her eyes adjusted, she saw the krootymoosh – row after row of the beasts. Even though Imogen had been warned, even though she knew they weren't real, fear slithered down her spine.

There were voices at the far side of the cave. Imogen and

Perla drew back as three men came into view. They were well dressed, with long red cloaks.

'It's not fair,' said one of the men. 'Why don't I get to go? I spend twice as long underground as the rest of them.'

'Stop your complaining,' said another. 'We're not missing much. Surovetz will snap the boy's neck. It'll be over before it's begun.'

They were talking about the duel. Imogen didn't dare breathe. She pressed herself against the cave wall, but the men didn't even look her way. They were clearly used to being alone.

'I heard the boy's been drinking buvol milk,' said the third man, and he started to undress. 'He might be stronger than he looks.'

'Bet there'll be a big party. Bet there'll be music and wine and roast pig. Meanwhile, we're stuck down here, guarding the stupid mines.'

The men were standing in their underwear, their clothes in piles on the floor. They each took a krootymoosh costume and climbed into the furry suits. Then they put on the clawed paws and spiked helmets, fastening the armour across their chests.

The transformation was complete. Three krootymoosh stood in the gloom. Perla was breathing fast. Imogen put out a hand to her friend. *It's all right*, she wanted to say. *We won't be here very long.*

The krootymoosh stomped out of the cave.

CHAPTER 91

Imogen and Perla selected the smallest krootymoosh costume they could find, pulling it down off its stand. 'Do you think this will work?' asked Perla.

'I don't know,' said Imogen. 'But we've got to try.' She took hold of the helmet. A sneering metal face stared back, with teeth screwed into steel and holes drilled for eyes. Imogen poked her finger through an eyehole. 'Not so scary now . . .'

Perla clicked her fingers and a blue light appeared. It came from a minuscule fly. Imogen almost dropped the helmet with shock. 'How did you do that?'

'They're glowflies,' said Perla, smiling. 'They light up to snapping sounds . . . Don't ask me why. They're as strange to me as to you.'

Imogen clicked her fingers. Sure enough, another glowfly turned on. It drifted like a mote of dust. Imogen wanted to inspect it, to understand how it worked, but there wasn't time for such things. Imogen and Perla were on a mission: they had to break into the mines.

Perla held the map to the glowflies' light. After a moment's hesitation, she turned. There was a narrow passage at the side of the cave. 'I think it's this way,' she said.

Imogen followed Perla, lugging the krootymoosh costume with both arms. She decided not to bring the metal shoulder plates. They were heavy, and those spikes were sharp.

The passage the girls took was one strand in a system of cracks that spread like veins through the rock. Perla navigated slowly, counting each rift that they passed – branch after branch, twist after turn. 'Last time, this place was crawling with krootymoosh,' she said under her breath. 'Miro's diversion must have worked.'

Javelins of sunlight pierced holes in the roof. Sometimes, a bee bobbed down. Imogen watched one for a few seconds as she wrestled with the monstrous costume. She'd just hitched it into a better carrying position when Perla held up her hand.

They were at the edge of a large cave. A krootymoosh stood at the far end, guarding a pair of semicircular doors.

'I think that's the entrance to the mines,' whispered Perla, checking their position on the map.

She tucked herself behind a boulder and Imogen did the same. 'Great,' replied Imogen, although her belly squirmed with nerves. If they were caught, they'd lose everything: all hope of rescuing their siblings, all hope of getting back home.

Perla's mask of calm was slipping and fear shone in her eyes. 'You can do this,' said Imogen. 'For Tomil. For Luki.'

Perla nodded and closed her eyes. She was leaning against the boulder as if it was all that stood between life and death.

Imogen stepped into the krootymoosh costume. The plan was that Perla would sit on her shoulders – like a pantomime horse, but with the two children as top and bottom, rather than as back and front.

The costume was a dirty thing, like a onesie that had never been washed. It stank of old sweat and cheese.

Yuck, thought Imogen. *What a stink. I hope it doesn't rub off on me.* She paused. And what about the krootymoosh's actions? Could bad deeds rub off too?

Imogen brushed the thought aside. She pulled on the furry boots. They were too big, so the girls removed their stockings and stuffed them round Imogen's feet. Before long, she'd transformed into a krootymoosh – or, rather, the bottom half of the beast.

Now for Perla. She was small and light for her age so it was better for her to be up top. Imogen lifted the helmet over her friend's head.

'Can you see?' asked Imogen.

The krooty-child nodded.

It was time to join the two halves. Perla stuffed the map back into her belt and climbed on to Imogen's shoulders. Underneath the krootymoosh costume, Imogen held Perla's ankles tight.

Imogen was reminded of stealing plums with her sister. She'd carried Marie on her back, encouraging her to take their neighbour's fruit. 'Won't we get into trouble?' Marie had asked. 'Just take them,' Imogen had replied. She forced the memory down deeper, into the cave at her core.

Perla did up the buttons at the front of the krootymoosh costume. She left one undone so Imogen could see.

And then Imogen stepped forward. *Left foot. Right foot.* It was like walking on gigantic stilts. She made her way round the boulder until she could see the mine doors.

The krootymoosh guard turned in their direction. 'What do you want?' he grunted.

Perla answered in her deepest voice: 'We need to go into the mines.'

'We?' The krootymoosh tilted his head.

Perla felt heavier with each step that Imogen took.

'I,' gasped Perla – 'I need to go.'

'Wouldn't go now, if I were you,' said the krootymoosh. 'The yedleek are on the prowl.'

Imogen wondered what that meant . . . perhaps it was some kind of slang.

'It's Surovetz's orders,' blurted Perla.

And those were the magic words. The krootymoosh unlocked the half-moon doors. Imogen felt a whoosh of cold air. *Left foot. Right foot.* Her legs were shaking. Her face was too hot. The earth trembled as the doors rumbled shut. That was it. They were inside the mines.

CHAPTER 92

Perla dropped the krootymoosh helmet as gently as she
could. It landed with a clunk on the ground. Then she
scrambled down off Imogen's back. For a moment, they were
both trapped in the costume, fighting to find a way out.

'Ow,' hissed Imogen. 'That was my forehead.'

'Sorry,' whispered Perla. 'Where are the buttons?'

She must have found them because she crawled out of the
krootymoosh's belly. Imogen kicked off the clawed boots and
followed, shaking herself free.

The girls were in a long tunnel. The walls were chiselled
stone, the ceiling was supported by beams. Imogen didn't like
to think how many tonnes of rock they held up.

The only light came from a small swarm of glowflies,
hovering by the semicircular doors. Ahead, the tunnel stretched
into darkness.

'*This* is where they're keeping my sister?' said Imogen. She
couldn't imagine it . . . The mines were cold and damp and
dark. Those were not things Marie liked.

Perla removed the map from her belt, her fingers shaky and

slow. 'I don't know if I can do this . . . I wish . . . I wish Konya was here.'

'You *can* do it,' said Imogen, forcing certainty into her voice. 'We've already done the hard bit. Now it's just a question of reading that map – and no one's better at maps than you.'

Perla nodded, too focused to respond to the praise. She unfurled the parchment and pointed at the palest lines. 'We're in the upper level,' she muttered. 'The different blues *are* different levels, just like I thought, but, because we're underground, they go the opposite way. The ink gets darker the lower you go.'

Perla located Yemni's hand-drawn cross. That was where the kidnapped children were being held – deep in the guts of the mines. The ink near the cross was a rich midnight blue.

The girls set off down the tunnel. Imogen clicked her fingers and a glowfly sparked to life. The flies seemed to live in cracks in the rock. Their lights dimmed when the girls walked on.

Air sighed along the tunnel, as if the mines were trying to breathe. With it came the whispers of Imogen's worry creatures. *You'll never get out alive . . .*

How many were there? It sounded like thousands.

Perla paused to study the map. This part of the tunnel looked the same as the place where they'd begun. They could have moved five miles or five metres.

'How long do we keep going?' asked Imogen, eager to talk over her fears.

'I don't know,' said Perla. 'The map isn't to scale, but there should be another path soon.'

Imogen noticed a passage branching off to the right. This one had a lower ceiling and the floor was angled down. 'Like that?' asked Imogen, pointing.

'Yes,' said Perla, and she led the way. Imogen followed, keeping one hand on the wall. With the ground set at such a sharp angle, it would be easy to slip.

There was a square of light ahead. Sunlight sliced down a shaft. Imogen paused beneath it, blinking in the sudden brightness. When she looked up, she saw a pinprick of sky. The shaft made her dizzy so she wriggled her toes. It was strange . . . that normally only happened when she looked down.

'Imogen,' said Perla, 'we need to keep going.'

Imogen stepped out of the light. She followed her friend. Deeper, darker.

The passage joined other routes and the girls found themselves in the central layer of the mines, where the map was cobalt blue. Some of the tunnels were flooded. In others, the ceiling had collapsed. These sights felt like a warning – a reminder that space and air were the exception. The earth could reclaim tunnels whenever it wanted to.

The girls climbed down a ladder and entered the lower levels of the mines. Imogen noticed a flicker of silver in the rock. At first, there were just a few flecks. Then Perla found a great seam, running like a glittering river through the stone. There were chisels and hammers on the ground.

'We must be getting close,' said Perla. She seemed to grow more confident with each step. She checked the map, finger following the route. 'I think I'm getting the hang of this.'

Imogen was finding the opposite. The deeper they went, the more fearful she grew, the more her worry creatures talked. She saw one scuttle across the tunnel like a rat. *Turn back*, hissed the worry creature. *Turn back if you want to live.*

Imogen counted her breaths, tried to keep herself calm.

She didn't know how long they'd been walking when Perla stopped by a flooded passage. Imogen clicked her fingers, but no glowflies appeared. Perla hesitated at the edge of the water. 'It's through there,' she whispered. 'The place Yemni marked on the map . . . It's at the end of that tunnel.'

PART 5

CHAPTER 93

On the morning of the duel, King Ctibor's servants helped Miro get ready. They swept back his hair and cleaned his face. They fastened leather armour to his chest.

While they worked, Miro stood as if he was in a trance. He hadn't slept since his meeting with King Ctibor and the decidedly dead 'water dragon'. He was numb from exhaustion and nerves.

A sword was attached at Miro's hip. A shield found its way to his hand. He staggered out of the castle – out of the darkness, into the light – with rivergulls shrieking overhead.

Miro was half blinded by the sun. A man was waiting, silhouetted against the sky, and for a dizzying moment Miro thought it was his father come down from the stars . . .

But it was just another guard. 'Your Highness,' he said, 'follow me.'

Miro and the man walked away from the fortress, towards the natural bridge. Skret guards bowed. The river ran on.

Then Miro heard a warbling wail. It was coming from behind, from inside the castle. It sounded like the climax of a tragic ballad, but that was no human singer ...

The guard glanced at Miro. 'Isn't that your cat?'

Miro didn't answer. He didn't want to think about Konya, trapped in his chamber, clawing at the door, crying by the locked window. He'd *had* to leave her behind. He didn't have any choice. Perhaps she would tire herself out.

'We can go back and get her if you want,' said the guard. 'She can watch the duel from afar.'

Miro would have loved to have Konya at his side. He didn't want to make this journey alone. But the sněehoolark had been trained to defend children from krootymoosh. There was no way she'd just sit and watch. The yowl started up once more – a cross between a howl and a miaow.

'No,' said Miro, his decision made. 'Konya is staying behind.'

The guard led Miro to the Pevnee River, where a boat was decked out in streamers and flowers. Ribbons trailed from the mast; rosettes quivered at the bow. The boat's figurehead was a dragon, its wings spread against the hull.

So much for Odlive's advice, thought Miro. *King Ctibor's dragon is stuffed and this one's made out of wood. Neither will come when I call.*

Four skret and a man stood on the boat's deck. On another day, Miro would have laughed to see skret in wide-brimmed hats, with ribbons tied under their chins. But Miro was too afraid for laughter. He shuffled along the gangplank in silence.

He could still hear the siren call of the snĕehoolark – a long and mournful sound.

A lump formed in Miro's throat.

'Welcome aboard *The Champion*,' said a man who must have been the captain. 'We renamed the boat in your honour.'

The Champion. That was what they called Miro now.

The boat's sail caught the wind, and Miro grabbed the railings to stop himself losing balance. The deck shifted beneath his feet as the vessel cut upstream, ribbons trailing in the breeze.

Miro turned to the closest sailor, a skret in a baggy shirt. 'Do you think there's such a thing as a water dragon?' he asked.

'Why, yes,' said the skret. 'King Ctibor keeps the beast in his castle. Everybody knows that.'

It wasn't the response Miro wanted.

They sailed under a bridge, plunging into darkness.

'Are you afraid?' asked a crackle-hiss voice. It was only the skret, but Miro shuddered. The lump in his throat seemed to grow.

'Of course not,' he said. 'It's just a duel to first blood.'

The boat emerged into the fierce light of day and Miro had to shield his face. Vodnislav was diminishing – its buildings falling back – and there were shoals of people on the riverbanks.

They stood on upturned carts. They lined piers. There were hundreds of them, maybe more: fisherfolk, farmhands and shepherds. Some were silent, as if watching a funeral procession. Others waved flags and cheered.

Miro felt the weight of people's expectations, like a giant thumb pressing his chest. *I suppose*, he thought, *this is what it means to be king.*

There were red cloaks among the crowd too, and Miro knew what it meant. They were krootymoosh without their fur suits and armour, hiding in plain sight. Miro was relieved so many had come. He hoped the mines were deserted. He hoped his friends could escape.

Mlok Island was visible ahead, a blob of land with no buildings, people or trees. That was where the duel would be held. Miro's insides squeezed tight.

The boat passed a big wooden barge where the five queens sat on deck, their faces unmoving, their jewellery reflecting the sun. One queen wore a circular headdress. Another wore a face-net of pearls. They looked magnificent – like living statues. Miro *almost* forgot that they weren't on his side . . .

A second boat was anchored near the island. This one belonged to King Ctibor himself. Ctibor and Kazimira were perched in the crow's nest – a barrel near the top of the mast. Kazimira's dress was a bundle of bows. The king's cloak flapped in the wind.

They weren't on Miro's side either. Miro was sure of that now.

Ochi's words came back to him. *Think you can slay the krootymoosh and the world will fall at your feet? There's nothing in your future but blood and death . . .*

Miro's stomach clenched tighter still. The boat he was on approached Mlok Island and the captain yelled orders to his crew. The skret sailors lowered the plank.

'May the stars defend you,' said the captain to Miro. 'Our fates are in your hands.'

Here we go, thought Miro as he picked up his shield. *Time to make my parents proud.*

CHAPTER 94

Miro was alone on Mlok Island, heart hammering like an overwound clock. 'It's only a duel to first blood,' he whispered, trying to reassure himself.

Another boat approached the far side of the island. The Lord of the Krootymoosh was standing at its bow – a great hulking beast, much taller than the crew. In one hand it grasped a club.

The people on the riverbank shouted and Miro felt the heat of their rage. It was coming from within him too, radiating from his chest. He tried to take in his surroundings. A patch of reeds. The wreck of a boat. But he couldn't focus on any of it. His eyes kept returning to his foe.

The krootymoosh stepped on to dry land and Patoleezal's words had never felt so true. *You cannot possibly win . . .*

The krootymoosh stretched its furred neck. Then it swung its club, wrist rotating forward and back. Finally, it rolled its powerful shoulders, like a wrestler limbering up.

It moved with such ease. Was it really a costume? Could this beast be the real thing? Perhaps there were fake krootymoosh *and* real ones.

Miro's enemy wore metal armour – armguards and spiny shoulder plates, gleaming articulated gloves. Each piece was plated in silver. Miro knew where that silver had come from. He knew who'd dug it up.

His own armour was made out of leather. It was light. He could move easily enough. But the krootymoosh was so well protected . . .

Trumpets sounded from Ctibor's boat and all eyes turned to the king, who was still sitting in the crow's nest with his daughter. Ctibor stood up and raised his hand; the crowd went very quiet.

'People of the Lowlands,' he shouted, 'I know that you are angry. I'm angry too. We've lost so many children. We've suffered at the hands of these beasts.' He gestured at the Lord of the Krootymoosh. 'I would like to thank Miroslav for fighting this battle on my behalf.'

Miro did *not* like that. He wasn't fighting for King Ctibor. He was fighting for his friends and the children in the mines. He was fighting to be a good king.

'May the stars protect our champion,' finished Ctibor.

The trumpets sounded, and, when Miro turned, he saw that the krootymoosh was charging at him. Everything else seemed to fade.

The beast's jagged helmet dipped. Its paw-beats thundered on the ground.

Miro's limbs felt loose, like he might come apart any minute. Somewhere in the distance, people were chanting his name. The Lord of the Krootymoosh was almost upon him. Miro dodged to the left, dragging his sword in the mud. The beast's club swooshed past his shoulder.

The krootymoosh turned on shaggy paws. 'There you are,' it said, raising its club.

Miro was living on instinct. He lifted his shield, took the blow, and pain ricocheted down his arm.

Miro cried out and dropped the shield. The krootymoosh kicked it aside. 'The dragon won't help you,' it growled. 'It didn't come when we took the children from the villages. It didn't come when we raided the towns.'

'I know,' replied Miro. 'I was there.'

Through the helmet's eyeholes Miro thought he could see the flicker of a human iris. The krootymoosh took a step closer, swaggering with confidence. It swung its club and Miro ducked. The club whistled through the air above his head.

'What, then?' grunted the krootymoosh. 'You think Ctibor will come to your rescue? Between you and me, I think he'd rather like to see you skewered.'

Miro straightened, faced the beast. He raised his sword with some effort, directing the point at his enemy's face. The krootymoosh was almost twice his height and at least three times his weight. Miro wanted to attack, but his feet had other ideas. They kept on backing away.

They did two laps of the island like this – krootymoosh advancing, Miro in reverse; krootymoosh swinging, Miro dodging the blow.

'Fight me,' said the beast. Sweat darkened the fur under its armpits, but its movements didn't slow. Miro, on the other hand, wasn't sure how much longer he could keep this up.

'I've spent months chasing brats like you,' said the krootymoosh. 'Don't imagine you'll get away.'

Miro tripped and his sword flew from his grip, skidding to a halt by his enemy's paw.

'Come and get it,' whispered the beast. 'I promise I won't bite.'

There was a rivergull watching from the top of the wreck. The bird's wings were tucked behind its back. Miro wished he had wings. He'd fly far away if he could . . .

'Stand up and fight like a man,' boomed the monster.

But Miro wasn't here to fight. He got to his feet and started running – running towards the old upturned boat.

While the boy-king duelled with the krootymoosh, Ochi seized her chance. Most of the guards had left Vodnislav Castle to see the fight for themselves.

Ochi could hear the sněehoolark yowling as she approached the castle's land bridge. She waited, knowing the cat would wear itself out, and finally, when all was quiet, the witch slipped into the fortress.

She peered into chambers and rushed across halls. Eventually, she found the right room. The clock of stars was lying on a bed, next to some folded clothes.

The giant cat was asleep in the corner, exhausted by its own wails. Ochi scowled at the snĕehoolark. She had met it before, and she still had the bruises to prove it.

Ochi sneaked across the chamber towards the clock, more grateful than ever for her youth. It was much easier tiptoeing as a young woman than when your body was seven hundred years old.

The clock's face wore new scratches and none of its hands moved. *Poor thing*, thought Ochi. *You're no child's toy.*

She glanced out of the room's stained-glass window. *There* was the fast-flowing river. *There* were the tall willow trees.

The willows waved their branches at the forest witch. It was they who had spotted the clock. They'd seen it through the window. Ochi whispered her thanks.

Then she picked up the clock with both hands and stole out of the castle, unseen.

CHAPTER 95

There was no part of Imogen that wanted to step into the flooded tunnel. Was Perla right? Would it lead to Marie?

But Perla was already wading in. 'Come on, Imogen,' she called. 'We can do this – remember what you said! For Tomil and Luki. For your sister!'

Imogen took a deep breath and followed her friend, ignoring the shock of cold as water sloshed over her ankles – shins – knees. It seeped through the rocks overhead. *Drip, drip, drip; tick, tick, tick.*

And there, cutting through the damp air, came the whispers Imogen knew so well . . . a chorus of worry creatures, chanting her name, telling her she'd never get out. How many were there? It sounded like thousands. They were crawling like spiders along the walls.

Imogen started to hum. She wasn't trying to drown out her fears – there were far too many now for that – but the sound reminded her of what she was doing. It helped her walk into the unknown. *Left foot. Right foot.* Deeper and darker.

Marie always liked to hum.

Imogen could see stars ahead, reflected in the water. But that didn't make any sense. It wasn't night-time and there were no stars underground. Perhaps her eyes were going funny.

She kept walking. Water swilled round her knees – shins – feet. The flooded tunnel led the girls to a cave and, at first, Imogen wasn't very impressed. She'd seen enough caves to last a lifetime.

But as Imogen's eyes adjusted, she realised that this cave was different. For one thing, it was massive, as big as a football pitch. For another, it contained thousands of glowflies, tiny specks of blue light. *They* were the things she'd mistaken for stars.

Imogen clambered out of the flooded passage, stepping on to dry land. 'Crusty catfish!' gasped Perla as she gazed at the galaxy of insects. The glowflies swarmed by the roof.

'It's a cosmos cave,' whispered Imogen.

'What's cosmos?'

'All of the planets and stars,' said Imogen, glad that Perla had asked. Space was her specialist topic.

There were dribbles of rock hanging down from the ceiling and lumpy stone mounds rising up from the floor. *Stalactites and stalagmites,* thought Imogen. *That's what they're called.*

A stream wound through the middle of the cave, twisting round the pillars of rock. Some of the stalagmites were as tall as lamp-posts, others were no bigger than garden gnomes.

Imogen took a few steps across the cave and a rock pillar moved.

Perla almost jumped out of her skin. Imogen gave a strangled cry. For a long moment, both children stared. Could stalagmites turn into humans?

But it wasn't the stalagmite that had moved. There was something behind it. Something with fingers and hair. It was a child. A little girl.

'Hello?' said Imogen to the girl behind the rock.

There was a second child. A tall boy with sandy hair. He wrapped his fingers round the stone and peered at Imogen and Perla. 'New arrivals,' he said. Then he let his voice fill the cave – 'COME SEE THE NEW ARRIVALS!'

More children emerged. They peeped from behind stalagmites and blinked from dark holes. One girl even crept out of a pool. Soon, the Cosmos Cave was full of children: dirt-smeared girls and sun-starved boys, children with hollow cheeks and knotted hair.

The smallest child must have been about five years old. The tallest were teenagers – not fully grown. Their eyes were too large, their clothes worn to rags. The colour had gone from their cheeks.

'I saw them first,' said the tall boy. 'They're joining my group in the Deep Pits.'

'No,' said a girl, whose clothes were too small. 'You said I could have the next pair of shoes. I want those ones. They're my size!' She pointed at Imogen's boots, the ones Branna had given her.

Imogen took a few steps back and almost slipped into the flooded tunnel she'd just come out of. Perla had frozen. Her eyes darted from one child to the next.

'What about their ribbons?' said an older girl, who'd scaled a stalagmite to see over the crowd. 'I want ribbons like that.'

'We're not new recruits,' said Imogen, finding her voice at last. 'We've come to help you escape.'

The tall boy cocked his head. 'Escape? You can't escape from the mines.'

A small pale boy burst out from the crowd. He threw himself at Perla. Imogen was about to step between them when she realised that she knew his face. It was Luki.

'Perla!' he cried. 'You've been kidnapped too!'

Perla returned the embrace, clasping Luki with both arms.

There was a girl not far behind. She seemed to be chasing after Luki and she had a look that Imogen had seen before.

The girl paused when she caught sight of Imogen. Now Imogen could place her. The girl looked like a mini version of Branna – round-faced, with a rosy flush. Could this be her missing daughter? The one Branna said wouldn't return?

Imogen's fingers went to her skirt. She felt awkward. She was wearing the missing girl's clothes.

And Marie? she thought, like a scream inside her. *Where is Marie?*

Another boy stepped into view. He was brown-skinned, with the same expressive eyebrows as his sister.

'Perla,' said the boy. 'Is it you?'

'*Tomil!*' squeaked Perla. Her voice had gone ultrasound high.

Soon all four of them were hugging – Perla, Tomil, Luki and his sister – a circle of arms and big smiles.

But Imogen couldn't join in. She scanned the faces of the crowd, becoming more desperate by the second. None of the children had red hair. None of the children was Marie.

Imogen felt herself crumple.

Then a voice floated over the hubbub. It was distant and familiar, like in a dream. 'Hey!' it said. 'Get out of my way. That's my sister!'

CHAPTER 96

Imogen saw Marie and everything else seemed to drift. The other children faded, the glowflies went faint, and the sisters were drawn together, bound by a gravity of their own.

Imogen hugged her sister and Marie hugged her right back. 'You found me,' gasped Marie.

'Of course,' said Imogen. 'I'd never go home without you.' There were tears running down her face, tears on her chin and her neck. She didn't care who saw.

Imogen and Marie were two stars in space – out of words and in their own time. Marie's arms round Imogen's middle. Marie's hair tickling her face. It was real. *This was real!*

'Anneshka killed an old lady,' said Marie. 'I tried to stop her, but I couldn't.'

'It's okay,' said Imogen. 'I'll take you back home. You won't have to see Anneshka again.'

'But she's up to something, Imogen. She wants to be queen.'

What did it matter? Marie was okay. They were going back to their mum. The rest was only a void.

'Don't worry about Anneshka,' said Imogen, as she drifted

back down to Earth. 'We need to get out of this cave.'

'Wait a minute,' said the tall boy. 'Do you know the way to the surface?'

Marie's face had gone shiny and bright. 'This is my sister,' she declared. 'I *told* you she'd set us free!'

Imogen positively glowed with pride. 'It was mostly Perla,' she mumbled, suddenly wishing that she hadn't blubbed in front of all these people.

'But there *is* no way out,' said the girl whose clothes were too small. 'You'll get lost in the mines. And once you get lost, you've had it. You'll die with no food or drink. *This* is the only place with cavefish. That's why we're here and not working. It's almost time for our lunch.'

'Cavefish,' said Imogen. 'Is that what you eat?'

'Not always,' said the girl, crossing her arms. 'The krootymoosh drop bread down a shaft. Sometimes they drop cabbages too. But you shouldn't go wandering in tunnels you don't know. It's a labyrinth. You'd never survive.'

There was a murmur of agreement from the others.

'We won't get lost,' said Imogen. 'Perla's got a map of the mines.'

Perla was talking to Tomil. Her face mirrored his wide-eyed delight. Luki was twirling around them – a wild dance that involved lots of stamping and shouts.

A ripple of excitement ran through the crowd. 'A map?'

the children whispered. 'A map that shows all the tunnels and caves?' One of the smaller girls let out a squeal. 'We're going back to the surface!'

'Is it true?' said the tall boy, stepping closer to Perla. 'Do you *really* know the way out?'

Perla nodded and showed him the scroll.

The tall boy squinted in the glowfly light. 'You know how to read this? It looks like tangled wool.'

Hundreds of eyes were fixed on Perla. She blushed a deep berry red. Imogen guessed she didn't like the attention, but that's what you got for being a map-reader extraordinaire.

'I think so,' murmured Perla. 'It's worked so far.'

'But what about the krootymoosh?' said a dusty-faced girl.

'There are only a few of them here at the moment,' said Perla. 'If we go together, they don't stand a chance.' The cave was filled with excited chatter. Some of the more energetic children joined Luki's jig.

'But I'm scared,' said a small boy. He couldn't have been older than six. 'I don't want to go to the surface. It's safer down here in the dark.'

The tall boy took the child's hand. 'It's okay,' he said. 'I'll be with you.' Then he stood taller still. 'Come on . . . let's go back to the light.'

CHAPTER 97

Miro sprinted towards the upside-down boat. The rivergull was perched on the wreck's highest point. When it saw the boy hurtling towards it, the bird unfolded its wings and lifted into the sky.

'That's it!' snarled the krootymoosh. 'Run! Run like the coward you are.' The beast was in pursuit, armour clanging, each breath snorting out like a bull.

Miro may have lost his sword and shield, but at least his hands were free. He scrambled up the side of the wreck until he stood on the top, arms out for balance. He could hear the river at his back, feel the pull of the crowd.

He knew what he had to do.

The krootymoosh hesitated at the base of the boat. It glanced over its shoulder, towards the barge where the five queens watched.

Miro seized his chance.

He flung himself at his enemy – hands grabbing armour, feet fumbling for grip. The krootymoosh faltered. 'That's no way to fight,' it bellowed, swinging its club at Miro and almost striking its own head. 'Fight like a man! Fight like—'

Miro had his feet on his enemy's shoulders, wedged between metal spines. His fingers were wrapped round the spikes on the helmet. The krootymoosh threw down its club and drew a dagger from its belt.

Miro would have to be quick. He wrenched the helmet and it lifted up. Miro fell back, back – *smack!* – into the mud-squelching earth. The helmet thudded on to his chest.

For a split second, there was quiet. A silent echo of shock. The Lord of the Krootymoosh wasn't a krootymoosh. It was Surovetz of Valkahá, his true face exposed.

'Why, that's a man!' cried King Ctibor.

The crowd on the riverbank roared. It was a rolling, wrathful sound like a gathering wave. It crashed on to the island, washing over the place where Miro lay.

Surovetz lurched in his big-clawed boots as if dazed by the light and the noise. Then he rounded on Miro, dagger in hand. 'You will pay,' he growled, lunging with the knife.

Miro lifted the krootymoosh helmet. The dagger pierced an eyehole. Surovetz came at him again, and this time the blade hit its mark. It sliced through Miro's leather armour, biting the flesh on his arm. It didn't hurt. Not much. But when Miro put a hand to his shoulder, his fingers came away red.

Blood.

He'd lost . . . The duel was over . . .

And instead of feeling sad, Miro felt an incredible lightness. He was free! The battle was done. Far above, rivergulls cried.

But Surovetz didn't seem to be stopping. He stood over his prey, knife glinting.

Miro lifted a bloodied hand. 'I'm wounded,' he called. 'You win!'

'Did you really think I'd let you live?'

Surovetz stabbed and Miro rolled sideways. The blade missed his face by an inch.

'But those are the rules,' cried Miro as he jumped to his feet. 'You *have* to stop at first blood!'

'Rules are for peasants,' sneered Surovetz.

There was another angry roar from the crowd. Miro had unleashed something powerful when he'd shown them the krootymoosh's face. The people's fury was palpable.

But there was a river between Miro and the crowd. They couldn't save him right now. Miro glanced at King Ctibor, perched high in his crow's nest. Surely Ctibor would make the duel stop? But the king was watching in silence. Kazimira was watching too. Neither of them moved to help.

As Miro staggered away from Surovetz, Odlive's voice seemed to float on the wind. *Spill your blood in the river.*

Well, he had nothing to lose . . .

Miro splashed into the shallows, running as fast as he could. Cold water tugged at his knees. He could hear the crowd on the other side of the river, see their fluttering flags.

He touched his wounded arm and plunged his bloody hand underwater. His fingers were splayed wide as if reaching, reaching for something – or someone.

The water accepted his blood.

'I'll kill you,' screamed Surovetz. He kicked off his krootymoosh boots in a fit of blind rage, shrinking to his true height. He looked almost comic – bulging eyes, bare feet and a big furry suit. There was nothing he could do to make people unsee him. No way to make them forget.

The ex-krootymoosh waded into the water.

If the dragon was real, Miro needed it. He needed it to appear right now. Odlive's words sailed downstream. *Your blood must mix with your enemy's . . .*

Miro picked up a stone from the riverbed. It was heavy and shaped like a fist. He flung it at Surovetz.

Missed. The stone plopped into the water.

Surovetz kept wading, dagger in hand.

Miro picked up another rock with his non-injured arm and threw it with all the strength he could muster. The stone pinged off Surovetz's metal shoulder plate.

That was closer, thought Miro. *Try again.*

He glanced at the people. They were cheering him on now, carrying him on their great wave. And, this time, instead of Miro feeling pressure, the crowd's love gave him strength.

He picked up a third stone and launched it. The stone struck Surovetz's nose with a crunch.

Got him, thought Miro, and he reached for more rocks, but Surovetz seized his arm.

'Nobody defeats the krootymoosh,' hissed Surovetz. Blood glooped out of his nose. He pulled Miro closer, as if to embrace him.

And then he stuck the knife in.

CHAPTER 98

Miro felt like he'd been punched in the stomach, but it was worse than that. He'd been stabbed. There was an open mouth in his belly, gurgling blood. 'You've killed me,' he whispered. He couldn't believe it. He wasn't ready to die.

There's nothing in your future but blood and death . . .

Swaying on his feet, he looked up. Red was streaming out of Surovetz's nose. It ran over his chin and dripped into the river.

'Help,' said Miro, and his voice sounded breathy. 'Somebody, please . . .'

The water throbbed, as if in answer. A shadow of fear crossed Surovetz's face and he scrambled up the bank. The water pulsed again and, this time, there was no mistaking it.

Thu-thud, thu-thud.

It was the beating of a heart. The pounding of the Sertze Voda. Its power shuddered through the water and Miro fell to his knees. The river was rising and falling, swelling in great humpbacked waves.

Somewhere, not far away, Kazimira screamed.

Miro was only dimly aware of anything outside his body.

He let himself slide into the waves. There were stars in the water, stars in the sky, more stars than he'd ever dreamed . . .

Perhaps dying wouldn't be so bad. Perhaps then he'd be with his parents. But the pain was intense. It was opening him up, turning him inside out.

Something brushed against his fingers and Miro made himself focus. The thing by his hand was a frog. No, not a frog . . . a newt. Where had he seen it before?

There were stars crowding his vision and, as the water around him turned red, Miro's world faded to white.

CHAPTER 99

The children left the Cosmos Cave, with Perla leading the way. Everyone wanted to walk close to her, to see the map and ask how it worked.

Imogen took a final look at the cave, with all of its glowfly lights; at the slippery rocks and the twisty underground stream.

They'd done it. They'd found the missing children. She couldn't wait to tell Miro how well his plan had worked. In the end, it had almost been easy. Imogen linked fingers with Marie and, together, they walked out of the cave. They followed the others through the flooded tunnel, the children's voices echoing in the dark.

'Your friend's like the Pied Piper,' said Marie.

'Yes,' laughed Imogen. 'Except the opposite because she's taking children back home.'

Slosh, slip, slap went the water. Imogen gave her sister's hand a squeeze. She wasn't going to lose her again.

'How did you find me?' asked Marie.

Imogen smiled in the darkness. 'It's kind of complicated . . . We used a star-reading clock. You know, the one from Miro's tower, the one Ochi had in her hut?'

'That clock's magic?' gasped Marie. 'All this time, and we didn't know! It's so nice of Ochi to let you have it.'

'Mmm,' said Imogen, marching on. She didn't feel like telling that story today.

The sisters stepped out of the flooded tunnel and glowflies illuminated their way. A procession of children was visible now, following Perla and her map.

The sisters walked up through the caverns and clefts, up through the bone-brittle rock. And while they walked, they chatted. Imogen kept a wary eye on the others – the last stragglers in Perla's line.

'Did you meet Princess Kazimira?' asked Marie.

'Yes. She's a proper snot bomb.'

Marie giggled. 'She is a bit . . . And her dad, King Ctibor, he made me eat fish.'

'He sentenced us to death! What was it like with Anneshka? Did she . . .' Imogen paused, tried to force the words out. 'Did she hurt you?'

Marie gave a tiny head-shake.

The girls were still holding hands when they entered a cave. The ceiling was supported by beams, arched in the middle like ribs. The other children were on the far side.

'What's that?' asked Marie, stopping dead.

'What's what?' said Imogen. She tried to tug her sister along, but then she heard it too. A low rumble. It came from below. No . . . from above. A shuddering groan ran through the rock.

Marie looked terrified.

'It's okay,' said Imogen. But Marie knew the mines better than her sister. The glowflies began to go out.

The other children scrambled out of the cave, slipping through a passage on the opposite side. The beams in the ceiling were splitting. But Imogen and Marie were too far back. If they tried to sprint to the passage, they risked getting crushed on the way.

'It's not okay,' cried Marie. 'That's the sound the rock makes before—'

Imogen didn't hear the rest. The beams snapped like toothpicks. Imogen stumbled back, retreating the way they'd just come. Her fingers slipped from her sister's.

'Marie!' she yelled. But stones fell thick and fast. One struck Imogen's head and she staggered to the ground.

The last thing she saw before the world faded, was a curtain of tumbling rock.

CHAPTER 100

Imogen opened her eyes. It was dark. Not the kind of dark you get at bedtime when you can still see streetlamps outside. This was a heavy, ancient dark. A dark with no promise of light.

Imogen wondered if her eyes were still shut. She scrunched them closed and counted to ten. Then she opened them for a second time. Darkness pressed in from all sides.

I'm dead, she thought with a mounting horror. The air smelled of minerals and mud.

I'm dead. I'm dead!

Something wet slithered down her face. She licked her lips and the wet stuff tasted like blood. *Do dead people bleed?* Imogen didn't think so.

There was an ache in her head that grew sharp when she moved. She sat up and the pain took her breath. She paused, head throbbing.

Dead people don't feel pain.

And then Imogen remembered. It came back to her in flashes – a great rumble – falling rock. The cave ceiling had collapsed. Imogen groped in the darkness. There was stone on all sides.

It doesn't matter how hard you try, fate always wins in the end.
Those were the words of Odlive, the river sprite. Imogen batted
the thought away.

She tried to stand but there wasn't enough space. Pain
exploded in her head and she was forced to sit very still. A
memory of Mark stirred in the darkness. He was standing with
his hands on his hips. *Nasty, angry thing*, he said. *Must take after
her father.*

'I'm nothing like my dad,' muttered Imogen. 'I'd never leave
my family behind.'

What about your mother? said a worry creature.

An image of Mum rose in her mind. Mum alone and
anxious . . .

Then came an image of Marie.

. . . Marie.

Where was she?

Imogen couldn't feel Marie's body. She fumbled with both
hands, praying her sister had made it out of the cave. She
reached up and touched rock. It was hovering, suspended
in space. She traced a line along the boulder's belly until she
found a second stone. It was wedging the first one in position –
stopping it from falling on her head. Imogen was lucky not to
have been flattened.

Lucky . . . She scowled at the word. What could she do with
such luck? She was trapped in the mines, buried alive. Luck

had saved her from being crushed. A slower, more painful fate lay ahead. How long would she survive down here on her own?

'Hello?' she called through the blackness. 'Can anyone hear me?'

The worry creatures were ready to answer. *It's just you and us*, they whispered with glee. *Everyone else got away*. Imogen could hear the creatures scrambling over rubble. They were searching for her, feeding on her fear. And there was plenty of fear to be had.

Imogen tried to imagine the world above – the scrub and the free-flying birds, the endless space with clouds sweeping by. She tried to think of the stars.

But the worry creatures were controlling her thoughts. There was no world above. Only darkness and despair. One worry creature climbed up her back. Another burrowed into her chest, squeezing tight round her heart and lungs.

'They're killing me!' cried Imogen, and she curled in on herself. Each breath came shallow and sharp.

Fear and panic. Darkness and despair. Worry creatures swarmed all around. 'Stop it!' shrieked Imogen, tearing at her face. 'Go away! Leave me alone!'

A thin voice cut through the darkness. 'Hello?' it said, and the worry creatures froze. Imogen stopped struggling too. 'Imogen,' said the voice, 'is that you?'

CHAPTER 101

Imogen didn't know whether to be happy or sad. She didn't want Marie to be trapped down here, but it was *so good* to hear her voice. 'Marie!' gasped Imogen.

'Keep talking,' said her sister. 'I'm trying to find you by sound.'

'I thought you'd escaped,' cried Imogen. 'I thought I was the only one left!'

She plucked a worry creature from her neck and dashed it against the rocks. The others backed slowly away. 'Are you injured?' called Imogen.

'I don't think so,' said Marie. Her voice was closer this time. 'There's a gap – I'm just – climbing through—' There was a scrabbling near Imogen's feet. She reached with both arms, stretching into the unknown.

'Where are you?' she asked. She was afraid of the reply, afraid Marie might not be real. But something touched her hand and it didn't feel like stone. It felt a lot like her sister.

Imogen clasped Marie's fingers in hers. She held her arms – shoulders – face.

'I'm sorry,' sobbed Imogen. Her head really hurt.

'I'm sorry. I didn't mean—'

'Sorry for what?' said Marie.

'Sorry for *this*,' cried Imogen. 'I promised everything would be okay! I promised we wouldn't be long! It was my idea to leave the hotel and go through the door in the tree – and now we're trapped underground and no one will find us, and Mum will be sad and it's all my fault!'

There was a pause.

'You didn't make this happen,' said Marie. She spoke in such a matter-of-fact voice that even the worry creatures sat up. 'I chose to go with you. I wanted to go through the door in the tree.'

Imogen could picture Marie's face, serious and owl-like in the dark. 'But I'm the big sister,' she muttered. 'I'm supposed to make things okay.'

Marie almost laughed. 'You're not in charge of the whole world, Imogen. You do know that, don't you?'

Imogen's worry creatures shifted among the rubble. They hadn't disappeared. They were listening.

Marie shuffled closer, so the sides of the girls' bodies touched. 'Who were you talking to earlier?' she asked. 'You said something like, "Leave me alone."'

Imogen felt a stab of humiliation. *My imaginary worry creatures*, was the answer, but she could hardly say that. Marie would think something was wrong with her. That's what Mark thought already. That's what Mum and the therapist thought too.

No, Marie mustn't know. She wouldn't ever take

Imogen seriously again.

But then, thought Imogen, *maybe it doesn't matter . . . if we're both going to die.*

The worry creatures hissed a warning.

Imogen took a deep breath. 'I was talking to my worry creatures,' she said, and she kept her voice low, half hoping her sister wouldn't hear.

'What are worry creatures?' asked Marie. She didn't seem to be teasing.

'They're things that appear when I'm upset.' The nearest worry creature let out a squeak and Imogen realised it had vanished. She didn't need to see to be sure. 'They say bad things,' she continued. 'I keep trying to shake them off. Sometimes, I imagine throwing them out of windows, stamping on them . . . that kind of thing. But the worry creatures always come back.'

'A bit like sisters,' said Marie.

Imogen snorted. 'Not like sisters at all.'

Her worry creatures were squealing now – fizzling out one by one, like mints in a bottle of Coke. They didn't seem to like being talked about. Imogen was so distracted by this discovery that at first she didn't notice the light.

'Hey,' whispered Marie. 'Can you see that?' Imogen squinted into the darkness.

There was a flickering among all the debris. A flame in the endless night.

CHAPTER 102

Anneshka felt the barge move beneath her – a sickening lurch to the right. 'Is it supposed to do that?' she demanded.

Queen Blipla shook her jewel-shrouded head. She looked alarmed, or as alarmed as was possible with a silver centipede draped over her face.

Anneshka knew it had been a bad idea to borrow King Ctibor's barge. Everything in Vodnislav was shoddy: the people, the dragons, the boats.

She crossed the deck as it tilted towards her. 'Move out of my way,' she shouted and the skret sailors all stepped aside. Anneshka grabbed the boat's railing.

The other queens were nailed to their seats. 'What are you doing?' said Queen Zlata.

Anneshka did not respond. Through her pearl face-net, she took in the scene.

Something was happening to the river. It was choppy where it had been calm. It was surging, subsiding and blistering, as though something lived under its skin.

Miroslav's body floated near the island, surrounded by great plumes of blood. But the boy's death was no use to Anneshka. It had come at too high a price.

Now everyone knew that the krootymoosh were men. Even in death, the boy had won.

Never underestimate children, thought Anneshka. *Especially those you've had murdered once.*

King Ctibor's boat was in turmoil. It rolled in the water like a pig. Ctibor was shouting from the crow's nest. Kazimira was screaming from the rigging.

When Anneshka looked back at Miroslav's body, she was startled to see it had gone. In its place was a vortex, a circular current. It must have sucked the boy in. Anneshka did not like that . . . She had a deep-seated mistrust of water. Especially water that turned into something else. Was that a whirlpool?

The barge lurched in the other direction and Anneshka paced over the deck. *There* was Vodnislav in the distance. *There* was the mob with their flags, furious to discover that the Lord of the Krootymoosh was a human in disguise.

The river was expanding. It bubbled as it swallowed its own marshy banks. Surovetz's men turned and fled. They ran with a terrible desperation – as if the river was coming just for them.

Anneshka tightened her grip on the railings. Maybe it was.

'I know that man,' cried a voice from the crowd, pointing to the unmasked krootymoosh. 'His name is Surovetz. He works for the queens.'

The mob turned and Anneshka felt as if a great wave was summoning strength from below.

Surovetz was alone on the island, still wearing his krootymoosh suit. His face shone with sweat and blood flowed from his nose. 'No,' he rasped. 'It's not true.' But there was no power left in his voice.

The crowd surged towards the river. It wasn't just the water that was rising. The people were rising too. Their anger had been released by Miroslav when he'd revealed what the krootymoosh were.

If only he hadn't removed Surovetz's helmet. *If only* he'd fought like a king!

The boy had, once again, ruined everything.

'That man serves the queens!' shouted another voice from the crowd. They were still talking about Surovetz. 'I've seen him kneel at their feet!'

Flagpoles were lowered. Fists were clenched. The mob was out for revenge.

Surovetz stared at Anneshka from the island, his krootymoosh swagger quite gone. 'Queen Svitla,' he shouted, 'I thought we had a deal! Help me! HELP!'

Anneshka scowled under her pearls. If the crowd had any doubts that the queens were mixed up with the krootymoosh, those doubts had just been erased.

'We need to get off this barge,' said Queen Yeeskra.

Anneshka silently agreed. She looked around for an escape route.

Some of the crowd waded into the water, making a beeline for the queens. Others scrambled aboard little boats. 'You stole our children!' they cried.

Meanwhile, the river threw great soapy waves. They slapped against the barge, making it groan. 'Ctibor said this boat was safe,' snapped Queen Flumkra.

'It is,' quibbled the captain. 'It's the most stable boat in our fleet.'

'Then why is it sinking?' shrieked the queen.

Panic bloomed like blood underwater. Skret sailors jumped overboard. The human crew weren't much better.

Anneshka ran to the lifeboat, only to find it had gone. Queen Zlata was in it already, rowing away from the barge.

'Damn it,' muttered Anneshka.

But her envy faded as a fleet of fisherfolk intercepted the lifeboat and threw Queen Zlata into the waves. That circular headdress looked heavy. So did those crystal-encrusted robes. Queen Zlata sank like a stone.

Anneshka did not want to share the same fate. *But I'm not a real queen*, she thought. *The krootymoosh weren't my idea. Damn that boy and his revelations! Damn this whole waterlogged place!*

The barge plunged, and Anneshka's world flipped. She skidded down the deck, flailing. Her body slammed into the mast. It was at the wrong angle, tilting sideways. Anneshka clung on for dear life. Above her, the deck sloped like a mountain. Below, the wild water seethed. The river was waiting with open arms, but it wasn't a friendly invitation.

Anneshka couldn't hold on for much longer, feet dangling, fingers turning white. *That's the problem with masks*, said a voice in her skull. *If you wear them for too long, they get stuck.*

And, with that, Anneshka surrendered.

She fell into the wrestling waves.

CHAPTER 103

When Miro came to, he was at the bottom of the river with stones digging into his back. He should have been drowning, but, somehow, he wasn't *in* the water – although water rushed all around.

Miro turned his head to the side. A great liquid wall met his gaze and there were things moving within. A piece of fiddleweed whipped past. It was followed by a pebble and a fish. *There* went an anchor. *There* went a crab.

Miro rolled his head to the centre. A column of air rose above him, tunnelling up through the waves, capped by a blue ring of sky.

But this was impossible. How could there be a hole in the river?

There was silt between Miro's fingers and droplets of spray on his face and that was when he realised – he was inside a whirlpool, right at its core.

Miro scrunched up his eyes. This didn't make sense! Where had the whirlpool come from? And how had he got to its centre?

His nurse had told him tales about the lands beyond the

mountains. None of them had been as strange as this.

He didn't even understand why he was still alive. He thought he remembered being stabbed . . .

Then Miro became aware of something cold on his stomach. It was small and soft and wet. It was in the same place as where Surovetz's knife had gone in. Miro gritted his teeth, preparing for pain, as he propped himself up on his elbows. But the pain didn't come.

The cold thing on his belly was a newt. It was lying across Miro's wound, feet suckering on to his skin. Strangest of all, the newt was glowing . . . and Miro knew where he'd seen it before. It was the same one they'd rescued from Kazimira.

The newt unsuckered its toes – *pop, pop, pop*. Then it crawled off Miro's stomach, revealing a scar where Surovetz had stabbed him. The scar was shaped like a mouth, sealed shut.

Miro touched the new skin. It felt real enough. The cut on his arm had healed too. 'How did—?' he began, but he stopped because he knew. He knew what the little newt was.

Miro got to his feet, being careful not to touch the water that swirled on all sides. For he was in the eye of the whirlpool; the one safe place in this storm.

'It's you, isn't it?' said Miro with wonder.

The newt flicked its long tongue. Then it closed its eyes and went still. Miro could tell it was concentrating, although *on what* he wasn't sure. The light it emitted grew brighter, rising to an unnatural green. Only its outline was visible.

Miro stared at the fluorescent newt. It was small – about the length of his foot.

But this was no black-spotted salamander.

It healed wounds.

It moved rivers.

And that was when Miro knew for certain: he was in the company of a water dragon.

CHAPTER 104

'What is it?' asked Imogen, crawling forward. She peered through a gap between rocks.

'A yedleek,' replied Marie. 'I heard the other children talking about them, but this is the first one I've seen.'

The flame was coming from a figure, rising from the top of its head. It didn't seem to be in pain. It was shaped roughly like a human – as if someone had given a toddler a lump of clay and asked them to make a man. But this lump of clay was eight-feet tall, and its body was sculpted from stone.

'It must be searching for bodies,' said Marie.

Imogen's skin tingled with fear. 'What kind of bodies?' she whispered. The figure was lifting boulders and checking beneath each one, before tossing them aside like tin cans.

'Don't worry,' said Marie. 'Yedleek only eat grown-ups . . . and a few of the bigger boys and girls. Even the krootymoosh are afraid and avoid the deep parts of the mines.' Marie seemed to think for a moment. 'I suppose it's like the opposite of us eating veal. Yedleek like their meat *old*.'

Veal . . .? Imogen's head swam with pain. A stone must have

struck her during the rockfall. And there was a funny smell in the air, like a freshly lit match.

'But why are the yedleek here?' she asked.

'I think this is their home,' said Marie.

Imogen remembered what Yemni had told her. *Miners kept disappearing . . . There were tales of monsters that lived in the rock.* So this is what the adults were afraid of. This is why they put children here instead.

The yedleek turned. It must have heard the girls talking because it stared with smouldering eyes. Imogen drew back, but the yedleek didn't come any closer. It resumed its business, shifting rocks.

At least now Imogen could see her surroundings; the yedleek's flame cast enough light for that. The air was thick with dust and she could make out some shapes in the haze. There was a huge pile of rubble where the ceiling had collapsed. There was no way Imogen and Marie could follow the other children. The escape route was totally blocked. Their only option was to turn back.

'Do you remember the way to the Cosmos Cave?' asked Imogen, ignoring the pain in her head. 'You know? That place with all the glowflies?'

'I think so,' said Marie. 'There's clean water in that cave, and fish. We can try to catch one if we get hungry.'

Imogen almost smiled. She was still the older sister, but she was beginning to think that being older didn't mean very much. Perhaps she didn't have to keep her worry creatures secret . . . Perhaps she didn't *always* have to save the day.

'Why do I have this feeling,' said Imogen, 'like I've come all this way to rescue you – across mountains and lowlands and scrub – and now that I'm finally here, it's you who's rescuing me?'

The Cosmos Cave greeted the girls with its canopy of glowflies. There was a familiar face waiting for them – or rather, a familiar pair of wings. The shadow moth was perched on a stalagmite.

Imogen should have felt happy. She should have rushed to say 'hi'. But her head hurt each time she moved. She let herself sink to the ground.

The moth twirled its antennae.

'We need your help,' cried Marie. 'Please, show us the way out!'

The insect crawled down the stalagmite, opening and closing its wings. It was moving in a pattern, similar to the way it had marched across Branna and Zemko's kitchen table. But Zuby wasn't there to interpret and Imogen didn't know what the dance meant.

The moth fluttered up above Marie's head. It was flying towards the cave roof. 'Where are you going?' called Marie. 'We can't go up there!'

The shadow moth didn't seem to be listening. Imogen lost sight of it between the glowflies – a grey shimmer among blue stars.

'Why won't it help us?' cried Marie.

Imogen shook her head and the pain made little fireworks go off behind her eyes. *The moth didn't come to help*, she thought. *It came to say goodbye.*

CHAPTER 105

Anneshka plunged down through the cold fizzing water, down through the white foaming waves. Her costume was heavy, making her sink, so she tore off her headdress and kicked with her feet.

Off with the glittering breastplate.

Off with the face-net of pearls.

She fought, harder, fiercer.

Wrenched and rent.

I am not Queen Svitla, she thought, *I will not die for her crimes.* All around was the roar of the water, but, beneath it, she heard something else.

Thu-thud, thu-thud.

It was a sound that Anneshka remembered, a sound that she felt with her bones, yet there was no time for reminiscing. The river was dragging her down.

Anneshka snapped the belt from her waist.

All of it. Take all of it.

A gift for the waves.

She yanked the silver chain from her neck and gave one

final thrust up. Her head broke the surface, she drank in the air. 'I am – not Queen – Svitla!' she gasped.

Anneshka was light now. All she wore was her smock. It inflated around her like a jellyfish and she turned her breathless face to the clouds.

Thu-thud, thu-thud.

Surely . . . that couldn't be the Sertze Hora? It was coming from the water below.

And then Anneshka saw the whirlpool. A hole, not far from the spot where she swam. Anneshka started to panic. She didn't have much energy left.

The whirlpool reeled her in.

But there was a boat – just a small one – with a man rowing hard and fast.

'Help,' cried Anneshka.

The vortex reached for her toes. There was a girl's voice and the man kept on shouting. He was repeating the same single word. What did he want? Who were they? How could Anneshka get in their boat?

A hand grabbed Anneshka and heaved her aboard. She lay spreadeagled and gasping – as helpless as the day she was born. She rolled over and peered at her saviours. The man looked a lot like King Ctibor. The girl wore a dress made of bows. It was Princess Kazimira.

Anneshka touched her own face. No headdress. No face-net of pearls.

Pavla. That's what King Ctibor was shouting. *Pavla. Pavla.* The name of his daughter. Anneshka retched, and up came a bellyful of water. She managed a weak yellow smile.

'Pavla,' cried Ctibor. 'It's you!'

When Anneshka felt strong enough to sit, she leaned against the side of the boat. Kazimira was shivering and, for once, she was quiet.

Anneshka peered at the scene beyond. In the distance there were circular boats – tiny fishing craft. In the foreground was the island, or what was left of it. The earth had been swallowed by the river and the whirlpool was sucking things in.

The water tilted towards the whirlpool. If they were to escape, the little boat would have to travel uphill. But Ctibor was a surprisingly strong rower. He bared his teeth with each stroke of the oars. He was bright red, ferocious, determined.

There was someone else in the water. A man. He grabbed the edge of the boat. 'Hey!' the man shouted. 'It's me!'

Ctibor hesitated. 'Pavla . . . do you know him?'

Anneshka eyed Surovetz. She saw the wildness in his expression. The blood had been washed from his face.

'Come on!' he called. 'We're partners!'

But Anneshka had warned Surovetz not to fight the boy . . . Now everyone knew he was a krootymoosh. Everyone knew what he'd done – and Surovetz was no use to Anneshka.

She glanced at Ctibor. 'Daddy,' she whispered in her most

feeble voice, 'that's the man that kidnapped me. *That* is the Lord of the Krootymoosh.'

Ctibor's face puffed up like a blowfish. He got to his feet and the boat wobbled. Kazimira let out a whine. Ctibor freed an oar and Surovetz reached up, thinking he was about to be helped.

But Ctibor was done with rescuing. He brandished the oar like a weapon, raising it high above his head. 'Look away, girls,' he instructed.

Of course, neither girl did.

Ctibor brought the oar down. A great whoosh. A sickening crack. And Surovetz sank into the waves.

CHAPTER 106

Kazimira followed her father, King Ctibor, and her long-lost sister, Pavla, into Vodnislav Castle.

'There's been an uprising,' said the king to his servants. 'The river . . . the people. It got out of control . . . Prepare a hot bath for my daughters.' Then Ctibor turned his attention to Anneshka. 'Pavla, my plum cake, what happened in Valkahá? I was worried you wouldn't return!'

Kazimira could tell that her father was busy, so she took the opportunity to leave. She had seen Miroslav getting stabbed. She'd seen him go under the waves. And Ctibor had promised that if the boy died, Kazimira could have what she desired.

The princess stomped through the fortress, leaving a trail of river water in her wake. She knew she shouldn't be doing this alone, but her father was fussing over Pavla, and Kazimira had waited long enough.

She dismissed the skret at the entrance. She didn't want guards in her way. Then she burst into the guest chamber – the room where Miroslav had slept.

'Kitty, where are you?' said the princess. She had come to claim her prize.

Kazimira pushed the door shut behind her. The kitty was asleep on the floor. 'There you are!' shrieked Kazimira, and Konya opened one eye.

The snĕehoolark seemed to sense what was happening. She got to her feet and slunk under the bed, pressing her belly to the floor. Kazimira tried to follow. She crawled under the bedframe, reaching with one outstretched hand. 'You're MY kitty now,' she grunted.

But Konya shot out from hiding. She ran past Kazimira, quick as an eel. The princess grabbed her tail. '*Stooooop,*' shouted Kazimira as she was dragged across the room.

Konya bucked with her back legs, trying to shake the girl off. But Kazimira had been here before and, this time, she was not letting go. *This time* she was getting her kitty.

Konya shook her tail and the girl was tossed into the air. Room spinning – ribbon dress twirling – Kazimira landed on the wolf-cat's back. She was so surprised that she fell silent. She was facing the wrong way, but that didn't matter; she was riding the kitty!

Konya twisted and arched her back, but Kazimira sensed victory was near. She dug her fingers into the cat's fur and squeezed her legs very tight. Konya turned to the window.

'Good kitty,' said Kazimira, thinking the snĕehoolark was

about to give up. But Kazimira had severely underestimated Konya's desire to be free.

The sněehoolark bounded towards the window, clearing the sill with one leap. She smashed through the stained-glass panes. The princess and the sněehoolark were flying – out of the castle, in a great leaping arch. A rivergull swooped to avoid them.

And then their flight path curved down.

Kazimira was still facing backwards so she didn't see what lay ahead. She didn't see the river rushing closer. Didn't see Konya stretch out her front paws.

The water embraced the princess and, at last, she let go of the cat.

CHAPTER 107

Miro stood in the centre of the whirlpool. His wounds had healed and his heart was full of joy. The duel was over. He'd summoned the great water dragon – which was as powerful as it was small.

The little dragon stood by Miro's feet, continuing to glow bright green.

Miro stared at walls of water; at the things the dragon had caught. It was like the whole river was swirling about him, with all of its weeds and wonders on show.

An otter was riding the waves. An eel looked far less relaxed; it thrashed with its tail and snapped with its jaws as it was swept round and round.

But among all the feathers and the fish, broken oars and scraps of net, were some larger pieces of wreckage. Drowned people floated like driftwood.

Miro moved closer to the water. One of the bodies belonged to a queen. She wore a stiff beaded dress and her shoulders were clasped in metal. She'd been weighed down by her wealth, sunk by her silver.

The dead woman drifted aside and Miro saw another queen. Their faces were ghostly white. There was no life in their bodies, but the dragon made them dance. The river turned to the little creature's will and so did the people who'd drowned in its waters.

Bad queens, thought Miro. *They deserved it.* But he couldn't quite make himself believe . . . couldn't quite stop that creeping sense of horror.

Did bad rulers always have to die?

The dragon clearly thought so. It turned greener than an alchemist's workshop.

Two more queens appeared. The whirlpool drew them in. One queen had a silver centipede dangling over her face. Another wore jewels across her forehead. That made four in total.

Four dead queens waltzing round and round.

In the distance, where the water was murky, Miro noticed more shapes. The shapes had arms and legs. As the whirlpool carried them closer, he saw they were the bodies of men.

Bad men. Wicked men. Men who'd done evil – just like Miro's uncle. And, as the bodies drew nearer, Miro started checking their faces, looking for Drakomor's stare.

But the drowned men weren't related to Miro. Their mistakes were not his. Their bad thoughts, words and actions were nothing to do with him. They were krootymoosh; Miro could tell from their red cloaks. The men joined the dancing queens.

Miro glanced at the dragon. It had saved him. It had placed him at the centre of the whirlpool and healed his wounds. But why? Why had it decided to help?

Maybe Miro was a good king after all.

Surovetz's men tap-danced on the riverbed.

'I want to leave,' said Miro to the dragon. But the newt didn't respond. It was far too busy controlling the river and, was it Miro's imagination, or were the sides of the whirlpool closing in? He shuffled closer to the centre.

Something tapped Miro's shoulder and he turned to see Odlive, the sprite. She was on the other side of the great wall of water, swimming hard to stay still. Her tail was longer than Miro had expected and there was no fin at the end. Her scales were the colour of riverbed silt.

In one hand Odlive grasped the thick stem of a lily. The giant leaf bobbed on the surface, way above both of their heads. Miro could make out its dark ring against the sky.

'Why are you here?' he asked the river sprite. She thrust the stem his way, pushing it through the wall of water. The sides of the whirlpool were close now. One false move and Miro would dance with the dead.

Odlive was talking – moving her mouth – but Miro couldn't make out the words. 'I can't hear you,' he cried. He looked at the lily stem. It was covered in prickly hairs. Then he looked back at Odlive, at her watertight eyes. He'd trusted her this far . . .

Miro grasped the lily stalk.

'Hold on!' mouthed Odlive, before pulling back. And then the whirlpool closed.

Water hit Miro from all sides. He didn't see what happened to the dragon. The stem jerked forward and Miro was lifted up. Water rushed over his skin. A dead queen's hand batted his face. Then Miro was blinded by bubbles.

He gripped the stalk as he rocketed through clouds of fiddleweed and mud. He knew the lily pad was up there, so he started to climb the stem – moving one hand, then the other, fighting the whiplash current as it tore at his hair and his clothes.

Finally, Miro's head found the surface. He drew breath after spluttering breath. Brown water churned all around, but Miro held on to the lily pad. This was his lifeboat, his rubbery raft. He heaved himself on top of the leaf and lay face down, breathing hard.

When he had the energy to look over the leaf's rim, Miro saw that the river had burst its banks, flooding Mlok Island and the ground on either side. There were dozens of round boats being paddled nearby. They all bore Lowland folk, who cheered and waved when they saw him. 'Look! It's the Champion!' they called. Miro raised a tentative hand.

The water moved with relentless force, carrying him towards the city. The number of little boats dwindled. They were being paddled towards the shore, but Miro had no means of steering his craft. He went where the river wished.

Currents strained like muscles, tensing and slackening beneath the giant leaf. The lily pad slipped over the water, navigating each swell with ease. It was even bigger than the leaf he'd travelled on before.

Miro couldn't see Odlive or the dragon. He hoped that they were okay.

The river carried him through the outskirts of Vodnislav, where the buildings were wooden and small. He travelled under piers and bridges, but now the water had risen and Miro had to lie flat to avoid being knocked off the leaf.

Some of the fishing boats had broken free from their moorings and a waterwheel lay on its side. Bits of everyday life had been turned into surreal sculptures by the flood – a hatstand was suspended in a willow, a rocking chair lay in the reeds. Most of the townsfolk were too busy saving their belongings from waterlogged homes to notice Miro passing by on his oversized leaf.

As he was carried round a bend in the river, Vodnislav Castle came into view. It was crouched on the peninsula, above the water's reach. Ctibor's ancestors had known what they were doing when they built their house on high ground.

Miro felt the leaf rise beneath him, skating over a particularly big wave. He wanted to lie down and sleep. He'd been drenched and stabbed and saved, and he thought he'd seen just about everything, but nothing could prepare him for what he saw next.

Ctibor's fortress loomed before Miro. *There* was the land bridge. *There* were the castle's thick walls. And *there* – jumping out of a window – was a shape that Miro knew well.

'Konya!' he screamed as the sněehoolark hit the water.

Was that a girl on her back?

CHAPTER 108

Imogen didn't know how long she'd been sleeping when she heard Marie shriek. Wooziness washed over her as she scrambled to her feet. She could still feel a pain in her head, and there was rock dust and dried blood on her hands.

Marie was standing in the middle of the Cosmos Cave, but she wasn't shrieking with fear. She was jumping and whooping with joy. When Imogen looked up, she saw why.

There was a rope hanging down between glowflies – a rope with a man on the end.

Imogen stumbled closer, head pounding. She gripped a stalagmite for support. The man was being lowered to the cave floor. He wore a Lowland jacket and his trousers were tucked into his boots. There was a pack on his back with supplies, tightly fastened. He looked like some kind of explorer.

Imogen pulled her sister back. Better to stay clear until they knew what he wanted, but Marie struggled free. The man's feet touched the ground and he stepped out of the rope loop. Imogen saw a fuzzy beard and small twinkly eyes . . .

But that was no explorer. Marie rushed at the man,

throwing her arms round his waist.

It was Mark.

Mark, their mum's boyfriend.

Mark I-hate-children Ashby.

Imogen couldn't believe it. How did he find them? Where did he get those clothes? She never thought he'd come all this way . . .

'Hello, girls,' said Mark, and he knelt, returning Marie's hug.

Imogen opened her mouth. She didn't know where to begin. 'How did – why did—'

'A little moth said you might be here,' said Mark. The shadow moth fluttered into view, circling the rope and landing on Mark's shoulder.

Imogen must have looked surprised because Mark went on, 'I know, I know. I said I don't believe in magic moths – Imogen, are you okay? There's blood on your—'

'I'm fine,' cut in Imogen. 'I just don't understand how you found us.'

Mark smiled. It wasn't a full-on grin. He seemed nervous. 'Perla's parents got a letter. Their friends said they had you – said you were staying in their house. But by the time we arrived, you'd disappeared.'

Branna said she was going to write, thought Imogen.

'I was in Valkahá when the moth found me,' said Mark. 'I'd almost given up hope, but the moth looked just like the one you'd described – big antennae, grey wings. I thought to myself, *Imogen says those moths are intelligent. She says they can show hidden things . . . I'd better give it a go.*'

Give it a go? Imogen did not associate those words with her mum's boyfriend.

'You followed the moth!' piped Marie. She was beaming.

'The moth took me out of the city, and there was this young guy with white-blond hair. He said he was waiting for some children.'

'Yemni,' whispered Imogen, wincing as her head throbbed again.

'We followed the moth together,' continued Mark. 'It led us to a hole in the scrublands. It didn't look very inviting, but the moth was insistent. Kept flapping in my face.'

The shadow moth was still resting on Mark's shoulder, wings folded over its back.

'I gave the young man my rope and he lowered me into the pit . . . I hope we can trust him.' Mark glanced up. The top of the rope was engulfed in darkness, but there must have been a hole somewhere in the cave roof – an opening that led to the light.

'I'm so glad I've found you!' Mark said to the girls. 'You've no idea how frightened I've been.'

Imogen couldn't process his story. Her mind kept circling back on the same thought. 'You came all this way, for us?'

Mark hesitated. He rubbed his hand across his beard. 'Look,' he said. 'I know I've got things wrong in the past . . . I'm not your father. I never will be. I just want to make your mum happy. And I want to make sure that you're safe.'

Imogen could smell something funny. It was the smell of birthdays, of blown-out candles. The pain in her head was intense. 'Mark,' she said, 'can we go home?'

'Yes,' cried Marie. 'Let's go back!'

Mark smiled – a proper smile this time. 'Of course. That's why I came.'

Chapter 109

Imogen took hold of the rope that hung from the cave's ceiling and stepped into the loop at the end. It was like sitting on the world's longest swing.

Marie perched on Imogen's lap, facing the other way. She clasped her arms and legs round her sister. Imogen held the rope for them both.

Mark gave it three sharp tugs. The moth circled upwards. The rope tightened and Imogen's toes left the floor.

'What about you?' Marie called to Mark. 'How are you going to leave?'

'There's only one man pulling the rope,' said Mark. 'He can't take us all at once. Just make sure you throw it back when you're done. I don't fancy staying down here!'

Imogen caught another waft of burning. She glanced over her shoulder, looking for the source of the smell.

'Don't let go,' warned Mark. The girls were several metres above his head.

Imogen could see the underground stream coursing around stalagmites. She could see the holes in the rock where the kidnapped children had lived and there, in the cave wall, she saw something else – something moving.

'Erm, Mark,' called Imogen, 'what's that, behind you?'

The rope continued to rise. The girls were high now, feet dangling.

The thing in the cave wall twisted and writhed, like a person trapped under a sheet. A rough hand reached from the stone.

'What the—' Mark stumbled backwards.

And Imogen recognised the smell. It was the scent of burnt matches – of smoke. The hand was followed by a stone-sculpted arm.

'It's a yedleek!' cried Marie. 'Mark, don't let it catch you!'

But the girls were too high to help. The underground stream was a thin silver ribbon and Mark was as small as a mouse. Imogen tugged at the rope, hoping to make it stop, but Yemni kept pulling and the girls rose up.

Two arms stuck out of the rockface. The yedleek was clawing with a slow but unwavering desperation. *There* was its lump-of-clay head. *There* was the pit it had for a mouth.

Its eyes burned red when they turned towards Mark, and Imogen's heart froze with horror. *Yedleek only eat grown-ups.* She remembered Marie's words well.

Imogen tried to think. There must be something they could do, but her headache made thinking painful, and if the girls

slipped from this height they would die. 'Don't squirm, Marie,' she cried.

'But Mark's going to get eaten!' sobbed Marie.

The sisters were near the cave roof. Glowflies drifted all about, and finally Imogen could make out an opening – a hole with the rope threaded through.

She looked down past her feet. 'Run, Mark!' she screamed. The yedleek was out of the rock. It stood still and its skull ignited, shooting fire like a blowtorch from its head. 'Run!' cried Imogen. 'RUN!'

The monster advanced. Its movements were sluggish as lava, but more yedleek were surfacing from the stone. Soon, Mark would be surrounded.

Marie clung to Imogen, shrieking. Imogen clung to the rope.

Mark stood very still and looked up at the girls. 'Tell Cathy I love her,' he called. His face was a pale white dot. It was the last thing Imogen saw before she was pulled through the hole in the roof.

CHAPTER 110

Plants grew from the walls of the tunnel. Roots knuckled deep into rock. Leaves batted Imogen, like a pagan blessing, as she travelled towards the light.

Yemni drew the girls from the ground. Marie was sobbing and someone kept screaming, 'Run!' It took Imogen a few seconds to realise the voice was her own.

Yemni set the girls down, at a little distance from the hole. Then he prised the rope from Imogen's fingers. Her hands had made claws round the line.

'Please, Imogen,' said Yemni. 'I need it.'

He passed the rope back into the pit. He had the other end tied to a boulder. 'The yedleek,' said Imogen weakly.

Yemni nodded. He understood.

Imogen's head was throbbing with pain. Her eyes burned in the light. She peered into the dark pit as Yemni lowered the rope. 'It's hit the cave floor,' he muttered, 'but I can't feel his weight.'

Mark had come all this way – all this way to make sure they were safe.

Yemni knelt and shouted to Mark down the hole. 'Hey! Can you hear me? Take hold of the rope!'

But there came no reply.

Imogen was dazed and drained. She didn't know what to say. She stared at Yemni and her sister. She stared at the space all about. The Scrublands were so blindingly bright and there, in the distance, before the bulk of the city, was a long line of children. They were traipsing across the scrub. 'Perla,' whispered Imogen. 'They made it.'

The sun was high and the sky was boundless. The moth, for once, stuck around. Bees buzzed in the bushes and flowers bloomed as if all was right with the world. But Mark had risked everything.

'Why won't he take the rope?' sobbed Marie.

Imogen held her tight. She remembered Ochi's words from many nights ago: *Fear the men of burning light. Fear their molten forms. Fear their deep volcano eyes and yawning, hungry jaws.*

It was a long time before Yemni stopped shouting down the pit. He sat heavy on the earth. 'I'm sorry about your father,' he said to the girls.

He's not my father, thought Imogen. Yet that was not what she said. Because what did it matter any more? She opened her mouth, but there was nothing worth saying.

Instead, she started to cry.

CHAPTER 111

Princess Kazimira had vanished, snatched from the very castle she called home. Servants checked every chamber. Skret looked under tables and chairs.

'I want Kazimira found,' yelled King Ctibor.

But nobody thought to look downstream.

Miro took hold of Kazimira by a giant bow on her back. He lugged her out of the water and dragged her on to the leaf. Konya scrambled up behind her and the lily pad lurched. For a horrible moment, Miro thought they were too heavy, but the leaf stabilised.

'BAD KITTY!' screamed Kazimira.

Miro was taken aback. He had no idea how the princess came to be riding a snĕehoolark backwards, jumping from her own father's castle, but he was pretty sure it was her fault, not Konya's.

Kazimira was on all fours, dress dripping. She was ranting and raving at the world. If Imogen had been there, she might have given her a shake. Perla would have dealt a hard stare.

But Miro waited for the girl to quieten. He knew what it

was like to be alone – to want company so badly that, when a friend comes along, you seize them with both hands and squeeze tight. 'Are you all right?' he asked the princess.

Kazimira blinked at the boy. Her ribbons and bows sagged with water. Her hair was stuck to her face. 'You're supposed to be dead,' she replied.

Miro couldn't help being offended. It was like she was disappointed. 'If you're not going to be nice, you can get off my leaf.'

Kazimira looked at the water flowing fast on every side. She crawled to the centre of the lily pad. 'I'm nice,' she said.

Konya sat next to Miro. She looked half her normal size with her fur sopping wet and her whiskers drooping. Her body language shouted, 'Don't touch.'

And so the three unlikely companions were carried out of Vodnislav on a leaf. Miro couldn't wait to tell Imogen and Perla that the newt they'd saved was the dragon. Would either girl believe him? Did Miro even believe himself?

He wondered how his friends were doing. There was no way for him to find out. The Scrublands were west of Vodnislav, and although Miro's geography was hazy, he was sure this river went somewhere else.

'I want to go back to my daddy,' whined Kazimira. But the river was running wild, chopping and swirling, still full of the dragon's power. There was no way to make the leaf stop.

The lily pad swept on and Miro spotted the Ring of Yasanay, high on a hill. He only saw it for a second before it zipped out of sight.

'Where are you taking me?' cried the princess.

Normally Miro would have been upset to be asked a question like that. He hadn't kidnapped Kazimira. The girl had kidnapped herself. But Miro was curiously happy. He felt lighter than he'd felt for months. He'd unmasked the krootymoosh. He'd summoned the water dragon. He'd stood in a whirlpool and lived.

Miro didn't have to be a champion. He didn't even have to be king. From now on, Miro decided, he was going to focus on being a child.

Kazimira eyeballed Konya. The princess's journey out of the castle window seemed to have cured her desire to touch, but her snĕehoolark fascination had not quite disappeared.

Konya pretended not to notice the princess, although she kept one ear tilted her way. The giant cat turned to the horizon ahead of them. She lifted her nose and sniffed the wind.

There were strange mountains in the distance, so faint they almost weren't there. An idea floated towards Miro. He knew he should return to Yaroslav . . . but he was tired of doing what he *should*, tired of worrying about what 'his people' might say.

Miro glanced at Kazimira, heart skipping with excitement.

'I know where I'm going,' he cried. 'I'm going to the Nameless Mountains!'

'Why would you want to go there?' sneered the princess.

'Because I can,' said Miro. He was so happy, almost light-headed. Perhaps it was the thought of a new adventure. Perhaps it was the lack of food.

'My mother was from the Nameless Mountains,' he continued. 'That's where her family live. I think this river goes in that direction . . . if I follow it for long enough.'

'I don't want to go to the Nameless Mountains,' cried Kazimira. 'Make the river stop!'

Miro smiled at the mountains on the horizon. He remembered Odlive's advice. 'Sometimes,' he said to his sodden companion, 'it's better to go with the flow.'

CHAPTER 112

The dragon swam with the current. It wriggled from side to side, slipping between driftwood and fiddleweed. The river was thick with mud, but that was no problem. The dragon knew where to go.

There was a hole in the side of the river – the mouth of an underwater cave. The dragon floated in. The water was clear in here, sheltered from the chaos of the flood. And there, at the far side of the grotto, huddled around a blue stone, were ten precious eggs.

Ten baby dragons were packed tight inside their transparent wobbly sacks. The dragon fanned the eggs with its tail, ensuring they got enough oxygen. Then it turned its attention to the Sertze Voda. The stone was fantastic blue. *Thu-thud, thu-thud.* Each pulse made a shockwave.

In a few hours, the Sertze Voda would be calm. The dragon lay down on top of it, suckering on to the magic stone's strength. It was time for the dragon to recharge. After all, it had been quite a day.

CHAPTER 113

The last kidnapped child stepped out of the mines. Sunlight broke over his head and he blinked, stunned by the brightness, dizzied by the sharp-winged birds.

It had been a long time since he'd felt sun on his face. The sky seemed impossibly big. The horizon, an invitation to roam. The child thought of his parents. He could remember their voices and the warmth of their smiles. He tucked his hands in his pockets and walked east.

And so the missing children returned. Luki and his sister set out for home. All across the land of hills and rivers, families were made whole again.

Perla's father, Michal, was in Valkahá. He'd travelled across the Lowlands and the Scrublands with Mark. His face lit up when he spotted his daughter.

But Perla was not alone. 'Papa?' said Tomil, stepping out of the shadows.

Michal's jaw went slack. He reached for his children and there weren't any words. Father hugged daughter and son.

Then Michal held Tomil at arm's length, looking him over

in disbelief. 'My boy,' he said. 'I should have known you'd come back. How did you manage to escape?'

Tomil's eyes darted to his sister. There was a mischievous look on his face. 'It was Perla,' said Tomil. 'She saved us. And she did it all with a map.'

The next day, Imogen and Marie joined them. Greetings and stories were exchanged. Imogen tried to explain about Mark and found her words going too fast.

She stopped mid-sentence, suddenly remembering Mark's upturned face – small and far away. Yedleek were closing in on all sides but Mark hadn't taken his eyes off the girls.

Marie filled the silence that followed. 'He didn't take the rope,' she whispered.

'Your father was a brave man,' said Michal. 'He loved you both very much.'

Imogen nodded her head. Mark was brave. It was true.

'Why don't you travel with us?' suggested Perla.

Imogen hesitated. It felt wrong leaving Valkahá without Mark, but what choice did they have? They'd waited for hours by the pothole. Imogen had called his name until her voice was a croak. Then, just before the sun set, Yemni had ushered the sisters into the city and tended the wound on Imogen's head.

'But what if Mark survived?' Marie had asked late that night.

'The yedleek are eaters,' replied Yemni. 'They don't let grown-ups go.'

So Imogen and Marie joined Perla, Tomil and Michal. Together, they left Valkahá. They only had three horses between them and progress across the Scrublands was slow. They stopped when they needed food or shelter.

The shadow moth journeyed on Imogen's shoulder. It had stayed close, ever since the yedleek attack. It seemed to be determined to escort the sisters back home. That was good. Imogen would need the moth's help if she was to open the door in the tree.

Whenever they met travellers going in the other direction, Imogen asked if they'd seen the duel. Everyone had a different story to tell. It was as if they'd witnessed six different fights. Some people said the krootymoosh had won. Others said victory was the boy's. He'd shown that the beast was a human. He'd made the people rise up . . .

But no one knew what had happened to Miro. He'd been injured, that much was clear.

'He must be alive,' cried Marie. Imogen had to agree; she didn't think she could take any more bad news.

They'd been trekking for several days when they came to the Bezuz River. It cut between the Lowland hills. Imogen stooped to refill her waterskin and the shadow moth fluttered nearby.

'Hello, fingerlings,' said a voice from the river.

Imogen looked up. It was Odlive. She was lounging on a rock

with her tail flopped over the edge. 'I bring news of your friend.'

'Miro!' cried Imogen. 'He's alive?'

'Of course,' said Odlive. She started brushing her hair with a fish skeleton, running its ribcage through the stands. She was trying to look indifferent, Imogen could tell, but her eyes kept flicking back, eager to see Imogen's reaction.

'Imogen,' squeaked Marie, running over, 'there's a mermaid in the river!'

'I'm not a mermaid,' snapped Odlive, and her watertight nostrils flared. 'Do I look like a fairy-tale creature? Prissy little things, always singing.'

Imogen noted Odlive's sharp teeth. She noted her sludge-coloured tail. Oval scales were embedded in her skin and covered in a thin layer of slime. 'No,' said Imogen. 'You don't look like a mermaid.'

'Sorry,' said Marie. 'I didn't mean to be rude . . . Did you say you'd seen Miro? Is he okay?'

Odlive tossed her fishbone comb into the water. 'Yes,' she said. 'He is fine. He's with the big cat and a small shouty girl.'

Perla was at the riverside now, with Tomil hot on her heels. 'Do you mean Konya?' asked Perla. 'You've seen my snĕehoolark?'

'Yes,' snapped Odlive. 'Everyone's fine. Everyone's breathing and splashing and laying eggs. If you'll let me finish, I was going to tell you—'

'Hey!' called Michal, running towards them. 'Stay back from

the water. River sprites are dangerous!'

Imogen was reminded of Mark, who'd said something similar. She pushed the memory down, deep down. She didn't want to think of Mark now.

'It's okay, Papa,' said Perla. 'We know this river sprite.'

'It doesn't matter if you know her! Sprites drown children for fun!' Michal tried to pull his daughter away, but she struggled free from his grip.

'Papa!' cried Perla. 'I've come all this way on my own. Please . . . can't you trust me on this?'

Michal's left eye twitched. 'Okay,' he said, 'but if she comes any closer . . .'

The children turned back to the sprite. 'Please, Odlive,' said Imogen. 'Tell us what you saw.'

So Odlive described the duel. She told them how Miro had been injured, how he'd summoned the dragon and escaped on a leaf.

'Hang on a minute,' said Imogen. 'You're saying the newt we saved from Kazimira – the one she'd got dressed as a doll – is a water dragon?'

Odlive shrugged. 'Why not?'

'Aren't dragons supposed to be . . . big?'

'Dragons are not *supposed* to be anything,' said the sprite. 'Dragons are like humans and fish and flies. Dragons just *are*.'

'I don't understand,' whispered Perla. 'That newt couldn't save itself from Kazimira . . . How did it make a whirlpool?'

'The water dragon is tied to the Sertze Voda,' said the sprite. 'It draws its strength from the jewel, but the stone is not kept in the castle. When you met the dragon, its powers were worn down.'

Marie poked her head between Imogen and Perla. 'What's a Sertze Voda?' she asked.

'The heart of the river,' said Tomil. 'Nobody's seen it for centuries . . . not that we haven't tried.'

'And the fishermen talk of it often enough,' put in Michal.

All this time, the shadow moth stayed close to the children. Perhaps it sensed that Odlive had a long sticky tongue and a taste for flying insects.

Perla looked at the sprite through her lashes. It was hard for her to meet Odlive's gaze, but she seemed determined to ask this question. 'Where are Miro and Konya now?'

'Far away from Vodnislav,' replied Odlive. 'Last time I saw them, they were travelling east.' She started sliding off her rock, retreating tail-first into the water. 'I expect they'll be near the flooded meadows. Who knows where they'll end up.'

Perla swallowed hard. That wasn't the answer she'd wanted.

'But didn't Miro say where he was going?' cried Imogen. 'Can't you make the lily pad stop?'

'I did hear him mention some mountains,' replied Odlive. 'But I don't travel that far.' Her head bobbed above the water, algae-green hair spread wide.

'Why would Miro want to go to the mountains?' said Marie.

Imogen turned to put this question to the sprite, but Odlive had disappeared. There was only a ripple where she'd been.

CHAPTER 114

Days later, when the children returned to Perla's hometown, her parents threw a party at the Water House. There was elderflower cordial and baked apples, music, and games with boats. They even made a bonfire by the river.

Perla shone with happiness. Her parents wouldn't let her or Tomil out of their sight, but that was okay. The siblings had a lot to catch up on.

Imogen had never seen her friend so chatty. Perla was sitting by the river with Tomil, bare toes skimming the water. '. . . And then we pretended that Konya ate the newt,' she was saying, eyes sparkling.

It was only once, when Tomil went for more food, that Imogen caught Perla looking sad.

'I think she misses her cat,' said Marie. 'I met it when I was here with Anneshka. They used to do everything together. Perla even let it sleep in her bed.'

'I know,' said Imogen, smiling.

Imogen and Marie sat on the edge of the party, where the

firelight faded to black. They watched the Lowlanders dance and sing. There was joy all around – long-lost parents and newly found children. The town had many reasons to celebrate.

But Imogen and Marie were subdued. They were happy for their friends, yet they couldn't quite bring themselves to join in. Imogen's mind kept returning to Mark. He'd travelled all that way, just for them . . . and now he'd been eaten by rock monsters. How would she explain that to Mum?

The shadow moth sat on Marie's lap, cleaning its feathered antennae. It was ready to take the sisters back home. They'd leave for the Kolsaney Forests in the morning. Perla's mum had arranged a guide to make sure the journey would be safe. But Imogen felt a little sick each time she remembered they'd be going without Mark.

As night drew in and the bonfire burned low, the party moved into the tavern. Perla's mother opened jars of sweet pickled trout and served it with bread and soft cheese. Perla's father poured a long row of beers.

The children took a table in the corner. Tomil brought out a plate of fruit-stuffed dumplings covered in sugar and soured cream.

Marie ate hers with sticky fingers. Imogen tried to gobble one whole. Perla cut hers into neat halves, revealing the apricots inside. Tomil demolished one after another. He was like a dumpling bulldozer.

I suppose, thought Imogen, *he didn't have any dumplings in the mines.*

The shadow moth settled on the side of her plate and sucked up the apricot juice. For a moment, Imogen almost forgot about Mark.

'Is this how you celebrate back home?' asked Perla.

'Kind of,' said Imogen. 'Except we don't really have bonfires and Mum would probably make a giant cake.'

'What, no dumplings?' Tomil looked horrified.

But Imogen's reply was cut short. The tavern door burst open and a figure stood outside. Every head turned in the stranger's direction.

'Hello?' said Michal. He spoke the word like a question.

The stranger stepped over the threshold. He walked with a slight limp and Imogen felt a shiver run up her spine. It spread across her scalp like cold fingers.

'Please, come inside,' continued Perla's dad.

Nobody else said a word. The stranger stepped into the tavern. He put one arm on the wall, as if he was about to collapse.

When Imogen saw his face, she felt like the blood had drained from her body.

No.

It couldn't be.

It was.

'Mark!' screamed Marie and she scrambled across the table, knocking plates with her knees. The man looked weary beyond sleep, old beyond his years. But he smiled when he saw Marie. Imogen followed at a little distance. She didn't know why she felt awkward. She thought she was past all of that.

'Imogen,' said Mark, fixing his eyes on her face. 'It's good to see you too.'

Imogen made herself give him a hug. He smelled like charcoal and fire. But he felt like flesh and blood.

'We thought you'd been eaten!' squeaked Marie. 'We thought the yedleek got you!'

'So did I,' said Mark.

Imogen was *so* relieved to see him. She couldn't quite process it, couldn't find the right words. 'How did you escape?' she asked.

'Enough questions,' said Michal, forcing his way through the crowd. 'Can't you see the man's exhausted?' He helped Mark across the room towards a high-backed chair. Imogen and Marie gathered on either side.

The shadow moth fluttered near Mark's head, but it didn't land on his body. Instead, it perched on the edge of the chair. It opened and closed its wings. Imogen recognised that movement. It meant the moth was thinking. She was thinking too.

'We didn't mean to leave you,' mumbled Imogen, feeling a

stab of guilt. 'Yemni said there was no hope.' She didn't want Mark imagining they'd done it on purpose – that she'd wanted to leave him behind. Because she didn't. Not any more.

'It's okay, Imogen,' said Mark. He sat back in the chair and closed his eyes. 'You did the right thing. I just need a good night's rest. We'll leave first thing in the morning.'

CHAPTER 115

A sense of shame settled on Valkahá, cold and quiet as snow. From judges and priests to playwrights and servants, now they all knew the truth about the mines.

Some of them wondered in private why they hadn't worked it out for themselves. Where did they think the new silver had come from? Perhaps they should have asked more questions and trusted a little bit less.

Others said that was ridiculous. They couldn't possibly have known.

Either way, the fashion for big silver headdresses disappeared almost overnight. Those ornate lumps of metal, inspired by the queens, were no longer paraded in the streets. As the landlady of the Courtyard Inn explained, 'They just don't look right any more.'

For many noble families, the kidnap of Lowland children was not news. Indeed, it was their sons who'd done the kidnapping, their coffers that had been the most generously lined. Some of the nobles fled the Scrublands, taking what riches they could. Other stayed and lay low, hoping that whoever came next would be in need of a little silver . . . hoping they'd be willing to forget . . .

For now, the five queens' palace lay empty. No footsteps echoed across the hall. The people who had feasted there every night stayed away. The minstrels and courtiers disappeared.

And even though the hall was plated in silver, it seemed to shine greasy and thick. No amount of light – natural or otherwise – could cast the shadows from that place.

Nobody in Valkahá dared claim the thrones. The city was holding its breath. It wouldn't be long before other kingdoms heard that the palace was without any rulers. How loyal would Valkahá's old trading partners be when the news reached their ears?

Many miles east of the Scrublands, Anneshka lay in a hot bath. She was staying in King Ctibor's castle, pretending to be Pavla again. She'd started taking baths every day to get some quiet time to think.

The bathwater was silky with birch oil. Anneshka sank deeper and steam cloaked her head.

Valkahá was not the greatest kingdom. Of that, she was sure. She'd seen the queens drown under their silver. Their wealth hadn't helped in the end.

Anneshka remembered the water all around her, the weight of her headdress and robes. She gripped the edge of the bathtub. She didn't want to go under again.

At least Miroslav Krishnov was dead. Anneshka hated the boy. He'd always seemed to appear just before things went wrong. If he hadn't pulled off that helmet—

But there was no point holding on to regrets. The greatest kingdom must be somewhere else. Anneshka just needed to work out one thing . . . what was 'greatness'? What did that word really mean?

It wasn't a dragon.

Nor was it silver.

Petals floated at the end of the bath and Anneshka crushed them one by one with her toes.

I'm from another world. That's what Marie had said.

Anneshka sat up too fast, and water slopped out of the tub. What if she'd got it all wrong? What if Marie had been sent to her, not as a servant, but a sign?

Anneshka cursed her stupidity. All these weeks, she'd been thinking too small. This kingdom or that kingdom. What did it matter? The realms were all much the same.

But another world?

That was true greatness.

Who knew what wonders it held! Marie had said that the queen in her world had very little power . . . But perhaps Marie's world was great in other ways . . . in ways that Anneshka did not yet understand, in ways that she couldn't imagine.

Perhaps, thought Anneshka, *I could be someone else.* She let the water close over her head, resurfacing a few seconds later.

The stars had sent Marie to open her eyes, and Anneshka was looking at last. She could see the possibilities spread before her – the possibilities of ruling other worlds.

CHAPTER 116

Imogen, Marie and Mark stood in the Kolsaney Forests before a large tree. There was a door in the trunk – half hidden by ferns and brambles that must have grown since the girls had come through.

'So, this is it,' said Mark. 'Time for home.'

The shadow moth flew to the door. It had travelled with them across the mountains – always keeping ahead, showing them which way to go.

'Do you still have the pictures?' asked Marie. Imogen couldn't think what Marie meant. 'You know, the photos you took on Mum's phone. You wanted to prove that Yaroslav exists.'

Imogen put her hand in her pocket. There was no phone. She didn't even remember where she'd last had it. This adventure had stopped being about evidence a very long time ago.

'Oh,' said Imogen, 'I don't think that matters . . .'

A flock of velecours padded through the trees. Imogen could see their feathers against the green of the forest. A glimmer of purple. A flash of pink. They weren't very subtle birds.

The moth made its way to the door's handle. It folded its

wings across its back. Then it wriggled through the keyhole and the lock clicked.

Mark nudged the ferns and brambles aside. He pulled the door open wide. Although it was daytime in the forest, it was gloomy on the other side of the door. Mark looked at the girls. 'After you.'

Imogen and Marie led the way through the gardens. Mark followed, a little way back. It was dark and cold, and the ground was laced with frost. Imogen shivered in her Lowland clothes. She wasn't dressed for winter.

The sisters and Mark crossed the river, going slowly over the fallen tree trunk. Imogen could see a light on in the Haberdash Mansion. Mrs H must be getting ready for bed. There was light in the garden too. At first, Imogen thought it was Christmas lights, but too much time had passed for that . . . The light in the garden looked more like a torch. As they got closer, Imogen could see it was coming from inside a tent.

Imogen held Marie back and pointed.

'What is it?' mouthed Marie.

'I don't know,' whispered Imogen. 'Perhaps it's the police. Let's go and see.'

The tent was under the boughs of a tree. Imogen had only ever been camping in the summer. She didn't fancy it now. Not when the dew was freezing. Not when the ground was so hard.

A shadow shifted inside the tent. It was human, that much was clear. The tent was large enough for a family, but there was only one figure within. There were things stacked up – maybe books – and what was that in the corner? It looked like the silhouette of a telescope.

'Mark,' hissed Imogen, 'you go first.' She thought it'd be better if they didn't appear all at once. She was beginning to think that the figure in the tent was up to something very odd.

The sisters waited in the darkness. Mark approached the encampment alone.

The person-shaped shadow moved in the tent. A zip opened and a woman stepped out. She was wearing a headtorch, but she didn't look up. Imogen knew her in an instant. The woman was wrapped in a big winter coat and her gloved hands clutched a mug and a flask. Her hair was scraped back from her face and she looked a little tired, a little cold.

It was Mum. Imogen wanted to rush at her, but she hesitated. *Let Mark go first*, she thought. *Don't want to give Mum a heart attack.*

Mum was pouring coffee from her flask, frowning with concentration. She must have heard Mark's footsteps, but she didn't glance up. 'No photos,' she said. 'I'm not here to fill your papers. Isn't it a bit late for all that?'

'Cathy,' said Mark. 'It's me.'

Mum looked up. How strange Mark must have seemed. His

481

face was half masked in beard. His body was leaner than before. And as for his clothes . . . no suit. No shirt. No more squeaky shoes. He wore a Lowland jacket, loose trousers, leather boots.

Perhaps Mum wouldn't recognise him. Perhaps there was none of the original Mark left.

Mum froze, flask in hand. It kept pouring and coffee overflowed. Hot liquid slopped over Mum's fingers. She cursed and dropped the mug in the grass.

'Mark?' For a second, Imogen thought Mum would retreat, but no. She took a faltering step. 'Where the hell have you been?' she demanded.

Mark flinched. It was a question with more anger than love. Now it was his turn to hesitate. *Go on*, Imogen willed him. *Speak.*

'I've been with the children,' croaked Mark.

Mum's eyes darted left and right and Marie rushed out from hiding. 'Mummy!' she cried.

Mum raised a hand to her mouth as Marie went hurtling towards her.

She threw her flask aside and gathered Marie in her arms, picking her up as if she was still small. Imogen watched from afar. 'What about your sister?' asked Mum. 'Where is she?'

Marie pointed to the shadows. Imogen stepped into view and Mum shrieked. Imogen ran, wordless. She flew towards her mum and they hugged for a very long time.

'Where have you been?' sobbed Mum. She was holding

Imogen so tight it hurt.

Imogen pulled back a little. 'I'm sorry,' she said. 'I'm so sorry we left.'

'But where did you go? And why? Are you . . . are you okay?'

Imogen bit her lip. A pair of worry creatures were sitting on the branch of a tree. *It's your fault*, they said in a chorus. *It's your fault your mum is sad.*

'I wanted to show you that Yaroslav's real,' whispered Imogen.

Mum looked concerned and, in spite of herself, Imogen felt that old frustration – that desire to be believed, to make her mum *see*.

But Mum was listening.

'I wanted to take some photos.' Imogen looked at her toes. She scuffed the frozen grass with her boots. 'I wanted to gather . . . evidence.'

'I've been gathering evidence too,' said Mum. She gestured at the tent.

Imogen could see through the open-zip door. The tent was full of books and old crisp packets. There was a camera with a long nose. There was even an illustrated chart of moths.

What had Mum been doing out here? Mum didn't like insects. Mum didn't eat crisps.

'I've been studying your moth,' said Mum. 'I've been trying to learn about the door in the tree.' Imogen's guilt swirled with pride. Had her mum become some kind of moth expert? Was *that* her fault too?

'Your moth appeared in the kitchen,' said Mum. 'It did this incredible dance.'

Imogen remembered her message, the one she'd asked the shadow moth to deliver, telling Mum she was okay.

'It was beautiful,' said Mum. 'I tried to record the moth's movements, but I'm not sure I captured it all.' She fumbled in the tent for a notebook and flicked to the very first page. There were arrows going in different directions, like a mind map without any words. It looked curiously scientific.

'I didn't know what the dance meant,' said Mum, 'but I got this feeling, I can't explain why, that everything was going to be all right. After that, I took things into my own hands. The police weren't interested in the movements of moths. I think my therapist was a little concerned.'

'Therapist?' asked Marie and she peeped over the notebook.

'Yes, I've been seeing someone too,' said Mum, as if it wasn't a big deal, as if people went for therapy every day.

Imogen glanced at her worry creatures. Maybe people did . . .?

But something had happened to Mum. She was talking so fast that she was running out of breath. She wasn't just relieved to have them home. She was something else too . . .

Excited? Yes, that was it! Mum was excited about moths.

'After the visit from the shadow moth, I set up camp here,' explained Mum. 'Mrs Haberdash gave me special permission, and I've been coming every night after work. Sometimes Grandma joins me. Mrs H is still worried about the monster. She makes me keep her old rifle in the tent.'

Imogen's jaw dropped, just a little. Her mum had some kind of gun?

'I've been trying to study this place – the stars, the moths, the trees.' Mum gestured at the telescope behind her. 'I sold a few things to buy equipment . . . I knew that you girls love this garden. I knew there was something going on and I thought, perhaps, if I could just understand, if I just knew enough—' Her words slowed. 'I thought it might help bring you home.'

Imogen wasn't sure what to say. She'd never felt so many emotions. Guilt and pride, excitement and love. Her insides were like a big 'feeling' soup.

'We took photos of the magic world,' said Marie. 'But your phone got sort of lost.'

'It's okay,' said Mum. 'You're back. Nothing else matters.'

'But you believe us?' asked Marie. 'You believe the other world exists?'

Mum hesitated.

'I know what you're thinking,' said Mark. He'd been so quiet that Imogen had almost forgotten he was there. 'It doesn't make any sense. Moths opening doors. Forests that fit inside trees. It's against the laws of physics.'

Imogen took a sharp breath. Was Mark going to betray

them? After everything they'd been through? She couldn't make out his expression in the dark.

'But it's real, Cathy,' he said. 'I've seen it.'

Imogen let her breath go.

'And, Cathy,' said Mark, shifting on his feet, 'I'm sorry about our fight. I didn't mean the things I said.'

Imogen had almost forgotten what Mark had told her in the mountains – about how he'd argued with Mum on the night they'd left the hotel. That was why he'd still been awake and sitting alone in the bar. That was why he saw them sneak out.

'You were right,' Mark continued. 'About all of it. You can't keep people safe if you don't listen to them.'

Mum looked unsure and Imogen realised two things. First, Mum was still cross with Mark. Second, Imogen didn't want them to argue.

'Mark saved us,' said Imogen. 'We wouldn't be here if it wasn't for him.'

'Yes,' cried Marie. 'He was like a ninja! He came down this big hole on a rope and we thought the yedleek had got him, but they hadn't! Mark was like, *POW!*'

Mum looked from Imogen to Mark to Marie.

Please don't let her cry any more, thought Imogen. But Mum didn't cry.

'Come here,' she said, and she reached out her hands to them all. 'I want to know that you're real.'

CHAPTER 117

Marie climbed into Imogen's bed. They were home. They were in their pyjamas. But neither girl wanted to spend that first night alone. Imogen lifted the duvet and Marie snuggled underneath. It was *so good* to be together.

Mum and Mark were talking in the lounge. Their voices travelled through the floorboards, although Imogen couldn't make out the words.

There was a worry creature on the windowsill. A pot-bellied thing with a sour, scrunchy face. Imogen thought about telling Marie – about mentioning the fears that still lingered. But the worry creature must have heard her plan because it didn't say a word. It didn't even put up a fight. It slid down from the windowsill and padded out of the room.

'Do you think there's something different about Mark?' asked Marie, wriggling closer.

Imogen laughed. 'Everything's different about Mark. He's way less annoying than before.'

Marie was quiet for a moment. Imogen could feel her breath on her cheek. 'Yes,' said Marie. 'I like him. But that's not what I meant...'

'Go on,' said Imogen. 'What *did* you mean?'

'Sometimes he walks really slowly.'

'That's old people for you,' said Imogen, although Mark wasn't that old.

'Oh, right,' said Marie, but she wasn't done. 'And this evening, when we were having tea, he was just staring into space. His eyes almost looked like they were glowing. I'm sure they didn't use to do that.'

'Marie . . .' Imogen reached for her sister, found her hand, squeezed it tight. 'Do you know what Dr Saeed said, the last time I saw her? She said it can be hard to accept someone new in the family. She said, sometimes, we put our feelings on other people, like a cinema projector. And it can change how we see them.'

'You think I changed Mark's eyes?' asked Marie.

'No,' said Imogen. 'I don't think that. But I think we're both looking at Mark a bit differently. And we're a bit different too. So of course we're going to see new things . . . notice stuff we hadn't noticed before.'

Marie tucked the duvet under her side and Imogen did the same. They were cocooned in a cave for two.

'Imogen,' said Marie. Her voice was a whisper. 'Sometimes I think about the old queen.'

'Huh?'

'The queen Anneshka and Surovetz . . . you know . . . *killed*.'

That took Imogen by surprise. She wanted to tell Marie not

to worry, to put the dead queen out of her head, but she knew you couldn't tell people what to feel. It didn't make the feeling go away.

'I shouldn't have broken into the private bit of the palace,' continued Marie, voice getting louder. 'I shouldn't have let Anneshka in, but she told me . . . she said if I did what she asked, she'd let me . . . she'd let me go home.'

Imogen twisted round in the bed so she was face to face with her sister. 'Marie,' she said, 'it's not your fault that the queen died.'

But Marie didn't seem to have heard. 'I knew Anneshka could be really mean. I knew she did bad things, but sometimes I thought she was better. Sometimes I thought . . .' Marie gulped. 'I didn't know she'd do *that*!'

'It's not your fault,' said Imogen – more fiercely this time.

'It keeps playing in my head,' said Marie.

The realisation came to Imogen with a jolt, like someone had spun the bedroom upside down and she was sleeping on the ceiling. It was a world-flipping idea.

What Marie was describing was a worry creature . . . or something very similar.

Imogen wasn't the only one who had them.

Still reeling from this brain-bending thought, she tried to imagine what might make Marie feel better. 'I know,' she said. 'What you need is a story.'

'What kind of story?' asked Marie.

'How about the legend of a boy who summons a dragon?'

'That sounds like a good story,' said Marie. 'Tell me that one.'

Imogen smiled in the darkness. Her bedroom wasn't completely pitch-black. There was a light on in the landing and a streetlamp outside.

Beyond the clouds must be stars.

EPILOGUE

Let's wind the clock back – just a little . . .

Before Imogen and Marie returned to their world, Ochi was sitting in her cottage. The witch was old and contented, nestled deep in the Kolsaney Forests. Her chicken purred in its drawer, her snail slimed up a chair, and the clock of stars rested above the fireplace.

'Don't you worry,' muttered Ochi to the clock. 'We'll soon have you working again. Together, we'll collect hundreds of souls.'

The pots on the nearby shelf rattled. They were packed tight as starlings on a branch.

'Don't you worry either,' wheezed Ochi. 'There's always room for a few more.'

There was a new clay pot on the windowsill. It was empty, waiting for Anneshka's soul.

Ochi was busy drying some herbs when she heard voices outside. She hobbled to her window and looked out. There, marching through the forest, was the girl that had stolen her clock.

The girl was walking with a great sense of purpose. There was another child at her side, with hair the colour of autumn leaves. Together, they followed a moth.

Ah, thought Ochi. *So the travellers have returned.* This time, the witch kept her house hidden.

A man was following the children. Mark – that was his name.

'I thought he got eaten by the yedleek,' whispered Ochi, for she had foreseen the man's death.

The forest witch decided to investigate. She rooted her feet to the floor and looked through the eyes of the trees. Bark lids opened and Ochi saw Mark. She was looking out of a birch tree.

Ochi asked the birch to lean down. Mark ducked to pass under a branch and several leaves brushed against his face. Ochi and the birch both sensed it.

A scent was oozing out of Mark's pores. Sweat. That much was normal. Some cheese he'd eaten last night. And a very subtle smell of burning . . .

The roots crackled deep underground, passing the message from tree to tree.

Not quite a human, this one. Something else . . . Something that doesn't want to be found.

The witch opened her real eyes. She was back in her cottage once again. She heaved a book on to her desk and turned the pages until she found the right bit.

Here lies all that is known of the yedleek.
Also known as 'eaters' and 'rock folk'.
Yedleek dwell underground and have
the ability to travel through stone.
They cannot come to the surface.
Nor do they wish to.
They gorge themselves on human flesh,
consuming those who travel too deep.
The older the human, the greater the nourishment.

Ochi couldn't stop trembling. She was the most ancient human alive and yedleek were her greatest fear. To them, she'd be delicious – a most tender and mature cut of meat.

The only time yedleek let their prey escape
is when they wish to start a new hive.
They lodge their spawn in the human gut.
The eggs are smooth and hard.
Here they stay, in the darkness,
until they are ready to hatch.

Ochi sat down on her stool with a bump. She suddenly felt her great age. All of the years were rushing at her, crushing her with their cares. This was not good news. Not good news at all.

Ochi closed her eyes. She rooted her feet to the ground and spread her wrinkly toes wide. She opened the eye of a hazelnut tree and peered at the forest nearby.

The girls and the man had opened a door – the one that led back to their world. Ochi watched as the first girl stepped through the portal. She watched the small girl do the same.

The witch made her tree shake its branches. She had to stop them! No one deserved this fate!

Mark glanced at the hazelnut tree.

And yet . . . it wasn't Ochi's world in danger . . . it wasn't her forest under threat. Wouldn't it be better if the yedleek eggs went somewhere else to hatch?

The hazel tree went very still.

Mark gave a small shrug. Then he stepped through the door and pulled it shut.

'I am sorry for you,' whispered Ochi. 'Sorrier than you will ever know. For I am fairly certain you take more than two children home.'

Beyond the Mountains

It's not the darkness that I fear
nor the world below.
For darkness has a loving touch
and kindly ways to go.

But there are creatures shaped by fire,
who hunt for human meat.
They say the young are under-ripe.
They say the old taste sweet.

It's not the darkness that I fear –
it's being fully grown.
For yedleek like to gnaw upon
time-hardened adult bones.

I fear the men of burning light.
I fear their molten forms.
I fear their deep volcano eyes
and yawning, hungry jaws.

It's not the darkness that I fear
nor the world below.
For darkness has a loving touch
and kindly ways to go.

– Nursery rhyme from the Scrublands

Thank you to . . .

All my family and friends who have brightened a sad, strange year. Especially Mum and Dad, for your love and encouragement.

Mini and Bonnie, who've both helped make this book. Your sticky paw prints are on every page. I hope you realise this?

Joe, mé lásce. You are the world's only pongoose, carrier of snacks, bringer of joy and ovary of original ideas. Thank you for travelling with me.

Seb for the speed-reading, second opinions and first-rate feedback.

Nick Lake for killing the hermit. Thank you for making this book so much better than I thought it would be – and for believing that I could write it.

Claire Wilson for all the head strokes and advice. You are still the wisest adult I know. Thank you also to Safae El-Ouahabi.

Chris Riddell for the beautiful, brilliant art.

Aisha Bushby and Rachel Faturoti for your kind words and helpful suggestions.

Stephanie Turley for making the time to discuss the most unlikely scenarios.

Nicola Skinner. You know what you've done. Thank you for bouncing into my life.

Writers of WOW. Even in digital form, you've been such an incredible support. Thank you especially to Donna Rosenberg.

Everyone at HarperCollins Children's Books – including Samantha Stewart, Julia Sanderson, Laure Gysemans, Tina Mories, Louisa Sheridan, Jessica Dean, Alex Cowan, Jasmeet Fyfe, Jo-Anna Parkinson, Elorine Grant, Matt Kelly, Hannah Marshall, Deborah Wilton, Nicole Linhardt-Rich, Julia Bruce, Sarah Hall and Mary O'Riordan.

And last, but certainly not least, thank you to my readers.